The recording was poor, but there was no mistaking the words:

"Timmy is alive. He is safe. I will not physically harm him if you do what I say. But you must do exactly as I say. In exchange for Timmy's life, this is what I want: I want the hands of Jordan Stone. Both of them. I want them delivered to Locker 255 in the International Terminal of Kennedy Airport by 5 P.M. on August 20. No tricks . . . I will allow no second chances."

PLOT TWIST

ERIC ADAMS

St. Martin's Paperbacks

The characters and events in this book are fictional. Any resemblance to those living or dead is purely coincidental.

PLOT TWIST

ISBN: 0-312-95609-6

Printed in the United States of America

St. Martin's Paperbacks edition/October 1995

10 9 8 7 6 5 4 3 2 1

To my mother,
who taught me to love poetic truth

Acknowledgments

For thoughts weaved into every page: Ronnie Benjamin, Nancy Beckus, John Anderson, Todd Keithley, Carolyn Minionis, Betty Anne Greco, and Mel Berger. And to Kathy, who knows.

Words are deeds.
—The Talmud

PART 1

PART I

ONE

Jailers at the Nassau County Jail often mistook Jordan Stone for a criminal attorney. Perhaps it was his sports coat, grown a little ratty, or his attorney's swagger, one of the easiest gestures to imitate. More than likely, it was simply that criminal attorneys were the only males out of uniform or handcuffs to bother frequenting the place at all.

Whatever the reason, Stone didn't mind the misconception. Playing attorney was one of the fundamental prerequisites of the true crime author. Insurance agent, distant relative, Hollywood producer—whatever it took to get a phone number, a name, or a confession—Stone found a way or a persona to acquire it.

But the rule's corollary said don't fake if you don't have to, and Stone didn't need to play attorney this hot summer morning. No one cared who he was. The overweight female prison guard with the bleached blond hair and ring of keys dangling at her side waved Stone through with an indifference so consummate that even Stone paused to admire it.

Like everyone else she couldn't stand the humidity, thick as jail walls. The month was a thirty-one-day communal sentence and everyone in the city was pissed off about it.

"I'm here to see Chester Tenden, 1-B-122," Stone said.

"That's your problem," the guard replied, gesturing toward Jordan's shoes and belt for inspection.

Even with the morning temperature sizzling, Stone sensed the cold of the metal around him. He handed her the items.

"Going to be a scorcher," he said.

With barely a cursory glance, the guard handed back the shoes and belt. She buzzed open door number 1, and Stone slipped through the opening while fitting on his soft Italian loafers. He refastened his belt and walked the final two hundred paces to the visiting station.

Chester hadn't been convicted. Not yet. But Jordan had no doubt Chester would be tagged by week's end at the conclusion of his trial. So incriminating was the evidence that the prosecution had smugly refused to bargain away the kidnapping charge. Sexual assault *and* kidnapping carried twenty-to-life. At Chester's age, and in the god-awful shape he was in, he'd be mighty lucky to make ten with his will to live intact.

The tabloids had missed Chester's story, giving Jordan the inside edge. It's easy to miss good crime. There is no police log that reports the collusions, intrigues, and inducements that prompt people to transgress in the creative ways they do. Police logs divulge just the facts. In Chester's case, the log reported a simple charge of sexual abuse occurring sometime in early February, and dropped the following day. Several months later, Chester's name surfaced again for sexual abuse, this time with a kidnapping rap attached. Standard police beat stuff, even kidnapping charges, which are invariably dropped by prosecutors without time to prosecute.

Jordan picked up on the story due to that distinctive name, Chester. The first time Jordan had read it he had joked with the desk sergeant about *Chester the Molester*. When the name reappeared in April, Jordan remembered the name and the joke. On a lark he called the sergeant for the sketchy details.

It seemed that Chester had abducted a neighborhood Chinese girl. "A real fortune cookie," said the sergeant. Chester kept her locked up for two weeks, sexually abusing his "chink toy," as he bragged about her to his friends. Ling, as her name turned out to be, risked her life in a daring escape, but declined to press charges, afraid that her illegal-alien status would get her deported. Nothing unusual so far.

Then Chester, God knows why, decided to kidnap Ling again, two months later, this time off the streets in a warehouse district in Hempstead where she worked. The same girl. Naturally the second time he was busted swiftly. The trial was on now, but no one in county lockup was laying down a bet that Chester would ever see the outside again. And that's where Jordan liked his criminals, behind bars.

"He's coming," said the jailer wearing the obligatory New York cop mustache. He keyed Jordan into the visiting room and pointed to the thick metal door to the "inside."

The sparse room was furnished with three wooden chairs and a wooden table carved with the initials of countless inmates. Jordan took a chair, blew the dust from the table top, and laid down his soft leather briefcase. The black satchel was old and tattered. But that's the way Stone wanted it. You can't look too rich or they'll want more money.

The inside door thundered open and Chester appeared, casing the visiting room with darting eyes. A hairy little man with a paunch, Chester was the kind of guy who broke into a sweat at the slightest physical effort, like buying a pack of smokes from a vending machine. The guy looked scared shitless. Chester's pre-

vious jail stint had been twenty-two years earlier for
petty theft. Plenty had changed since then, mostly
Chester's age. It's one thing to be in prison at twenty-
five, quite another at forty-seven. Chester had grown
accustomed to his worldly little luxuries, cheap as they
were. Now he was one verdict away from becoming
some goon's little luxury in Attica.

"Chester, sit down," said Stone, skipping the formal-
ity of a handshake.

Stone opened the briefcase and pulled from it a single sheet of paper. He drew a thin silver pen from the
inside pocket of his jacket, laid it carefully on the paper, and slid them both toward Chester.

"And if I don't sign?" said Chester.

"That's your loss." Stone leaned back in his chair.

"Maybe I can cut a better deal."

"If you're convicted this week, no one will touch you.
No one will need to."

"Maybe I'm innocent."

Stone couldn't help but let out a chuckle.

"Your attorney didn't tell me you were a comedian,"
said Stone.

"It's not funny."

"Tell me you can't use two grand right now for your
wife." Jordan leaned forward slightly. "Or is it your
wives?"

Chester moved closer to the table and for the first
time gazed at the document. He scratched his forehead
like a gorilla.

"What does it say?"

"It says you're giving me the rights to your story, in
book or movie form. Exclusive rights."

Give them the cost with no hesitation, just like a car
dealer. Chester rolled his eyes and wiped the sweat
from his furry brow.

"It's your chance to tell the truth," added Stone. If it
costs nothing, make them feel good, too.

"Truth ain't got shit to do with this," said Chester. He went to finger his oversized pinky ring, then realized it had been checked at the gate. "This is about money, man."

"Well then, I'm offering two grand," said Stone.

"Five."

"You ain't got a leg to stand on."

"Four."

"My offer is on the table."

"Thirty-five hundred."

"You're wasting my time," said Stone.

"What do you think, I'm a punk? I made two grand a day on the outside. I'm a productive member of society."

Stone leaned forward.

"Maybe once in your life you made two grand in a day, and that was when you ripped off your mother."

Chester scratched his unshaven face. "Three grand."

"I'm out of here." Stone thrust the chair backward and marched to the door to the inside, pounding on the tiny window. "You don't want it, fine, I'm just covering my ass."

On cue, the jailer opened the door for Chester.

"Wait," pleaded Chester.

Jordan sat back down and peeked underneath his fingernails. They were squeaky clean.

"All right," Chester mumbled. "I'll do it."

With his chubby fingers, Chester picked up the silver pen, felt its weight, and scrutinized the document.

"Hurry up, it's not the Declaration of Independence," said Stone.

Chester scribbled his name. The sweat from his arm dampened the paper and smudged his signature. He slid the release form back to Jordan.

Stone tucked the pen in his suit. He lifted the release form, careful not to touch Chester's sweaty mess, and returned it to the folder in his satchel.

"I'll have the check sent to your lawyer."

Jordan tapped on the door to the outside. The jailer opened it immediately. No wait today, and for a moment regulations were violated when both doors were open at the same time, Chester on the way in and Jordan on the way out.

"Hey, Stone," Chester called, just as Jordan was about to walk.

"Yeah?"

"Fuck you."

Jordan turned to face the molester.

"Let me ask you a question," said Jordan. "Why the hell did you kidnap the same girl twice?"

Chester flushed red. "I don't know. I just kind of missed her."

"You kind of missed her," said Jordan, shaking his head in disbelief. "Your attorney was right. You are a fool."

With that, Jordan vanished from sight.

"You'll get yours, Stone. You'll get yours," shouted Chester. His words bounced off the enameled cinderblocks and echoed down the hallway and back. But Jordan was long gone.

The ride from Nassau County to Manhattan is rarely a problem at eleven o'clock in the morning. Once in Manhattan, though, traffic is a bitch, as Stone discovered again halfway across the Williamsburg Bridge. From the bridge it took another forty-five minutes to Chinatown and another fifteen to find a garage with space available. Twenty bucks.

Ling had given her address as 501 Canal Street. But there was no 501, just 503 and 499, as if something had sucked up a building and compressed what remained together. Stone stopped in a ginseng shop at 495 Canal. The little-men roots were piled high in display jars like bodies after a holocaust.

"Wu? Do you know a family named Wu?" asked Stone.

The old Chinese man looked at Stone as if he were crazy.

"Who?"

"Ling Wu."

"Ling who?" he asked with a hand cupped to his ear.

"No, Ling Wu."

"Sorry, no Ling Wu."

Stone stepped out. He passed a few restaurants and a butcher shop with chickens dangling in the windows, their twisted heads still attached and their rubbery feet awaiting the chopping block.

The odors of the neighborhood—garlic, soy, frying pork, dry cleaning solutions—mixed with the steam escaping from the street vents. It smelled so exotic, as if anything was possible here in this tiny world within a world, any contraband attainable, any perversity easily arranged.

It was hotter in the city than on Long Island by ten degrees at least, and the hottest part of the day was yet to come. Stone walked in the thin shade thrown by the shop awnings, then crossed the street to try 510 Canal Street. Maybe Ling had flipped the 1 and the 0 when she had given him directions—510 instead of 501.

Stone was right. It was 510 Canal. The name Wu had been scratched in ballpoint pen on the nameplate next to the buzzer for Apartment 10. By its mushy feel, Jordan knew the buzzer was broken. No loss, the lock was busted and Jordan let himself in.

It was a typical Chinatown tenement, although Stone had discovered long ago that tenements were universal. All the clichés fit—dimly lit corridors, broken windows, smell of yesterday's dinner, exposed wires, stench of urine wafting from the stairwells, a junkie lurking in a dark corner. Ling's building was no different.

Jordan climbed the three flights to Ling's flat. He

rang and this time the buzzer worked. He heard a rattle inside.

No answer. Jordan rang again, but before he could withdraw his finger from the button, the door jerked opened the length of the short chain.

It was an old Chinese woman, small, and sinewy as a rat. Stone could hardly see her eyes through her wrinkles and indignation.

"I'm here to see Ling Wu. Does she live here?"

"You go away," snapped the woman.

She slammed the door shut.

Not the most welcome reception Jordan had ever encountered, not the coldest either.

As Jordan contemplated a new approach, the chain slithered off its rack and a lithe hand peeled open the door.

"Mr. Stone?"

If this was Ling, Jordan knew why Chester had abducted her twice. She was petite with the demure beauty bestowed chiefly on Asian women. Her eyes were the color of walnut, her hair black and lustrous.

Jordan winced at the thought of Ling's escape from Chester's apartment. The resourceful girl had bitten through the leather thongs tethering her to Chester's bed. Naked, and despite a 22-degree-below-zero wind chill, Ling climbed down the fire escape eight floors. It took some forty-five minutes for Ling to navigate the icy metal walkways to the street below, where she ran into a Woolworth's, begged a blanket and a quarter, and called her family amid the stares of late-night shoppers. Except for one frostbitten toe and an abortion, Ling made out all right.

The second time Chester abducted her, Ling's ordeal was briefer and far less hideous. This time Ling's uncle knew all about Chester, his whereabouts, and his peculiar sexual appetites. Lucky for Chester, the uncle called the police and not the Chinese mafia, or Chester would have been reduced to bits of wonton filler floating in a ceramic bowl. In a matter of hours, police picked up Chester and freed Ling. Justice prevailed, just as Hollywood likes it.

Ling bowed her head slightly, almost unconsciously. She entreated Jordan to enter as if he were an ancient Chinese warlord demanding homage.

The stern old lady had not disappeared by any means. Nor did she make any attempt to hide her displeasure.

"Mother, this is the writer."

Ling spoke English well enough, though her accent was stiff. Jordan extended his hand to Ling's mother, not sure if she would shake it or bite it off. She did neither.

The studio apartment had a bathroom and an alcove that served as a kitchen. That was it. The floor was covered with mattresses wall to wall.

"Come in. Sit down," said Ling.

Jordan tiptoed around the mattresses to one of only two chairs around a wobbly kitchen table. Ling walked with a noticeable limp. No toe. Water boiled in a huge aluminum pot on a camping stove. Despite the heat, the windows were tightly shut. Jordan looked at Ling and her mother. He was the only one sweating. Ling picked up a large chopping knife and resumed her chore, dicing vegetables for twenty.

"Ling, I'd like to write you a check right now for $15,000."

Jordan glanced up for a reaction. He was hoping for a jaw drop. Ling paused only momentarily from her task.

"Mr. Stone, I'm so sorry but I can't."

"I'm sure that's more than you make in one year at the factory."

Ling lowered her eyes. "I don't work there anymore. I can't. You're very kind, but I cannot accept."

Ling moved the pile of chopped purple eggplant to a cooking bowl. She changed knives to a small dicer and picked up a knot of fresh ginger. Her hands worked in short little strokes peeling off translucent slices.

"How about other girls? If you tell your story maybe you'll prevent other immigrant women from being abducted and sexually abused. How about them?"

With the hand holding the knife, Ling wiped a solitary tear from her smooth cheek. Jordan wasn't sure if the tear was prompted by his offer or the nearby yellow onion diced into a thousand tiny squares.

"Mr. Stone, you don't understand, I am so sorry."

"I do understand. I want to help."

"There is no help," whispered Ling.

"Certainly $15,000 can help."

Fifteen grand was a lot of money for a life-rights agreement, far more than Jordan usually began negotiations with, but Ling *was* the story, and if she agreed, it would be worth every penny.

"It's not a question of money," said Ling.

"We have to tell your story, then, for the sake of justice."

When all else fails, turn it on thick. But Ling wasn't buying.

"I know this is difficult," said Jordan with all the empathy he could muster.

"You don't understand. I have brought shame to my family. I cannot bring more."

"I offer you redemption then. You can move your family to a bigger apartment, a safe apartment, with $15,000."

Ling's mother needed to hear no more. The old woman grabbed Jordan's jacket sleeve and wrenched him from the chair. Jordan was startled by her strength.

"Go! Go! Go! You leave now," thundered the old lady.

Ling's expression told Jordan that she was sorry, but

she couldn't do the book, couldn't prevent his eviction. The forces were too great, too powerful, whatever they were. She said it all with her sad, beautiful eyes.

"Ling, I'm just trying to help. They'll do it without you."

Ling's mother led Jordan away from her daughter. He tripped over a mattress on his forced march to the front door.

"Go. Get out. Now. We want honor. We want respect. Leave. Don't come back."

With one final push, Ling's mother expelled Jordan from the apartment. The door slammed on his tail. It wasn't the first time.

Jordan descended the rickety stairs to the sweltering street below. He thought it a shame that Ling didn't take the money. For her sake, Jordan promised to try again, though it wouldn't change a thing. Ling's honor or not, Jordan was going to write this story.

Two

Naturally the idea disturbed him. It wasn't his nature to commit a crime in the first place, and then to request something as abhorrent as—

But what choice did he have? Society needed to learn a lesson, and he had been called upon to teach it —he and Jordan Stone. He felt compelled to act for the sake of the children, not only his child, but all the world's children. It was the perfect opportunity to champion one of society's more ignored afflictions, one in which Jordan had played a significant role and shortly would play victim or, should he say, object as well.

He longed to share his thoughts with Stone, to explain how Jordan's sacrifice would better the world. As someone who ostensibly sought to expose society's ills for remedy's sake, Jordan would understand. Under different circumstances he and Jordan would get along fine, he thought. Both were educated, family men, top echelon of society in terms of earnings and prestige. He longed to chat with Jordan over a snifter of Courvoisier and a fat Macanudo.

But such a chat was not to be. He would never have the opportunity to shake Jordan's hand, not at least in the traditional sense. No, he and Jordan were destined to share a more unusual relationship, forged by a bond of uncommon service to humankind. Later Jordan would thank him, not during the first few days, understandably, but later, when the virtues of the ordeal could be appreciated. Then Jordan would be grateful for the opportunity to contribute to society in such a—what was the word—*creative* way.

But there was work to be done, last-minute details. The route was familiar to him, nevertheless he checked with the highway department for road closures of which he should be aware. He checked the van's coolant level again. After having witnessed the swell of overheated vehicles littering the roadside these past few days, he dared not become a victim of the insufferable heat. Then he made a final visual inspection of the apparatus packed neatly in a locked box in the van's rear. In the morning he would retrieve the anesthetics from the refrigerator and pack them on ice in a cooler.

The major work was already done. He had use of the apartment in Manhattan, and of course there was the hunting lodge far out on Long Island, each stocked with ample provisions. He gazed out the window beyond the August oppression and saw a train rush by. Even the train fit neatly into his arrangements.

He had to chuckle when he thought of the plan, a masterpiece both logistically and poetically. He had painstakingly attended to every contingency like a surgeon before an untried procedure. And the broadstroke concept, well, he liked to think it bordered on genius. Then again, there had been so much time to mull it over, so much energy to focus on the problem, so much heartache to transform into an appropriate response.

As he dabbed the sweat from his brow, he pondered his surprising serenity and overwhelming sense of invincibility. The sensation came not from an excess of self-confidence, though he felt supremely confident, rather it emanated from the utter superiority of his moral position. He relished having no choice but to act in the specific manner dictated by his convictions. He felt so exhilarated, so liberated, like Jesus must have felt confronting the money changers or Moses before Pharaoh. Nothing empowers like purity of mission.

He took a deep breath and smiled, the first time in a long time. He felt so alive today, so close to God, as if he could touch divinity with his fingertips. Best of all, Jordan Stone would soon understand.

The fastest way to get around New York midday is by subway. Even rich people use it during the day. Rather than take his car out of the Chinatown garage, Jordan hopped the number 6 train to Wanda's Upper West Side apartment.

The timing was perfect. Wanda had just two hours off, half an hour to travel back and forth from her East 66th Street television studio—she insisted on a taxi—and ninety minutes with Jordan.

She was waiting when he arrived.

"Won't you tell me?" Wanda teased as she unraveled her smoke-colored pantyhose. Her legs were long and her ankles chiseled to perfection. Jordan never missed an opportunity to appreciate them.

"Not a chance. And let you run with the story?"

Jordan unzipped her crimson dress. It fell to the ground without a sound.

Though Wanda's apartment was a simple three-room, she had decorated it elegantly with Oriental rugs and soft white leather sofas. The small bedroom was dominated by an oversized bed. Behind it hung a huge mirror, which doubled the image of the room but did nothing to increase its square footage. Why the extra-large bed, Jordan didn't ask. Outside their occasional trysts, Wanda's private life was her business. Jordan guessed she didn't sleep around much. At the same time, he dared not fool himself into believing he was the only one.

Jordan clearly fit Wanda's criteria for a lover. He was nonthreatening due to his marriage to Allie, yet intimate due to their former working relationship. Although Wanda rarely talked of her childhood, Jordan gathered it wasn't a happy one. It was never said, but both Jordan and Wanda understood they were cut from the same ragged cloth, and each zipless fuck celebrated this affinity.

"You never give it away," said Wanda, teasingly. "One of these days you'll tell me what you're working on."

"I'll tell you when I've got all the releases sewn up," said Jordan. He reached around the front of her body and released the snap of her bra.

Wanda turned and loosened Jordan's tie.

"Anyway," he added, "you have enough material for your TV show to last a lifetime."

"But I always lust for more," she said.

Jordan smiled. "You're wicked, from your work to your private life."

"Don't you just love it?"

They had met while working at *Newsday*, rookies together on the police beat, an assignment that no reporter with talent wants for long. But it is on this tour of duty—at grimy police stations, poring over tedious police logs, and interviewing victims and their families fresh with pain—that young journalists hone their craft. Who, what, when, where, why, and how—these questions may be elements of every news story, but they are the corpus of the crime story. Who inflicted pain on whom? What was the instrument of suffering? When and where did it transpire? How was the devious act carried out? And often the most difficult question to answer: Why did it have to happen?

Oddly, Jordan and Wanda left the newspaper the

same week, propelled in different directions by the same force. It was a crime. This one involved a little girl in Mastic, beaten by her parents, abused by her uncles, and violated by her siblings. Her name was Cindy, and the tabloids dubbed her Cinderella. Greedy for cash, Cindy's parents rented her to a pornographer in New Jersey for $5,750 cash. Not bad, the parents figured, for a week's work by their daughter. By a stroke of luck, the FBI was investigating the pornographer at the time on an unrelated charge of mail fraud. Little Cindy was delivered by her parents C.O.D. to the pornographer just hours before his arrest. Cindy was rescued, still untouched or photographed, and hailed as a hero. The tabloids went berserk over the story, rambling on about a fairy godmother alive and well and living in Teaneck.

Jordan and Wanda were the only reporters allowed to interview the child, a bright but timid girl who wore her scars with uncommon dignity. After the spotlight faded, Wanda sold the "inside" story to a network, and Jordan's book proposal for *Up from Ashes: Cindy's Story* was snatched up by Clarion Books. Both reporters left the newspaper the same week for their new media.

Jordan was glad to go. He had made the foolish mistake of lifting a few sentences from a copyrighted magazine article and using it verbatim in one of his pieces. A reader with little else to do caught the transgression and alerted newspaper management. Reporters plagiarized all the time, out of laziness more than anything else. Still, Jordan's boss scheduled an employee review, in which Jordan was sure to face a stiff reprimand. By slipping out before the scheduled meeting, Jordan hoped to put the unfortunate incident behind him and keep it quiet. "P" for plagiarism is the scarlet letter for journalists. There was another good reason to leave. Jordan's wife, Allie, had nearly caught Jordan and Wanda in the act. As long as his desk abutted

Wanda's in the newsroom, Jordan's marriage was in jeopardy.

It wasn't long before Jordan wrote a second book, then a third. And Wanda rose in rank to on-air reporter and then producer and anchor for *Crime Current,* the television show with three true-crime segments nightly. Wanda was perfect for television with her high cheek-bones and green eyes. The television added ten needed pounds to her gaunt frame and hid her freckles. More than that, Wanda had a gift that can't be taught or learned—an unforced intimacy in front of the camera, a gift possessed by only the best in the business. A studio set was Wanda's natural habitat.

"Won't you give me just one tiny clue?" Wanda whispered in Jordan's ear.

The lovers fell together onto Wanda's large bed and their mouths met for the first time. Her thin lips tasted like strawberry lipstick and cigarettes.

"It's about sexual abuse," Jordan confessed finally.

Wanda grunted. "What else is new?"

She rolled on top of him. Her breasts dancing in the afternoon light.

"Nothing," said Jordan.

Jordan had to hurry if he was going to catch the end of Timmy's birthday party. It was, after all, his youngest child's seventh. Jordan and Wanda left the apartment at three o'clock on the dot, she in her yellow taxi and he down the stairway to the labyrinth of tunnels under the city. The subway was crowded but fast, and Jordan was in his car and over the bridge before four, and off the Long Island Expressway by five.

Jordan had known about the house that would be his in Rocky Cliff ever since he began delivering cigars on bicycle to his father's wealthy customers. Cuban cigars, fat, round, smelly, and illegal, which made Jordan feel delightfully criminal as he weaved along the sidewalks past the estates built when George Washington roamed the countryside.

To a fourteen-year-old's eyes, the old Rocky Cliff house looked like a movie set, with its back against the water, its ornate porch columns, and the pink hue of the clapboard siding. The inlet in back led to Rocky Harbor, then to the Sound, and then the open sea for anyone with a small boat brave enough to dare. How different it was from the left side of the brick duplex that Jordan's family called home when he was young.

But for Jordan the real charm of the place was the spacious room above the detached garage that overlooked the front yard and the road beyond. He had converted the room into an office equipped with computer, copy machine, fax, three phone lines, a couch, and enough desk space to spread out an epic. The intercom linked him to the house, so Allie could leave the kids without having to worry.

The Victorian had only one drawback. It was situated on Sand Castle Drive at a bend so deceivingly sharp that it regularly caused drivers to screech their brakes to keep from colliding with the painted white fence surrounding the property. Aside from the location, the house was perfect. And so was Rocky Cliff, one of only a few North Shore villages to inexplicably escape encroachment from the city and its suburbs. Perhaps it was the town's hilly terrain, which didn't favor subdivision building, or its high cost of living, or its distance from the main traffic arteries of the Island. Whatever the reason, Jordan and Allie both savored the New England feel of the little town, with its bucolic main street, and the wave-at-everyone attitude of its residents.

As he approached home, Jordan slowed down at the sharp curve and turned carefully into his driveway. More than once he had narrowly avoided collision with cars speeding from the opposite direction. He parked behind a line of minivans and station wagons. Just in time.

Inside, the party was in full swing. Seven-year-olds chased each other. Mothers chatted on living room couches. Colored balloons and streamers hung haphazardly from the tall ceiling and doorways. The heat had subsided and everyone apparently enjoyed a second wind.

Jordan spotted Allie across the way in the dining room putting out cupcakes. Even from that distance, Jordan could see the sparkle in his wife's dark eyes. Her Spanish grandfather had left her with an olive complexion and a penchant for the dramatic. Jordan gave her a wink, and she threw back a kiss before disappearing through the swinging door to the kitchen.

Timmy came running up holding a baseball mitt, still stiff with newness.

"Look, Daddy, look!" Fueled by his pure excitement, the small boy leapt into Jordan's arms.

The youngest and frailest of the three children, Timmy had been born, quite unexpectedly, two months early and weighed just four pounds one ounce at birth. His first two weeks of life were spent in an intensive care nursery, surrounded by the controlled environment of a Plexiglas isolette. IVs pierced the crown of Timmy's head, and cardiac electrodes clung to his little chest. The only vestige of the premature birth was asthma, serious enough to keep Timmy from participating fully in activities he loved, like baseball.

"Well, let's see it." Jordan admired the glove's fine workmanship and its obvious magical qualities.

"You got a special one, Timmy. This mitt will catch you a whole lot of fly balls."

"Like Cal?"

"Just like your brother."

Timmy squirreled down. The excitement of the party was too much for him to stay put for long, even in his daddy's arms. Jordan navigated through the shredded gift wrapping paper and brightly colored plastic toys. He stopped at a sullen little girl in a frilly dress. He had known the girl's name once.

"Do you have something in your ear?" Jordan asked.

The girl nodded no, barely picking her chin up from her chest.

"I think I see something." He touched the girl's ear and pulled out a shiny quarter.

The girl's eyes brightened. "How'd you do that?"

Jordan handed the quarter to the girl for her awed inspection. "Magic," he said, and continued on.

Jordan found Allie at the kitchen sink rinsing dishes. Her short-chopped black hair bobbed at the collar of her blue cotton jumpsuit.

"There's just something about you and chocolate icing," said Jordan.

"You just don't want to do these dishes," she replied with a smile. "How'd it go?"

"Chester? A real sweetheart."

"And the girl?"

"Ling's coming along." It was a lie.

Jordan picked up a bowl lined with traces of chocolate icing. He used his finger.

"We got a royalty check today. For *Invasion of Privacy,*" said Allie.

"How much?"

"Eight-thousand-something."

"Not enough. Where's Sarah?"

"On the phone."

"Not talking to that Jimmy Buconti kid again?" Jordan asked.

"All day, everyday."

"And Cal?" Jordan asked.

"Soccer."

Jordan swiped another line of chocolate. Allie came

over to give Jordan the first peck on the cheek of the day. She hesitated.

Did she smell Wanda? "What's the matter?" Jordan asked, masking his trepidation.

Allie picked up another tray of cupcakes and pressed her way through the swinging door. "Nothing, I have a party to throw. Got to go. And, hey, you're in charge of dinner tonight."

Jordan smiled until she was gone. Allie was too smart not to find out. She had forgiven his indiscretions with Wanda once, a few years into their marriage. The episode had scared Jordan straight for years. If Allie discovered the renewed affair she would leave Jordan in a heartbeat.

But more than Allie finding out, Jordan knew the affair was wrong. He often wondered what compelled him toward complicity. Allie had given up her career as a magazine editor in the city to be a full-time mom. She never resented it. She was smart, free of emotional hang-ups, great in bed, looked fantastic, a born mom, independent as hell but not hellbent on the idea. Jordan's friends lusted after her—in Jordan's presence. She was his lucky star, and Jordan was lucky to hang on.

On top of that there were the kids, all wonderful in their kooky ways. Sarah with her recent discovery of boys, Cal with his teeth so crooked that Oreo cookies fell whole through the gaps, a condition $10,000 worth of braces had failed to correct. And Timmy, sweet Timmy.

How could Jordan face them with his transgressions should they find out? Jordan had promised himself before, he promised himself now, and he was sad to think that he would promise himself again: Wanda was over. No more.

Jordan searched the refrigerator for something to cook but couldn't find a thing. Behind the microwave he found a take-out menu for The Seven Immortals, their favorite Chinese restaurant in Rocky Cliff, the only Chinese restaurant in Rocky Cliff.

Jordan leafed through the menu for Allie's favorite dish, then Sarah's, Cal's, and Timmy's. He circled the selections with a dull pencil.

It would be Chinese food tonight, Jordan's treat.

THREE

Although no one believed it could grow more humid, the following day was far muggier. The sky had turned a pewter gray and the branches of the tall maple, poplar, and ash trees surrounding the house hung low, burdened by the weight of moisture. Even the usual breeze off the Sound was turned back by the damp thickness.

Sarah had sped off somewhere with Jimmy. Cal was at soccer practice. And Allie as always had something on her agenda. Only Timmy elected to stay behind and despite the weather had asked to play outside.

From the office window Jordan held a sweeping view of nearly all of the front yard. Only one little corner on the down-sloping side near the road was hidden. Jordan checked on Timmy. He hadn't let go of his mitt since the party yesterday, and Jordan vowed to stop work later and throw the ball around with Timmy if things cooled down.

Meanwhile, Timmy didn't seem to mind the solitude. With his mitt tucked underneath his arm, Timmy dragged a birch switch along the grass. Capote, the Stone's black and white cat, chased it as only a cat can. From his view above the scene, Jordan stopped to watch the graceful dance of play.

Timmy wore a colorful tie-dyed T-shirt, a birthday present handmade by the mother of one of his buddies. Like a lilliputian matador, Timmy teased Capote with short strokes of the stick. As soon as Timmy captured Capote's interest, he broadened the strokes sending the cat into a tizzy, racing side to side to snatch the stick. Then Timmy himself twirled around in circles with Capote chasing in wild abandon. Nothing could distract the cat from his relentless pursuit. Timmy slowed the circles down, slower, slower, giving Capote the chance to pounce on the stick. The gentle warrior that he was, Timmy always let Capote win in the end.

It was hard for Jordan to concentrate on the blue screen of his computer. The office was air-conditioned, but just the thought of the humidity outside distracted him. Jordan was outlining Ling's story, as of yet untitled. The task was somewhat premature since Clarion had yet to make an offer. Jordan had no doubt they would, the New York publishing house had never passed on one of his proposals. But Jordan wasn't sure how editor Tom Cryer would react if Ling's release didn't come through.

The unsigned release worried Jordan on another count. Clarion might fuss, but they'd eventually buy the story without the release. Jittery Hollywood, however, wouldn't touch the property without exclusive commitments in place. And that's where the payoff was—on television. For every one person who read a book, one hundred watched the movie of the week. Jordan had optioned four of his books, three had made it through development and on to broadcast. The money was great, and the kicker was book sales afterward; it never hurts when 20 million Americans tune in.

The phone rang. Jordan took one last glance at Timmy and picked up the receiver.

"Good day, Jordan," said Evelyn Ashford, Jordan's

agent, a grand old dame with an English accent so perfect it sounded fake.

"I've just spoken with Tom at Clarion," Evelyn said. "They like the story very much."

Evelyn was tentative, not like her.

"Then what's the problem?" asked Jordan.

"I'm afraid, you're not going to like this."

"Tell me."

"He's offering thirty thousand for the advance."

"Don't kid me. I got sixty-five for my last book. He can't be serious."

"He is."

"Then tell him we're going to Simon & Schuster. They've been hounding you to sign me, haven't they? I'm ready for a change anyway."

"I would, Jordan, but honestly I don't think it's in your best interest. It's not you, nor is it the book. And you know Tom doesn't want to lose you."

"Than what is it?"

Jordan strolled the length of the phone chord. He glanced through the window. Timmy twirled in circles with Capote in pursuit.

"The market is saturated," Evelyn continued. "For what it's worth, my advice is to take the sacrifice on the advance and we'll make it up in royalties. It all evens out in the end, you know that. I already have a Hollywood producer interested in a movie of the week.

Jordan heard a terrible screech of tires outside. He jumped to the window. Timmy and Capote, still entranced in their game, hardly seemed to notice the disturbance.

"I don't like it. He's messing with me," Jordan continued.

"Jordan, be reasonable. The dollars have stopped flowing. Advances are down, believe me. No one *reads* anymore. You haven't even received the release from the girl."

"I'll get it. Tell him fifty-five minimum. Call him. Tell him that's the best I can do."

"Jordan, you're putting me in an unenviable position."

"I can't do less, that's what it costs me to write it. Tell them to fire an MBA or something."

"I'll give it a try, but I wouldn't get your hopes up."

Jordan hung up the phone and gazed out the window at Timmy. Capote stalked the switch from left to right and back again. Jordan fell into his highback leather chair. He stared at the screen, the blue void. Even without the release he would write the story. Ling would just have to suffer. He would get her money on a TV deal. She would have no choice by then.

Jordan had time to type only one or two thoughts before the phone rang again.

"Jordan, it's Evelyn."

"Yeah?"

"You're fearless."

"What did he say?"

"Or lucky," she said.

"I told you."

"I'll send the contract."

"Evelyn, thanks."

Jordan punched the air in celebration. No matter how many books he had sold, it always felt great to sell another. "Yes."

Jordan glanced outside. Capote played with a solitary leaf. Timmy was gone.

Jordan bent down to get a better view through the window. No Timmy. He probably stepped inside for a drink or decided finally to part with his beloved mitt. Jordan reapplied himself to the work at hand and jotted down the first notes of the afternoon. Now he was ready to get started.

It came in spurts, it always had, ten minutes on, five minutes off, but now buoyed by the win over Clarion,

Jordan worked furiously laying down a basic structure. When he glanced at the clock he realized that a half hour had elapsed. He peered out the window again. Capote had found a sticky pinecone to bat around, but Timmy was nowhere to be seen. Strange.

Jordan walked down the stairs, along the side of the garage and into the house. He entered through the kitchen.

"Timmy?" Jordan called. But the house was silent.

"Timmy?" he called a bit louder.

No response.

Jordan stepped again into the humidity outside. He walked around back to the inlet, where Timmy and Cal often set broad leaves to sail before pummeling them with acorns.

"Timmy?"

Nothing.

Around the house he walked, past the crumbling treehouse and beyond Allie's flower garden that sprung to life with tulips in the spring and died in late fall with the last yellow chrysanthemum. He strolled into the front yard, with its wide green lawn on which many a touch-football game had been played.

"Timmy?"

The name bounced against the hill beyond the road. Jordan heard his own faint echo but no response from his son.

Maybe he went to Aaron's house, Timmy's friend down the street. Or Colin's, even closer. It was possible, but not like Timmy. He knew better than to go anywhere without saying something first.

"Timmy."

Jordan walked out to Capote. The cat ceased batting the pinecone and looked up at Jordan asking him to play.

"Timmy?" Louder now.

No answer.

Jordan saw the birch switch laying on the grass closer to the road. He walked to the spot and picked it up. He saw the scratches left by Capote's claws. A few cars drove by. No Timmy.

"Game's over." Jordan shouted into the air. But this wasn't Timmy's game, never was. Jordan eyeballed his office, gauging the view he had from there to here, this spot where he last saw his son. An unobstructed line of sight.

"Timmy," Jordan shouted again.

Only the echo returned.

Then Jordan saw it, beyond the white pine fence, on the black asphalt soft with heat. Jordan dropped the stick and bolted. He vaulted the fence and raced to it. It was crushed like a small animal on the crooked double yellow line. Timmy's new mitt.

"Timmy!"

A car careened around the corner and headed for Jordan. The driver swerved and slammed his brakes. The shriek of the horn blasted Jordan to his senses and he jumped away in the nick of time.

"Asshole." The driver honked as he drove on.

"Timmy. Oh, God."

Timmy had never once ventured beyond the property without permission. There was too much of interest to him inside the small world within the fence. He preferred to discover with his mind more than his eyes.

Jordan cupped his hands around his mouth. He shouted to the sky, long and slow, so his words would scale the juniper-covered hills and curve around the bend in the road.

Capote watched inquisitively from the yard.

A taste of adrenaline filled Jordan's tongue and numbed it.

"Timmy, where are you?" Jordan whispered.

Jordan turned north, east, south, west. He called in each direction, but Timmy did not call back.

What had Jordan done wrong? He had watched from the window as always. Hadn't he glanced out often? Indeed, today he had watched all the more closely, captivated by the little game between Timmy and Capote. And when Jordan had heard the tires screech, hadn't he looked out immediately to check on Timmy? But there had been nothing wrong, no car, no problem. It was only when Jordan was on the phone with Evelyn, wrapped up in talk.

But even that episode was short. What could it have been, two, three minutes, maybe? Timmy had played countless times out front for ten or twenty minutes without Jordan checking on him.

The mitt in the road, that's what frightened Jordan. No one had to tell Timmy to stay away from the road. He feared it, always had. Timmy would not have been there on his own accord, no less near the double yellow line. Timmy didn't like things hard or angular. He loved the soft, the round, the pretty, the fair. And the mitt. Timmy loved that mitt. He had kept it close all day, not setting it down for a moment even when not playing with it.

Jordan realized the mitt must have had made it onto the road in some strange forceful way; a shiver ran up his spine. Jordan flashed briefly on all the times he had written that hackneyed phrase, *"a shiver ran up his spine."* Now it was his story, his spine, his shiver.

A van slowed on the road. Allie's.

"What in the world are you doing?" she asked.

"Timmy. He's gone."

"Gone? Where?" she said calmly. Then she saw the panic in his eyes.

"Look." Jordan held out Timmy's mitt as the only proof needed. "I found it in the road."

"The road?"

Allie pulled the minivan into the driveway and slammed it into park.

"Weren't you watching?"

"Yes, but I—"

Allie didn't wait for an answer. She shouted his name hoping her voice traveled on different channels to her son. A car slowed. Allie approached the driver. It was Nan, a neighbor from down the road.

"Have you seen Timmy?" Allie asked.

"Is he missing?"

"Yes. No. We don't know. Did you see him down there by your place?"

"No."

"Timmy," Allie shouted once again.

"Please call us if we can help." Nan crept away, watching in her rearview mirror.

"Timmy!"

A thousand scenarios raced through Allie's brain. He's wandered to a friend's house. He's in the trunk of a car tied up and screaming. He's just beyond, playing in the cattails near the inlet. His limp body rests under a juniper up on the hill.

Is he alive? Dead? If he was in the hands of a stranger, a terrible stranger, would she prefer him alive or dead? Where is he? Goddamn it.

"Timmy!" How much louder could she scream? How much more could she want her son?

"What do we do?"

"Okay, let's not panic," Allie said.

How many crises had the two faced together? There was Sarah's bicycle collision with a truck not twenty paces from here that broke her collarbone. Allie thought Sarah was dead when she first ran from the house screaming. There was Cal's concussion from slamming his head on the shallow inlet bottom. He almost drowned then.

But nothing held the terror of the unknown like this.

"I'll call Aaron's and Colin's," Allie said.

"How about the police?"

She thought for a moment. "You look for two minutes. If we don't find him, we'll call."

Allie dashed into the house. Her hands trembled, fumbled over her address book. She dialed a wrong number, then started over again. Come on, come on, she prayed, pick up, pick up. Thank God.

"Deb, have you seen Timmy? Please tell me he's there."

"Why no, we haven't seen him," said Colin's mom. "Something wrong?"

"I'll call you later."

Allie called Aaron's mom. "Aaron's at camp, left this morning."

Timmy, where are you?

Silversteins'. No answer. Timmy wouldn't be there. Why would Timmy be there?

Allie checked the living room, den, garage, dining room, the bedrooms upstairs. Timmy, please.

What do you do when you've lost your child? How many television shows had Allie seen on stranger abduction? Family abduction? How many articles had she read?

But now her mind was blank. Her sheer will was not enough to bring her baby back, and she didn't know what else to do.

Jordan raced inside, breathless.

"Nothing."

The adrenaline had spread now to Jordan's cheeks and eyes. He felt the blood pump to his fingertips and the balls of his feet.

"Let's call the police."

Allie fumbled with the phone again. Nine-one-one.

Jordan looked at his watch. One minute, two.

"Why aren't they here yet?"

Three minutes.

"I'm going to call again," said Allie.

"Call."

"An officer is on his way," said the dispatcher. "Rocky Cliff is off the beaten path, you know."

Goddamn Rocky Cliff.

Four minutes.

"I can't stand this," said Jordan. He ran from the house and called into the air again. "Timmy!"

Five minutes. Jordan saw the Nassau County Police squad car slow down near the driveway.

Slow, he's driving so slow.

Allie rushed out to greet her savior.

"It's Timmy," said Jordan. "Our six-year-old. He's gone."

"Seven years old," Allie corrected him. "He turned seven yesterday."

"How long has he been gone, ma'am?" asked Patrolman Dibbs.

Allie looked at Jordan. "I don't know, thirty minutes, forty-five minutes, maybe."

"Maybe twenty, I don't know," said Jordan.

"If it's just been twenty minutes I wouldn't panic. Most of the time, they just come home by themselves."

"You don't understand, officer," said Jordan.

"Friends? Relatives? Think where he could be."

"Please, listen," said Allie. "Timmy would not leave. He's weak. He has asthma. He's not the kind of child to just go. The glove, show him the glove," she told Jordan, remembering the most compelling evidence of all.

Jordan had almost forgotten it, too. He held it still.

"This glove. He got it for his birthday. I found it in the middle of the road. He would never let it go."

"Okay." Dibbs sighed. "I'll tell you what I can do. I'll radio for another car to look around the neighborhood. Meanwhile, I'll come in and take a report."

"Report?" said Jordan angrily. "Our boy is out there and you're going to write a fucking report?"

"I don't even know what he looks like."

"Light brown eyes, light brown hair," said Jordan.

"An angel," Allie added.

"You don't understand," said Jordan.

"Let's step inside, please."

Dibbs radioed in. A few minutes later a second patrol car stopped in for a moment, then left in search of a Caucasian child, male, seven years old, light brown eyes, brown hair, approximately forty-seven pounds, four feet tall, last seen wearing tie-dyed T-shirt, green shorts, white sneakers and socks.

As Dibbs scribbled the pertinent information, the adrenaline in Jordan slowly transformed from an electric fluid to a solid lump of fear stuck in his throat.

One hour. Allie made more phone calls, Billy, Bobby, Alyssa, Zoe, Hank, Richie. Every friend she could think of. Everywhere Timmy wasn't.

Officer Dibbs asked questions endlessly. Any suspicious cars recently? Weird phone calls? Was Timmy having trouble in school? Had he had a fight recently with Jordan or Allie? Drugs—did the parents suspect drugs?

Two hours. Jordan drove the neighborhood looking around the sides of houses, in parking lots, schoolyards. He drove slowly looking for a flash of that distinctive T-shirt, for Timmy's disarming smile. Nothing. In the town of Rocky Cliff, nothing. How he prayed for a glimpse of his son. Jordan vowed anything that God demanded for his son back.

Three hours. Cal took off on foot through the brush and trails only he and Timmy knew. Sarah made more calls, Matthew, Christopher, Katie, Janette, Jessica, Trevor.

Four hours. The evening breeze returned on schedule and the shadows grew long. Capote slept soundly on the den couch.

Five hours. Dibbs was replaced by Sergeant Pena and Patrolman O'Brien.

Six hours. Dusk came with a few sprinkles.
Seven hours. A shower of summer rain.
Eight hours. More tears.
Ten hours. No Timmy. No Timmy at all.

FOUR

At 8:00 A.M. sharp, Jordan walked briskly through the halls of the regional office of the Federal Bureau of Investigation in Melville, Long Island. Though he knew the place well, it seemed strangely unfamiliar today.

The secretary was new. That was good. Jordan couldn't recall what guises he had used to persuade the former secretary to do his bidding, but surely he had played them out with impunity. His vulnerability today precluded any games.

During the previous night, the long night, the police had fanned out into the woods surrounding the house. In their heavy boots moving silently on the bed of pine needles, the men and women searched, first within 50 yards of the house, then 100 yards, then 200 yards, always enlarging the perimeter until their shouts through the trees were distant and indiscernible and they were forced to communicate by handheld radio. Whatever the medium, the message was the same.

"Agent Julius Waters, please," Jordan bid the secretary, a slender brunette with a mole above her right eye.

"And your name?"

"Stone, Jordan Stone."

The secretary dialed the extension and spoke a few words, then turned back to Jordan.

"I'm sorry, Special Agent Waters is unavailable. Is there someone else who can help you?"

Jordan crouched down to eye-level with the woman. His first impulse was to fabricate a story. Habits are hard to break.

"Would you please call him back and tell him this is a personal matter, a grave personal matter."

The secretary sensed the urgency, honesty, or both. Her long red fingernails tapped out the numbers quickly.

"He will see you now."

"Thank you."

Normally Jordan would be sure to get the secretary's name for future use, but today he had no time, no courage.

Of all the agents, Jordan shared the most history with Waters, and it wasn't surprising that Waters had attempted to shun Jordan.

Jordan strode past the trophy cases and framed photos of agents congratulating one another for jobs well done. He rapped lightly on Waters' door and it swung slowly open.

"Well, if it's not the book dude," said Waters, a man as large as he was black. "We haven't had the pleasure since, when, that nasty little case about the gardener who tended more than just the family lawn."

Jordan feared Waters would bring that up. Jordan's book *The Tended Garden* was the true story of a gardener, a hunky Greek named Spiro, who couldn't resist the advances of an aging heiress of the Southampton estate he tended. After a few months, Spiro grew tired of the affair. But the heiress clung like a vine to her Adonis, which triggered several ugly verbal fights between them, according to her husband, who apparently was delighted to have his wife's attention focused elsewhere. At the gardener's trial, the prosecution argued that Spiro murdered the heiress with a middle A wire ripped from a grand piano that graced the estate's salon, all in a clumsy attempt to untangle himself from the affair.

The gardener wept throughout the trial and professed his innocence at every possible juncture, but his denials failed to sway the jury. They found him guilty of first-degree murder and sentenced him to life. The papers dubbed the case "A Greek Tragedy," and called Spiro "the garrote gardener."

Much to Waters' chagrin, Jordan's book was published a year later. It included transcripts of taped interviews the bureau had made with the husband of the victim—transcripts that conveniently never made it to trial. They included a number of alarming discrepancies between the husband's original story and his courtroom testimony—enough to cast doubt on the verdict and on Waters' investigation.

The gardener was retried and found not guilty. He thanked Jordan with a wet kiss on the cheek, then fled back to Greece the very next day, apparently having had his fill of American justice and women. The husband tried to flee but was nabbed at JFK and is serving time somewhere.

Jordan knew that nothing peeves law enforcement officials more than seeing their work unraveled, rightfully so or not, particularly by a writer or journalist. Cops and special agents cherish convictions, and Waters, who worked long and hard on the case, never quite forgave Stone for his meddling. But Waters was the best agent on the force, and Jordan needed no less.

"If you're still upset about that book, you have a right to be," said Jordan.

Waters let out a bellow, the kind that can only be learned from growing up barefoot in the Caribbean Islands or Jamaica, which was the case with Waters.

"Do I detect contrition?" said Waters in his deep syncopated voice, as if he were ready to begin a sermon or break into song. "For you to employ contrition means that you want something fairly badly, Mr. Stone."

"It's my son, he's missing."

"Come now, I wouldn't have suspected even you to stoop as low as to include family members in an attempt to extract information."

Despite his roots in poverty-stricken Kingston, Waters had been educated privately, the token darkie in a school on an island run by racists. He fooled everyone by graduating at the top of his class, going on to Cornell, and graduating from the FBI Academy with top honors. He worked a bureaucracy and a ghetto with equal aplomb. If he had one flaw it was impatience. He jumped too quickly to snatch the quail, as one of Waters' colleague described it.

"This is no scheme, no joke," said Jordan.

Waters pondered Jordan's urgency and saw this was no ruse.

"Have you met Ron Deleese?" Waters pointed to a shadowy figure standing near the door.

Jordan turned and saw the man for the first time. Jordan extended his hand, slightly startled by a presence he hadn't felt.

"Mr. Deleese comes from our Lincoln, Nebraska, office."

Deleese did, indeed, look like a farm boy with his wide-set blue eyes and sandy hair. He gestured to Jordan with a tip of an imaginary cowboy hat. Deleese squeezed Jordan's hand as if drawing milk from a cow.

Waters leaned back in his chair. Jordan could hear the leather strap of Waters' shoulder holster stretch under his jacket. "How long has your son been missing?"

"Since yesterday afternoon."

"Exactly when?" asked Waters. Jordan now remembered Waters' obsession with precision.

"Three-thirty, four o'clock, about then." Jordan retold the events of the afternoon.

"I'm sure the local police are doing all they can," declared Waters.

"They've done a good job searching the area, but they're not equipped to do much more. You know that."

"I do, indeed. But we can't take the case. I'm sorry." Waters leaned forward and began officiously shuffling papers, as if to suggest that Jordan's time was up.

"Look, you can't hold *The Tended Garden* against me. This is a felony. This is my son."

"It has nothing to do with your book, I assure you. It's simply that we don't get involved in missing children cases unless there is evidence of stranger abduction or a bona fide ransom request. It's routine."

"There's nothing routine about this. I told you I saw—"

"What, Stone?" Waters interrupted. "What precisely did you see? You saw your son one minute and the next he vanished. It might be anyone, for any reason—if he were abducted at all."

"I know he was. I feel it in my gut."

"Are you familiar with the statistics? Ninety-eight percent of all missing children cases clear as runaways or parental abductions."

"Timmy wouldn't run away, and my wife and I certainly didn't abduct him."

"Perhaps, but policy prevents us from taking the case until we are presented with a solid lead or motive. I'm sorry, Jordan."

"I have money.. People will do anything for money these days."

"Delusions of grandeur, Mr. Stone. Many people have money, and quite a bit more than you."

"Then help me as a friend."

Waters sighed. "I'll tell you what we can do," said Waters. "If Timmy isn't found by tomorrow morning, come back and we'll reassess the situation. Fair enough?"

Jordan whipped the table with his fist. He could feel his jawbone unconsciously flex. "I'm not leaving here until you do something. I swear."

"Please spare me, Stone. I've had my quota of martyrs for the week."

"We're losing precious time. There's a clear motive here," said Jordan.

"And what's that?"

"Profit."

Waters laughed again. "You've been reading too many of your own books. It sounds as if you have this case already solved. Perhaps we should let you catch the kidnapper."

"Don't make me beg, Julius. This is my son."

Waters leaned back, and once again the holster strap creaked as it strained around his large body. Unlike most agents, Waters dressed impeccably, from the handkerchief in the top pocket of his dark blue suit to the buff on his Oxfords. Jordan could see him sweating underneath his handmade cotton shirt with the accented collar.

"What do you think, Deleese?"

Deleese moved from the shadow of the door. As he stepped forward, he touched the back of the vacant guest chair, as if to indicate that this was his seat and soon he would have the gumption to sit in it.

A moment of silence passed before Deleese spoke.

"I think we need m-more information from Mr. St-t-tone."

Oh, great, a stutterer, Jordan thought. How the hell did the FBI allow a stutterer to join its ranks?

"What kind of information, Ron?" Waters asked.

"The type of threats he and his f-family have received and from whom."

"Fine idea."

Water picked up the phone and punched three numbers. "Ask Sherard to join us please."

Waters clasped his hands on the desk and turned to Jordan.

"I'll tell you what I am willing to do. We'll take a few notes and see what we have here, but I'm not promising you anything. Understood?"

"Understood," said Jordan.

Jordan eyed Deleese, back in the shadows. For the first time Jordan studied the quiet man with the thick hands. There was an angelic quality to him, as if he had yet to learn of the perversities of the world.

"Thank you," Jordan said to him. "Thanks."

Deleese nodded. The corner of his mouth moved up slightly, but the movement was so brief and subtle, Jordan wasn't sure if it was a smile or a twitch. A knock on the door broke Jordan's concentration. It was Sherard, notebook computer in hand.

"Now Jordan, we need you to tell us about each individual that you feel may hold a grudge against you and why."

"No one holds a grudge against me."

Waters laughed. "Please, you write books revealing the most intimate secrets of people's lives and you think no one holds a grudge against you? You're fooling yourself. Why don't we start with your first book?"

The subjects of his books were suspects by association if nothing more. Jordan had thought about the prospect, naturally, but somehow he always regarded it as little more than a remote possibility. He took a deep breath and recounted the tale of Cindy, the prepubescent who escaped the pornographer's camera by a stroke of luck.

"The prime suspect in Cindy's story has to be John

Kent, the child pornographer who arranged to rent Cindy and all her modest charms for the week," said Jordan.

"Tell me more."

"Kent worked with others, I don't know who, under the cryptic name of YPI, a profitable group that sent some 2,000 pieces of child pornography through the mails each week.

"What does YPI stand for?" asked Waters.

"You don't want to know."

"I do."

Jordan paused. Sherard's fingers took a rest from the keyboard.

"It's stands for Young Pussies, Inc."

Waters cringed with revulsion.

"I told you you didn't want to know."

"How about the girl's parents?" asked Waters.

"In prison, both of them. Fifteen to thirty."

"Siblings?"

"There was an older brother and sister, but I hardly mentioned them in the book, even though it was common knowledge they had a hand in Cindy's abuse."

For the first time, Waters loosened his silk tie. Jordan took it as a good sign. Early as it was in the morning and despite the air conditioning, the wooden chair stuck to Jordan's pants, and he felt the heat slip through the slats of the blinds behind Waters. Another sweltering day.

"*Invasion of Privacy,* my second book. Dotty O'Dougherty, a boarding house matron kills her guests to get their social security checks. She's in the Fed Pen in Lompoc, California."

"Does she have children, brothers, sisters, a husband?"

Jordan remembered that Dotty had a long-lost daughter, Kitty, married to a biker named, by coincidence or design, Doggie. He had never met them but he saw a picture of Kitty and Doggie after their arrest at a methamphetamine lab set up in their garage. Kitty had a tattoo on her cheek of a cat's paw ripping away the skin under her eye and freeing a trickle of blood to drip down her cheek. Doggie was covered with prison line art, indistinguishable green designs of demons, pistons, and seminude mermaids faded and wrinkled over time to become splotches of green mange.

"Find all the pertinent info: last known address, aliases, social security numbers, prison identification numbers, and physical description. They're worth a check," said Waters.

"Next book. Number three, *Carrie's Confession*. A young woman, Carrie Richter goes to prison after confessing to the death of her eight-year-old niece. Only she didn't commit the crime, her father did. It seems he had been abusing every female in the family for three generations. He was even doing it with his wife's mother. With a psychiatrist's help, Carrie was able to unshackle herself from the delusion and point an accusing finger at her father."

"And what about him?"

"Harold Richter. Corporate type, white shirt, middle-aged. Worked for a number of hi-tech firms always in the finance department. He was a real wiz with numbers, I understand."

"Where is he?"

"In Attica last time I checked."

"Any relatives?"

"He had a brother, Amos or Aaron, or something like that, a soft-spoken professor, who seemed night-and-day different from Harold."

"Did he testify at the trial?"

"No, but he was there. He sat at the defense table the entire time."

"He sided with his brother, the murderer?"

"Strange family."

,"Check it out. And Carrie?"

"She's happy. She got money and married the therapist. Though Carrie's mother, Lillian Richter, took an
odd position at the trial. She stood by her husband's
side, said it was impossible that he had done all those
horrendous things. During testimony, she painted Harold as a saint and tore her daughter to shreds, calling
her a whore and a traitor. She sounded good until the
prosecution brought in her doctor."

"What happened?"

"He came armed with a stack of medical records revealing years of vaginal trauma to Lillian. It turns out
Harold was abusing Carrie's mother on a scale far
more ambitious than anyone else. He had brainwashed
her to the max."

"And the status on Lillian?" asked Waters.

"Don't know. But I don't think she is the vengeful
type."

"Not unless she's still under his thumb and doing his
bidding," added Waters. He nodded to Sherard to
make a special note of Lillian's name. "Go on."

"*Slaughter Alley,*" said Stone.

Waters glanced at Jordan in disdain.

"Well, that was the name of the road where the murder took place."

"I was making no judgment, I assure you."

"Three boys gang rape a sixteen-year-old girl, then
bludgeon her to death. Two are doing time, Ron Gallagher and Richie Walters. Ron, the oldest, had a previous—an attempted murder charge bargained down to
involuntary manslaughter for which he spent seven
months in a JV facility. Ron's definitely the toughest.
I'm sure he was belt-whipped by his father. He had that
edge to him.

"And the second boy?" asked Waters.

Richie. His specialty was burglary. Police found his
parents' garage filled with over $100,000 of merchan-

dise, from stereos to jewelry, even an Alpha Romeo covered with a tarp. The kid also had a knack for computers. Investigators discovered notebooks filled with lists of stolen telephone access codes.

"The third kid was Josh Hedlund. The kid swore to police that he had acted merely as a lookout. But investigators didn't buy it. They found fresh semen stains in the boy's jeans after the arrest. Police surmised Josh had attempted to rape the girl only to have an orgasm before he could get himself unzipped. The cops took to calling him Preemie for premature ejaculator."

Waters leaned back in his chair. "How about relatives?"

"All three boys came from broken homes—rich, apathetic homes. That's the way it seemed anyway. If I had to choose a suspect from *Slaughter,* it would be Richie's father, Paul Gallagher, an attorney and a right-wing religious fanatic who audits his holiness by the number of abortion clinics he protests each month. The girl's parents didn't like the idea of the book at first because their daughter wasn't exactly the Virgin Mary, but I've heard little from them after the initial grumbling."

"Check them all out," Waters instructed Sherard.

Then there is *The Tended Garden.* I don't think I have to tell you the major players there."

"Certainly not," said Waters without looking up.

"Next," said Jordan, *"Mind's Eye,* my latest in print. It's about a cult leader named Satchel Arness. His group started out as your typical fundamentalist cult—paranoid, gun-collecting. They bought 130 acres in southern Indiana, outside of Greensburg, and built tunnels and bomb shelters, garden-variety stuff. But Arness was no ordinary Christ figure. He's brilliant but certifiably insane when off lithium. A real snake-charmer. He convinced several of his lighter-skinned followers to sell their babies to some Kuwaiti baby broker for arms—grenade launchers, antiaircraft munitions, everything short of Sherman tanks.

"He wrote me a letter once full of threats. I have a copy at home, but I didn't pay much attention to it. He's made a cottage industry out of threatening people. Last I heard he was being transferred to solitary. It seems he got to preaching to the inmates and some were proclaiming him God. Prison is dangerous enough without true believers of a false messiah.

"Several lieutenants attempted to keep the cult going with limited success. The standout is a guy named Charlie Spike, a tall, dark-haired fellow who never travels without an entourage of worshipful seventeen-year-olds and some of their mothers, too. He has an older brother named Willy, a quiet but intense guy who lives off the human surplus his brother can't find the time to screw."

Waters looked out the faded venetian blinds onto the parking lot and then back at Jordan.

"Anything else?"

"I'm working on a book right now. It's untitled." Jordan recounted the passions of Chester Tenden and the poor fortune it brought to Ling Wu.

"I saw Chester just last week in jail," said Jordan.

"Threaten you?"

"Mildly."

"Why am I not surprised? Anyone, else?"

"That's it," said Jordan. "That's all."

"Quite a distinguished body of work, Stone. You must be proud."

"I'm not anything but concerned about my son. I'm sure you can understand that."

Waters sighed. "All right. We'll take the case. But on one condition."

"What's that?" Jordan asked.

"That we have your full cooperation, you work with us and through us. "No hanky-panky, Stone."

Jordan nodded.

"Do we have your word?"

"Yes."

"Okay. Sherard, I want backgrounds and status quos on everyone. Give the Arness group and Richter top priority. Deleese get ready to set up shop at Stone's home. If it's one of these people, we should expect contact in the next few days."

Sherard flipped the lid down on his computer and exited with military precision. Waters creaked back in his chair and lowered his voice two notches.

"Let me prepare you, Jordan. Ransom abductions are extremely rare, despite their hallowed place in film and popular culture. Stranger abduction is the much more likely scenario. And when a stranger abducts a child, his motive is fairly predictable. You understand that?"

"Yes."

"You must be ready for the worst. And prepare your wife."

"I know."

"Now, any questions of us?" Waters asked.

"What do we tell the media?"

"We tell them nothing. We keep it absolutely confidential."

"You know, I'll do anything to get my son back," Jordan said.

"I understand."

"No, you don't. I mean anything."

FIVE

The bed was hard in Timmy's room, far harder than his bed at home, but it felt safe. The man had left two blankets. Timmy didn't need either because it was hot. He folded them neatly and laid on top of the blue sheet. It was hot, really hot. The window was covered with a piece of plywood and nailed shut. Everything was neat in the room. There wasn't much: A bookcase filled with children's books, a nightstand with a light, a little potty with a roll of tissue paper beside it. Timmy was free to turn the lights on and off whenever he wanted. On the first day the man had asked Timmy what he liked to drink and eat. Timmy said Yoo-Hoo chocolate drinks and Twinkies. The man left and came back later with lots of both. Timmy was a little sick of them now. Three times a day for three days and anything will get you sick. Timmy remembered his mom saying that too much of a good thing could hurt. She was right.

Timmy had been scared at first, he still was, but not like the first day. Not like when it happened. The van slowed to a stop on the road. Timmy didn't notice it at first. But he looked up after someone called. The man leaned out and asked if this was Timmy Stone's house. This was it, said Timmy. Did he know Timmy Stone?

the man asked. Timmy explained that *he* was Timmy Stone. The man sounded surprised. Really? Are you sure? He said he had a package for Timmy Stone, a birthday present. Timmy did his best to assure him that he was Timmy. Good, said the man, then you can take the package. Timmy was excited. He wondered who the package was from. Timmy moved closer to the fence. For me? he asked. Well, if you are Timmy Stone it's for you, the man replied.

The man stepped out of the van and held out a clipboard to Timmy. The man said Timmy had to sign for the package. Timmy climbed the fence two rungs to sign his name. He had never signed for anything in his life, but he had seen his dad sign for packages a zillion times. Timmy took the pen in his left hand. He reached over for the clipboard.

That's when the man grabbed him. He grabbed tight around Timmy's wrists. Timmy didn't understand. Let me go, Timmy shouted. He struggled, but the man was strong. Timmy pleaded with the man. Before he had looked so nice, had a present for Timmy. Now he looked mean and angry, like a thief. Let me go! Timmy shouted. But the man didn't listen.

He pulled Timmy over the fence and dragged him across the street. Timmy's mitt fell from his hand. The man lifted Timmy up by his armpits and threw him into the van. Timmy felt his elbow sear with pain as it scraped on the ribbed metal floor. The door slammed shut. Timmy screamed for his daddy, but the man put his large hand over Timmy's mouth and told him that if he didn't shut up somebody was going to get hurt. Timmy thought the man was talking about his dad, so Timmy stopped struggling.

The man got into the driver's seat and drove two blocks. Then he stopped and tied Timmy's hand and legs with speaker wire. Timmy knew it was speaker wire because he helped his father install the new stereo last

year. The man pulled a long hypodermic needle from a
bag. Timmy closed his eyes and felt a sharp pain as the
needle entered his bottom. It hurt bad.

There was a curtain between the back of the van and
where the man sat in the driver's seat. Timmy couldn't
see anything. He wanted to open the sliding van door
but he was afraid he would fall out while the van was
going fast. Timmy tried to stay awake but he couldn't.

When Timmy awoke he found himself in the room
with the hard bed, the plywood covering the window,
and the little potty that looked like the one at
Ephraim's house for his little sister Eliana. Timmy
couldn't tell if it was night or day when he awoke. His
elbow ached. He was thirsty. The light was on. He
didn't know if the room was attached to a house, or if it
was in an apartment building, or whether he was in the
middle of Alaska in a hut or something. He wondered
if anyone would ever find him again. He tried the door
but it was locked. He never felt so alone. He turned the
light off just to see what would happen and the room
turned pitch black. He flipped it on quickly again and
was glad it worked.

He knocked softly on the door. Nothing. He knocked
harder. He heard footsteps moving to the door. He
heard keys jangling and then he saw the doorknob wiggle. And now he was sorry he had knocked. Timmy
stepped back. Suddenly he remembered the man, the
ugly man and his ugly face when he pulled Timmy over
the fence. Please don't let it be him.

The door squeaked open. It was the man. Timmy
covered his face with his hands to protect himself.

"Don't worry, I won't hurt you," said the man.

Timmy looked at him through his fingers. The man
didn't look frightening anymore. Timmy got a quick
glance of the living room. It was old and musty with a
big overstuffed blue chair, like in the basement of

Timmy's house. The man moved into Timmy's room quickly and shut the door behind him.

"Timmy, how are you feeling?" asked the man.

"I'm scared."

"I hope I didn't hurt you, your wrists I mean."

Timmy had forgotten about his wrists and felt them now. They hurt.

"No," said Timmy.

"I'm sorry." The man had little hairs growing out of his nose. His eyes were blue and he had a little brown mole on the side of his neck. But it was his bad breath that Timmy noticed most.

"That's okay." There was a moment of silence. Timmy didn't know if he was supposed to say anything more.

"Timmy, you may be here for a long while, many days. And I want you to be comfortable. Anytime you need something, you just knock. When you're hungry, knock. When you have to empty your potty, knock. When you want to, you know, just talk, knock. Okay?"

Timmy nodded yes.

"Good," said the man. "I don't want any trouble from you and I promise I'll be good to you, *if* you do as I say. Do you understand?"

Timmy nodded yes again.

"Sir?" Timmy asked.

"Yes, son?"

"Can I ask you a question?"

"You may."

"How do you know my name?" Timmy asked.

"I know you just had a birthday, that you have an older brother and sister, that you like art in school. I know your dad."

"You know my dad?"

"Well, let's say I'm familiar with him."

"Do my parents know I'm here?"

"No."

"When can I go home?"

"You ask a lot of questions."

"Sorry."

"I'm going to lock the door and I'll be back in a while. Okay?"

Timmy nodded yes.

"Don't be afraid. I think you and I will get along just fine." The man patted Timmy on the head, tussling his hair slightly.

"Mister?"

"Yes?"

"What's your name?"

The man stopped to think.

"Wally," he said. "You can just call me Wally."

Wally slipped out and pulled the door shut behind him. Timmy heard the doorknob click and then a padlock settle into place. After some movement, he heard what sounded like a front door open and close. Then silence.

Timmy looked at the books on the shelves for the first time. It looked like they were all brand-new. He was familiar with many of them. He had some at home and had read others at school. But he didn't feel like reading now. He touched the plywood over the window. It was fastened tight. Timmy paced the floor, then tried the doorknob again. There was no way out. Suddenly he had an urge to pee. He lifted up the potty and started to urinate. The urine hit the potty and splashed back on his pajamas. So Timmy stopped peeing for a moment, got down on his knees so the pee wouldn't hit the potty with such force. He looked at the yellow urine. It smelled. He closed the lid, but it still smelled pretty bad.

"Mommy," Timmy heard himself say. He looked around but nobody was around to hear. He missed his family so much. He wondered what they were doing now and if they missed him. He got back in bed and pulled the sheet over his face. He watched as his quick breaths lifted the sheet momentarily before it fell again. He wanted his mom so badly. In the distance he heard the low moan of a train whistle, then it was gone. What had he done wrong? Timmy pulled the sheet tighter around him and tucked his knees to his chest. And then he cried himself to sleep.

From a phone booth outside the Bureau office, Jordan called his office for messages. There was only one. He hesitated to listen, thinking he should wait for the Bureau to monitor the call. But since the call was now forever saved on tape, the agents could listen to it all they wanted later. Jordan couldn't contain his curiosity. Maybe this was Him.

The tape rewound quickly; the message was short.

"Jordan, Arnie Sinkowitz here. "We have to talk. Give me a call or stop by. It's urgent."

If Sink said it was important, it was.

The *Newsday* offices weren't far off, and Jordan drove there with urgency. A sprawling building accommodating hundreds of workers, few people outside the New York region realized how big a paper *Newsday* was. Aside from covering nearly four million Long Islanders, the paper published a city edition and found a quiet but large readership with New Yorkers whose demographics placed them somewhere between the highbrow *New York Times* and the lowly *Post* and *Daily News*.

Jordan was forced to sign in at the front desk. Procedures had apparently tightened since he had walked the halls as a reporter years ago. Now laminated badges dangled from the employees' necks, as if they worked for the Defense Department.

The newsroom hadn't changed, still a vast sea of identical desks, each topped with a computer terminal, accompanied by the purr of phones ringing continually.

As Jordan walked through the maze of desks, he felt like he had been let loose in a house of mirrors. He remembered experiencing the same dizzying sensation the first several days on the job.

Jordan spotted Sinkowitz across the room, his jacket off and his sleeves rolled up. Sink had replaced Jordan on the police beat seven years earlier, and despite Sink's obvious disdain for the "battered wife patrol," as he called it, he had never known another tour of duty. With his timid manner, Sinkowitz was an odd choice for the beat. He possessed the unconscious habit of rocking gently when he wrote or thought deeply, like a Hasidic Jew in prayer. His eyeglasses were cut from a fishbowl and he still sprouted zits like a teenager.

The desks around Sink were unoccupied. Jordan pulled up a chair and drew close to his former colleague.

"Jordan, I know what's going on," Sinkowitz said, his head bobbing.

"Know what?" Jordan did his best to appear puzzled.

"Please, Jordan. Don't make it hard."

Jordan bowed his head. "How'd you find out?"

"I saw it on the police log yesterday, I mean we live in the same town, two blocks away. I recognized your address. I made some calls, you know, the usual."

"And the others?" asked Jordan.

"The TV stations didn't catch it. The *Times* doesn't care. And the tabloids miss everything that doesn't punch them in the nose. It came over as a missing child. I mean, you know how frequent they are. There's never a story there, really."

Sinkowitz was right. When Jordan had started on the beat he made the mistake of chasing down every missing child report until he discovered that most children found their way home by dark, returned the next morning drunk, or called from places like Philadelphia or Boston, professing their hatred, often deserved, for their parents. Jordan had learned quickly to let missing children reports slide, along with domestic altercations, assaults with a deadly weapon, and burglary. Dead ends, all of them.

"Look, Arnie. I know you have a job to do, but please help me keep it quiet. I can't have this guy panic."

"Is the FBI in on it?" A true journalist, Sink was always digging. Jordan nodded yes.

"Any leads?"

Jordan's expression held the answer.

"You must have a database or something," Sink said.

Without him having to say a thing, Jordan knew that Sinkowitz understood what was happening, who was suspected here.

"We're investigating."

"I'm in a bind, Jordan. They don't like it upstairs when we hold stories back. Not one bit. You know that."

"I know."

Sink looked around to make sure no one was watching, then drifted into a gentle rock. "If I let it slide I could get fired."

"I know."

The management was fairly liberal at *Newsday*, but some things absolutely didn't fly. No fabricated quotes, no personal insinuations, and never let a story slide for personal reasons, politics, or other allegiances. Despite his solid performance for years, Sink would be fired without an afterthought if he held back and management found out.

Jordan waved at a reporter across the newsroom. An old colleague in a sea of young, unfamiliar faces.

"How's the beat?" Jordan asked.

"Same as always," Sinkowitz said. "Hard edges, short stories."

"Tell them you want out," Jordan advised.

"They know."

"The squeaky wheel gets the grease."

Sink shrugged. He was not a complainer.

"I need this one favor, Sink. I wouldn't ask if it wasn't my son, you know that."

Jordan wondered how he would have reacted seven years ago had a colleague come to him with the same request. This was a potentially big story: *Famous author's son kidnapped.* A scoop could garner recognition, perhaps a pay raise, maybe even a bump to a new beat. Jordan couldn't answer his own question and was glad no one was posing it to him now.

Sinkowitz looked over the legion of computer terminals, as if searching for the answer. The light from the morning sun outside refracted at odd angles on the desks and walls.

"Look, Jordan, I'll lay off for awhile, as long as I can. But if the story breaks, I have to go with it, full force. You know that."

"I know."

"You'd do the same, I'm sure," said Sinkowitz.

"You bet." Jordan said, not so sure. "Thanks. You're a good man."

"Don't thank me, yet. Thank me when it's over."

"I will."

"And Jordan, if there's anything I can do . . ."

"Thanks."

As she waited for Jordan's return, Allie couldn't help but return often to the front door to check for signs of Timmy. The yard was a sweep of green grass, save for the wide magnolia tree and an occasional burst of yellow dandelion, but Timmy was nowhere to be seen.

Allie thought about the losses in her life. Her mother had died of breast cancer when Allie was a teenager, no more than Sarah's age. Allie still pondered the bitter irony of her mother losing breasts to surgery just as

Allie was developing hers. Allie had spent the last two years of high school shrouded in a fatalistic fog. She emerged from it in college, with its fresh surroundings and rush of new faces and ideas.

That's when her father died. He checked in for routine prostate surgery and suffered a massive stroke on the table. Allie received the call while she and Jordan were frolicking in her dorm room. Her father had always been Allie's rock. She was an only child and that left no one.

No one except Jordan. During their college years, Jordan and Allie ventured in and out of other relationships but they always gravitated back to each other.

After they started a family and Jordan took to writing books, Allie often thought of Jordan's work, its ethical implications, and the danger it posed. But she drowned such thoughts under the flow of daily life. She swore to live in the present, soaking up every moment of existence. She was not about to question life, not when so much good and happiness surrounded her. As she searched the front yard for her youngest child, Allie swore not to entertain the thought of losing Timmy. There was no telling if she could survive a loss one more time.

Allie glanced out the front door just as Jordan pulled into the driveway. With her arms folded across her small waist, she stepped out and met him halfway up the path.

"Anything?" Jordan asked.

"No," she said without hesitation. "We called some more, and Cal ran the paths again. Nothing."

"Anyone from the papers or television stations called?" Jordan asked.

"No."

"Good."

"And the FBI?"

"They're coming."

Allie nodded. Nothing could make it better.

"We'll get through this," Jordan promised. "Whatever the kidnapper wants we'll get it. We'll sell the house. We'll borrow money. It doesn't matter," Jordan said, motioning to the house. "None of this matters."

On cue and without fanfare, Waters and Deleese pulled in behind Jordan in their brown, windowless van. It could have been a carpet cleaning van, or a delivery van, or some high school kid's dream ticket out of town. The vehicle wouldn't rate a second look from passers-by. But the abductor, should he cruise by to scout the house, would know. He would understand. That's the way Waters wanted it; keep speculation down, but send a clear message to the mark: We're here, talk to us.

Deleese, dressed in a polyester Western-cut suit with no tie, stepped out and began unloading the unmarked boxes. The equipment was standard: three trap-and-trace devices, one each for the three phone lines coming into the house, four tape machines, two cellular phones with encryption capabilities, and a modem-equipped notebook computer. Waters had requested a private fourth line be installed for a computer linkup to the National Crime Information Center and other criminal databases.

"Mrs. Stone, I'm sorry about your son," said Waters. "We have agents working on all possible suspects back at the office. We'll stay until we find Timmy."

Deleese moved into the house with a box full of wires and jacks. After a brief tour, Waters settled on the dining room for headquarters. The table was big enough for Deleese to set up the equipment, and a large bay window, flanked by two casement windows, offered a wide view over the front of the house, never a bad asset. Waters ordered a temporary one-way covering installed over the window so the view in was not as conspicuous as out.

Allie passed the day working in the kitchen, preparing food and cleaning up like a nanny at a wake. Each phone ring sent everyone scattering for their positions. Deleese to his trace machines, Waters to the headphones, and either Jordan or Allie to pick up the receiver. Then, when everyone was set and eye contact was made, Jordan or Allie lifted up the handset, and per Waters instructions, waited a moment or two before saying hello. Every fraction of a second gave Deleese a better chance of tracing the call in the likely event that the kidnapper had blocked Caller ID from the local phone company.

Most of the calls were from friends checking back to see if Timmy had returned safely. A few calls came from solicitors, and Sarah's boyfriend Jimmy called in.

But the call everyone so desperately waited for did not come.

SIX

As usual, Raoul the mail carrier slowed his jeep to a stop at the corner of Sand Castle Drive and Woodbury Lane. The Stone's landed fourth on his route, but since the houses fell far apart Allie knew it would be six or seven minutes before she heard his dangling keys signal his approach.

Strolling up the path, Raoul checked his bag for magazines, then flipped through his sort for handpieces.

"Good morning," said Raoul.

"Buenos días," said Allie, completing their near daily ritual. She reached out to grasp the mail, but from behind the partially closed front door a black hand snatched the mail away.

"I'll take that," said Waters stepping out of the shadows. His large, dark presence wiped the smile off Raoul's face.

"Thank you," Waters said cordially.

"De nada," said Raoul, startled into his native tongue by the surprise of a burly black man intercepting Allie's mail. Raoul tipped his cap and jangled down the path to the street.

Cradling the mail in the palm of his left hand, Waters used his pinky fingernail to flip through the corners of the envelopes. He worked quickly until he came to a small.manila envelope with no return address. The package had some weight and bulk, its corners were sharp and uncreased, and it was addressed with a typed or computer-generated label to *Jordan Stone, True Crime Author.* Allie was taken by the package's tidiness, as if a secretary had bundled it for her boss. A short piece of Scotch tape kept the flap secure on the back side.

Waters picked up the envelope daintily, and held it aloft from one corner as if it were contaminated. As it twirled slowly in his fingers, Allie caught a glimpse of the postmark: Brooklyn, N.Y.

"Deleese," Waters shouted. "Get me an evidence bag."

Deleese brought over a large Ziploc plastic bag, like the ones Allie used to freeze meats, and Waters plopped the envelope into it. He zipped the lock until the bag closed airtight.

"Aren't you going to open it?" asked Allie.

"Back at the office I will. Our criminalists need to examine it unopened. There are clues all over this thing."

"When will we know, I mean, what it says?"

"Give me two hours."

"Two hours?"

"Two."

With bag in hand, Waters and Deleese hustled to their van and sped off. As Allie watched them disappear around the bend she realized she was holding the remainder of the mail in her hand. Waters had evidently handed the mail to her without her realizing it. While her mind focused on that envelope traveling away in the clear plastic bag and its mysterious contents, two streams of emotion ran through Allie's body. The first was relief that Timmy was alive. He had not been snatched randomly for sex, like so many unfortunate children. His abductor had purpose, motive. And the package—if it were from the abductor, and Allie prayed that it was—was an indication that he was ready to negotiate for the return of Timmy. That meant that Timmy was some material possession away from safety. Thank the Lord. Instinctively, or maybe it was habit from twelve years of Catholic education, Allie crossed herself and brought her hands to her lips in gratitude. Timmy was alive!

Then the other stream, the dark stream, rushed through. The feeling emanated from the envelope itself —the neat, Nazi-like fastidiousness of the package. Allie sensed the package was prepared by someone surgically cold, devoid of emotions, lacking in empathy. This was not a howling lunatic, but a calculating psychopath. She imagined Timmy under the reign of such a person and a chill raced up her spine to the tip of her tongue, causing the letters to spill from her hand onto the stone walkway.

Allie retreated to the porch out back. Over the years, the jasmine had crept up the porch posts to the lattice above and laced through the slats to form a fragrant canopy. On summer days the aroma was so thick and heavenly that often Allie sat alone, eyes closed, with no other desire than to grow intoxicated by the flowers' perfume.

Jordan joined her and the two sat silently on the wrought-iron porch chairs covered with fuchsia-colored cushions, which Allie had sewn herself. Allie glanced across at Jordan, his face drawn from lack of sleep, the distress lining his usually shadowless face. Allie reached out and took Jordan's hand. His blue eyes were sadder than she had ever seen them, and she knew his pain was deep because he made no attempt to hide his sorrow.

Jordan's eyes infused with a trace of hope with the sound of Waters' van pulling up in the front of the house. Three hours had passed since the lawmen had vanished with the package. Jordan strained a smile, squeezed Allie's hand gently, and stood to greet the ultimatum.

Waters carried with him two file folders and a handheld cassette recorder. From his strut it was obvious he was not interested in small talk. Beads of sweat crowned his thick forehead and he looked decidedly uncomfortable in his tweed jacket. Deleese followed with folded hands across his abdomen like a mourner at a wake. Waters took a seat at the round glass table, laid down the file folders, and loosened his already loose tie.

"It's from him," said Waters.

There was no need to clarify who the *him* was.

"And?" asked Jordan.

Waters pulled out a Polaroid photograph. He slid it across the table to Jordan.

"It's Timmy!"

In the photograph Timmy stood shoeless against a wall. He wore light blue pajamas with little antique airplanes printed on them and right-out-of-the-package creases up the legs. With one hand he held a teddy bear to his chest, and his other hand fell limply at his side. The camera's flash had turned Timmy's eyes red, making it difficult to read his expression. He wasn't smiling, neither did he display fear.

Jordan handed the photo to Allie. She took it with both hands. Her first impression was that Timmy was okay, that he wasn't being harmed, not physically. But his expression worried her. It wasn't like Timmy not to show emotion. This was a ghost of Timmy, a single dimension of her little son. Allie held the picture with two hands in her lap, occasionally rubbing her thumb gently against the slick surface of the photograph caressing her son's face.

"Have you ever been arrested?" Waters asked Jordan.

Jordan was startled by the question. His first impulse was to answer no. He had conditioned himself to respond negatively the few times he had been asked at job interviews and such. But there was no margin for fibbing here.

"Well, once. Yes."

"Want to tell me about it?"

Surely Waters was privy to the information. "Don't you know?"

"I want to hear it from you."

"It was at a rally in Manhattan, in support of First Amendment rights. Things got a little out of hand. The police and demonstrators were tugging and tussling, and before I knew it I was led off with about twenty others in a paddy wagon. The judge dropped the charges the next day. No big deal. But that must have been ten, twelve years ago. What's it got to do with anything?"

"It was *eight* years ago," said Waters. He slid a file folder across the table to Jordan. Jordan flipped it open and saw a single item, a photocopy of a fingerprint card, complete with the mandatory ten prints and a repeat of the primary four fingers of each hand in unison.

"What's this?" asked Jordan.

"It's a copy of an arrest fingerprint card."

"I can see that. Whose?"

"Yours."

"Mine?"

"We checked them against the file. They're yours."

"What's this all about?" asked Jordan.

"You better sit down."

"That's all right, I'll stand. Whatever he wants, we'll get it," said Jordan. "Money, whatever, anything for Timmy."

Waters sighed and shot one last glance to Deleese hovering in the lattice shadows. Even with the breeze from the Sound beyond, it was hot.

"He doesn't want your money, and he doesn't want your son."

"Well, then, what does he want?"

Waters pulled a cassette tape from his jacket pocket and slipped it into the compact tape machine. He pushed the play button. The recording was poor and the kidnapper obviously had employed a voice-altering technique, but there was no mistaking the words.

Timmy is alive. He is safe. I will not physically harm him if you do what I say. But you must do exactly as I say. In exchange for Timmy's life, this is what I want: I want the hands of Jordan Stone. Both of them. I want them delivered to Locker 255 in the International Terminal of Kennedy Airport by 5 P.M. on August 20. No tricks, and this tragic irony will end. I will allow no second chances.

As the tape drifted into background noise, Jordan sank slowly into the cushion of the chair. He felt a pulse throb all the way to his fingertips. The sweat oozed from the pores of his palms and his wrists ached slightly, as if he was sensing the existence of his hands for the very first time.

Allie looked at Deleese for confirmation, just to make sure this wasn't a trap or some ruse to confuse them. Deleese's somber expression told her it wasn't so.

Jordan searched Allie's eyes for guidance, but found only a confused anguish. He walked to the edge of the deck. He could smell its salt of the Sound as it mingled with the aroma of jasmine. It was a scent unique to this spot at the edge of the porch.

When he was a very young boy, Jordan remembered wanting only one thing, a hug from his father. Now that he was a father himself, Jordan satisfied that longing with hugs from his own children. Often, when in an embrace with Cal, Sarah, or Timmy, Jordan felt that same feeling, a readiness to die, but not from unrequited love, rather from pure fulfillment.

Jordan would give his life for his children. His hands? They were trinkets in trade for Timmy. Jordan straightened his shoulders and walked back to the group.

"How do we go about doing this?" Jordan said.

"We don't," said Waters. "What if he wants your feet next? Your arms? Your testicles?"

Waters had a point. The kidnapper obviously had planned this out well. The fingerprint card was proof of that. What if this request was only the first of many? There were no assurances whatsoever he would stop at Jordan's hands. He could request body parts until Jordan was reduced to a torso.

"I'm not going to lose Timmy," said Jordan.

"The FBI is not in the body parts business, Mr. Stone. We have three days to figure out who this guy is. Regardless, we have a plan underway to snare the kidnapper. I'm not at liberty to say what, but I will say that the exchange is always the most vulnerable moment in an abduction, and we plan to exploit this vulnerability to the utmost."

"And if I'm willing to take the chance, to cut off my hands?"

"If we thought we could get Timmy back by trading in your hands, we'd consider it, believe me. But that's not the case here. You'd be insane to gamble based on the information before us. And if I feel you're making an attempt to do so behind my back, I will take all the necessary precautions to keep prevent you."

Deleese stepped forward. Everyone looked up at him, surprised that he was readying to speak. Finally, the words left his lips.

"Trust us, please. We have criminologists b-back at

the field office poring over the originals, putting together a profile. We have techniques."

Jordan sighed. "What do we do in the meantime?"

"We wait. Every m-minute, every hour we get closer to him," Deleese said.

"What about Timmy?" asked Allie.

"Ever hear of the Stockholm Syndrome?" said Waters.

"The what?"

"The Stockholm Syndrome. Kidnappers grow fond of their hostages. The longer they hold them, the more difficult it is for them to harm them. It's documented."

"So we just wait?" asked Allie.

"Yes," said Waters. "It's the hardest job of all."

Dusk came lazily, as if it too was slowed by the heat. The sky took its time cycling through its shades of blue, then purple, then gray, but never black; the lights from the suburbs and the city beyond never allowed the heavens to turn black—just a weary gray. With the darkness came a chorus of ten thousand cicadas anticipating the moment when they shed their skin.

Occasionally a car screeched along Sand Castle Drive as it hit The Curve. Jordan paused each time it happened. *Why didn't I hear it? Why didn't I see it?* Jordan envisioned the scenario. The abductor using some diversion to draw Timmy to the fence. Timmy never suspected the motives of others, but no way would Timmy have climbed over the fence by himself: he had been well-drilled on the importance of not talking to strangers. Maybe this wasn't a stranger? Maybe it was someone Timmy knew.

Whatever the case, Timmy got close enough so that the abductor could snatch him. Surely there was a moment when Timmy looked up at Jordan's office window, signaling his distress, crying out for his dad.

And where was Jordan during the glance? With his

back to the window, the phone cord wrapped around him, caught in a numbers game. "Daddy!" Timmy had screamed. But Jordan didn't hear, he couldn't have heard through the tightly shut window and the hum of the air conditioner.

But why wasn't Jordan looking out the window at that moment? Why had he chosen so many other moments to gaze at Timmy, but not that fateful one? Why couldn't he have been so lucky?

The thought sent Jordan jumping up from bed. Still fully clothed, Jordan knew he wasn't going to get a wink of sleep. He roamed the upstairs hallway for the millionth time. He opened the door to Cal's room. The boy's room was covered with posters of sports stars. Trophies lined his shelves. Cal, the baseball/hockey/basketball/soccer fanatic, was fast asleep, snoring lightly.

Jordan opened the door to Sarah's room. She had posters of TV and rock stars pinned on the walls—typical heartthrobs with their shirts off and hard bodies gleaming in the sun. No longer a little girl, Sarah now talked about dating, periods, college. But like a vestige of her prepubescence, Sarah's stuffed animal collection slept with her on the bed.

Jordan tiptoed into Timmy's room, strangely vacant. Timmy would be happy to know that Allie had made the bed, a chore Timmy completed each day with great reluctance. On his little blue desk, Timmy had set up a student microscope, a gift from Jordan and Allie for his birthday. While Cal loved to explore wide swaths of territory, Timmy loved to look at things closely. Timmy had stacked his unopened birthday presents neatly near the desk. After great deliberation, Timmy had decided to exhaust the thrill of each one before opening the next.

Timmy's walls were covered with posters: a panda bear, turtle, alligator, and a Noah's ark full of creatures. But Jordan was drawn to a plaster cast of

Timmy's hand dangling from a nail. The imprint of his little hands were spread wide, like wings, and painted blue. Timmy had made the cast in first grade as a school project. Every so often, Timmy would drag over his desk chair, climb up to the cast and place his hand over the imprint just to see how much his hand had grown. It was never much, but enough to convince Timmy that he was indeed getting bigger.

Jordan closed his eyes and touched the plaster cast. He tried to imagine Timmy's hand, little and warm, slapping him in a high-five or wrapping affectionately around his. Jordan pulled his hand away and stepped out. There was little use indulging in fantasies.

Jordan returned to the master bedroom. Even though the alarm clock read 2:12 A.M., Jordan knew that Allie was awake. She faced the wall away from him, breathing slightly out of rhythm. The green of the clock light illuminated the smooth olive skin of Allie's back. She was beautiful, and days ago Jordan might have swooped down to ravish her. But that was then, now everything was different.

"It could be random, it happens all the time," said Jordan. He knew immediately the words rang false.

Allie knew better and felt partly responsible for the deed. She knew the risks, yet she didn't stop him. She didn't send back the fat royalty checks. But that was just it, the risk never was stated. In talks with friends over lunch, at meetings with editors, at parties with fellow authors and fans, no one had mentioned the risk, no one had warned her of the cost of dabbling with the profane. Jordan and Allie received only adulation and encouragement.

Tonight, when she wasn't thinking of Timmy, Allie recalled the events that started Jordan writing true crime books. *Up from Ashes* was a good story. It helped Cindy secure her future with the money from the book rights. Sure Cindy's parents were exposed, but their indiscretion justified the exposure. During the writing, Jordan investigated the Social Services Department and brought attention to its weaknesses. The book was hailed as an "investigative achievement."

After the first book, Jordan's agent and editor screamed for more. You're on your way to fortune and success, they said. You've got fans, a following, a future. You've touched the vein.

But the vein sucked Jordan in. After *Up from Ashes,* the cover of the next book was nastier, with blood spatters ripping across the page. Then the next book came out, and the next, and soon they all started sounding alike with lurid titles and banal story lines. But sales swelled with each one and Allie never complained. Silent risks, all of them.

"Where did we go wrong?" Allie said.

Jordan turned Allie around to face him.

"One promise, Jordan. I want one promise from you."

"What?"

Allie seldom asked for promises, and when she did they rarely were small favors like take out the trash, but large ones, like promise you'll never sleep with Wanda Gentry again.

"You'll do what they say," Allie said. "You won't try anything on your own. I know you. Promise?"

"I promise."

Would he try anything on his own? Jordan honestly hoped it wouldn't come to that, but he knew this promise would be easy to break if it meant getting Timmy back. Jordan would sell his soul for Timmy.

Jordan slid his arm under Allie and snuggled behind her. "We'll get through this. I swear we will. I only hope—"

But his sentiment was interrupted by a terrifying scream from Sarah's room. Jordan and Allie instinctively ran into the hallway and burst through Sarah's door.

Sarah sat up in bed, her back arched sharply as if an electric current ran up her spine. Still asleep, her eyes were fully open and staring at whatever demonic vision filled her mind.

Allie shook Sarah until she emerged from her trance. Sarah gazed at her parents, angels who snatched her away from the torment of her nightmare.

"Shh, my baby," said Allie, gently stroking Sarah's hair. "It was only a dream. Only a dream."

With that welcome notion, Sarah sunk her head into her mother's breast and sobbed. Allie wrapped her arms around Sarah and rocked gently.

"My baby, my baby, it's all right."

Deleese had heard the commotion upstairs and popped his head in the door.

"Everything al—, is everything all right?"

"No problem," said Jordan. "Just a bad dream. Everything is fine. She has them often."

It was true, Sarah often woke up screaming, a trait she had inherited from Jordan. Deleese withdrew, and Sarah whimpered for a few moments more before capturing enough air to speak.

"It was horrible," she blurted out. The vision sent her chin quivering.

"It's okay, darling," said Allie. "Relax, everything is okay."

Sarah wiped her cheek with the sleeve of her nightgown. Her blue eyes filled with tears, a deep, clear pool of sadness.

"I dreamt that—" But it was too soon to speak, and she sought refuge in her mother's embrace once more.

"What?" asked Jordan impatiently. "What did you dream?"

Sarah caught a deep breath.

"I dreamt our house . . . . I dreamt it was on fire."

Sarah spoke as if each word was tethered to a heavy weight and it took all her energy to draw a single one to the surface.

"It was burning to the ground. The flames were so high. I could feel them. I could feel the heat burning my face. It was so hot. And I didn't know where you were. I didn't know where Cal and Timmy were. I was alone and the house was burning and I didn't know who to run to, who to tell. I felt so helpless. And then . . . ."

Sarah wiped a tear.

". . . and then I felt someone pulling at my sleeve. And I looked down. It was Timmy."

Sarah stopped.

"And?" asked Jordan.

"It was Timmy in his pajamas. Except . . ." she stuttered.

"Except what?" asked Jordan. "Tell us."

"Except he had no face."

Sarah's expression turned to anguish.

"He had no face to talk to me with. He kept tugging on my sleeve like he had something to tell me. But he had no face, no face at all."

Sarah broke into tears again.

"Shh, my baby. Dreams can be scary, but they don't mean anything. Soon you'll forget about it. It was nothing, honey. Only a dream. Go back to sleep now, sweetie."

After a few minutes Sarah nodded that she was all right. She gave her mom a peck on the cheek and her dad a hug, then pulled up the covers around her.

"Mommy?" she called. "Is Timmy going to be okay? I mean is he coming back?"

Allie kneeled and stroked Sarah's cheek. "We'll do everything we can to get him back. Everything. It's in God's hands after that."

"Daddy? Is he coming back?"

"Yes, honey. He's coming back."

Sarah pulled the covers tighter.

"Good night, honey," said Allie.

Allie pulled the door softly shut. She glanced at Jordan, but no words were exchanged. Allie walked down the stairs into the kitchen, knowing it would be foolish to attempt to sleep, wanting a cup of coffee and a cigarette, even though she hadn't smoked since college.

The pot of coffee was on. Allie poured herself a cup but stopped midstream when she felt a presence behind her. She turned quickly.

"You startled me," she said.

"Forgive me," said Deleese. "Couldn't sleep?"

"Not a wink. I'm sorry, I've forgotten your name."

"Deleese. But please call me Ron."

Allie looked over Deleese for the first time. He had been invisible earlier, consumed with his equipment. Now she noticed his large hands and slightly bowlegged posture, his rough but gentle face, and his blue eyes.

"Would you like a cup?" asked Allie.

"Yes, thank you."

"You must be tired, being here all night," she said.

"There's no choice."

Allie pulled a cup from the cupboard and poured the coffee for Deleese. "Cream or sugar?"

"Black, thank you." Deleese took a sip. "I can't say I know what it's like. I can only imagine."

"Do you have children of your own, Ron?"

"No, I've never been married. But I believe children are gifts from heaven."

"They are." Funny he would say that, Allie often referred to her children as *my three gifts*.

"And I also believe we'll get Timmy back," Deleese added firmly.

"Really," Allie turned to him, "or are you just comforting a grieving mother?"

"No, I truly believe it."

Allie sipped on her cup. The aroma smelled good. "I'm too afraid to think about it. I'm too afraid to pray."

"We need your prayers. Honestly, we need them."

"That's very nice, but with your equipment, your computers—you don't need my prayers."

"Prayers may not bring miracles, but they have powers which can't be denied."

"Perhaps."

"It doesn't hurt to pray."

"You're right, it doesn't hurt anything."

"Thanks for the coffee." Deleese smiled and bowed his head as he retreated into the dining room.

No longer craving coffee, Allie returned to bed.

"I just talked with Mr. Deleese," she said to Jordan. "Very nice man."

"Too bad about that stutter," said Jordan, staring at the ceiling.

"What stutter?"

"That stutter when he talks."

"He didn't stutter."

"Listen carefully. It's there. Believe me. It's there."

Allie didn't answer. She wanted to, but she fell asleep before the words left her lips.

SEVEN

By the time Waters returned to the Bureau's regional office, the midafternoon humidity had thickened considerably. As he walked the carpeted corridors past the desks of the administrative staff, he noticed a slight but perceptible slowness in the movements of everyone, as if gravity had taken a turn for the heavier and people were still unfamiliar with the new equation. Ties hung loosely around necks, skirts stuck to buttocks, moist circles of sweat ringed armpits. Even sound seemed to tarry under the weight of the moisture before reaching its destination. In his office Waters kicked up the air conditioner, though for all its rattle it did precious little to cool the room. The office faced southwest and the hazy afternoon sun poured in through the venetian blinds onto Waters as he slumped at his desk. Leaning back in his chair, Waters stretched to close the blinds fully, but little lines of light still managed to penetrate the blinds and strike his back. In his nineteen years as a law enforcement officer, Waters couldn't remember anything as mysterious as the ransom note for Timmy.

Among his many cases Waters recalled four dismemberments, one post-mortem evisceration, and three willful amputations, during two of which the victims were kept alive during the amputation. Savage murders all, but savage murders were far more common than ransom kidnapping. Criminals, even brilliant ones, no longer possessed the patience to plan and execute kidnappings. It was far easier to extort money, develop a con, or fiddle with a financial database than to wade through the messy details of a kidnapping. Waters knew that most kidnappings were family related, involving feuding parents in child-custody cases. Less than five percent were stranger abductions, and the great majority of these were sexually motivated. Unfortunately, the victims were nearly always killed and rarely found. Ransom kidnapping was a statistical blip and even among the few dozen cased reported yearly most were fraudulent claims: kids trying to extort money from their parents, vengeful lovers, business partnerships gone sour. True Lindbergh-style ransom kidnapping had vanished like the prop plane.

Waters heard a rap on the door.

"Are you ready?" It was special agent Rochelle Roe accompanied by psycholinguist Anne Fortunato.

One of the new breed of agents coming up from Quantico, Roe was sharp, precise, confident, and unencumbered with personal baggage. Whatever they were doing in recruiting was working, thought Waters, and the poised Roe was evidence of that.

"What have you found?" Waters asked.

Roe looked down briefly at her yellow pad, crossed her legs, then began her recital as only a criminalist can.

"The label was computer generated on a 24-pin dot matrix printer. Based on font generation, we believe it's a Panasonic 1124 or one in that series. According to ink tests, it's even the original printer cartridge or a replacement from the original equipment manufacturer. The plain sheet of paper wrapped around the audio cassette was National Paper. We conducted an electro-

static detection analysis, but it proved negative—no in-
dented writing from a previous page.

"The audio cassette is a sixty-minute Sony, bottom of
the line. No discernable interior background noise,
though we picked up something we're still working on."

Roe paused to flip over the page.

"What's that?" asked Waters.

"A whistle in the distance. We believe it's a train
whistle. Unfortunately we weren't able to isolate
enough to compare the tone with local train lines, but
we're fairly sure it emanated from a train."

"Well that rules out the Antarctic and Sahara Des-
ert," said Waters.

"All the rest—envelope, paper clip, Polaroid film, all
standard and available nationwide."

"Fingerprints?"

"We lasered everything. Not a trace. No fibers, inci-
dental human hair or tissue. The only remnants we
found were trace particles of latex rubber consistent
with materials used in surgical gloves. Again, these are
readily available nationwide and no surprise that the
suspect was using them. You can pick them up at paint
stores."

"In sex shops?" asked Waters.

"There, too."

"How about Stone's fingerprint card?" asked Waters.

"The card came from the New York City Police Department. I talked to a Sergeant Philip Johnston there.
He said no one had a request on file for this particular
set. But you know how they operate. We did get a little
from the photograph. The wallpaper behind the boy is
from a company called United Designs. Big outfit in
Omaha."

Waters recalled the wallpaper from the photo. It was
purplish in color with a repeated print design of a large
cream-colored flower, a rhododendron, perhaps. It reminded Waters of his grandmother's house in Jamaica.

"The production manager told me the style is called 'Country Home,'" continued Roe, "but they stopped making it thirty-two years ago after a fourteen-year run."

"It's an old house then."

"An old house or apartment, hunting cabin, lodge, something to that effect," said Roe.

"Near train tracks."

"Near tracks," Roe confirmed.

"Anything else?"

Roe nodded no. "He didn't make any mistakes. Everything was clean as a whistle."

"Thanks."

Waters turned to Fortunato. At first, Waters, like so many veteran agents, was skeptical of Fortunato and the few other agents certified as psycholinguists and trained in criminal profiling with the Investigative Support Unit at the Bureau's National Academy. "Psychobabbles" is what the veteran agents called them initially. But after working with Fortunato on a number of cases, Waters joined the converted. Once she had built an accurate criminal profile based on two words. A bank robber brandishing a .45 caliber handgun had entered a Savings and Loan in Astoria, Queens. He wore a dime-store gorilla mask and brown leather gloves. He didn't say a word and the teller never caught a glimpse of his skin color. The robber nervously handed the teller a note scribbled with the phrase "Gimmay monay." The teller handed over the money, and the robber dashed out the door with some $3,200 in cash, discarding the mask a block away. No witnesses.

Fortunato theorized from the misspelling that the culprit was from Louisiana, of Cajun descent, and therefore white. She also speculated that, given his education level, he would have no idea that the bills would be marked. Because he didn't speak a word to the teller, Fortunato surmised that his distinctive accent was thick. And since the note was scribbled on a bank deposit slip, and the mask purchased from the Woolworth's next door, she inferred that this was an impulse crime, and the robber would be spending the loot freely and quickly not far from the bank. Two hours later, based on the profile, agents picked up Thomas Beaudaux at an Off-Track Betting parlor three blocks from the bank. They overheard him betting on a horse named "Dixie Whistle" in that unmistakable Cajun accent. Beaudaux was white, from a farm town 80 miles northeast of Lafayette, and had been in town just two weeks after spending most of his teenage years in a youth detention facility in his home state. Fortunato had been right on the money, and though luck played a part in Beaudaux's apprehension, it would never have occurred without Fortunato's sharp profile. Now Waters hoped that she would be just as good or lucky in sketching a profile of Timmy's abductor.

"What have you learned from the tape?" asked Waters.

"He used a voice-altering device so we had to play with it a lot. From what we could tell, we analyzed his accent. We think he's originally from the Midwest, Ohio Valley. Definitely male, mid-forties to mid-fifties, and white. We have the voice print to match against future tapes for verification. We're running the print now against other voice prints in the database, but it's doubtful we'll find anything since the voice was altered.

"As for content—sentence structure indicates a good education and abstract thinking well above average. He is extremely precise, perhaps an engineer. We don't believe he was reading a script, but there were no glitches in presentation. He's thought long and hard about what he was going to say."

"Psychologically?"

"We ran the usual battery of psych tests on word

choice, phrase emphasis, and diction. And again, nothing much. He is bitter, but not withdrawn. No glaring indication of severe psychosis, paranoia, or psychopathic or antisocial behavior.

"There are indications, however, of a narcissistic personality disorder. The message contained 76 words, seven of which were the pronoun *I,* that's nearly one of every ten words. For instance, the kidnapper says 'Timmy is alive. He is safe. I will not physically harm if you do what I say.' A non-narcissistic personality would more likely have phrased it as 'Timmy is alive. He is safe. He will not be physically harmed if you do what I say.' It's subtle, but there. According to the DSM-IV, the essential feature of a narcissistic personality disorder is a pervasive pattern of grandiosity. The kidnapper is more consumed with his own personal power over Timmy than with Timmy himself. Narcissists are preoccupied with fantasies of unlimited success, power, brilliance, beauty, or ideal love, and a chronic feeling of envy for those whom they perceive as being more successful than they are."

"So, then, it might even be another true crime writer," suggested Waters, "someone without a scrapbook as fat as Jordan Stone's."

"It's not out of the question," said Fortunato. "Narcissists can be, and very often are, genuinely brilliant. Look at politicians. I'd venture to say that many are undiagnosed narcissists. There is no correlation between intelligence and personality disorders. My guess is that we're dealing here with a high-functioning individual with an above-average I.Q."

"Go on."

"Narcissists are distinct for two other reasons. First their self-esteem is unusually fragile, thus they tend to be hypersensitive to the evaluation of others. Secondly, they lack empathy. They have no true understanding or compassion of how others feel. Consequently, narcissists have a very difficult time maintaining interpersonal relationships. Odds are the abductor is divorced, several times perhaps, estranged from his kids or parents, living alone. Maybe he's doing very well in his chosen profession, but he's on the periphery when it comes to social groups and alliances."

"Every criminal lacks empathy," said Waters.

"True, but for narcissists it's unavoidable. They can't help but objectify those around them, using them as vehicles for profit or pleasure. Criminals lack empathy, narcissists are incapable of feeling empathy, period. And there's one more thing."

"What's that?"

"Narcissists are prone to episodes of brief reactive psychosis."

"You've lost me."

"If pushed into a corner, or stressed out, narcissists can really lose it. With his back against the wall, a narcissist is capable of doing anything, including the most violent crimes you can imagine."

"Pushed how hard?"

"That is the sixty-four-thousand-dollar question."

"You think he has a criminal record?" asked Waters.

"All I can give you is my gut on this, but I don't believe he does. He may be committing a crime, but I don't think he's a criminal."

"Why's that?"

"Disturbed as he is, this is someone who has learned to play the game well. His ransom message is clear, perfect grammar, spelling, typing. He's literate, smart, maybe even a leader in his field. Even the package was put together with mechanical precision. I don't think he's committed a crime before because he hasn't had to. Society has rewarded him for his delusions, his self-worth. Society often does. Look at cultists like Jim Jones and David Koresh. Among other things, they were narcissists as well, you can be sure."

"Is he working alone?"

"I'd venture a yes. Narcissists don't make good partners."

"Think he's got sexual intentions?"

"I'm afraid I can't rule that out."

"Why?"

"Listen to the tape. The abductor says Timmy won't be *physically* harmed. What does this mean? The abductor is unconsciously signaling his limits. He won't physically harm the boy, but he won't guarantee the boy's emotional or sexual safety. I think he's struggling with the idea. He's interested in a sexual relationship but fearful it would complicate his mission, which appears to be motivated by something other than sexual gratification, if we're to believe the connotation of the ransom message."

"Victimology?" asked Waters.

"Timmy is the youngest of the three children, the most vulnerable. Why did the perpetrator pick Timmy? Three possibilities come to mind. One, the abductor is inexperienced and he knows that Timmy is the easiest mark. Two, he's sexually motivated and Timmy meets this additional criteria, consciously or not. Or three, he knows Timmy and likes him."

"What do you mean knows him?"

"I don't know, a friend, acquaintance of the family, perhaps."

"Or maybe someone who has watched the family for a long time, someone who knows all its members well," added Waters.

"That, too. It could be any reason or any combination."

The air conditioner rattled as it automatically kicked down to low. Finally the room was getting cooler.

"Now the most important question of all," said Waters. "Jordan's hands. Why does he want Jordan's hands?"

Fortunato sighed. "Ever hear of a story called *The Handless Maiden?* It's an old fairy tale, origin unknown, though it was popular in Europe for a few centuries. Jungians have a field day with it because of its mythological significance. It's the story of a miller who spends all day at the grindstone producing flour. Then one day the Devil comes and says he'll teach the miller how to grind his wheat with little effort, all the Devil wants in return is what's behind the barn. Skeptical, the miller walks to the back of the barn and finds nothing but an old apple tree. The miller makes the deal, and sure enough, he turns out flower twenty times faster than before.

"Several years later the Devil suddenly reappears asking for his part of the bargain. The miller, now a very rich man, walks to the back of the barn and, there, sleeping under the apple tree, is the miller's beautiful daughter. The miller can't bear the thought of parting with his daughter and he argues with the Devil through the night. Finally, as the sun cracks the horizon, they reach an agreement. The Devil will leave the maiden behind but will take away her hands. The moment the agreement is made, the Devil slices off the girl's hands and vanishes in thin air."

"You tell a good story."

"Thanks. I was an English major in college."

"But what does that have to do with anything?" asked Waters.

"Well," explained Fortunato, "the maiden isn't necessarily a woman, it also represents the feminine, nurturing, creative quality in all of us, and we loose that ability to nurture when we make deals with the Devil, when we machinate our lives, like the miller did. Jordan Stone made a deal of sorts with the Devil by writing crime books. Perhaps the abductor wants Stone's hands to signify the loss of that element within all of us."

"Too abstract," said Waters. "I don't think he would depend on an obscure reference to a medieval fairy tale to do so. He wants more out of this."

"Chances are he doesn't know about the fairy tale," said Waters. "His request is from deep within his subconscious. That's what the Jungians would say."

"That's why there are no Jungians on the force. This guy is concrete, you said so yourself."

"I didn't say concrete, I said precise. Even highly abstract or theoretical people can be precise, often more so."

The air conditioner turned on to high again and filled the room with a lot of noise and a little cool air. Waters peeked out the blinds to see if the weather had changed, but the haze hung over the parking lot like some vision of hell.

"You don't understand what I'm saying," said Fortunato. "What do writers do with hands? They write. The abductor wants Jordan's hands so that he'll never write another book again."

"You're absolutely sure it was a subject of one of his books then?" asked Waters.

"Either that or someone who was affected, hurt in some secondary manner, a judge, prosecutor, police officer—someone who didn't like what Stone has written. Remember this is a narcissist we're dealing with. What may seem like a minor slight to us would feel catastrophic to the narcissist. For all we know he could be reacting to even a single line or a passing reference in one of the books."

"If that's the case, then it could be anybody. Stone has written six books. If you were to compile a list of everyone mentioned in the books, you would find scores, perhaps hundreds of suspects."

"True," said Fortunato.

"It's impossible to investigate all of them."

"We have one more criterion," said Roe with a wry smile.

"What's that?" asked Waters, hoping for a handle.

"He lives near train tracks."

"A smart, meticulous narcissist near a train?" said Waters.

"That's our man."

EIGHT

Directly across the street from Chester Tenden's building, among a line of about a half-dozen retail shops, Special Agent Ray Russo found an Original Ray's Pizzeria. Since his first name was Ray, Russo knew the location of nearly every Ray's Pizzeria in the city. There were plenty of them and they all claimed to be the "Original Ray's." Sleuth that he was, Russo knew exactly where the original Original Ray's was located, in Greenwich Village. But he wouldn't tell anyone at the Bureau just because everyone there called him Original Ray, a nickname he detested. So he kept the knowledge to himself, visiting the original Original Ray's whenever an assignment landed him in the Village, and comparing the pizza served up by impostors when his assignments fell elsewhere.

As he ordered a slice, Russo kept an eye on Chester's building, a dreary fourteen-story bunker built with red-brown brick, stained from the drippings of leaky air conditioners and the accumulated soot of fifty years of smog. Many of the building's small windows were barred with iron, even windows on the higher floors not attached to fire escapes. The roof was circled by a tangle of barbed wire. Evidently a few residents had found life in the building sufficiently dreary to end things before the next rent period by taking a quick fourteen-story plunge. All in all, the building was no different than hundreds of others in this section of Brooklyn, populated by Puerto Ricans, Pakistanis, Iranians, some Cubans, a few Italians and Jews left over from a generation ago, lots of drugs, and an unhealthy dose of prostitution, nothing more than in most other parts of the city.

But the pizza at this Original Ray's was good, not as good as the original Original Ray's, but better than most. Russo folded a steaming hot slice and took the best bite of all, the first.

With the hot oil of the mozzarella cheese burning his palate, Russo saw Chester exit the building. The lucky stiff had been freed on a technicality a few hours after visiting with Jordan. This was the first time Russo had seen Chester come out. According to reports that Russo had read from other shift agents, it was the first time Chester had left the building in the last seventy-two hours, since surveillance began. Chester moved briskly away from the building, waddling like a castrated Penguin as he pushed a fold-up grocery cart.

Russo wasn't sure what to do with the slice. He took another bite, knowing full well the cheese would sear his palate, but he wasn't going to waste a buck-fifty. He laid down the slice and hustled out of the pizza joint, drawing in a breath of warm air to sooth his tortured mouth.

Russo tailed Chester as he turned down Baxter Street and into a Korean-owned corner grocery store. Russo waited outside, berating himself for inflicting so much pain on himself for the price of a slice of pizza. Twenty minutes passed before Chester emerged from the store, his roll-along cart half filled with three sacks of groceries. Ray couldn't see much, but he did spy a box of Trix cereal in one of the plastic bags. Chester continued his stroll down Baxter Street until he came to The Pussycat Adult Store.

Russo wasn't going to miss this. He slapped on his shades and followed Chester in. It would be easy to keep undercover in the store; the place was crowded with men lurking in the corners. Chester stopped at the ten-dollar-a-pop magazine rack, ogling over titles like *Titty Whippers, Butt Holes,* and *Pregnant Mamas.* Chester took his time leafing through each one, despite the proprietor's prominently displayed admonition to "Buy If You Want to Look." The free peeks apparently were enough for Chester.

He returned the soiled magazine to the rack and waddled up to the video rental rack. Russo was unable to read the titles on the video covers, but he did see a generous flash of flesh on each. Chester chose one video and walked to the glass display case filled with dildos, leather collars, strap-on vaginas, and other sundries. Chester scanned the offerings and pointed to a set of metal handcuffs. With a look of abject boredom, the proprietor pulled them out for Chester's inspection. Chester ratcheted the cuffs closed then keyed them open a few times. He pulled out his wallet, paid for the cuffs and the video rental, counted his change very carefully and left the shop. The proprietor hadn't seen Chester, the little thief that he was, slip a tube of Sure-Lube lubricant into his front left pants pocket.

Chester left the store and retraced his steps back up Baxter. Though Russo felt positive about the identification, he took the opportunity to snap a quick photo of Chester from across the street. Then Russo pulled back, and from a safe distance watched as Chester vanished inside his building.

Russo turned into the pizza shop once again. He dropped a quarter in the pay phone and called Deleese to give him the news. Then he ordered another slice of pizza. This time he let the slice cool a few moments before taking the first bite.

It was good pizza, but it wasn't the real thing.

Just as Jordan and Allie loved the back porch, the kids, all three of them, loved the den with its wide-screen television. Jordan had purchased the TV set after selling the movie rights to *Slaughter Alley* with the excuse of wanting to watch the made-for-TV movie when it aired on the "big screen." Once installed, however, Jordan and Allie knew they had made a mistake. Whether it was the odd dimensions of the Victorian room, or the peculiarities of the lighting, the screen dominated the room, converting it from a quaint parlor to a larger-than-life-sized shrine to what Allie declared as the shallowest of endeavors. Perhaps its grand presence was why the kids loved the television so. Despite protestations and bribes from Jordan and Allie, the three spent much of their time in front of the tube.

That's where Jordan and Allie found Cal and Sarah shortly after their meeting with Waters. Cal shuffled his baseball cards on the floor, bringing the Mets and Yankee players to the top of the deck and then reshuffling the cards back into the stack. Sarah was curled up on the couch with Capote watching the local news.

Jordan paused to look at the large face on the screen. Years ago the news anchor would have been considered too young to have passed as a serious journalist. Not now. The anchor paused momentarily before switching camera angles, shuffling papers, then, in a ruddy deep voice brimming with earnestness, he began the next story.

In just a few days Prince Andrew will arrive in the U.S. Meanwhile, the royal family was rocked by more scandal today. A rumored lover of Prince Andrew stepped forward with revealing details about her love affair with the second in line to the throne—

Jordan pushed the off button and the wide face of the anchor shrunk instantly to a tiny white blip in the center of the screen and then to nothingness.

"We have to talk," Jordan said.

Cal carefully laid his cards aside and Sarah pulled Capote closer to her. The cat found a new position in Sarah's lap and resumed his purr.

It wasn't Sarah that worried Allie. It was Cal. Sarah would cry out her emotion, talk it out. But Cal was not a communicator. He held things in, tortured himself, just like his father. When Cal was younger, around Timmy's age, he and Jordan had passed through a difficult period. "A stage" Jordan called it then, but Allie knew it wasn't a stage, nor was it Cal's fault. Jordan's fathering skills were the problem, or rather lack of them. Jordan expected too much of Cal, cut him little slack. He grew hot tempered with him at the slightest provocation. At first Cal tried desperately to please his father, but when his efforts failed, Cal simply withdrew into his video games and Saturday cartoons.

Part of the problem was that Cal and Jordan shared few common interests. They were simply different, physically and emotionally. They knew it, everyone in the family knew it, though it was never admitted openly.

Jordan's relationship with Sarah, on the other hand, was easy. Jordan never had a problem parenting Sarah, even though she was the oldest. She was his girl. There were arguments, sure, but always tearful reconciliations followed by long talks and sweet hugs.

These past few days when Allie had tried to connect with Cal, he had looked through her, vacantly. One of her therapist friends called it a "disassociative stare." Allie brushed it off at first, primarily because she was in no emotional condition herself to deal with it, and secondly because she knew that this was Cal's way of dealing with things, and she wanted to honor his space. Cal had always felt a tinge of jealousy toward Timmy because he and Jordan had such a naturally close relationship. Allie wondered now if the jealousy persisted just a bit—that in some weird way Cal wished that he had been the one kidnapped just so he would be the recipient of his father's worries and tears.

"Cal, are you all right?" Allie whispered.

Cal shrugged his shoulder and lowered his eyes. Allie decided not to push it. This was unfamiliar emotional ground and she didn't want to make a mistake.

"Well, whenever you're ready to talk," she said, leaving it at that.

Jordan paced the floor in front of the television, searching for the words he wanted to use.

"I just wanted to— Your mother and I— There's been a development that we think you should know about. We received a package from the kidnapper. Timmy is alive and safe, thank God."

Jordan passed around the photograph of Timmy. The kids studied it, each in turn.

"There's more," said Jordan. "We received a ransom note."

"What does he want?" asked Sarah, her joy suddenly subdued.

"Get ready for a shock," Allie said. "He wants something of your father's. It's ugly and mean. And I'm so sorry to have to even tell you."

"What? Tell us," pleaded Sarah.

"He wants your father's hands."

"Hands?" asked Sarah.

"Cut off."

"Oh God," Sarah moaned.

Allie looked for Cal's reaction, and surprisingly she found one. Cal looked up, his shoulders straightened, he became interested, almost animated, as if the request touched some primordial emotion in him.

"The point is," said Jordan, "we are going to be in a

tough situation for the next few days until the FBI can figure all this out. In the meantime, we can't tell anyone one about this, not your friends, not your acquaintances. It's bad enough everyone already knows he is missing."

"It's only with your help that we'll get Timmy back," said Allie. "That's why we're telling you everything. We have to stick together now as a family."

Allie felt that both children were old enough to understand the gravity of the situation and the strangeness of the abductor's request. "Understood?"

Cal and Sarah nodded yes simultaneously.

"How could someone be so sick?" said Sarah.

"We think it may be someone your father has written about," said Allie.

Cal shuffled his cards nervously until all the Mets were on top.

"Dad?" he said.

"Yeah?"

"What did you do wrong? I mean, why is somebody after you?"

"I didn't do anything wrong. It's just some bad people. The world is filled with them," Jordan explained.

"Why did you write about them in your books and everything?"

"Cal, the public wants to know about these things. It's my job to tell them."

"I don't want to know," said Cal.

"Cal, please," said Allie. "We can't argue now. You guys are old enough to understand that."

Cal reshuffled and the Mets players disappeared into the stack.

"Dad?"

"Yeah?"

"Are you going to do it? I mean, cut off your hands."

"What do you think I should do?"

"I don't know. I guess if you had to—for Timmy."

"For any of you, I would," said Jordan.

"Then why don't you just do it, I mean, get it over with?" asked Cal.

"Maybe I will."

Even though the door to Jordan's office was partially open, Waters knocked anyway. The office floor was littered with cardboard boxes, manila files, video cassettes, and thick court transcripts tied up with fat rubber bands or stuffed into oversized shoe boxes. On the walls, Stone had pinned several dozen photographs, some were mug shots, others surveillance photos or snapshots of happy families.

"May I come in?" asked Waters.

"Certainly."

Waters studied the gallery of photos. He recognized some from Jordan's books. Waters hadn't the time, nor the inclination, to read any of them, but he had asked Fortunato and Roe to take the stack of books home to read.

"Not a pretty bunch," said Waters, examining the photos.

"No, they're not."

"Anyone here you suspect? Gut feeling?" asked Waters.

"I wish I did."

Waters stopped at a photo of an elderly woman, handcuffed and pushing a walker through the halls of a courthouse.

"Who is this?" asked Waters.

Stone came over for the identification. "Dottie O'Dougherty from *Invasion of Privacy,* the old matron who killed her boarders for their social security checks. That's her during her trial."

"They cuffed her?"

"I guess."

"One can never be sure about people sometimes," Waters said, shaking his head.

"What do you mean?"

"Take, for instance, Mrs. O'Dougherty. I'm sure she has a healthy bank account, certainly only a few years left to live. She's too ill to enjoy whatever money she pilfers, yet she commits the most heinous crimes for pocket change. Why does she do it?"

"You want an answer?" said Stone.

"Sure."

"That's her pleasure," said Stone. "She loves the planning and the execution of her deeds. That's what she told the psychiatrist assigned to the case. It wasn't the money. It was the crime she loved. You know how some people have affairs not because they want the sex, but because they love the thrill of adultery. Dottie was the same way about murder."

"I believe I know the type. It must be fascinating work, writing about crimes. You must spend a lot of time away from home researching all this, or even locking yourself up to write."

"Every profession has its disadvantages."

"True enough." Waters moved on to another batch of photos. "May I ask you a personal question?"

"Sure."

"Does it ever bother you?" Waters asked.

"What?"

"Intruding on people's lives?"

"Not really."

"I'm sure most people want to live their miserable lives in privacy, without a writer exposing their failings for all the world to see."

"That's the pot calling the kettle black. You expose people, too," said Jordan.

"My work has purpose to it. I save lives, punish criminals, uphold the law."

"I tell the truth. There's precious little of that these days."

"Truth? Is it for truth's sake that you write?" asked Waters.

"What does this have to do with getting Timmy back?"

"Well, maybe if I can understand your motivation, I can better understand the motivation of the abductor."

"Is that so, or are you using the opportunity to settle an old score?"

"You're reading me wrong. I harbor no ill will toward you."

"You've done a great job of hiding it so far, but you're still upset about *The Tended Garden*. You're the one who screwed up on that case. I only reported the facts."

"I actually like you, Jordan. I really do. Perhaps it's you who doesn't like yourself. Maybe that's the problem."

"I hope you're a better detective than you are a psychologist."

"Sometimes it amazes me how closely the two are related."

The conversation was interrupted by a knock on the door. Deleese took two steps in.

"We checked out Satchel Arness."

"And?" asked Waters.

"He died two years ago. S-Stabbed in prison during a riot."

Waters turned to Jordan. "No more threatening letters from him."

"But we did get this from Ray in the Bronx," said Deleese, handing a grainy photograph to Waters.

Jordan peered over Waters shoulder.

"Know him?" asked Waters.

"Chester Tenden. I spoke with him last week. He got convicted for kidnapping."

"No he d-didn't. He walked," said Deleese. "A technicality. Ray thinks it might be him."

"Couldn't be," said Jordan. "I know him, he's not that smart."

"He was on your list. You told us he threatened you," said Waters.

"He did, but he didn't mean it. It was a spontaneous remark. Believe me, Chester couldn't plan something like this if he tried."

"Where's he from originally?" asked Waters.

"Cleveland, if I remember correctly," said Jordan.

"That matches the regional accent identification made by our psycholinguist," Waters said.

"Ray has reported some strange activity from him," Deleese added.

"Like what?"

"Typical abductor behavior. Hurried entries and exits. Observing for surveillance. Holed up."

Deleese hesitated to speak and Waters caught him.

"Spit it out," said Waters.

"He bought handcuffs and lu-lubricant in a sex shop."

Jordan's face turned pale.

"That wasn't his voice on the tape," protested Jordan.

"The kidnapper used an altering device. Or maybe we are wrong. Maybe there is a partner involved."

"I'm telling you, not Chester," said Jordan.

"Anything else?" asked Waters.

"Trix cereal. He bought Trix cereal."

Waters turned to Jordan. "What's Timmy's favorite?"

Jordan whispered, "Trix."

"It's shaping up a little differently than we thought," Waters whispered back.

Deleese nodded a sad yes.

"How could Fortunato be so wrong in her profile?" asked Waters.

Deleese shrugged his shoulders.

Waters took one last glance at the surveillance snapshot of Chester. He found a thumbtack on Jordan's desk and pinned the photo to the wall next to the others, then he turned to face Jordan.

"It looks like we'll have to take a closer look."

NINE

Waters and Deleese spent the night sleeping in Waters' dark green Ford Thunderbird fifteen yards southwest of Chester's building awaiting any sign of movement. There were none. The night was filled with passing sirens and fitful dreams until morning dawned rusty in the city. At the height of rush hour, Deleese stepped out for donuts and coffee and returned a few minutes later. Now the coffee was cold and Waters could feel the sugar from the donuts eating away at his unbrushed teeth.

The hardest chore of the evening had been convincing Chester's neighbors across the hall to let the Bureau use their apartment for surveillance. The peephole in the door of Apartment 11H had a bird's-eye view of Chester's apartment door. Knowing that most people don't appreciate a black man knocking at their door at eleven o'clock at night, Waters declined to negotiate himself, instead sending Deleese. The occupants, an elderly couple clothed in tattered bathrobes, spoke only broken English. Deleese shouldered his way in as soon as the husband cracked the door a bit. At first, the couple thought they were in for a mugging or worse, but Deleese allayed their fears with his badge and honest face.

Once the couple understood what was happening, they pulled up two kitchen chairs and spent the night watching Agent Rotondaro as he leaned against the door with one eye glued to the wide-angle peephole keeping a vigilant eye on Chester's abode. Except for frequent trips to the bathroom, the couple rarely moved from their front-row seats.

Waters had assigned Special Agent Ray Russo to the coffee shop across the street, and when it opened later, to the Original Ray's pizzeria. Agent Riley was positioned in the apartment stairwell with a small periscope to turn his view around the corner. He clothed himself as a homeless person just in case Chester decided to walk down the stairs rather than take the elevator, an unlikely scenario given Chester's physical condition. Agent Ellsworth waited in the lobby in UPS garb. And since Chester's apartment faced the back of the building, Special Agent Krauss hung out in the back alley among the discarded hypodermic needles and beer cans. Playing a junkie was Krauss's specialty.

In the event the Bureau had to move fast, Waters had stationed a four-man SWAT team, led by Agent Levin, one flight above Chester's floor. The NYPD had been alerted and were ready to supply units in case of apprehension. Waters' top priority was surveillance, but he wasn't about to lose the opportunity to snatch Timmy if he could. It wasn't scribbled on any contingency report, but Waters secretly hoped to have this thing wrapped up by evening.

At 10:37 A.M., Waters' radio crackled. He sat up and ran his fingers through his hair and licked the donut sugar off his teeth. The voice of Agent Rotondaro stationed in apartment 11H broke through the static.

"I've got movement on the door. It's opening. It's him. Chester is coming out the door. Blue shorts, man's white sleeveless undershirt, black socks, black shoes. He's locking the top lock. Moving toward the elevator.

He's got a video in his hand. Porno. It looks like a porno video."

In his car, Waters turned to Deleese.

"He's returning to the porn shop. The asshole doesn't want to pay a late charge."

Rotondaro continued on the squawk box. "He's leaving my sight now. Moving to the elevator. Out of view."

Waters jumped on the radio. "Levin, stand by."

With Levin's affirmative response, Waters could hear the safeties clicking off the SWAT team's assault weapons.

Riley in the stairwell checked in at a whisper. "Moving toward the elevator . . . There . . . Down button . . . Waiting . . . Waiting . . . Waiting . . . Slow elevator . . . Waiting . . . Open . . . Walking in . . . Closed . . . Out of sight . . . Down, down. Going down. Over."

Waters rolled up his car window and slumped in his seat. Deleese followed suit in anticipation of Chester's passing. The porno store was in the opposite direction, but no one could predict Chester's route for the morning trip.

Then Waters dropped the bomb.

"Levin, we're going in," he ordered into his handset.

Levin's dead air time on the radio indicated his startled response.

"I said we're going," said Waters.

"Julius," said Deleese. It was the first time Deleese had called Waters by his first name. "Let's wait until he leaves the building."

Under the third contingency plan developed late the previous evening, if Chester left the premises, the plan was to wait until Chester was sufficiently away from the building before raiding the apartment.

"He's in the elevator. He can't hear a thing. I want that boy."

Waters returned his concentration to the radio. He

lifted his arm and looked at his watch until the second hand swept by the quarter past mark.

"In thirty seconds," he instructed Levin.

"This is wrong," said Deleese.

"Let's wrap this thing up," Waters replied firmly.

Deleese picked up the NYPD channel and instructed Detective Harris that a raid was imminent.

The Bureau SWAT team stood up, tested their boots on the dirty linoleum floor, and checked the fasteners on their bulletproof vests. Stairwell Riley drew his hand gun from his coat. Junkie Krauss came to consciousness ready to secure the rear exit, and Ellsworth in the lobby did his best to act like a United Parcel route driver.

Waters and Deleese had one foot out the door ready for Chester's apprehension away from the building when Ellsworth radioed in.

"He's going up!"

Waters jaw dropped as he looked at Deleese.

"What do you mean he's going up?" said Waters incredulously. He looked at his watch. Eighteen seconds to go.

"He's going up," Ellsworth came back with the same unwelcome message. "The elevator stopped on the second floor and now it's on its way back up."

"Shit," Waters exclaimed. He checked his watch again. Fourteen seconds.

"Call it off. Let him go," said Deleese.

"No," said Waters. "I want that kid."

"We don't even know if he's in there," said Deleese.

"He's in there. I'm sure of it," Waters snapped. Then he returned his attention to Ellsworth. "Where's the elevator now?"

"Fifth floor," said Ellsworth. "It's slow as hell."

Nine seconds. Eight.

"Go. It's a go, Levin in . . . Seven, six—"

"You're crazy," said Deleese.

"Let's go."

Waters and Deleese dashed from their car into the building. They rushed passed Ellsworth, eyeing the elevator indicator. Seventh floor. It *was* slow, Waters thought.

"Ellsworth, Rotondaro, take the elevator," Waters barked. "I want him in cuffs before he knows what hit him."

Rotondaro slipped out of the apartment after instructing the old couple to stay inside and away from the front door. He met Ellsworth at the elevator. They stationed themselves on either side of the elevator, backs against the wall, watching at a severe angle the indicator, which showed the elevator now approaching the ninth floor.

Waters shot up the first set of stairs, checking his watch again: two, one, zero . . .

"Go!" yelled Agent Levin on the twelfth floor. His four-man team bolted down the stairs in twos, with Levin at the fore carrying a battering ram.

One blast with the ram was all it took. The front door splintered open and its remnants slammed against the foyer wall, sending a shower of splinters and dust into the room.

"FBI!" Levin shouted. The team stormed the apartment itching to blast away. But all was still.

As he huffed his way up the stairs on the fifth floor, Waters listened to the reports.

"We're in," reported Levin. "No activity. Going for the bedroom."

The bedroom door was fastened shut with a thick padlock. Levin picked up the ram and charged, but the lock held firm.

He slammed the ram again, and the lock flew off its hinge. One more thrust and the lock surrendered completely. Levin and his men burst into the room, guns drawn.

"We have a subject," Levin reported into the microphone pinned to his collar. Purposely, he said nothing more.

"Great," said Waters in between huffs, he was at the seventh floor now and slowing considerably.

"Tenth floor . . . and . . . eleven," said Ellsworth, still tracking Chester's elevator.

The elevator lurched to a stop. The doors separated slowly. Just as Chester stepped out, Ellsworth and Riley converged from each side. Ellsworth struck Chester on the back of the neck, sending him to the floor.

"What the fu—" Chester cried. But before he could finish his sentence, the agents had him cuffed, frisked, and eating the filthy carpet.

"You're under arrest."

"What the hell? Who are you guys?"

"FBI."

"What the fuck?"

The door to the stairwell opened and Waters and Deleese emerged, huffing like wolves.

"Great," said Waters. He was so relieved that their mark was in custody. "You're finished, Chester."

"I don't know what you're talking about."

Waters looked down the hall. Levin was waiting outside the apartment. "You'd better come in here."

Waters hustled down the corridor and into the squalid apartment, littered with beer cans and pizza boxes. The only furniture was a red couch with the stuffing long gone from the arms, a television, and a VCR.

"Do we have the kid?" Waters asked.

"Better come with me," said Levin. As he walked to the bedroom, Waters heard the first sirens of the NYPD surrounding the building. Soon the entire block would be cordoned off.

Waters was expecting the worst when he entered the bedroom, but he didn't know how bad.

It wasn't Timmy.

"Who in God's name are you?" Waters asked. The woman obviously had been woken from a deep sleep. Her hair was frizzy and knotted and her sagging breasts rested on her beer belly. About forty-five years old, she had junkie written all over her. Probably an ex-prostitute, though nobody would screw her now. Her eye had been blackened by a healthy blow. She had a homemade tattoo of a cobra on the inside of her thigh, right next to her stained yellow panties. She made no effort to cover herself.

"Who the hell are you?" she answered back.

"I asked you first," said Waters.

"None of your fucking business."

Deleese walked in to the apartment followed by Chester and his escort of Ellsworth and Riley.

"She's my wife," said Chester.

Waters moved closer to the woman.

"You're married to him?"

"Just my frickin' luck, huh?"

"Where did you get the black eye?"

"Where do you think, that creep over there," she said, nodding toward Chester.

"What for?"

"For being nasty. Is that a crime?"

"Do you want to leave?"

"What are you talking about. I live here."

"You don't mind being locked up?"

"Chester, what the fuck is going on? I thought you told me you were clean this time."

Chester gestured his utter astonishment.

Waters turned to Chester.

"Where were you going right now?"

"To the video store, to return a video."

"Why'd you turn around on the elevator?"

"I forgot my wallet. Look."

Chester turned so Waters could see his back pocket, devoid of a wallet.

Waters pushed his perspiring face menacingly close to Chester's.

"Where's the boy?" he said.

"What boy?" Chester asked with sincere bewilderment. "I don't know what you're talking about."

"You don't know anything about the Stone boy?"

"Who? I swear to God. I'm clean, man, I'm not getting in anymore trouble. I ain't going back," said Chester.

"I'm telling you, Chester, I need the truth now and I need it quick. Who were those handcuffs for?"

"What, you guys been following me?"

"Fucking A we have," said Ellsworth.

"We saw you steal that lubricant in that trash store yesterday."

"Oh, God. Is that what this is about? They send out the Bureau for shoplifting?"

"You goddamn know what this is about. Who are the handcuffs for?"

Chester motioned toward his wife. Waters moved toward her and lifted her wrists. They were red and sore, just like Waters had seen on plenty of prisoners in the past.

"Law against kinky sex?" she said.

"What's your name," asked Waters.

"Valerie."

"You're real name, not your streetwalking tag."

"Glenda."

"Glenda, shut up."

"Where are the cuffs now?"

Glenda pointed to the ancient radiator in the corner, caked with about a dozen layers of peeling paint. The handcuffs laid on the floor, one of the cuffs still attached to a radiator coil.

"Damn," said Waters. He turned his gaze back to Chester. "And what about the Stone boy?"

"The *what* boy?"

"The Stone boy. Jordan Stone's son."

"Jordan Stone's son? I didn't know he had a son, but that asshole owes me two thousand bucks."

The sirens on street level screamed now.

"Fuck," Waters said.

"Do you know who kidnapped Timmy Stone?"

"Look, like I told you. I don't know a goddamn thing about anything. I'm just happy as hell not to be in that fucking slammer anymore. Honest."

Chester wasn't fooling. Waters could spot bullshit a mile away and Chester was telling the truth.

"Now what?" Waters whispered to Deleese.

"I don't know. Let him go, I guess. Keep him under watch."

"Fuck," Waters repeated, then he moved to Chester's face and stuck his index finger into his chest.

"I'm going to keep on you like hair on pussy, and if I find out you got one goddamn little thing to do with the kidnapping, I'm personally going to drain your worthless little balls. You got me?"

"I hear you. But I'm telling you, you got the wrong man."

"You fucking better hope so," added Waters.

He paced the floor and looked out the window below. On the side street he could see the crowds forming. New Yorkers loved a good crime show.

"What do we do now?" asked Ellsworth.

"Let him go, that's what we do. Let the asshole go."

"Take him with you," said Chester's wife. "He's worthless."

Back outside the police had cordoned off the block on each side of the building. Crowds packed up against the yellow plastic tape that sealed the area. Those lucky enough to get a late-morning slice of pizza at Original Ray's had the best seat in the house. Detective Harris had arranged squad cars, blockade style, in front of the building and sharpshooters took aim from behind the cars.

The press corp had arrived in full force, perfect timing for the electronic media's evening newscasts and still time enough for afternoon editions of the paper.

Waters walked out to a blazing sun, which had just topped the building across the street, and a pack of reporters pressing at the front door.

"You look like shit," said one reporter.

"Up all night," said Waters. He realized how bad his breath must have smelled. But his thoughts were interrupted by reporters barking questions.

"Did you get your man?"

"Who were you looking for in there?"

Waters was flustered. He had forgotten the trigger that sets off the media with each stakeout.

"We'll have a statement for you within the hour."

The reporters let out a chorus of boos.

"You can't surround a building and not talk to us," said one reporter, as if the Bureau had negotiated media rights to its operations.

But Waters knew they were right. He hadn't prepared for this scenario, so sure he was that he would come out triumphant with Timmy. He hadn't planned on screwing up.

"Did this have anything to do with the Stone kid?" said another reporter.

"Who told you that?"

"Inside source. Word's out. Don't you listen to the radio?"

Waters turned to Deleese. "Shit."

"It's the Stone kid!"

The word rumbled through the pack of reporters as they pressed harder to hear Waters.

What else could he do? Word was out and any further delay would only stimulate the media appetite. Waters had no choice but to tell the reporters, gathering in strength every moment, everything he knew about Timmy's disappearance. Everything, that is, except any hint of a ransom note and a few key details that would be necessary to weed out the inevitable pranksters.

"So what did you find inside?"

"Nothing," said Waters. "Absolutely nothing."

As the reporters scurried away to file their reports, Waters rubbed his tired eyes and passed his tongue over the grimy layer of sugar caked on his teeth. Not a good way to start the morning.

When the doorbell rang at the Stone's home minutes later, Allie thought it was an agent with news of the operation. It was obvious from the buzz among the agents around the dining room table that something momentous had just occurred. Allie rushed to the door. She even indulged herself with the prayer that it might be Timmy himself, the operation a success.

With quivering hands, Allie opened the door, her heart pounding. But the visitor wasn't a kind agent with news of the stakeout, nor was it her youngest child returning to a mother's grateful arms.

Rather, it was the striking Wanda Gentry, crime reporter extraordinaire.

Wanda wore a crimson dress, the same dress she wore days before during her midafternoon tryst with Jordan. Jordan recognized it immediately, and his face turned a pale hue of the same color as he turned the corner to greet the news of the stakeout only to find instead his mistress standing at his front door.

Allie was startled. The last person she had ever expected to see at this precarious moment was the woman who nearly ruined her marriage years earlier. Nevertheless, here was Wanda, as slender and as menacing as Allie remembered.

"I thought I told you never to set foot in my house again," said Allie.

"This is business, not pleasure," Wanda said, stamping out her lipstick-stained cigarette on the slate porch. "May I come in?"

Jordan always fancied himself a good juggler, but this was too much.

"What do you want?" he asked as benignly as possible.

"I'm sorry about the news," said Wanda regretfully. She took two uninvited steps into house.

"They'll be here soon. I think we should talk," she said.

"Who will be here soon?" Allie asked.

"Hasn't anyone told you?"

"For God's sake, what are you talking about?" Allie implored.

"You mean you don't know?" replied Wanda, truly surprised. "They didn't find Timmy at Tenden's apartment. They didn't find anything."

The news stung Jordan like a dagger. Even though his gut had told him Tenden wasn't involved, he had hoped he was dead wrong, that Waters was one up on him this time, that he would see Timmy approach the house excitedly in the back of an unmarked squad car.

"The story is out. The media know he's been kidnapped," added Wanda.

As if on cue, several television news vans squealed to a halt in front of the house. Cameramen disembarked like paramedics as they hurriedly grabbed their equipment and hustled to the house. The first two mobile units belonged to local independents, soon joined by well-equipped microwave trucks run by the affiliates of ABC, CBS, and NBC. The van from Fox looked like it was ready to tip over under the weight of the large satellite dish perched on its roof.

The first reporter to reach the door was a scrawny

kid with an Adam's apple the size of a plum. He wore
the expression of every young reporter sent into battle
only to find, surprisingly, that he leads the pack, and
therefore the story as well. Jordan vaguely remembered
the same heady sensation when he was young, running
amok far too earnestly with a reporter's notebook and
Bic pen in hand.

. The cub reporter was ready to pee in his pants as he
waited anxiously for his cameraman to trudge up the
pathway. When the cameraman was close enough to
roll some tape, the reporter flashed a nervous smile
and extended his foam-covered microphone like a pon-
tiff's scepter.

"Did the stakeout of Chester Tenden have anything
to do with your son?" His voice trembled.

Jordan and Allie looked at each other incredulously
as Wanda slipped into their home.

The kid reporter's disappointment was visible when
Jordan didn't gush his answer in appealing sound bites.

"No comment," Jordan said. He had been on the
other side long enough to know not to speak when startled, confused, or unsure. He had always marveled that
people actually spoke to the press at times like these.

The kid was distraught when two other camera crews
joined him on the crowded stoop at the Stones' front
door, ending his brief moment of exclusivity.

"Has the kidnapper contacted you?" asked a reporter.

"Who said anything about a kidnapper?" Jordan
snapped back.

"How much money does he want?" asked Wade
Deply, who Jordan recognized as the Channel 8 news
anchor who had suffered a embarrassing demotion after showing up sloshed on the set. His snide smile indicated that his attitude toward the business hadn't
changed much.

"Who told you?" Allie asked.

Jordan immediately realized his wife's slip.

"Then you have received a ransom note," Deply surmised. "It's true."

Jordan slammed the door on the faces. Why had he waited so long?

Wanda emerged from the interior shadows, her heels clicking on the hardwood floor of the foyer as she surveyed the house like a real estate agent.

"I think we need to talk," she said.

PART II

TEN

An agent summoned Allie to the phone. It was Waters explaining the nightmare, apologizing for not having Timmy by his side.

Jordan took the opportunity to prod Wanda privately.

"How can you do this to me?"

"Oh, listen to you," she said. "As if you don't know what my job is."

"Yeah, but this is my family we're dealing with, Wanda."

She chuckled and threw back her hair. "They didn't seem to be much of a consideration during our visits together."

"How did you get here so fast?" Jordan asked, truly curious.

"Scanners, radio. I'm surprised you don't have one."

Jordan thought of a thousand things to say from the snide to the crude. "No, I don't," he said, settling on the neutral, always the best policy when your back is nailed to the wall.

"Wanda, I'm asking you . . ." but Jordan's voice trailed off with the sound of Allie's quick footsteps approaching. Allie recounted Waters' explanation, careful to be as vague as possible, so as not divulge any information to Wanda.

"So what is it you want?" Allie asked.

"What everyone wants. Your story, exclusively. Of course, we're willing to pay. We can offer $25,000, but the exclusive holds only if you don't talk to the other media outlets until forty-eight hours after your son's recovery," Wanda said.

"You make me sick," said Allie.

"Just doing my job."

"Do you really think we would stoop so low?"

"Stoop so low? Aren't life-rights agreements the meat and potatoes of this household? I didn't realize you had changed professions, Jordan. Aren't you supposed to send out a postcard or something?"

"Very amusing," Jordan said.

"You haven't changed one bit," said Allie.

"Seems to suit your husband."

"What's that supposed to mean?"

Wanda responded with only a mysterious smile. She was toying with Jordan, and the repartee edged too close to their secret.

"I'm sorry, we're not interested," said Jordan, again maintaining neutrality.

Allie gazed at Jordan, astonished at her husband's cordiality. She knew Jordan to fight like a jackal when cornered. Jordan noticed Allie's puzzlement but chose to ignore it. His concern was the ace up Wanda's sleeve.

"Not so fast," said Wanda. "I don't think I have to explain it to either of you. Your story is out. The media will get it, one bite at a time. You know that. All I'm doing is offering you control."

Jordan had used the argument many times himself. Wanda was right, control came through exclusivity. The media could be played like an orchestra, though true maestros were few. The cacophony came when each reporter copped a piece of the score at random, then played their tiny snippet for whatever audience they happened to entertain.

But Jordan couldn't fathom working with Wanda on this one. Allie would rather die than hand over her life to Wanda.

"Thanks for your consideration, but the answer is regretfully no," Jordan said.

Allie again threw Jordan a gaze of disbelief.

Wanda started to speak then cut her words short with a droll smile. She searched for her purse, pulled out a business card and placed it neatly on the glass coffee table.

"If you change your mind," she said. "And Jordan, I know you're capable of that."

Wanda sauntered through the foyer to the front door. The media army outside was in full drill. The buzz of questions drowned out Wanda's good-bye as she slipped into the frenzy. Reporters swarmed around her like a queen bee as she walked gracefully to her car, leaving the honey of her smile but uttering not a single word.

Jordan slammed the door shut but continued peering through the peephole until he could see Wanda's crimson dress no more.

And then, for the first time, he paused to mourn over the dashed prospect of seeing Timmy back home today. When Jordan returned to the living room, Wanda's business card was ripped into little pieces and heaped in a neat pile.

"What's going on?" asked Allie angrily.

"Can't you see what she's trying to do?" Jordan said. "She's trying to force a wedge between us. It's a beginner's game and a bad one at that."

"I only hope so," said Allie.

When Allie lowered her eyes, Jordan knew she had given him the benefit of the doubt. He hugged her, more to banish any remaining doubt than to give comfort.

That's when a glint of refracted light caught the corner of Jordan's eye. It came from a television camera a few feet from the house staring into the living room window like a clumsy cyclops. Jordan saw a flash of the cameraman's Rangers cap and Van Halen T-shirt.

Jordan raced through the kitchen door to the backyard. He turned the corner behind the house and surprised the cameraman with a swift kick to the camera, flipping over the tripod.

"What the fuck?" the cameraman exclaimed, not sure whether to protect the camera or himself. Jordan shoved the cameraman into a prickly juniper bush and kicked the camera again, more symbolically than with any force. The tripod legs settled skyward like the stiff members of a carcass.

"I catch you again and you're dead meat," Jordan said. "And the same goes for those assholes there," he added with a nod toward the throng of reporters on the road.

"I'll sue you. I'll sue your ass," the cameraman threatened as he delicately extricated himself from the bush. But Jordan remained unfazed as he waited for the cameraman to hurriedly gather his wounded gear and flee.

"I mean it," Jordan yelled as the cameraman jogged away. "I mean it. Fucking pigs."

Jordan returned inside and pulled down all the shades of all the windows. Every few minutes he peeked outside to see what was happening. More trucks and cars arrived. The churning generators of the microwave trucks obliterated the peaceful quiet of the neighborhood. Cameramen strapped on Portapaks and television reporters fixed their hair. A few curious onlookers, mostly neighbors, stood on the periphery gawking in their slippers.

A snack truck stopped in the middle of the road, the vendor busy making quick change on five-dollar ham-and-cheese sandwiches and bottles of Snapple at two bucks a pop. All this in twenty minutes.

Jordan noticed a bank of lights power on for the start of a live news report with the Stones's house serving as the backdrop.

"Hey look," Cal yelled from the den. "It's our house!"

The family circled the big screen television, watching the stand-up report emanating from just beyond their front lawn. The segment was reported by the sardonic Wade Deply, the demoted alcoholic now serving up the news at any godforsaken location in the tristate area that happened to please the assignment editor of the day.

Cal jumped to the window during the telecast to confirm that the remote broadcast was actually occurring live and was not some electronic sleight of hand. It was real, all right. Outside Deply swayed and gestured simultaneously with his television image as he spoke. Deply wore his signature snicker and a polo shirt unbuttoned, as if he had been hastily summoned away from a singles club and his martini was just out of eye shot of the camera.

"Behind me is the Rocky Cliff home of Jordan Stone, the preeminent crime writer in the country. In a bizarre twist worthy of one of Stone's own books, authorities believe the kidnapper may very well be someone Stone has written about. If that's true then the FBI have plenty of leads. Stone is the author of six bestsellers."

Deply paused momentarily to let the irony of his comments sink in for his audience. Then he continued, "Rocky Cliff town folk are shocked."

The remote producer, sitting in the steamy truck on the road, cued on the word *shocked* and signaled to control to cut to a prerecorded segment taped earlier on the streets of Rocky Cliff and emceed by a middle-aged female reporter. Jordan recognized The Seven Immortals restaurant in the background.

"I can't remember anything happening like this in Rocky Cliff," said the first man on the street, a disheveled construction worker held up by faded red suspenders. "People are pretty quiet around here, family types."

"Sure, I know Jordan Stone," said a store clerk cloaked in a greengrocer's apron. Nice prop, but Jordan had never seen the grocer before. "He's very secretive, kind of mysterious."

"Do you think he has something to hide?" the reporter asked inquisitively.

"I don't know, maybe so. I mean, why be mysterious if you don't have something to hide?"

Jordan resented the insinuation. He glanced through the window to see Deply standing by for a tag cue. Jordan wanted to run out there and ring Deply's neck, but he knew better.

Deply perked up for his tag.

"Timmy was described by teachers as a good student but with little physical stamina. All are hoping this *Tiny Tim* has the emotional fortitude to endure this terrible ordeal. Reporting live from Rocky Cliff, I'm Wade Deply."

Wrap, lights, pack it up. Cal watched the near-instant dissolution of the set while his father fumed inside.

"Tiny Tim," Jordan mumbled. Deply had emphasized the phrase, hoping the handle would stick so he could later claim credit for it. Jordan remembered the moniker "Cinderella" tagged onto the subject of his first book *Up from Ashes,* and how he had latched on to it.

Allie had expected coverage but wasn't prepared for its nature. The swiftness of the coverage, its shameless intrusiveness, left her realizing she didn't understand the nature of media after all, despite her association with Jordan and his cronies. Sarah sat stunned, slightly in awe of the technicality of the event much like Cal, but old enough to sense a threat, though she couldn't begin to verbalize it.

Perhaps it wasn't the best timing for Waters and Deleese to enter the house, but then, Waters' timing had been off all day. Waters entered first, without knocking. This was, after all, command central. He immediately caught whiff of Jordan's displeasure.

"I'm sorry. It was my mistake," said Waters.

"You told them, didn't you?" said Jordan.

"Told who?"

"The media."

"Nothing they didn't already know. Word was out."

"You condemn the media, but you don't mind a little spotlight yourself," said Jordan.

"I thought you were the big defender of the freedom of the press. The view is a little different from the other side, isn't it, Mr. Stone?"

Jordan prepared to rip into Waters but he stopped abruptly at the ringing of the phone. Everyone scurried to their places. Upon Waters' hand signal, Jordan picked up the receiver slowly.

"Hello?"

"I know who has your son. He's being hurt."

The muffled voice spoke with a foreign accent, Eastern European perhaps.

Waters pressed the phone extension closer to his ear, while silently signaling Deleese to monitor the trap and trace device.

"I want ten thousand dollars for the information," the caller continued.

Deleese scribbled a message on a piece of paper and passed it to Waters. It read, "Pay phone, South Bronx."

"I'm hanging up now. You'll get a future message."

"Wait," Jordan begged.

Waters grabbed the phone from Jordan.

"Why should we believe you?"

"This is no hoax. I have information."

"Prove it."

"I have a lock of Timmy's hair."

"What color is his hair?" said Waters.

"Brown."

"What's he wearing?"

"I don't know. I only said I have information."

"You'll have to give us better proof than that."

Click. The caller was gone.

Deleese returned instantly with the reason for the abrupt hangup.

"Police m-missed him by seconds."

"An imposter," said Waters. "Give me a voice print and tell them to dust the receiver. Then hand it over to someone else. I don't have time to deal with charlatans, we've got a kidnapper to catch here."

"How can you be so sure he's a fake?" said Jordan.

"They come out of the woodwork with every broadcast. Trust me."

"We have, and look where it's got us."

Waters ignored the comment and for the remainder of the evening, he and Deleese busied themselves with reports. Paperwork was always hell and Waters had to be extra meticulous after this morning's fiasco. The days were long gone when you could bust through an innocent person's door without suffering dress downs from above, ridicule from below, and lawsuits from outside. Waters had to cover himself but good, especially in this case with the coverage already beyond expectations.

Jordan and Allie spent the evening watching the coverage unfold on the television. Each update dredged up yet another detail of their personal lives, Jordan's business affairs, or Timmy's medical history. Some truths, some near-truths, and some outright lies, Jordan wanted to call and correct the falsehoods himself, but he knew that would only give rise to another round of speculation and fabrications. Jordan understood the guiding principle of newsrooms, he was a master of the technique. It was the *story* that was important not the facts.

As evening turned to night, the initial buzz outside ebbed, but there was still plenty of activity. Banks of lights cranked up regularly as reporters filed live updates for local affiliates in the East, Central, Mountain, and Pacific time zones. By the time the sequence of evening news programs had passed, it was already time for the late news round of reports.

By two-thirty in the morning, the West Coast updates were done and a skeleton crew settled down in their bivouac on Sand Castle Drive, some in sleeping bags, others playing cards or exchanging war stories. The next round would start in a few hours with the early-morning news programs followed by late-morning talk shows, noon newscasts, and afternoon talk shows. Then it was right into the evening newscasts and nightly news magazines, followed by the late news, not to mention continuing coverage on the cable news channels.

Right now it was time for a brief reprieve as everyone dug in for the long siege ahead.

ELEVEN

"Are you ready?" asked Wally.

Timmy nodded yes.

Wally sat down on the mattress next to Timmy. The weight of the man's body sank the center of the bed, hard as it was, and Timmy had no choice but to lean up against Wally. Timmy did his best to wiggle away but somehow always ended up sliding closer to Wally than he would have liked.

"How the Grinch Stole Christmas," Wally began reading. "By Dr. Spock."

"Dr. Seuss," Timmy corrected him.

"Yes, of course, Dr. Seuss." Wally smiled.

Timmy thought it kind of funny that the man should be reading *How the Grinch Stole Christmas*. It wasn't even Christmas. It was August and the heat was so bad. But it was okay. Timmy liked Dr. Seuss books. He had read most of them by himself, and before he had learned to read, his parents had read them to him lots of times. He liked the books still, especially *Cat in the Hat*, and *How the Grinch Stole Christmas*.

Timmy listened intently about *Who-pudding* and *Who-roast beast* and the things the Grinch couldn't stand in the least. But then Timmy's mind wandered to his parents and his home. He remembered what his mother looked like, her big brown eyes and the affectionate way she smiled at him, the taste of her vanilla pudding, and the scent of her skin, which smelled better than any of his friend's mothers. He remembered the freckles on the back of her hand and the oval shape of her fingernails. And Sarah, too, he remembered, especially the way she bounced up and down and bit her fingernails while talking on the phone to her boyfriend, and the way she scrunched her nose when trying to figure out a math problem. Cal's face was clear, too. Timmy was sure he could draw a map of every freckle on Cal's face. And how could Timmy ever forget Cal's windup on the mound? The way he grimaced in a crouch, brought the ball and mitt together to his chest, checked second base, stared down the plate, kicked his leg high, leaned back, and let the ball fly with all his might. Timmy could play the windup over in his mind with ease. But he couldn't exactly picture his father's face for some reason. He remembered it vaguely, yes, but he couldn't draw it in his mind, not like the faces of the rest of his family. And that made him sad because he loved his father and he felt bad that he couldn't remember him clearly.

So much of Timmy's former life seemed distant now, like a cloud or a dream. His room, his friends, the yard, school, everything seemed like a movie Timmy had watched a long time ago. Timmy wondered if his family remembered him or if he was beginning to fade from their minds. Were they still looking for him? Had they given up? Would they care to take him back?

Timmy worried about Capote, too. He feared that the cat had wandered onto the road looking for him after Wally had taken him away. Capote followed Timmy anywhere he went. Timmy would die if something happened to his best friend. If only Timmy could have Capote with him right now, everything would be better.

Wally was a good reader, but he just read through it, he didn't make it sing like Timmy's mommy. Timmy looked Wally over again, his soft hands, the large ring on his finger with a flurry of diamonds, his soft shoes that reminded Timmy of his father, and the foul breath.

Finally in Who-ville the Grinch's small heart grew three times that day, and he brought back the toys and the food for the feast, and he himself, the Grinch, carved the roast beast.

"Well that's it," said Wally. "Anything to drink?"

"No, thanks." Timmy figured in about a month he would be ready for another Yoo-Hoo, but he swore he'd never eat another Twinkie again.

Wally stood up and carefully replaced the book on the shelf, then he kissed Timmy on the forehead and walked to the door.

"Light on or off?" Wally asked.

"Off."

"Good night."

"Good night, sir," Timmy said. He closed his eyes and quickly went to sleep. He was so tired of worrying about his family back home and he found in his dreams he was closer to them than when awake.

Wally closed the door and bolted the padlock, twice making sure the latch caught. He had been well trained to pay proper attention to the details. Life or death depended on attention to details.

Wally walked into the living room, beat some dust out of the old chair, and picked up the day's newspaper. He had devoured the stories on Jordan, and now read back to front, sports section first. The Mets were in fourth place and making no great drive for first. The weather forecast called for hot, hot, hot. The dollar was lower against the yen. There was trouble in some central African country. And everybody railed against the president.

Ah, there it was, on page thirteen, an article on

Prince Andrew on his way to America for a visit. Some sex scandal traveling with him. Poor prince, Wally thought. What an woeful existence, rich, handsome, desired by women, free to travel the globe, unfettered by the exigencies of life, yet utterly unable to enjoy these privileges due to the bubble of publicity that encircled him at every turn. Analyzed, criticized, reproached, and scorned for every wrong move, every inadvisable word —what a plague, fame. The gout of our century. And how particularly virulent the modern form of it was. Cameras, tabloids, paperbacks, news magazines, radio talk shows, dailies, weeklies, monthlies, local news, national news, and on and on and on.

Still people craved fame. How odd to desire such a condition, Wally thought, to be recognized wherever one traveled, terrorized by psychopathic stalkers, unable to relax save in the prison of one's own home. How ailing the ego must be to desire the affliction of fame. No healthy person could sincerely care for fame, only the weak, the tortured, or the undeserving.

That's why Wally had devised this little plan for Jordan. Stone already enjoyed a certain degree of fame, this was true. But it was his books that were famous, his name, not his face. Soon Stone would no longer own his face. It would belong to the filthy proletariat that contaminated the lives of the famous with its squalid curiosity. Fame, fame, fame, what a wonderful form of injury. What a terrible affliction. You sucker, Jordan.

Suddenly the phone rang.

The phone. Why would it ring? And then he remembered, he had forwarded calls from the Manhattan apartment here. But even in the apartment, calls were so rare that they tended to startle him.

He looked around, expecting someone in the room to be waiting for a call, but he was alone. Three rings, four. He never planned on using the phone, that would be foolish considering the speed with which calls were traced in this electronic era. He had Caller ID blocking installed, as a precaution, but the phone had been for emergency use only.

And now it rang again. Five, six, seven. Perhaps it was a wrong number, or a solicitation. Wally put his hand to the receiver and felt the vibration of the ring. Eight, nine. He could restrain himself no longer and he lifted the receiver. He held it to his ear for a moment before speaking, hoping to gain some insight into the nature of the call, the intent of the caller.

"Hello?" he spoke calmly. Wally was shocked to hear the caller use his real name.

"Yes, that's me." No need to panic, he thought.

"I was just about to hang up," said the caller. "I'm glad I found you. My assistant spent half the day tracking down your number. It seems you've just moved."

"I see." Wally said cautiously. It wasn't true, but Wally was not about to give away any information. "Who is this?"

"My name is Wanda Gentry. I'm a reporter from *Crime Current,* the television show. You're familiar with our program, aren't you?"

"Yes, yes, of course." He lied.

"Good. And I know you're familiar with Jordan Stone."

Wally waited a moment. Was this a trap? The caller knew his name. Certainly she also knew of his association with Jordan. If he lied he would only be setting himself up for suspicion.

"Yes," Wally said. "I know Jordan Stone."

"We're preparing a show for tomorrow night on Jordan Stone, *the writer*. We're inviting guests whom he has written about, some more extensively than others. Obviously you're one of them. I know it's short notice, but would you be available for tomorrow night's show?"

"Well, I . . . ."

"We're able to pay an honorarium. It's not much, $500."

"What's the focus of the show, if I may ask?"

"Many of those Jordan has written about feel they were unjustly portrayed in his true-crime books. We thought it would be a good time to air these grievances, in light of the situation."

"I see," said Wally.

"Are you available? It's your chance to tell your story."

"What time?"

"The show starts at eight, but we ask you to be at our studios at six for makeup, preparation, and to answer any questions you may have. We rarely go live and we're trying to avoid complications."

"I'll have to think about it, of course."

"Of course, but we have slots for only four guests and I've arranged for three already. Could you call back within the half hour? I'll give you my private number."

"Certainly."

Wally hung up the phone. He weighed the pros and cons. Going on the show would mean unnecessary exposure. On the other hand, an appearance could also alleviate any suspicion the FBI may harbor toward him. Certainly investigators would surmise the kidnapper would not dare be brazen enough to appear on a television show about Jordan Stone. No one could be that audacious. And then there was the delightful opportunity to pontificate upon the vile Mr. Stone. Yes, what a delightful invitation, an unexpected treat.

Wally called back within minutes. "I'd be happy to star on your show."

"Excellent," said Wanda. She gave Wally directions to the studio in Manhattan. "And if you have any questions, just call. I look forward to meeting you."

"Likewise."

Wally laid down the phone and picked up the newspaper. Good fortune comes to those who persevere. He ruffled the pages of the paper. Where was he? Ah, yes, Prince Andrew, the poor soul.

North Shore Hospital is a sprawling jumble of buildings continually under construction and a stone's throw away from the Long Island Expressway. Once a small community hospital, it had grown to titanic proportions along with the rest of the health care industry.

Jordan walked past two elderly volunteers chatting pleasantly behind the information desk. He didn't need the ladies' help. He knew where he was going, to the office of Dr. Truman Emerson, a towering man with soft blue eyes and a voice so melodic it lulled babies to sleep. Jordan and Truman had been roommates in college, and despite their dissimilar backgrounds and interests they had remained friends, or at least in touch, during the ensuing years.

Jordan had last spoken to Truman some six months earlier. Truman had called, interested in writing a book on medical ethics and seeking advice from the famous author himself. Trying not to sound too pessimistic, Jordan explained that there simply wasn't a market for such a book. If Truman was lucky, perhaps he could find a publisher to advance a modest sum and print a few thousand hard copies, but no more. No one read books on ethics anymore. Jordan gave Truman the name of his agent and offered to review the material, but he had warned Truman there would never be any profit in such an endeavor. It would be a labor of love. Truman listened attentively then softly vowed to continue writing in his spare time.

Truman hadn't changed. The two were still as different as they had ever been. In college Jordan had been apolitical, Truman championed every liberal cause that came his way. Jordan partied his way through school,

Truman burned the midnight oil in the library. Jordan screwed every girl he could get his hands on. Truman remained loyal to his college sweetheart, even though she was known to tangle it up herself. When she dumped Truman in their junior year, Jordan was secretly relieved he would never have to tell his buddy that he had slept with her, too. Anyway, Truman deserved better than her and eventually got it with Judy.

Jordan followed the blue line on the floor through the maze of hallways until he reached the Orthopedic Department. With a well-rehearsed expression of preoccupation, Jordan slipped past the station nurse and down the short hallway to Truman's office.

The door was slightly ajar and Truman sat in his desk chair cradling a tiny portable computer in his lap. His huge fingers fumbled over the compact keyboard.

"Why don't you just get a desktop computer?" Jordan said as he stepped into the carpeted office.

"I should, but then transferring files, cables. Technology, it's the problem, not the solution."

They had always started with small talk and today they needed the ritual more than ever.

"Sit down," Truman gestured awkwardly, wondering what to say to someone whose child has been kidnapped. "I'm so sorry about Timmy. It was such a shock when we saw the news last night."

"Thanks."

"You know Judy and I will do anything that's necessary."

"We appreciate that."

"I mean it, Jordan. If you need a place to stay, or if you need us to take Sarah and Cal for awhile. You name it. Anything."

Jordan nodded appreciatively. "There is something," he said.

"Shoot."

"We got a ransom note from the kidnapper."

"And?"

"He's willing to negotiate for Timmy."

"Money? Judy and I have already talked about it. We're willing to help you out. We can pool our resources and—"

"It's not money," Jordan interrupted.

Jordan wasn't quite sure how to say it. So instead he lifted his hands and slowly twirled them in the air like two antennas searching for a signal.

"It's these," said Jordan.

"What?" Truman said with a look of puzzlement.

"He wants my hands, both of them."

"Jordan, please, no jokes."

"I wish it were."

"Your hands?"

"We—the FBI and I—believe it's someone I wrote about, someone upset with the way I portrayed them. This is their revenge, rogue justice, I guess."

"Jordan, I'm so sorry."

Jordan shrugged. "Risks of the business."

"But I don't understand. What can I do?" asked Truman.

"You're a surgeon. I want you to cut off my hands."

"You want what?"

Jordan leaned forward and looked into Truman's eyes. "I need you to cut off my hands."

"You can't be serious."

"I am."

"What does the FBI say about this?"

Jordan hesitated, but he couldn't lie to Truman. "They don't know I'm here."

"Then presumably they don't want you to amputate."

"They don't have a son whose been kidnapped. I want Timmy back."

"We all do."

"Well?" asked Jordan.

Truman set down the computer on the messy desk. "I don't think you realize what you're asking of me."

"I have no choice."

"Do you know what the hospital review board would do to me if I went ahead with something like this? I could lose my license."

"What if they didn't know, if they didn't find out?"

"Even if I agreed, I'd need nurses, anesthesiologists, assistants. It's a complicated procedure. This isn't the Civil War."

"This is my son. It's Timmy. Think about Amy and Susan. Tell me you wouldn't gladly give up your hands for your kids. Put yourself in my position."

"You know I'd give anything for my children. And I understand your desire. But you're asking me to perform an illegal act, to jeopardize my career."

"I understand that."

"If I had any guarantee that it would help Timmy, I might consider it, despite the consequences. But I'm not convinced, nor does it seem the FBI is convinced, that amputating your hands guarantees anything but your dismemberment."

"And Timmy? What about Timmy? Doesn't he deserve to live?"

"Jordan, please. It's not a question of who deserves what. It's a question of what's right and wrong, what's possible and what isn't."

"I'm asking as a friend."

"You know I'd do anything in my power. But this isn't in my power, Jordan."

Jordan stood. He could sit no longer. What would he do if Truman declined? How does one go about cutting off their hands?

"Truman, please, just think about. Don't answer me now. Just think. Will you give me that much?"

Truman leaned back and sighed. "That much I can."

"I don't want to lose him, True. I can't lose my son."

* * *

It didn't take long on the drive home for Jordan to spot
the unmarked car following him. The brown Chrysler
with the moon hubcaps and black-wall tires stood out
like a hobo among the sleek and colorless BMWs and
Acuras of Rocky Cliff. The driver, Agent Rocky Bales,
a stocky fellow in sunglasses and a drab gray polyester
suit apparently didn't seem any more interested in in-
visibility than style. Just to check, Jordan pulled onto
the shoulder of the road. Sure enough, the Chrysler
pulled off, too, a few hundred feet behind him. When
Jordan jetted back onto the pavement, the Chrysler began the tail again. And as Jordan drove the curvy
streets of his neighborhood, he caught peeks of the
boxy car in his rearview mirror all the way home.

So this is how it was going to be.

A handful of reporters perked up when Jordan approached. They sat in lawn chairs shaded by umbrellas
on the shoulder of the road. Jordan drove slowly
through the group with a scowl on his face.

"Did you find the kidnapper?" a reporter shouted.

"What's the ransom?"

"Is Timmy safe?"

"Any leads, Jordan?"

"Jordan, talk to us."

They kept a respectful distance as they shouted questions, remembering full well the incident with the cameraman yesterday. Jordan parked and scurried into the
house, slamming the door behind him. The reporters
returned to their lawn chairs and ice chests. Shitty assignment unless you wanted a suntan.

Inside, Waters was busy at the dining room table. He
was dressed impeccably in a soft blue cotton shirt,
double-breasted suit of light wool, a blue-green silk tie
with Australian Aboriginal designs, and a matching
blue-green handkerchief in his jacket pocket. Not a

thread was out of place. Jordan felt like tearing him to pieces.

"What the hell are you doing?" Jordan demanded.

"What are you talking about?"

"You're having me followed," Jordan said.

"How perceptive."

"I have my rights, goddamn it."

Waters let out a slight chuckle. "Your rights ended when you called us."

"You pull your bulldogs back or—"

"Or what? Look, we have a ton of suspects in this case and everyone is checking out okay. We're not any closer to finding the perpetrator than when we began this operation. Can you blame us for following you?"

"I'm not the kidnapper. I haven't done anything wrong," said Jordan.

"I don't believe you are the kidnapper. But I know what you're thinking, Stone. You're looking for an end run around this case. You're looking to fix it yourself, quick and dirty—just like your books."

"What's that supposed to mean?"

"You're the writer, I'll let you read into it."

"I don't owe anybody apologies," said Jordan.

"I don't want apologies. I want your help."

"Well, I'm not a team player."

"Then don't blame me if I have to bench you."

Allie watched the skirmish from beyond. She had felt the animosity between the two the moment she had met Waters. He was too much like Jordan, identical poles of a powerful magnet. Jordan didn't like others running his affairs. He was a lone wolf, always had been, just like Waters, she surmised.

"Stop it. Stop it, for God's sake," she said. "Timmy is who-knows-where, and you two are arguing like little boys."

The point was well taken by both men, who stepped back.

"We have Timmy out there. I think that should be motivation enough for you two to put your personal differences aside," she said.

Jordan knew Allie was right, but he couldn't help believe that he had a better chance of getting Timmy back than Waters. He had promised Allie to cooperate, but that was then.

"Look, we have forty-eight hours to deadline," said Waters. "We have a plan. A good one. It's simply not possible for him to pick up a package at JFK without us seizing him. We're going to catch him."

"How?" asked Allie.

"I don't want to discuss details. But believe me, we're going to catch him."

"Guaranteed?" asked Jordan.

"I don't normally give guarantees, but this time I will."

TWELVE

Cal grabbed his mitt and hardball and wandered out to the front lawn to play a game of catch with himself. His parents wouldn't allow any friends over and they had forbade him from leaving the property. He understood. Like them, he was terribly upset about Timmy and had cried the night of the kidnapping. Now that Timmy was gone, Cal suffered pangs of guilt for having had ignored Timmy so often before the kidnapping. Cal hadn't always been the best of brothers and he vowed to change that when Timmy came home.

Still, Cal was bored out of his mind. He missed skipping down to the inlet with his friends to see what had floated ashore or to scurry the paths along the cattails and pine trees at low tide in bare feet until the wet sand squashed through his toes. Since the kidnapping, Cal had missed two soccer practices, one game, and Tony's birthday party, which had included a trip to Shea Stadium and a Mets game. He felt guilty for missing all these things because he knew that Timmy was in great danger and all these things were meaningless in comparison. He missed them nevertheless, and he couldn't change that.

The first day after the kidnapping, Cal remained transfixed by the FBI agents and their equipment. Once he realized that the agents did a whole bunch of sitting around, their jobs didn't look so cool anymore. From day two on, Cal isolated himself in his room, playing computer games and watching videos.

So today Cal figured he'd venture outside for a catch, despite his parents' admonitions and the reporters hanging around just beyond the fence. It felt great to be outside. Cal felt self-conscious at first as the reporters perked up to watch him, but after awhile he forgot the spectators and threw the ball straight into the air as high as he could, blocking the sun with his glove for the catch.

Cal didn't realize he was slowly drifting toward the far corner of the property, away from the crowd of reporters and near the fence and the road. He flung the ball skyward and drifted into place to catch it, but the ball landed with a thud on the road just beyond the fence, dribbled across the street, and came to rest on the far shoulder in a thicket of crab grass. Cal began to climb the fence like he had a thousand times before, then he thought better and slowly descended to ponder his alternatives.

One of the reporters who had wandered away from the pack to take a leak saw the ball roll across the street. He ambled over to the ball, picked it up, and eyed it like an umpire looking for scuff marks.

"This your ball?" the reporter asked. Cal saw a long, thin notebook stuffed into the reporter's back pocket and a pencil behind his ear.

"Yeah, thanks."

Instead of chucking the ball back to Cal, the reporter checked for traffic both ways then slowly crossed the street juggling the ball in one hand.

"You're Cal, aren't you?" said the reporter.

"Yeah."

"I'm Sal Delano, a good friend of your dad's. You

and I met before at a party, right here at your parents' house."

"I don't remember."

"Hey, I don't blame you, with all the people you must meet." Delano plopped the ball into Cal's glove.

"Thanks," said Cal, turning to leave.

"I bet they've been ignoring you these past few days."

Cal stopped and eyed the reporter. "Kind of."

"Yep, it's a shame. I mean, what happened to Timmy is really terrible, but they can't just forget about their other children."

"I'm okay."

"Why, I bet they don't even tell you what's happening. I mean, like if they've gotten a ransom note yet, and what the kidnapper wants."

"They tell me stuff. I know all that."

"You do?"

Delano reached down for a blade of grass and picked his teeth with it.

"But I'm not supposed to tell anyone."

"Sure, I understand. I'd be tight-lipped if the kidnapper wanted a ton of money from my dad."

"He doesn't want money," said Cal.

"No kidding. What does he want?"

Cal eyed Delano then glanced to the stately Victorian in the distance.

"I don't think I'm supposed to tell you," said Cal.

"That's all right. I didn't think you knew anyway. I'll just ask your dad later."

Delano turned his back to Cal and began retracing his steps across Sand Castle Drive.

"He wants his hands," Cal said softly.

Delano stopped on the double yellow line and spinned around.

"What's that you said, kid?"

"The kidnapper," said Cal, "he wants my father's hands."

"You're shitting me." Delano's jaw dropped.

"That's what they told us last night."

"Who?"

"My parents."

A huge semi truck in low gear turned the sharp corner catching Cal and Delano by surprise. Delano backpedaled to let the semi pass. The driver squealed his brakes bringing his load nearly to a halt, then picked up speed and continued on slowly. When the truck passed, Cal searched for Delano on the far side of the road.

But the reporter was nowhere to be seen.

Jordan was oblivious to the quiet conversation taking place on the far end of the property. With cardboard boxes and manilla envelopes surrounding him, Jordan was too involved in the work at hand, reviewing the notes he had amassed during the writings of his six books, building a personal list of possible suspects. The FBI could take care of the prime suspects, Jordan targeted his search to lesser-known possibilities.

The files for *Up from Ashes: Cindy's Story* took up to six crates alone. As a first-time author, Jordan had overresearched the book, a common error. Jordan spent less research time on each successive book, so that his last book, *Mind's Eye,* was little more than a dramatic retelling of the court transcripts plus some snippets from telephone interviews with families of the cult members. Some critics claimed a decline in the quality of each successive book, but Jordan didn't agree. It's just that he had become more astute at fleshing out the story without resorting to painstaking interviewing, and keen to the fact that the audience is not interested in veracity as much as drama. In *Cindy's Story,* Jordan spent three chapters discussing the federal government's war on child pornography, but after numerous conversations with readers, Jordan had discovered that readers turned off the dissertation somewhere into the second chapter on the subject. By contrast, *Mind's Eye,* garnered the largest number of sales despite the critics' rejection. If Jordan occasionally highlighted the dramatic at the expense of the truth, well, such is the price one pays for entertainment.

With list in hand, Jordan dialed up Fred Griff, detective with the Nassau County Police Department, Sixth Precinct. One of the few detectives who would talk to Jordan anymore, Griff was a would-be mystery writer who stood in awe of Jordan and his success. With reverence Griff handed over his unfinished manuscripts to Jordan for his review. The work had potential but was the sure stuff of an amateur. Jordan pumped up Griff nonetheless, telling him he was one draft away from a best-seller. Griff in exchange, worked the inside computers for Jordan, tracking down people and saving Jordan countless hours of skip tracing.

The call rang through. "Griff, I need a favor," said Jordan, then he explained the situation and his B list of suspects.

"Why not just hand it over to the Bureau?" Griff's attitude was cooler than usual.

"They've got their list of suspects, I'm just hoping to glean what falls through the cracks."

Griff fell silent.

"What is it, Griff?"

"Waters was in here this morning, met with the captain. The memo went out that no one is to help you or interfere with the Bureau's work. Strictly hands off."

"I'm asking as a friend."

"There's more. Captain called me in personally. Said he knew I was hankering to be a writer and had asked you for help. Said I should forget about it—both the writing and helping you, both were worthless causes, he said."

"I need this. This is my son, Griff."

"Give me the list, but I can't promise anything."

"Thanks," Jordan said, cursing Waters under his breath. He read the names off the list.

"Don't call me, I'll call you," said Griff.

Just as he hung up with the detective, Jordan heard the house intercom buzz.

It was Allie in her serious voice. "Better get down here."

Jordan locked the room as he left and hustled to the house, where Cal waited in the living room, his chin glued to his chest.

"Cal has something to tell you," said Allie.

From the boy's inability to take his eyes off the floor, Jordan knew it was serious. "Tell me, Cal."

"I'm sorry."

"About what?"

"He tricked me."

"Who tricked you?" asked Jordan.

"A reporter."

"You talked to a reporter? Where?"

"Outside by the fence."

"I told you not to leave the yard."

"I didn't," said Cal angrily, looking at Jordan for the first time.

"Who was it, did he say?"

"Sal something."

"Sal Delano, *New York Post*. The weasel."

"He said he was your friend."

"In another life maybe."

Cal scraped his sneaker along the carpet.

"You didn't say anything to him did you?" asked Jordan.

Cal's nonresponse was his affirmation.

"And *what* did you tell him?"

Allie stood by. As much as she was angry at Cal, she was prepared to defend him in the face of Jordan's imminent wrath.

"I told him the truth."

"What truth?"

"About the kidnapper."

"They already know about him," said Jordan.

"Cal," said Allie. "Tell your father."

"I told him about the ransom, about your hands."

Jordan stepped back to ponder the ramifications of Cal's response. Then without thinking he grabbed Cal by the shoulders and shook him fiercely.

"You what?"

"I told him. Okay, I'm sorry. He said he was your friend."

"Didn't we say nobody? Tell nobody."

Cal ripped away and picked up his glove and mitt lying on the floor. "It's not my fault."

"Then whose fault is it? You tell me that," Jordan said. "Whose fault is it?"

Cal's face contorted and grew florid. He pulled the hardball from his glove and with a swift windup threw the ball at full speed through the closed living room window, sending shattered glass everywhere.

"It's your fault," he yelled at Jordan. "Yours."

Cal ran from the house into the yard.

"You better go apologize," said Allie.

"Apologize? Me? He's the one who—"

"He's a boy, for God's sake. You can't ask him not to make boy mistakes. He isn't the cause of all this."

Through the broken glass, Jordan saw Cal running toward the fence. The cameramen outside perked up.

Jordan raced from the house in pursuit. "Cal, wait."

Lights.

"Cal!"

Camera.

"Cal, get back here."

Action.

Cal slowed to a walk. Jordan caught up to him and attempted a hug, but the boy resisted and squirmed away.

"Cal, now you listen to me."

Cal heard that tone of voice and knew there was little mercy in it. He spinned around and raced toward the fence.

"Cal, you get back here!"

Cal leapt the fence with one swift bound. Like a deer escaping a hunter, he darted into the bushes beyond the road and disappeared. Only then did Jordan notice the swarm of cameras bearing down at him.

"What the fuck are you looking at?" Jordan said savagely as he pressed through the pack.

Undaunted, the cameramen kept the tape rolling long after Jordan returned to the house and vanished behind the slammed front door.

Cal returned about an hour later through the back door. He headed straight for his room, slamming the door shut. He turned on his Nintendo and put on his headphones. Loud. He vowed never to talk to his father again.

One bedroom over, Sarah faced her vanity mirror, a tray of cosmetics on the counter before her. The bright vanity lights illuminated her reflection, zits and all. A string of rosary beads, black and silver, with Jesus lashed passively to his crucifix, hung on the left mirror post. The right post was decorated with colorful strands of plastic Carnaval beads, which Sarah had snatched off the streets of New Orleans after battling an uproarious Mardi Gras crowd two Februarys ago with her parents.

She had already applied the mascara, thick and black, and much to her dismay, crunchy. She had rarely applied mascara before, only when playing with girl-friends, and certainly she had never scrutinized the results so closely. With a tweezer she attempted to remove the little crumbs of black gunk but succeeded only in painfully tugging a few eyelashes.

Sarah uncapped the lipstick tube, *Plum Passion,* and twisted up the crayon. She licked her lips wet, puckered once, then rolled on the flavorful color, careful not to overrun her lips, and quite amazed at what a little color can do to a face, from girl to woman, from virgin to babe. She hoped Jimmy would approve. Sarah had never worn makeup out; her mother frowned on it, and Sarah never felt quite right with cosmetics, except for a little blush, maybe.

Why she broke her rule tonight, she wasn't sure. Maybe because she was going out against her parents' wishes, which added an element of danger to the evening. Maybe because she was ready to forget this whole kidnapping thing. Or perhaps she needed a mask to cover the shame of her family.

She thought about all these possibilities only briefly before reaching for the aqua blue eyeshadow with sparkling highlights. The applicator was soft and clean and she loved the cool tingle of the powder as it colored her eyelids. It made her feel sexy. Why hadn't she done this before?

She reached for a bottle of Charlie and dabbed a dash on her neck, her wrists, and what little there was of her cleavage, certainly not enough for Sarah's liking, though Jimmy didn't seem to mind the few times she had allowed him to fondle her. Finally she reached for the foundation cream and once more dabbed a drop on her chin in a vain attempt to hide the pimple that seemed camped there forever. Pimples were the worst. No, she reminded herself. Timmy's kidnapping was the worst. She would endure a face full of pimples forever in exchange for Timmy right now.

One last check in the mirror and Sarah went to her closet filled with nothing to wear. She pulled out a pair of black stretch pants and a faded sweatshirt, which she immediately rejected as too baggy. She found a mauve cowboy shirt that had just the right appeal when tied around her waist above her navel. Thank *God* for her flat stomach. She modeled the outfit in her long mirror behind the door, striking alluring poses. The shirt's color clashed with her blue eyeshadow, but what the heck, it was summer, it was hot, and it was forbidden.

She heard the doorbell ring and raced downstairs hoping to beat her father to the door. But it was too late. Her boyfriend stood frozen with Jordan mastering over him.

"What's going on?" asked Jordan.

"I'm going out," said Sarah defiantly.

So this was how it was going to be, Jordan thought. The family is in crisis, his son flees into the woods, and his daughter dolls herself up and goes out against his wishes. Jordan understood Cal's reaction, but from Sarah this really hurt.

"Absolutely not," he said.

Sarah stiffened and pushed her hair away from her eyes.

"Sorry, Daddy."

"Why are you doing this to us?"

"I'm doing nothing to you. I just need a break, okay? I'll be back."

"And what's all this?" Jordan motioned to Sarah's makeup. He knew immediately he had said the wrong thing as soon the words left his mouth. Sarah's integrity was never in question. Nor had he ever forbidden her from wearing makeup. Making it an issue now would only give her justification for her behavior.

"Nothing. I'm just going out for a few hours."

"Let her go," Allie said, walking in from the kitchen. She understood Sarah's reaction. This whole unfortunate affair was too great a burden for the children to handle. Allie herself felt like running off sometimes. This moment with Sarah was inevitable and Allie felt if

she and Jordan didn't play it right, the trust they had
built with their daughter would quickly erode.

Jordan looked silently at his little girl.

"You come back by midnight. Do you understand,
young lady?"

Sarah slipped her arm in Jimmy's, and the two
skipped down the path past the runway of lights and
cameras that awaited them like royalty.

Jimmy fired up his old convertible Camaro, and Allie
and Jordan watched their little girl vanish down the
road, her arm around Jimmy's shoulder, her head bop-
ping to the tunes, and her chestnut hair whipping in the
August breeze.

THIRTEEN

Just as Sarah departed, the opening theme for *Crime Current* trumpeted from the big-screen television in the den. Allie knew she shouldn't watch, but the compulsion was too strong. What would Wanda concoct this time? As Allie slid into the plush sofa, she felt a sinful tinge of pleasure mixed with nausea, not unlike her brief days of binging and purging in high school. Jordan posted himself on the edge of the couch and all too consciously placed a hand on Allie's knee.

"Coming up on *Crime Current*," said the announcer in his urgent voice, "Timmy Stone—who has him, who wants him, and why. After these messages."

Off camera, Wally patted his head with a handkerchief and readjusted his buttocks on the hardwood chair. The three other subjects summoned hastily by Wanda did much the same thing, anything to ease their pre-show jitters. Wally had never been in a studio before and he was struck by the high ceilings, the tremendous amount of equipment that seemingly did nothing, and the cramped set, which looked so lavish when viewing the show from home. The floor director was easy to spot due to his continual state of panic. Wanda spent every moment up to the top of the cast looking over her producer's shoulder and his clipboard.

An assistant director, whom Wally thought was dressed entirely too casually for a nationally syndicated show, gave the guests instructions.

"You can relax the first segment. You're seg two at twenty-one after the hour. Look at Wanda. *Listen* to her questions. Answer succinctly. And give it all you got, let's nail the bastard."

Wally, naturally, had only seen Wanda on television, and he was struck by her beauty in person. She appeared far more intense and intelligent than she came across on the tube. He quickly developed a little crush on her and felt a rise in his pants as she walked his way. As Wanda took her seat among the guests, she smiled at Wally. He took it as a sign that the feeling was mutual.

Three, two, one.

The AD signaled Wanda silently, and she adjusted her posture. When the "on air" sign lit up, Wally watched admiringly as Wanda turned it on like a go-go dancer, fully aware of her audience yet pretending it didn't exist.

At the Stones, Wanda's image materialized on the screen larger than life, like the Wicked Witch of the West in Dorothy's crystal ball.

"Timmy Stone is missing and the nation is in shock," Wanda began solemnly.

"Everyone hopes and prays for his safe return. But as the FBI and the police search for the little lost boy, an anxious nation searches for answers. Why was Timmy kidnapped? What does the kidnapper want? And who really is the kidnapper? Our investigation has turned up some surprising answers.

"Tonight on this special *live* edition of *Crime Current,* we'll talk with some people who understand why someone may want to take revenge against the successful author of six best-sellers. But first we want to share with you some recent developments."

Wanda swiveled in her chair to aim her gaze at camera two the moment its red tally light brightened. She picked up a sheet of paper and began to read, as if the news was so hot the crew had had no time to transfer the text to TelePrompter.

Cheap prop, Jordan thought as he slipped a clean tape in the VCR and pushed record.

"Unconfirmed reports indicate that the Stones have received a ransom demand from the kidnapper. Our sources won't say if the Bureau believes the note to be authentic or a hoax."

Closeup.

"But *Crime Current* has learned that investigators aren't ruling anybody in—or out—as a suspect. And that includes Jordan Stone, according to sources close to the Bureau. Why Stone would arrange to have his son kidnapped—if indeed he did—is anyone's guess. But no doubt his publisher can only be pleased by the healthy boost in sales of Stone's books."

Pregnant pause. Dead-aim camera stare. Eyebrow lifted ever so slightly, head tilt to the right.

"Could all this be a Stone hoax?"

On the cue of *hoax*, the director cut to a mug shot of Jordan, taken many years earlier when his hair was long and he wore a mustache. Jordan recognized it immediately as the pose taken after his arrest at the First Amendment rally. He looked like a street jerk. But then, nobody looks good in mug shots.

"In fact," Wanda continued, *"Crime Current* has learned that Jordan Stone was arrested eight years ago and convicted of destroying public property during a riot in Times Square."

"I was never convicted," Jordan whispered.

Off camera, Wally smiled.

"Crime Current has also learned that Stone was reprimanded for plagiarism while he worked at *Newsday."*

"That's a lie." Jordan stood and pointed an accusatory finger at the TV, but it didn't flinch.

"Even the specifics around Stone's hasty departure from *Newsday* remain clouded in controversy, according to sources at the Long Island daily. While it may be debatable if Stone is involved in this diabolical scheme, one thing is for certain, his marriage is in for a rocky road ahead. Here's psychologist Norma Ginsburg."

Jordan searched for a judge to cry foul, but the oversized television held the floor.

Wanda swiveled in her chair to watch the monitor beam a remote of the esteemed psychologist from her office in Los Angeles.

Wally wiped his forehead and huddled closer to the monitor. What delightful and unexpected programming. He should watch this program more often, he thought.

Dr. Ginsburg sat in a high-back leather chair against a large bookshelf. Her glasses rested at the edge of her nose and her wrinkled face peered upward into the camera.

"Little puts as much strain on a marriage as the loss of a child, even temporarily," Ginsburg intoned. "But when tragedies such as this occur, marital problems that have been buried deep in the hurried pace of everyday life rise to the surface. Many marriages end in divorce when parents suffer a kidnapping, serious illness, or death of a child."

"Dr. Ginsburg," Wanda asked inquisitively, gazing at the monitor as if it were omnipotent, "and what about the strain on Timmy, psychologically?"

"Good question. All hostages—even mature adults— suffer great anguish during and after such a traumatic ordeal. For children it's even worse. We don't know if sexual abuse is involved here, but if so, Timmy will be traumatized as well as stigmatized for the rest of his life. He may distrust his parents, society, he may have trouble with commitment, even turn to crime. No one knows."

Wanda shook her head in consternation.

"And how about the Stones' other two children?" Wanda asked. "What affect will all this have on them?"

"Naturally, they will suffer, too," continued Ginsburg. "Grief is a debilitating emotion, and if the family can manage to stay together, they certainly will need counseling for many years to come. Don't be surprised, however, to see each family member run in his or her own directions."

On cue—and as if by total coincidence—the director cut to the tape shot earlier in the day of Cal fleeing the house with Jordan chasing behind. Let the audience see the family in crisis. See how Jordan chases his fine young son only to lose him to the bushes. Let the public experience firsthand the brutish methods Jordan Stone employs both at work and at home. Scrape away the successful veneer and reveal the corrosion underneath this man of letters.

Return to camera one.

"Heartbreaking," Wanda lamented, shaking her head.

Long shot of segment two guests. "We'll return in a moment with some surprising revelations about Jordan Stone the writer, and Jordan Stone the man."

"Bitch," Jordan mumbled softly. What an idiot he had been to believe that he held some special dispensation with Wanda. The Ice Queen. How many times had Jordan watched Wanda perform her black magic on others. And why wasn't he outraged then? Because others weren't him and then wasn't now.

After commercials, Wanda reappeared larger than life.

"We have in the studio with us four people whose lives changed dramatically after Jordan Stone wrote about them or someone they loved."

Jordan inched toward the television to watch the spectacle, to search for clues. Allie remained on the couch, legs tightly crossed, fearing what Wanda was cooking up now, hateful of her power, yet slightly in awe of it as well.

The first guest was Charlie Spike, the cult pimp from *Mind's Eye*. What women saw in this man, Jordan could never figure out. He looked like a middle-aged accountant, and a crooked one at that. He wore a permanent smirk that bordered on a sneer, and he combed his hair over his bald head, as if the deception fooled anybody. Charlie fiddled nervously with his hands, flicking the fingernail of his middle finger with his thumb.

Jordan also instantly recognized Amos Richter. He was the brother of Harold Richter, the murderer of their niece in *Carrie's Confession*. Amos was a soft-spoken college professor who stood by his brother's side during the trial. And he looked the part with his wool sweater and urbane demeanor. All that was missing was a thoughtful pipe. From Amos's expression, Jordan gleaned that Amos was not fully comfortable with his surroundings. He searched Wanda's face for clues, like a puppy on his first journey away from the den.

Jordan didn't recognize the two other guests. Wanda did him the service of introducing them.

"To my left is Arthur Hedlund, father of Josh Hedlund, one of three young boys convicted of murder and the subjects of Jordan Stone's fourth book *Slaughter Alley*.

Dr. Hedlund looked anemic, the type of guy who would collect stamps for thrills. During research on the book, Jordan had attempted to interview Hedlund several times, but the good doctor never returned phone calls. He looked like he had prepared a statement and couldn't wait until the moment was over so he could breathe again.

"And finally, on my right, Bill Kincaid, the now-released prison lover of John Tibett, the socialite convicted of murdering his wife with a piano wire in their posh Southampton estate."

Jordan was familiar with Tibett, but his prison lover? Kincaid was a big man. His squeaky clean skin glowed under the powerful television lights. Yet he possessed the pudgy cheeks and boyish grin of a preacher and Jordan imagined his handshake as limp and moist.

Wanda shifted back in her chair and tapped the rubber eraser of her pencil on the table.

"I want to ask each of you one question. Tell us, tell America, how Jordan Stone has affected your lives?"

Charles Spike leaned forward. His finger flicking increased in tempo until his started talking, then he hid his hands underneath the table.

"My family, and by that I mean my brother and the extended family of all the members of our congregation —we lived happily together. No one forced anyone to do anything. Everything we did, all the sacrifices we made were given up gladly in the Lord's name. Shorterly after the federal government leveled unfounded charges against us, it appeared the charges would be dropped. But then, as soon as it was learned that Mr. Stone was writing a book about us, pressure came from the highest echelons of government to make the charges stick. Mr. Stone then took the most scandalous lies circulating about us at the time and printed them as fact. I believe the Bible demands retribution for falsely accusing your neighbor."

"And what would you like to say to Jordan Stone now, Mr. Spike, assuming he's watching, and I have reason to believe he is."

How could Wanda be so cocky, even if she was right.

"I'd tell him to be prepared for the wrath of God. Judgment is swift and measured, and there is no place to run from the Lord."

Wanda wheeled her chair to face Bill Kincaid. "Mr.

Kincaid, I understand that Jordan Stone was instrumental in putting your lover behind bars."

Wanda damn well knew the story of how Jordan helped free the innocent Greek gardener and led police to evidence that incriminated Shirley Tibett's husband in *The Tended Garden*. If Jordan prided himself on anything it was his efforts to help free an innocent man.

"That's right," said Kincaid.

"And what would you say to Jordan Stone?"

The boyish grin disappeared. "I have nothing against the man personally, but John didn't kill his wife. He just didn't. He swears to me and I believe him. Lord knows I know the man well enough to know when he's lying. He suffers everyday, not only because of his incarceration but because his reputation was ruined by Jordan Stone. It's a tragedy. And my crusade will end only when John is freed. I'm thankful for this publicity, for the opportunity to state my case."

"And what would you say to Mr. Stone, if you had the opportunity to see him face to face?"

"I don't know. I have children, too. I can imagine the pain, but he can't say he didn't see it coming."

"Children. I thought you were gay?" asked Wanda.

"In prison I was."

"Thank you, Bill. Now, Mr. Hedlund. Tell us why you're angry with Jordan Stone."

"My son committed suicide."

"And you blame Jordan Stone for that?"

"I do. Like everyone here, it was Stone's publicity that turned us all into victims. No matter what the warden says, the boy killed himself because he couldn't stand being made a fool in Stone's book. I told my son to be strong, but he never listened to me."

"And what would you like to say to Jordan Stone right now?"

"I'd say, I blame you, Mr. Stone. But I know how you

feel. We've both had sons taken from us. Only problem is I will never get mine back."

Jordan shook his head in disbelief. Hedlund's son killed himself the day after being raped by a gang of older inmates. His father was lying. Jordan turned to Allie, seeking dispensation. Allie said nothing, her judgment held in check by the unfolding theater in front of her.

"Finally we have Amos Richter," said Wanda, turning to the professor. "How has Jordan Stone affected your life?"

Richter took a moment to gather his thoughts, much like he must do in class, Jordan thought.

"My brother may be guilty, I know that. But does that give people like Jordan Stone the right to exploit the tragedy? Even if my brother deserved the publicity or earned it, there are so many others affected by the telling of the story. Following publication of his book, my mother lapsed into a major depression from which she has yet to emerge. Harold's wife, Lillian, can't go to the store without people pointing fingers and whispering behind her back. My dead niece has sisters and brothers who deeply resent the book. It has earned them unwarranted notoriety. All these people and others have suffered twice now, once due to the horrible crimes committed by my brother, and twice by the shameless crime committed in the name of entertainment by Jordan Stone.

"I'm sure Jordan is suffering now, and I don't want to see anyone suffer. That's the point I'm trying to make. I have nothing against Stone. But I would like to address the thousands of writers, producers, publishers, directors, actors, and network executives out there who partake in this type of exploitation. Please, look at what you're doing. Think how it would feel to be in our shoes. If it's news you're reporting, that's one thing, we need a free and open society. But the right of free speech does not give you the right to profit from the pain of others, to exploit in the name of entertainment. You would be the first to protest if you witnessed circus animals being beaten. Yet here you are inflicting pain of a much crueler sort, deep emotional pain upon innocent people. All I have to say is *think*. Think what it would be like to be in our shoes. In Jordan Stone's shoes. That's all."

Wanda nodded knowingly, in complete agreement with the truth posited by the good professor.

"And so the saga continues. When all is said and done, and all America prays Timmy comes home safely, only one thing will be certain. Jordan's loving public will look at him with new eyes, perhaps a bit more critically. For *Crime Current,* I'm Wanda Gentry."

Jordan found the remote on the coffee table and zapped the show good-bye. He pulled out the tape and glanced at Allie. She shot him a strained smile that meant the pain ran deep. She vowed silently at that moment not to let this woman beat her.

"It's lies, all lies," said Jordan.

"Jordan, I have a question. And I need the truth."

"What is it?"

"The truth, Jordan." Allie eyed him directly.

"You have my word."

Allie took a short tour of the den, waiting for just the right moment and the courage to speak. Finally, she could wait no longer.

"Are you still sleeping with her?"

"With who?"

"You know darn well who."

Technically Jordan wasn't sleeping with Wanda. The relationship was over. But that wasn't the question Allie was asking. Jordan tried to comfort Allie, bring her closer, but she would have none of it.

"Jordan, please."

"The question is a little petty, I mean, under the circumstances."

"Don't do this to me, Jordan. I need an answer."

Allie's dark brown eyes were moist and she bit her bottom lip in anticipation. Jordan wasn't used to seeing her vulnerable. At this moment, under these circumstances, he felt he had no choice. He wanted to tell the truth, but he couldn't bear the thought of bringing more hurt into Allie's world. And he had to admit to himself that he couldn't bear the consequences should the truth be known. After all, this whole wretched episode would hopefully be over tomorrow afternoon when the kidnapper attempted to get near the locker at JFK.

"No," Jordan whispered. "No, I'm not."

"Tell me again."

"No, absolutely not." Jordan looked straight into her eyes.

"You wouldn't lie to me, would you?"

"I'm telling you the truth."

"I need to know."

"I've told you."

"I'm going to believe you, Jordan. I'm going to trust you. I just pray to God you're telling the truth."

"I am." Jordan smiled, but it took every fiber in his body to fake it.

Midnight, Sarah's witching hour, came and went with no sign of Sarah. At one o'clock in the morning, Allie woke Jordan and discussed the situation. They decided to call Jimmy's parents.

"He never comes home before four on weekends," said a cranky Mr. Buconti.

At 2:00 A.M. Allie could wait no longer. She called the Nassau County Police Department. The case sergeant was alarmed at first, considering the Stones' situation, then he heard Sarah had left on a date all dolled up.

"Kids stay out late," said the sergeant. "My daughter's no different."

Jordan promptly got on the line and enlightened the officer as to the differences between his daughter and Sarah. The sergeant reluctantly promised to have his patrols check the local teen hangouts for Jimmy's car. "But that's all I can do."

At 3:30 A.M., exhausted from waiting, Allie and Jordan fell asleep. The alarm woke them at 6:00. Jordan raced into Sarah's room and found her bed empty still. He began to truly worry for the first time.

Allie and Jordan contemplated their next move when at 6:06, a call came in from Nassau County Police. A patrolman had spotted Jimmy's car at the sand dunes near Port Washington. The vehicle looked empty so the officer got closer and found Jimmy and Sarah motionless in the backseat. He nudged Jimmy with his nightstick and the teenager didn't budge. Another nudge and Jimmy woke up. Sarah roused shortly afterward, unharmed and unconcerned over the agony she had put her parents through. Jimmy passed a sobriety test by a mere .01 percent and the officer instructed them to get on home, fast. So much for Jordan's daughter, the sergeant intimated.

Jordan took a steamy hot shower, dressed impeccably for his day's big objective, and cursed his lack of sleep just when he needed all his wits about him.

He was in the kitchen pouring himself his first cup of coffee when he heard Jimmy's car door slam shut. Spying out the window, Jordan caught sight of Sarah plant a big smooch on Jimmy's lips then pull herself out of the car, disheveled and groggy. She bent in the street to pick up the just-delivered *Post* and sauntered up the path, a few cameramen tagging along like puppies. Jordan waited until Sarah was well inside the house and out of earshot of the reporters before he spoke. He had learned his lesson well with Cal.

"Well, look what the cat dragged in," Jordan said. Sarah wiped the sleep from her eyes and handed the folded newspaper to her father.

"Can we talk later? I've got to get some sleep."

"This is not acceptable behavior."

"What are you going to do, *ground* me?" she said. She climbed the stairs slowly, her matted hair cloaking her eyes.

Jordan watched her vanish down the hall, then he carried the newspaper into the kitchen and poured himself a cup for the road. He slammed the *Post* on the table and it lazily unfurled. It was a moment before Jordan saw the banner headline befitting an outbreak of world war spread across the width and length of the front page. The shock caused him to spill coffee on his necktie.

Allie walked in a moment later and Jordan held up for her the dispatch that proclaimed in oversized type the news that Cal had delivered to Sal Delano just the afternoon before.

The headline read: *Hands of Stone!*

Jordan carefully ripped off the front page and posted it on the refrigerator with a magnet shaped like a Nathan's hot dog.

He kissed Allie on the forehead, walked from the house and hopped into his car. He nearly hit a cameraman backing out of the driveway. Never relaxing his steel grip on the gear shift, Jordan sped like a fury down Sand Castle Drive towards the expressway and the dense jungle of New York City.

FOURTEEN

Wally returned home from New York very late and flush with excitement. He hastily fed Timmy another generous helping of Yoo-Hoos and Hostess Twinkies, then locked the boy in his room. Wally rewound the videotape he had recorded earlier in the evening. Making sure to keep the television volume low, he sat down with a beer to relive the thrill of appearing on a nationally syndicated talk show. What a peculiar yet exhilarating sensation, almost a voyeuristic adventure to watch oneself on the tube. His head whirled with excitement, an inebriation of sorts that, much to his delight, did not dissipate as he played the tape again and again. He studied his every gesture, surprised by his demeanor on television. They say that television puts fifteen pounds on you, but Wally felt he looked strikingly slim and fit on the tube. He spoke confidently, calmly. He presented himself well and appeared sympathetic. What fun! He should do this more often.

And Wanda, the way she slung her arrows at Stone, never dirtying herself, always positioning herself as the emissary of truth. She was on his side! Wally would have to call the show tomorrow and request a publicity still to pin up on his wall.

During the sixth run-through, Wally concentrated on

watching Wanda's body language for clues of her interest in him. He detected a definite magnetic pull, but naturally she wasn't free to fully display her emotions on national television. At one point she tapped her finger on the table in his direction. Should he read meaning into this? Why not, what other method of communicating had she on the set.

It was late now, well past 3:00 A.M. Giddy still, Wally battled sleep, but on the seventh showing, he fell fast asleep in the big chair in front of the television. And he would have stayed fast asleep had Timmy not knocked on his door. Wally woke with a start and fumbled the lock open.

"What is it?"

"I'm so cold," said Timmy.

"Cold? How can you be cold, we're in a heat wave?"

"I just am." Timmy's lips trembled.

Foggy with fatigue, Wally groped for consciousness and realized that it was morning now, the pink hue of the early morning sun flooded the room. Wally returned with a blanket.

He closed the door on Timmy but decided not to latch the padlock, since he'd be back shortly to give the boy breakfast. And since he was up, why not watch the program one more time, see how an hour or two of sleep changed his perceptions of the event. He rewound the tape to the beginning—he loved the psychologist's analysis of the situation. But before Dr. Ginsburg could make her final observations, Wally slipped into deep and restful sleep, and his incessant snoring drifted under the tight door jam and into Timmy's room.

Timmy hadn't heard the padlock snap shut on the door's exterior, that was for sure. And for the first time since being brought here he heard snoring. Timmy listened to the rhythm, just as he had learned to do when his father took naps on the den couch. The rhythm was even, slow, unconscious, like his dad's. Wally was asleep.

And the door was unlocked.

Timmy sat up on his bed and concluded that it must be a trap. Wally had been so careful these past few days. How was Timmy to believe that Wally had forgotten to lock the door and was sleeping soundly just beyond. No way. Timmy felt safe in the room. Things would be okay. If he just waited, his father would find him surely. Just be patient and all things good will come to pass. That's what his mother always said.

But as the snoring grew louder, deeper, Timmy couldn't contain his curiosity. Carefully he tiptoed to the door and put his ear against the peeling wood. He heard the muffled voices of the television.

He retreated a step. Don't be stupid, he told himself. He placed his hand softly on the doorknob. The brass was cold and slippery, well worn with use. Timmy tested the play in the knob like safe crackers he saw in the movies. He twisted the knob to the left until he felt it catch the bolt. He turned the knob ever so gently, feeling the bolt slide along its track and withdraw into the door.

With a sharp click the lock gave way, and the door cracked open a few inches, surprising the heck out of Timmy. He gripped the knob. He listened to the snoring. The rhythm hesitated ever so slightly then resumed its monotonous pattern of inhale and exhale. Through the crack Timmy took his first prolonged look at the living room. Above the rock fireplace hung a head of a deer, a sight that had always frightened and horrified Timmy.

He widened the crack one inch more and strained to catch a glimpse of Wally. All Timmy could see was the crown of his head above the back of the overstuffed chair facing the television. Beyond, Timmy spied the entrance to the kitchen and its faded gray linoleum flooring curled up at the doorway. A crucifix with an unconscious Jesus hung near the front door. Pink curtains fluttered in the morning breeze and through the window Timmy took his first glimpse of the outside. A sea of cornstalks.

Timmy thought about closing the door and forgetting the whole idea. But the sound of the door closing might wake Wally and anger him. Plus, freedom lay just beyond one snoring man, and Timmy felt compelled to get help. He had to.

He nudged the door enough for him to slip out of the room and into forbidden territory. He took one step toward the front door, but each time he let go of the doorknob, the door swung open wide and threatened to hit the wall with a thud. Timmy lifted up an edge of the faded purple rug and used it to prop the door. Praying not to make a sound, he tiptoed behind Wally's chair. He eyed the front door lock, figuring out what it would take to open it. A simple twist, that was all.

But his mission was interrupted halfway to the door. The chair with the sleeping Wally no longer blocked Timmy's view of the television. He was startled frozen by the mention of his name.

"And what about the strain on Timmy, psychologically?" the lady said on television.

"Good question," said another lady. "All hostages—even mature adults—suffer great anguish during and after such a traumatic ordeal. . . ."

Why were they talking about him?

". . . Timmy will be traumatized as well as stigmatized for the rest of his life. He may distrust his parents, society, he may have trouble with commitment, even turn to crime. No one knows."

Who are these people?

"And how about the Stones' other two children?"

". . . if the family can manage to stay together, they

certainly will need counseling for many years to come. Don't be surprised, however, to see each family member run in his or her own directions."

Cal! There was Cal on television running in the yard away from Daddy. That's Daddy, Cal. Don't run away from Daddy. What was happening to his family? Why was this on television?

When the camera cut to the guest table for the second segment tease, Timmy got his first look at Wally on television.

There he was! There was Wally on the television program, sitting there with other people. Didn't they know? Didn't they know that Wally was the kidnapper? Didn't they care?

Unable to take his eye off the television, Timmy stumbled into a small table near the front door. It bumped against the dark-paneled wall, sending an ashtray clunking to the floor. Timmy fell to his knees to pick it up.

Wally grumbled and turned. Timmy held his breath clutching the ashtray, anticipating the worst. But Wally's snoring resumed its pattern. The sweat stung Timmy's eyes. His hands felt slippery and weak. He fiddled furiously with the door lock. It looked so easy to open from afar, but now it resisted all attempts to budge.

The lock gave with a jolt. So surprised was Timmy, his knee knocked the table once more and the ashtray tumbled loudly onto the hardwood floor and wedged behind a book case. Timmy bent to pick it up but he couldn't knock it free, and he heard Wally stirring in the chair.

Using both hands, Timmy clutched the doorknob. It was too late now to worry about making noise. With one swift heave he pulled open the door and caught his first breath of freedom. He twirled to take one last look at Wally, still asleep in the chair. Beyond on the television, Wally was talking about Timmy's daddy, saying awful things.

Timmy lifted his pajama legs and ran down the dirt driveway to the road. He tried so hard to ignore the pebbles stabbing at his bare feet. He reached the road and turned for one final look at the house. Timmy searched for a neighboring house, but saw none, just rows of corn and an empty road snaking toward the sun. He jogged in the direction away from the sun for as long as he could, but breathing was so hard. He slowed to a walk and each time he felt his lungs returning to normal, he jogged again.

As he topped a slight rise in the road, Timmy spotted a house. A house! He wheezed as he ran, and in his haste, he stepped on a shard of glass. He shrieked in pain. Timmy sat down and pulled out the splinter but could do nothing to stop the bleeding. He didn't have anything to clean his bloody fingers, so he wiped them on his pajamas.

Finally he reached the little red house. He left bloodstains on the door when he knocked. I'm sorry, he whispered. No one answered. He knocked again as loudly as he could. No answer. He thought about breaking a window and using the telephone. But he didn't want to break the law. Anyway, he saw another house across the street, further down. Maybe they would help.

Timmy limped to the road. He tried to run, but the pain stopped him from pressing down hard. The house was just a few hundred feet away. And a truck was parked in front. Somebody must be home. Please, somebody be home.

Timmy felt even luckier when a car breached the horizon. Timmy waved his arms. Please slow down, he pleaded. Timmy realized his bloody hands and pajamas might scare someone off, so he tried hard to smile.

The car slowed down and pulled to the shoulder just beyond Timmy. Thank God. Timmy ran to it, ignoring the pain in his foot, giggling with freedom. Escape! The passenger door opened wide and Timmy hopped in, ready to thank the driver for his help. But his smile vanished when he turned to the driver.

"Nice try," said Wally with a grin. "Let's go home, shall we?" Wally made a three-point turn and crept along the highway, stopping only near his driveway to pick up the newspaper, delivered daily, before parking the sleek car in the garage.

"We'll have to get you new pajamas."

A pickup truck passed. The driver waved a slow hand as if comforted to see another vehicle on the lonely road in the corn.

Parking on the Upper East Side was hell. Normally, Jordan would take the train in, then a crosstown subway to Wanda's office, but today he couldn't afford to be noticed, and everyone would notice him now, surely. So he donned shades, pulled down the sun visor in his Porsche, and battled the early morning traffic like everyone else.

His attorney Marty Roth greeted him in the lobby of the network's glass monolith. A lanky man with an Adam's apple so large it bordered on the curious, Roth first came to Jordan's aid during the First Amendment Rally. It was Roth who plucked Jordan from jail, and Roth who made the prosecutor realize it wouldn't be worth the hassle of trying to peg a rap on Jordan.

"Well, what are our chances?" Jordan asked.

"You want my real opinion or my $200-an-hour-attorneys-are-next-to-God opinion?"

"The real thing."

"She better have a soft spot for you because you don't have a chance in hell."

They waited for what seemed like an eternity in a soft green couch across from the receptionist, a chrome replica of the *Crime Current* logo on the wall behind her. She must have answered a dozen calls a minute. The tabloid TV business was apparently healthy. The wait sucked the courage from Jordan's stomach.

A young assistant appeared and led Marty and Jordan to the conference room overlooking the brown East River, the 59th Street Bridge, and gray Queens beyond. The door swung open on a long oak table occupied by Wanda and the silver-haired Dick Slater, the network's vice president of business affairs. The two sat against the far wall with the sun at their backs shining directly into the eyes of Jordan and Marty as they took their seats closest to the door. Against the backdrop of the sun, Wanda and Slater looked like dark apparitions, all outline and no detail.

Jordan sank into his chair and tried to adjust to the brilliant light, but the sun was overpowering and Jordan had to squint to eye his adversaries.

"Thank you for convening on such short notice," Marty began. "Jordan and I have discussed the situation and, believe me, the last thing we want is to file suit against you for last night's show."

"I'd be happy to sit down with you to rectify any errors," Wanda said to Jordan as an aside.

"Not anytime soon," Jordan said. A nervous quiver in his voice caught him by surprise. Usually he toughened up for meetings like this. He hoped Wanda and Slater didn't notice the uncertainty; they adored the smell of blood.

"We do, however, request that you black out the story until resolution," Roth continued.

"Come on, Marty," said Slater, dispelling the notion with a wave of his hand. "You're a lawyer, you know blackouts are a thing of the past. They went out with Eliot Ness."

Jordan had met Slater before only once at a party celebrating the network's first weekly ratings win. Though he was an attorney by training, Slater had crawled up the network ladder through the news division, where he championed a sensational style that relied on graphic footage. "In your face journalism" his competitors called it derisively, until their ratings began to slip and they moved quickly to mimic the Slater style, relabeling it "hard-hitting news."

At the party the network had handed out masks with life-sized photos of Slater's face. All the air-time sales reps, drunk to begin with and gleeful over their hefty commissions, ran around the party holding the masks to their faces chanting "in your face" in unison. Shortly afterward, Slater was upped to VP of programming where he created *Crime Current* and the network's two other top-rated strips. *Team Avenger,* in which a group of reporter vigilantes set out each week to strip the last shred of dignity from whatever two-bit criminal or shady politician they could get their hands on. The third show, *Crisis,* was a tightly edited compilation of footage gathered from amateur video photographers who happened on the scene of car accidents, domestic disputes, robberies, and other meager dramas in which blood and tears were shed in volume. Six crises per half-hour.

The three shows kept the network on top of the ratings heap on Tuesday, Wednesday, and Thursday nights. Slater studied the ratings each day like the Bible and his genius was in reading minor shifts in demographics and altering programming accordingly: Losing 18-to-25-year-olds? Get me a beer party slug fest for *Crisis.* Midwest is going to bed early? Get me a *Team Avenger* segment on a liberal democrat with a liking for little boys. California's channel surfing? Show me illegal immigrants marauding the border on *Crime Current.* Wanda subscribed to Slater's philosophy, and Jordan had always suspected that Slater was one of Wanda's paramours.

Marty walked over to the window and pulled down

the miniblinds, neutralizing the sun as network accomplice. Good move, Marty. Now Jordan could see Wanda and Slater's faces, tanned and expressionless, like yin and yang poles of the same merciless demigod. Wanda wore a silk two-piece outfit, gold with blue trim, tied neatly at the waist with a blue scarf. Slater wore an olive Armani double-breasted suit with a red power tie.

"Please don't force us into an unenviable position," Marty said, returning to his seat. "We hate court as much as you do."

Slater laughed. "What is this, Law School Tactics 101? On what grounds will you attempt to take us to court? Invasion of privacy? Libel? Jaywalking? You don't have a chance in hell of winning, and you know that."

"To start with, I know that you aired footage shot on private property, which you had no authority to film or air."

"Oh boy, we'll see you in small claims court," said Slater sarcastically. "Let's be real, shall we? Jordan is a public figure. We can say anything we even remotely believe about him. Ask Jordan, he's pushed the envelope a few times."

It was true. Jordan clearly qualified as a public figure since he had "put himself in the public eye" by becoming a successful author. Jordan was well-schooled in the intricacies of invasion of privacy law.

"Perhaps. But you won't get away with your reprehensible suggestion that this tragedy is some kind of hoax perpetuated by my client to increase book sales. That's despicable and it's libel," Marty said.

"Libel?" said Slater quizzically. "Do you know the last time anyone actually *won* a libel suit? Are you ready to prove malicious intent? Is your client willing to endure a full inquiry into his research and marketing practices—not to mention his nonprofessional pursuits," said Slater, with a knowing nod toward Wanda.

"Then we ask that at least you stop leading the coverage," Marty said.

"Should we take that as a compliment?" asked Wanda.

"Jordan, you have our best wishes," Slater said. "The entire media world is pulling for you. Hey, I've got kids of my own. But we've got to cover the story just to keep pace, you know that. The competition is vicious. We're a victim of the system, just like you."

"The almighty dollar," Jordan said.

"Oh, please, Jordan," Wanda said. "Hypocrisy doesn't suit you. Come on the show, then, and tell the truth. Be my guest. I dare you."

"It's quite a web you spin, Wanda. But never in a million years."

"And cowardly. I had more faith in you, Jordan."

"You don't know what faith is."

"Gee, I didn't know they offered crash courses in holiness. But I see you've graduated with honors."

"I'd never stoop to your level, you can count on that."

"I've seen you on your knees a few times."

"You make me sick."

"Well," Slater interrupted, "I think perhaps we should end this little chat before it becomes . . . personal. Gentleman, anything else on your agenda or have we sufficiently addressed your concerns?"

Marty shook his head no.

"Good, I'll walk you to the elevator." Slater smiled.

Slater and Marty exited the room first, leaving Jordan and Wanda alone.

"Jordan," Wanda called softly in a voice that Jordan recognized from another time and place.

"What?"

"I'm sorry about Timmy. I truly am."

"Fuck you, Wanda."

Jordan joined the other men at the elevator. Slater

pushed the down button, and the elevator arrived in no time at all. Slater thanked the men with a grin for coming and the doors whisked shut.

Moments later, the second elevator doors parted carrying a sole occupant.

It was Allie Stone.

"I'm here to see Wanda Gentry," Allie said to the receptionist.

"Is she expecting you?"

"I don't think so."

"One moment please."

The receptionist got on the phone then turned to Allie.

"Wanda is just finishing up a meeting, she'll be with you in a minute. She asked that you wait in her office."

Wanda's office was a study in cream. Cream leather couch, cream carpet, cream curtains. Only the silver and black of her numerous broadcasting and journalism awards and the few soft hues of the framed floral lithos on the walls broke the color code. As an editor, Allie had once ruled offices like these. It had been years now since she glided along carpeted floors in airconditioned suites high above the sweltering heat. These environments seemed so artificial now. Even the air smelled false, as if manufactured by some giant concealed machine that silently exhaled into these soundproof walls.

Allie pressed her face against the window to catch the street scene below. How comical the human rush appeared from above. She didn't hear Wanda crossing the threshold.

"Well, well, what a surprise. It must be my day to visit with the Stones."

Allie spun around. "I need to talk with you, please."

"My pleasure, sit down."

Wanda guided Allie to the chair across from the glass desk.

"And to what do I owe this honor?"

"I need to talk with you. Woman to woman."

"Woman to woman? I didn't realize we belonged to the same club," said Wanda.

"Please, no animosity. I'm here to ask you a favor. I'm asking you to stop it, the coverage. It's hurting our family. Sarah—It's ripping us apart."

"I'm sure you understand that this is my job. Ask Jordan what it's like, he knows all about it. Or don't you talk to your husband?"

"You'd understand if you had a family."

"And because I'm single I don't. Is that it?"

"Look, make what you want of it, but I can't play these games. I have a son, a son I love dearly who is in danger of losing his life. Can you understand that? Can you imagine what it means to lose a child? I'm just trying to protect what's important to me."

"And this job is important to me. Maybe I'm trying to protect it, too."

"It's not the same. We're talking about a human life."

"Tell me this then, how many times in the past have you asked Jordan to stop writing because of the damage it would cause someone he was writing about?"

"I'm talking about the life of my child."

"Answer me."

"A little boy."

"Answer me."

"Never."

"But certainly you've considered the downside of our work, his work. This is the business of exploitation with a capital E. You know that. You're not naïve, Allie, smart girl that you are. It comes with the territory."

"I understand."

"You understand. Now you understand. Now you want me to stop because it's affecting you and your family. Do you realize how selfish you sound, Ms. Stone?"

"Why are you doing this?"

"You're safe in your pretty suburban home, sure to support all the right causes, attend church. And then you sit idly by while your husband shamelessly destroys the lives of others. And now you have the audacity to pass judgment on me."

"Okay, maybe I didn't appreciate the consequences of Jordan's work. Maybe I was fooling myself. Now I do understand. My eyes are open. But what does that say about you? About your work? Obviously you understand the consequences of your job quite well; you put it so eloquently. But it doesn't seem to slow you down. Jordan wrote just one book a year. You keep pressing on, three segments a week, fifty-two weeks a year. How many lives ruined is that, Wanda, or have you lost count? You don't have the right to discuss morals with me. And let me tell you one thing more. And listen carefully. Don't you ever dare compare your job—any job—to the life of a child—anyone's child. And if you don't understand that, then you're damn right about one thing, we're not in the same club, and never will be."

"Whatever club I'm in, your husband seems to like it all right."

"What's that supposed to mean?" said Allie.

"You can't be that much of an innocent, or are you one of those woman too afraid to rock the boat?"

"If you're talking about your little fling with Jordan years ago, don't flatter yourself, that has no effect on me anymore."

Wanda looked out of the window on the tiny little people rushing along the sidewalk below.

"I was talking about the more recent one."

"You're lying."

"Am I?"

"Jordan told me nothing was going on and I believe him. Nothing you can say will change that."

"Suit yourself."

"And I'm warning you, stay away from my family."

"I don't take kindly to threats, Ms. Stone."

"This is no threat *Ms.* Gentry. It's a promise."

FIFTEEN

Locker 255 was painted blue, an ugly Kmart, Florida Marlins blue. It was located in a bank of sixty-four identical lockers, second row from the bottom, two lockers in from the right, adjacent to men's and women's rest rooms near Gate 63 in the International Terminal of John F. Kennedy Airport, which was forever under renovation. Special Agent Ray Russo had spent the better part of the afternoon fixated on the locker, waiting for someone, anyone, to as much as attempt an approach to the cubicle that held a nondescript attaché case placed there the previous day by Special Agent Ellsworth. The hard shell case with tumbler locks contained the following: three packages of dry ice; one pair of human hands vacuum sealed in a clear Ziploc bag; and one miniature global positioning transmitter sewn expertly into the palm of the left hand. The stitches securing the transmitter in place were camouflaged deftly by the hand's life line. How ironic, Russo thought.

Hands, if that's what the kidnapper wanted, that's what he was going to get. It just so happened that these hands didn't belong to Jordan Stone, they belonged to the latest homeless stiff near Stone's age to hit the county morgue without testing positive for AIDS, no easy chore. So what if the unlucky bum got buried without his hands, Russo figured. Nobody gave a shit about him when he was alive, why should they care about him when he was dead.

Russo was dressed to the hilt as an international businessman impatiently awaiting a flight. He loved the apparel because woman looked at him a nanosecond longer than usual, until he smiled and they caught sight of his crooked teeth. The shifts ran a fairly short two hours and eighteen minutes; Waters didn't want the kidnapper to spot Bureau faces lurking around the terminal for too long. And just in case Mr. X, as Waters called him, was wise to shift changes, Waters established the odd shift times. Russo had fourteen minutes to go and was dying to hit the Pizza Hut for a minipizza. It wasn't Original Ray's, but, hey, there's never much choice at airports.

Waters had spelled out his priorities in the strategy and logistic sessions held the previous day. The first priority was not to spook the guy. Let him take the bait. Let him get to that locker. Let him complete his mission. Waters took the liberty of not informing Port Authority Security about the stakeout. The move was strictly against procedure, but he couldn't chance some minimum-wage security guard blowing the action. Similarly, Waters ordered no more than two agents in the public area surrounding the locker at anyone time; one shift agent, Russo at the moment, and Special Agent Malinda Clark who manned the flower cart across the corridor. She sold overpriced bouquets and gave out airport information to harried travelers. The wire on her lapel pin kept her in contact with the rest of the crew cloistered in a security office near Gate 61, some 40 yards away.

The kidnapper could not have picked a worse place to make a pickup. The terminal dead-ended at Gate 69, some 75 yards north of the locker. All incoming passengers were routed to the U.S. Customs facility one floor below. All outgoing passengers were required to pass through a security checkpoint equipped with mandatory metal detectors and video surveillance cameras, not to mention plain-clothed U.S. Customs officials. Valid airline tickets for international travel that day were required for everyone entering the terminal. No good-bye kisses here.

Agent Levin had suggested that perhaps the kidnapper planned on picking up the package and continuing on to Rio or Moscow or wherever. Waters took the precaution of scanning the passenger lists of every flight scheduled to leave within 72 hours of the deadline and 24 hours prior, checking for names matching the suspect list. He could easily delay a flight if he had even an inkling of suspicion.

Should Mr. X decide to travel the other way—out of the terminal and into the airport itself, Waters was prepared for that possibility as well. The security surveillance cameras were hardwired into the security room. Two agents were assigned to monitor foot traffic on the screens. Two more agents stood guard at the metal detector checkpoint posing as, what else, surveillance technicians. Agents were stationed every 50 yards in every conceivable direction, wearing every conceivable disguise from cart handler to illicit limo driver. Other agents were stationed at the airport exits, in the parking lots, and even in vessels in the waters off Jamaica Bay. The tracking device hidden in the hands was the icing on the cake. There was no way the kidnapper could lose a tail if the transmitter did its job of pinpointing the location within a 20-yard accuracy.

The number two priority was to let Mr. X get away. Let him make the pickup. Let him walk out of the terminal. Let him get in his car and leave the airport. Waters had good reason for this. The pickup person could be nothing more than a messenger thinking he was earning his pay for a drug or weapons pickup. Happens everyday. After all, why would Mr. X take the chance of showing up himself. Smart guy that he was, he'd probably send some lackey and keep him in the dark, so if he got caught there would be no trail back home. The attaché case was locked tightly so the pickup person couldn't rip it open on site. He would have to at least take it to his car before trashing it to get to its contents. By then agents would have a clear vehicle description and be ready for a covert pursuit.

If the messenger was Mr. X himself, then he would lead them to Timmy. Psycholinguist Fortunato reminded Waters that the kidnapper was committing the crime for revenge not money. He was a terrorist not a criminal, and therefore they shouldn't expect him to confess easily. Catch the abductor before he gets to Timmy and he might decide to play martyr, button his lips, and let Timmy rot in whatever cage held him at the moment.

Waters was determined to let the kidnapper make the pickup and lead them to Timmy. That was the plan, period. And he wasn't going to allow another embarrassing situation like the lamentable Chester Tenden affair. Waters paced the floor of the tight security room under the glare of fluorescent lighting. He vowed to get the kidnapper and Timmy before midnight tonight, if the kidnapper had the courage to attempt a pickup. This would be Waters' grand moment and then he could rid himself of Jordan Stone and this wretched case forever.

Russo checked his watch. Twelve minutes to go. His mouth watered at the thought of the grease-stained cardboard box holding the pizza, but a commotion in the corridor took his mind off his upcoming meal.

A camera crew rushed by, Channel 8 stickers plastered all over their cameras and hardshell equipment cases. Russo recognized Wade Deply. Had someone leaked the stakeout? Russo had been instructed not to communicate with Waters under any but the direst circumstances. This qualified by any measure.

"We got a camera crew hustling down the terminal," Russo whispered into microphone concealed in his cuff.

"A what?" Waters' words blasted through Russo's earpiece. Waters would have loved to come out and look but he knew his face was an instant giveaway. He had to remain isolated.

"Television news cameras. Channel 8," Russo reported quietly.

There were five of them, the well-dressed Deply and four crew members in jeans and T-shirts, lugging equipment like tired tourists. They stopped directly in front of the bank of lockers that held the hands, not sure which way to proceed, as if awaiting further instructions. Then, apparently after receiving the word from a cell phone, they hurried down the terminal. Russo watched them bob and weave until they stopped and unpacked their gear near Gate 69, the last one.

Russo heard another commotion behind him. He turned to see a second camera crew rushing by. This one from Channel 4. It was followed by a crew from Channel 5. And now came throngs of people, scores of them, streaming into the terminal with faces full of anticipation, as if they've been promised a glimpse of the Holy Grail.

Holy fuck.

Russo radioed in his report. He strolled over to Clark at the flower cart. She was busy helping a customer. Russo smiled and examined a floral arrangement waiting for the customer to leave.

"Pretty exciting, huh," said the customer, a squat woman clutching a romance novel.

"What's all the commotion?" Clark asked innocently.

"Haven't you heard?" said the woman.

"No."

"They just announced it on the radio, that shock-jock guy. Prince Andrew is arriving right now, Gate 69. They kept the gate secret to the last minute, but now it's out. I feel so lucky."

"Prince Andrew?" said Russo.

"You know, from England. Royalty."

"And you're buying flowers for him?" asked Russo.

"When will I get another chance?" the customer said.

"Smart thinking," said Russo with a forced grin. He hustled over to the far window to get away from the crowds rushing in by the dozens. Down on the tarmac, Russo spotted plainclothes Secret Service agents, swarms of them, and NYPD blues securing the area. The terminal, a lazy lounge moments ago, now buzzed with paparazzi, media, and lucky travelers swept up by the excitement.

"We got a VIP arrival. Prince Andrew, Gate 69," Russo whispered into his cuff phone.

"What do you mean Prince Andrew?" Waters retorted, questioning the prince's audacity to arrive just now.

"I'm sorry," said Russo, wondering why he was apologizing for events out of his control.

"Keep calm. Proceed as planned," Waters said.

Russo took one last peek toward Gate 69 and was stunned by the size of the crowd and how quickly it had grown. Hundreds of people, appearing out of nowhere, held back by dour-faced Secret Service agents.

Russo retrained his eye on locker 255. He felt confident no one had reached the locker during the commotion. Sure, he had taken his eye off the locker, but for a split second each time. No one could have inserted a key, twisted it and retrieved the briefcase so quickly. But with all the people rushing by it was becoming ex-

ceedingly difficult to maintain a clear view of the
locker. As they tripped down the corridor, people
fished into their bags for cameras or slips of paper for
the remote possibility of an autograph.

Russo looked at his watch. Nine minutes to shift
change. But there wouldn't be a shift change now.
Russo vowed not to leave until this whole prince thing
was over. The boy wonder should be arriving any minute. He wasn't going to hang around the airport. A few
publicity shots and his handlers would stuff him into a
limousine and whisk him off to Manhattan. After the
crowd was gone, his mistress would deplane and take a
separate limo in. Standard procedure. All Russo had to
do was keep his eye on locker 255 until the tempest
subsided.

Russo caught sight of the prince's Lear jet, sleek and
light, quickly taxing to Gate 69. The crowd hushed in
anticipation. Locker 255, Russo told himself. Keep it
on locker 255. A late-arriving camera crew drifted by.
The crowd grew quieter still. Russo picked up a magazine from the seat next to him in a meager attempt to
appear indifferent to the royal arrival. Locker 255.

Even though he couldn't see down the terminal,
Russo knew from the girlish shrieks of "Andrew" the
instant the gate flung open.

Then the vibration began. The rumble of the crowd
moving in unison up the terminal corridor toward
locker 255.

The advance security team hustled by first, one hand
holding walkie-talkies, the other hand on their exposed
sidearms. A plain-clothed Secret Service agent turned
toward Russo, searching his expression. Russo froze in
place, feeling queasy, as if he secretly planned on blowing away the prince and surely would be discovered.
But the agent turned away and continued down the
terminal.

The din of the crown grew louder. And then they

came. First more government men and a few onlookers rushing down the corridor with hopes of locating a better vantage point for a brief glimpse of royalty.

Russo wasn't prepared for the size of the swarm as it marched between him and locker 255, a mass of humanity huddled together as if drawing warmth from the heat of the prince. First the latecomers jumping up and down for a peek, trying not to trip and fall as they maneuvered backward, jostling for position, stretching their necks, dying to catch a glimpse of Andrew's head so they could tell their friends back in the neighborhoods they saw the prince. Then the dedicated fans, wearing Andrew T-shirts and holding hastily made Magic Marker cardboard signs with slogans such as "I love you Andrew" and "Welcome to NY." One read, "Andy, Kiss My Candy."

Locker 255. Russo was losing sight of locker 255. Cameramen jousted for position and gaffers struggled to hold up their lights like flags in battle. Locker 255. A squad of plainclothes agents locked arms to form an impenetrable ring around the prince. Locker 255, get the fuck out of the way. Russo leaped onto his chair, pretending to be searching for the prince, but trying desperately to relock on the locker. Move, goddamn it, move! Locker 255, low in the bank, near floor level.

Russo rushed the crowd. He tried to squeeze through, but they wouldn't let him, the crowd, the agents. Locker 255 was lost. He reached for his badge, and thought about flashing it, demanding an opening. But that wouldn't work, no one would care.

Locker 255. Ten seconds, fifteen seconds, twenty seconds lost, obliterated. Finally the crown scattered. Only a smattering of ambling amateurs remained. Russo found locker 255 and sighed in relief, Until he looked closely.

The locker key was inserted in the lock and swung gently. The door was slightly ajar. Russo felt queasy to

his bowels. He opened the door and peered inside.
Gone.

"He's got it, Goddamn it!" Russo shouted into his
microphone. "It's gone."

Russo scanned the crowd for anyone suspicious, but
it was useless.

"He's still in your vicinity," Waters returned the message. "He's near you. Find him, damn it! Find those
hands."

Russo searched the crowd again, this time ready to
corral anyone carrying a bag large enough to conceal a
briefcase.

Still determined to uphold his cover, he strolled over
to Clark.

"What do you think?" he asked.

"Check the bathrooms."

"Let's do it. One at a time."

Russo wandered away, doing his best to camouflage
his panic. Clark calmly locked her cash register, popped
a stick of gum in her mouth and walked to the bathroom.

As he waited, Russo noticed Wade Deply shooting
his segment near an adjacent gate. One member of his
crew watched Russo intently. Russo winced.

Clark came out and walked by Russo without a hint
of acknowledgment. Then she whispered in her lapel
microphone "Nothing."

"The signal hasn't moved," said Waters. "He's in
your vicinity still."

Russo dashed into the men's bathroom, and took a
quick survey around the sinks, urinals, and unoccupied
stalls. Two stalls were taken, and Russo wasn't sure how
to proceed. What if Mr. X was in one of them at this
very moment ripping open the briefcase. As Russo
tried to think, one the toilets flushed and a Secret Service agent walked out. Russo saw the flash of his badge
as he slipped on his coat. One stall left. Russo looked

under the door. The man wore very expensive Italian
loafers and a pinstripe suit. Could be. Russo waited
impatiently, then finally he tiptoed into the adjacent
stall, stood on the toilet, and peered over the edge.

A silver-haired senior citizen jacked off energetically
to a ripped-out magazine photo of Prince Andrew. A
walking cane rested against the stall wall.

Russo groaned.

The cameraman from Deply's crew walked in and
eyed Russo suspiciously.

"What the hell are you looking at," said Russo. Then
he noticed something odd at the recently installed in-
fant changing table. He saw the corner of a clear plastic
Ziplock bag sticking out of the fold-up tray. Russo
looked back at the cameraman, busy urinating. He
pulled down the tray and took a peek.

"Bingo," Russo reported into his microphone.

He folded up the tray, smashing the hands inside. He
whipped out his bag and charged the cameraman.

"FBI. Get out of here."

"I'm pissing."

"I said get out of here. Now!"

The cameraman hurriedly zipped himself up but
couldn't help wetting his pants. Russo followed him to
the door and slammed it shut on his tail, then he hustled to the masturbator's stall and kicked the door
open.

"Now get out of here, you fucking pervert."

"Don't tell my wife!"

"Get out."

The man clutched his cane and fumbled out of the
stall. Just as he left, Waters and Deleese raced in, followed by a half-dozen agents.

"What do you have?"

Russo pulled down the changing table and the rigid
pair of severed hands bounced to rest on the padded
tray that smelled like baby poop and talcum powder.

"Shit," said Waters. "And the briefcase?"

"No sign of it," said Russo.

"Well, maybe it's good," said Levin. "Maybe he thinks they're Jordan's hands and he'll release the kid."

"Afraid not," said Deleese. "L-look."

Deleese pointed to the index finger on the left hand. Black ink filled the crevices of the wrinkles.

"He got a f-fingerprint before he left. He can check it against the file. We've lost him."

"Fuck," yelled Waters.

"What now?" somebody asked.

"Secure the area, I want everything dusted. Let's go look at the security tapes."

"One more thing," said Russo. "Get ready for a television news crew out there."

"What do you mean?" asked Waters.

"There was a cameraman in here before. I had to flash him."

"Did he see the hands?" asked Waters.

"I don't think so, but he knows something is up."

"I'll handle it."

Deply waited in ambush outside the lavatory door. Waters wasn't sure what to say, but Deply gave him his cue.

"What's this all about? Anything to do with Prince Andrew?"

"Bomb report. False alarm."

"A bomb," said Deply. "For Prince Andrew?"

"As I said. There was no bomb, just a package someone believed was a bomb and they alertly contacted us. We responded."

"Sniffing bombs now are you? That isn't your job, is it? It's NYPD Bomb Squad or the Secret Service."

"They were busy."

"This has everything to do with Jordan Stone and nothing to do with Prince Andrew. Isn't that so?"

"No comment," said Waters, turning chilly.

"Did you make an exchange with the kidnapper? Did you give him Jordan's hands?"

"I said no comment."

Waters began walking hurriedly with Deply and crew in tow.

"Is Timmy alive, do you have him now in custody?"

"Get off my back."

"You screwed up, didn't you? You screwed up."

"I said no comment," said an angry Waters.

"You don't have to speak. It's in your voice, loud and clear."

Waters throttled Deply by the neck and pinned him against the wall. Then Waters saw the cameras rolling in his face and he gently let the reporter down.

"I'll let that one slide," said Deply. "But you owe me."

"Don't hold your breath."

Russo glanced at his watch as he left the bathroom. His shift ended in two minutes, but he knew he wouldn't have time for pizza. It didn't matter, he felt too sick now anyway.

SIXTEEN

Allie and Jordan had learned to stop jumping each time the house phone rang, understanding now that the kidnapper chose not to communicate by telephone. The line had rung incessantly from day one with calls from family and friends offering support, inquiries from reporters, and crank calls from demented members of the electronic audience.

The only other call of importance came from Jordan's agent, Evelyn Ashford, with offers of money from book and magazine publishers, movie and talk-show producers, and tabloid newspaper editors from as far away as Sydney. Ashford said she could put together a $3.5-million deal within an hour, all she needed was Jordan's okay. "They'll do it with you or without you," she told him. "Without me," was Jordan's response.

But this call didn't come in on the home line. It arrived on the private line reserved for Bureau and official use only. A line which rarely rung. Agent Deleese answered the call, while Waters recited the litany of the day's folly to the Stones and groped for an explanation as to why Timmy was not home safe at this hour and his kidnapper no closer to capture then before the Bureau found it necessary to sever the hands of a homeless person and vacuum-pack them in a briefcase.

Deleese stuck a finger in his ear and turned away from Waters' apology to concentrate on the caller's message.

Waters, meanwhile, paced the floor, as close to a loss for words as he had been in his life.

"How could you let it happen?" Jordan snapped.

"We had the proper surveillance. Communications broke down. It happens."

"Didn't you know of the prince's arrival?"

"We had made the decision not to confer with Port Authority officials. The more people that knew, the greater the opportunity for failure."

"Looks like you didn't need any help."

"Please," interjected Allie. "How will this affect Timmy?"

"If he loses Timmy, he loses the ability to exact revenge. This isn't about Timmy, it's about Jordan."

"So what do we do?" asked Allie.

"We continue digging, following up on leads. And wait. He'll have to contact us again. How, we don't know, but he'll certainly give us a message, a sign, and we'll proceed accordingly. Meanwhile, we will continue to narrow our profile, discount suspects. We will find him."

Deleese hung up the phone gently. He looked at Waters, Jordan, and Allie, then around the triangle again, searching for the proper etiquette for a moment such as this. He realized there was no proper way to break the news.

His gestures spoke volumes of regret and sorrow even before the words stammered across his lips. "They found a b-body at Overland Park."

"And?" Waters asked urgently.

"It's of a boy. Timmy's age. T-Timmy's hair. They think. . . ."

Deleese allowed the news to sink in. "The face is

pretty beat up. They want you to g-go down for an identification."

The only sound came from the big screen television droning incessantly in the Stones' den.

"Was there a threat to Prince Andrew's life today? That's what royal-family watchers want to know after police cordoned off an area of JFK Airport shortly after the prince's arrival. Police won't say what they found, but as Wade Deply tells us, there was a mysterious package involved. . . ."

Waters motioned to an agent to shut off the television. An awkward silence ruled the house.

"You had better come with me," Waters said to Jordan.

Waters wrapped his arm around Jordan and led him to the front door. At first Allie gravitated toward Deleese but then she broke away to watch Jordan step into the night, telepathically transmitting all her desires to him. She couldn't bring herself to believe in Timmy's death. She had already endured such a fear during his premature birth, and his survival had been such a miracle that his life now seemed guaranteed, assured directly by the hand of God. Yet there was something heavenly about Timmy's being. Earth was not the proper dwelling for a half angel, half boy. Perhaps God wanted Timmy by his side to delight him, just as Timmy had delighted Allie and Jordan.

Allie watched Jordan slip into the sedan and vanish down the black road. She retrieved her rosary beads from her bedroom and fingered them unconsciously as she waited for The Call.

The precipitation wasn't quite rain, rather a mist composed of tiny particles that jabbed Jordan's face like warm daggers. The pinks and purples of the setting sun cast an unearthly glow upon the shrubs and trees glossy with rain. The windows of Waters' car fogged up during the slick ride to the park, a ride Jordan had taken many times before to drop Cal at soccer practice, or to push Timmy on the swings, or to leave Sarah to hang with her friends. All three children had had birthday parties in Overland Park, which sat on a hill overlooking the Sound. On clear days you could see the towers of the Throgs Neck Bridge to the west and the gentle Connecticut coast to the north.

Jordan's gaze this time settled no further than the yellow police tape that cordoned off a ravine near the far end of the park under a grove of sycamore trees. The police cars at the scene were still, no flashing lights, no whirling sirens. A few of the officers fished in their trunks for yellow slickers to keep the sticky rain from moistening their uniforms further. A crowd of curious onlookers gathered on the periphery. Beyond them, news teams had set up shop with thick cables running like umbilical cords from the dish trucks to the powerful banks of lights. Word had gotten out that this discovery was somehow related to Timmy Stone. The media lights powered on just as Waters crept to a stop. He got out and conferred with the sergeant in charge. Then Waters opened the door for Jordan and walked along side him, shielding him from the press of humanity.

The crowd yielded silently to impending grief. Even the news reporters fell into the hush. Jordan spotted Wade Deply, and Arnie Sinkowitz, his friend from *Newsday*. Arnie bowed his head respectfully as Jordan journeyed by. A spectator held up the yellow tape for Jordan to walk under, and then the crowd reoccupied the path they had made for Jordan. The sergeant in blue led the way to the shallow ravine. The body lay at the bottom behind a stand of junipers under a soggy police-issue blanket.

"We're done collecting evidence. We just need an ID."

Jordan nodded. The lawmen accompanied Jordan to

the very edge of the ravine, then stopped. The dese-
crated ground was reserved for Jordan only. Jordan
tread carefully as he inched down. The packed dirt had
become slippery with the rain, which had now turned to
a drizzle. Halfway down the ravine Jordan slipped, but
regained his balance by grabbing onto a juniper shrub.
A few juniper needles pricked his hand and Jordan
tried in vain to brush them off.

As he stood over the body, ready to lift the blanket,
Jordan thought of the biblical story of Abraham sent by
God to sacrifice his son Isaac. Timmy lay before him
now, an offering not to God but to a devil. Jordan
peered at the crowd hovering above him on the edge of
the earth watching his descent into hell.

Pearls of rain clung to the blanket and sparkled in
the artificial light from above. Jordan knelt near the
contour of the face, wishing that he could change
places with the still child, wishing so many things.

When he found the courage to pull back the cover he
did so slowly, first revealing the tussled hair, matted
with debris and mud, then the small ear caked with
dried blood, the cheek swollen purple with contusions,
the split lip, chipped tooth, shuttered eyes. Jordan did
not need to see anymore.

He climbed the ravine slowly, grabbing roots along
the way for equilibrium. The lights shone brightly and
Jordan had difficulty finding the narrow path until Waters' large figure blocked the beam of lights and Jordan
was blinded no more.

Jordan reached the top of the ravine, his hands
caked with mud. An unknown officer threw a blanket
around his shoulders. A few camera flashes illuminated
the crowd, turning night to day then to night again.
Jordan covered his face with his dirty hands and the
tears and sweat mingled with the mud. He wished for
the rain to pour down and wash his face clean.

Jordan wiped his face with the blanket. He took in a

deep breath of the moist air. He drew in a few drops of rain on his tongue, manna from heaven. Then he looked Waters squarely in the eye.

"It's not him," Jordan said.

"What do you mean?"

"It's not Timmy. It's not my boy."

"Are you sure?"

"I'm positive."

Jordan leaned against the sycamore tree and faced away from the glaring lights of the police and the media.

"All right," the sergeant barked at his men. "Let's get the body up. What are you waiting for?"

The officers hurried to their chores. Two men unfurled a thick black plastic body bag. Men clutched each other to prevent themselves from slipping down the hill. The coroner backed up his truck, angling it precisely to prevent the stationary news cameras from shooting footage of the operation.

Jordan remained alone, leaning against the sturdy sycamore. Then he remembered that God did not allow Abraham to sacrifice Isaac. Praise be to God.

The sergeant moved closer to Jordan but continued to monitor the operation below. "Poor kid," he whispered to Jordan.

"Who do you think he is?" Jordan asked.

"Beats me. Maybe the subject of your next book," said the sergeant.

Something in the ravine caught the eye of the sergeant.

"Hey Tony," he shouted. "His arm—shove it back in the bag, will you?"

By reflex Jordan glanced at the body. A tiny arm hung limply out of the bag as if waving good-bye. The officer stuffed the arm back in and closed the zipper tightly.

Slowly Jordan walked back to the car. The crowd

respectfully let him by, but the news hounds couldn't let a second opportunity pass.

"Mr. Stone, is that your son down there?"

Jordan didn't respond.

"Was he sexually abused?"

Jordan kept marching.

"Stabbed? Bludgeoned? Anything to say to the murderer?"

Jordan spurned them all.

"Any indication of mutilation?"

Jordan reached the car.

"How about satanic ritual?"

He let himself in the backseat, then closed the door behind him. But the barricade didn't prevent him from hearing the questions thrown at him like stones.

"What are you going to do now?"

"Anything to say to the kidnapper?"

"Jordan, tell us. How does it feel?"

Back at the Stones' home, Deleese let the phone ring twice before he lifted the receiver. He listened intently, trying hard not to show emotion, but keeping a keen eye on Allie, ready to intercept her should her reaction turn self-destructive.

When Deleese heard the news, he smiled.

"It's not Timmy."

Allie raced to his embrace. She stayed there, feeling the steady rhythm of his breathing for what seemed like hours but surely was just a few minutes. And then she cried, not due to the pain of the ordeal, rather the grace of the outcome. Timmy was alive, and she knew it, and a deep sense of accord overcame her.

Jordan returned within minutes, led by an escort of flashing police cars and followed by a convoy of media vehicles. He stepped out of the rain, into the house, and into the arms of his waiting wife.

"Are you okay?" Allie asked.

"I don't know. How about you?"

"I'm good. Very good," said Allie.

Allie wanted to talk, to comfort him, to *be* with him. But Jordan acted strangely aloof. Clearly Jordan needed space and despite her own needs Allie graciously gave it to him now.

The trauma had indeed set Jordan apart, but he felt compelled to withdraw for another reason. He didn't feel worthy of accepting Allie's intimacy or offering her solace or celebration, whatever the moment called for. He felt dirty because of Wanda and the affair. And he couldn't stand the thought of contaminating Allie, at this moment so vulnerable.

Jordan climbed the stairs of his office and sat in the dark. The night breeze calmed his body. It was hours before the trembling stopped. Jordan dozed in and out of that slender state between sleep and consciousness, the images rich and powerful. Suddenly he awoke with a gasp, startled awake by a terrifying dream, which he recalled vividly.

The dream flashed across his mind in two brief and seemingly unrelated segments, each with a rhythm and palette all its own. Jordan understood immediately that the two segments, dissimilar as they were, were connected in some mysterious way only his subconscious could divine.

The first image was tinged with a feeling of guilt, a terrible gnawing guilt. A body was hidden in the wall of an old house, a mining shack or some such dwelling. Suddenly Jordan realized that *he* was the murderer—he was responsible for the death of whomever was stuffed between the unseen studs. Dread overcame him. Certainly someone would discover his secret. Surely he would be caught, accused, convicted, punished. He wanted so desperately to run, but his feet would not carry him. Excuses stammered across his lips. He feebly denied any wrongdoing, despite the absence of observers to weigh his pitiful alibis.

Then came the smell, the putrid and unmistakable stench of a human corpse. Perhaps Jordan could have deceived with his words, but that rank odor would implicate him as readily as if the corpse laid warm at his feet. Jordan's shoulders slumped. Any hope of deliverance vanished with the odor of death. Resistance was futile. Surrender remained the only choice, and Jordan embraced it woefully.

As dreams often do, it shifted suddenly in time and place, mood and tenor. Jordan entered a cavernous building, a medieval church of some sort, with a long row of colorful stained-glass windows set in pointy lancet arches near a ceiling that stretched hundreds of feet into the air. The walls were fashioned from brown hand-hewn stones. Jordan was alone but surprisingly without fear as he entered.

He heard a scream. Faintly at first, then louder and louder until it filled the hall. It was the shriek of a madwoman howling as only the insane can. As it grew in pitch, the scream echoed off the walls, harmonizing in some demonic way with itself. Still, Jordan wasn't frightened. He ventured farther, his shoes clicking on the cold terra-cotta floor. He strolled until he came to a cell built into the stone wall and secured with thick metal bars. The howling came from inside the cage, from the inhabitant within. Jordan watched himself from above, as an uninvolved observer, while the cage door rolled open. He crossed the threshold and the unseen woman yanked him inside and commenced to devour him, limb by limb. From his vantage, Jordan could not see himself being eaten, but he could hear the woman's slurping as she sucked the flesh from his bones.

The madwoman nibbled the last morsel of flesh from a finger bone and deposited the bone with a clink into an empty brandy snifter. She extended her arm out the cage door, snifter in hand, and waited nonchalantly for someone to take away the last tiny vestige of Jordan Stone: a bone of no more than two inches in length. Then the madwoman let out the sigh of someone thoroughly satisfied with a hearty meal.

End of dream.

Jordan told himself it was just a nightmare, that nightmares were often grisly—everyone has them. He tried to convince himself that the dream was, at most, a message sent by his subconscious to torment him. But its persistence, and worse, its uncommon clarity suggested to Jordan that the dream held a far deeper meaning than a mere admonition from his damaged psyche.

Jordan sat in the dark many hours more. Well past midnight he turned on the light and pulled several books from his shelves. According to *Gray's Anatomy,* the human hand contained twenty-seven bones arranged in three distinct groups. The fingers were composed of phalanges, named for their resemblance to the marching columns of the ancient Greek army. Each finger possessed three phalanges, except for the thumb, which contained only two.

Next came the metacarpals, the long bones under the palm, five in all. These were attached to the eight carpal bones that formed the wrist, a peculiar arrangement unlike anything else in the human body. The carpals fit together tightly but haphazardly, like cobblestones disturbed by an earthquake.

These bones, along with skin, ligaments, tendons, muscles, glands, and nerves combined to make one of nature's most complex creations. Isaac Newton declared the thumb alone proof of the existence of God.

A human hand weighed approximately two pounds, or four pounds per pair. After all, what was one hand without the other.

Jordan closed the book, returned it to the pile, and walked to the window. He looked beyond his computer onto the yard where Timmy and his other children had played often. ·

It was late, three in the morning. Jordan could scarcely see the wide lawn in front of him through the darkness. Instead he was confronted with his own reflection in the window. His face appeared drawn. He had lost some weight these past few days. His blue eyes lacked their usual spark.

In the distance, on the Long Island Sound, Jordan heard a yacht bellow its horn as it traveled the silent black waters en route to the Atlantic. He closed his eyes momentarily and imagined sailing away. But it was late, and such thoughts were useless.

Jordan returned to his chair and picked up another book, an obscure tome on mythology. It said that hands represented justice and authority to some cultures, beneficence and generosity to others. Still other cultures believed the hands were equated with one's deeds, or the feminine aspects of life. The hand of God, the hand of the devil—mystics contended that the hand revealed all, like a periodic table charting the elements of one's soul.

Jordan gazed down at his hands, these instruments of creation. They appeared no different than other hands he had shaken or kissed—his hands, too, were fashioned of flesh and bone and blood. They moved in the wondrous ways only human hands can. But as Jordan inspected the shadows of their creases, their callouses and scars, and the soil underneath his fingernails, he wondered why his hands, so ordinary in every aspect, felt so terribly and utterly alien to him now.

SEVENTEEN

The morning came with two pieces of news, the identity of the boy found murdered in the park and a possible suspect in the brutal slaying. The child was seven-year-old Chaim Finkle, the middle son of Pam and Ari Finkle. She was a bookkeeper and he a mechanical engineer with the Long Island Railroad. Chaim was last seen at about 5 P.M. the previous day while riding his bicycle through a wooded field on his way to a friend's house for a sleep-over. The ride was less than a minute's duration and Chaim rode it nearly every day. Though instructed to call once he arrived safely, Chaim never did. He often forgot, his mother had told police. She had assumed he was fine.

One hour later, a teenager frantically called police after stumbling on the body. Even though it lay at the bottom of a ravine, the body was easily spotted from the well-traveled jogging path above.

The medical examiner determined the cause of death to be strangulation. He also concluded based on blood content or lack thereof near the skin surface, that the blows to Chaim's face were inflicted after death. As Waters recounted the findings, Jordan flashed on the moment he drew back the blanket to find that the dead boy was not his son.

The suspect was Larry Sawyer, a.k.a. Bummer, a fifteen-year-old dropout. As far as police could tell, the murder was over chump change, which didn't amount to more than three bucks in Chaim's pocket. The alleged killer boasted of his conquest to the wrong friends, who immediately called police. Sawyer had a history of violent assaults, and in his confession to police he said he hadn't intended on killing the boy, "just hurting him real good."

Allie and Jordan had spent the morning on the porch silently pondering the tragic coincidence. Jordan didn't say anything about the decision he had come to last night. He was tempted to tell Allie but stopped upon encountering her countenance that morning. She was calm, eerily so. Jordan noticed how much she resembled Timmy. He wondered silently if last night's encounter with death had affected her as powerfully as it had him. Jordan didn't ask and Allie didn't say.

By midday Jordan was ready. With Agent Bales dutifully following, Jordan eased into the traffic. He cruised leisurely onto the L.I.E. and then the Brooklyn–Queens Expressway.

The exit for the Williamsburg Bridge veers to the left, off the fast lane. It comes as a surprise even when looking for it. Jordan speeded up and at the last possible moment he swerved his Porsche onto the exit ramp. Bales, following close behind, never had a chance of pulling the same stunt. The agent's jaw dropped as their paths diverged, Jordan zooming off to Manhattan and Chinatown, the agent continuing on to Brooklyn. Bales was gone, traffic was easy and Jordan parked in the same garage as the last time he visited here. Twenty bucks.

Ling's building hadn't changed, squalor and misery as enduring as brick. The ground-floor door had yet to be fixed and Jordan stepped over a snoring drunk in the entryway before climbing the dark stairwell that reeked of urine still. Ling didn't answer the door, neither did her severe mother. Rather the door jumped open a chain length on a tough-looking Chinese man with a three-day stubble and a scar that ran diagonally across his upper lip.

"What the hell you want?" he said without a hint of Chinese in his New York accent.

"I'm Jordan Stone."

"I know damn well who you are. I asked what the fuck you want."

"Who are you?" asked Jordan.

"Ling's brother."

Jordan wasn't sure whether to believe him, but then he peeked in the door and saw Ling's tight-lipped mother leering back as she sliced ginger at the counter.

"I'd like to see Ling. It's not about writing a book."

"Take a walk."

"Please, I need her help."

"What for?"

"May I speak to Ling, please."

"I said what for?"

Jordan was reluctant, but he had no choice. "I need to find a doctor."

"Don't they have doctors out in fancy Long Island?"

Jordan peered down at his hands as if they were diseased. "I need a special doctor, one who—"

"Well, you're too late."

"I'll only take a minute of her time, I promise."

"You don't get it, do you?"

"Get what?"

"Ling is dead."

"Dead?"

"She committed suicide."

"But how? Why?"

"She shamed our family."

"She didn't do anything wrong. It wasn't her fault."

"That's not what she thought. And her thinking you were going to write a book didn't help."

"But I—"

"Take a hike."

"I'm sorry."

"Yeah, right."

"I truly am."

Ling's brother slammed the door in Jordan's face. He knew that door well.

Ling, dead. Jordan wandered the streets of Chinatown. For hours he endured the jostling of the harried shoppers laden with plastic bags, chattering in unintelligible languages. Jordan felt as lost as he could ever remember feeling in his life, as if he was an alien put down on earth, unable to communicate or comprehend, and worse, meaningless. Ling was a beautiful girl full of sweetness and soul. He could blame her death on stringent Chinese culture, on the hardships faced by immigrants, on the affliction showered on the indigent, or on the enduring curse of being a woman. He could blame it on all these things, but he didn't. He blamed it on himself, and he checked a few times to see if his hands were stained with blood.

Jordan rambled down Bowery through a seedy section in which liquor stores thrived to the detriment of all other establishments. He stopped in front of a peeling metal sign in a grimy restaurant window that read: PALM READER. PAST, PRESENT, FUTURE. GENUINE. UPSTAIRS.

He had no place else to go, no plan in mind, so Jordan climbed the narrow stairway to the apartment above. The sign in two languages on the apartment door read simply: RING BELL. Jordan assumed the Chinese characters spelled out the same message.

The door was answered by an older Chinese man, his face and hands truly yellow, almost jaundiced, and spotted with splotches of purple from hundreds of tiny capillaries too close to the surface of his skin. His teeth had rotted through and were grotesquely misshapen except for one glaring gold exception in front.

But Jordan was startled most by the man's nose, or rather lack of it. His nose had been lopped off and a puzzling piece of flesh flapped over a shallow dish where a nostrils rightly should have been. The man wore a brown pinstripe double-breasted wool suit, something off the rack of a vintage clothing store, and warm enough to endure a winter. The red rose in his lapel looked like it had been snipped this morning.

"Yah, come in, come in," the fortune-teller said with exuberance. He waved Jordan inside nervously as if afraid that yet another customer might turn at the sight of his tortured nose and retreat down the dark stairs.

"Yah, yah, you've come to the right place. Twenty bucks, twenty bucks."

Jordan sifted through his wallet for a twenty and pulled out two, laying them on the cloth-covered table at the front door. He never indulged in this sort of activity and he wasn't sure why he was doing so now.

"Ah, very good, clear picture of your future, clear picture, come sit down."

The man led Jordan to a small table at the window overlooking the awnings below covered with grime and pigeon droppings. The place smelt like incense, cigarettes and Vicks VapoRub. Jordan felt sick.

"Now, let's see. Left hand please."

The man examined the hills and valleys of Jordan's hand, the curvature of his fingers, the flesh of the palm. He turned the hand over several times then back again. With each breath, the fleshy appendage on his nose fluttered.

"I've seen you on TV," said the man. "Too bad about your son."

"Will I get him back?"

"Mmm, yes. Or no. Depending."

"Depending on what?"

"Many things. You're removed from the center of power."

"What do you mean?"

"It's out of your hands, excuse the pun. You've squandered power. Nature does not take kindly to that. It likes its creatures to remain true to their nature, to pursue their intended purpose. The river must flow to the sea, the grass must praise the sky."

"And what is the purpose of man?"

"To plow fields straight."

"And my son?"

"Your son's predicament is the price you pay for crooked furrows."

"Are you reading my hand or reciting what you heard on television?"

"I'd be crazy to ignore either one."

The fortune-teller flashed a grin, but Jordan couldn't stop staring at the quivering appendage partially obscuring the two holes in the center of the man's face that served as nostrils.

The fortune-teller saw Jordan's fixation. "Mao," he explained without a hint of animosity. "Cultural revolution is a bitch."

"Will I see my son again?"

"He's a special child?"

"Yes."

"Blessed?"

"Yes."

"Talks with animals?"

"Yes."

"He'll be okay. But find him fast. The man who holds him, he has squandered power, too. He is desperate, foolish, like you."

"Will he hurt Timmy?"

"Only if he has no choice. Even a cornered chicken will fight."

"What else?"

"Tell your wife."

"About what?"

"About your affairs."

"How did you know?"

"It's here in your hand. Plain as day. You don't think I know?" The man smiled. "You are a man who likes his pleasures."

"How about my hands?"

"What about them?"

"Should I cut them off like he says?"

"I wouldn't."

"Why not?"

"How will you hug your son? How will you teach him to work the earth without hands?"

"But my son is worth a pair of hands."

"Let me ask you, does the kidnapper really want your hands?"

"He says that's what he wants."

"Listen to my question. Does he really want your hands? I think not."

"What does he want, then?"

"What we all want. Honor, respect."

"How can I give him that? I don't even know who he is."

"I never said you didn't have a big problem, Mr. Stone."

A cooing pigeon landed on the windowsill outside. The palm reader tugged a soiled handkerchief from his pocket. After he blew his nose he made doubly sure to wipe the flabby appendage clean.

"Use your power."

"What power?"

"Your powers of persuasion, negotiation, ingenuity. The powers you've squandered. Direct your efforts."

"But how?"

"Good question. Let's see."

The fortune-teller studied Jordan's palm a bit more.

"You cannot defeat an enemy you cannot see. You must make him attack. Force a confrontation."

"How?" asked Jordan.

"This, I cannot help you with. This answer is not in your hands. It's in your head, in your heart. Draw him out, use his misguided power to bring about his downfall. Use your powers. And you'll see."

"See what?"

"He will be defeated by his own foolishness. The weight of vengeance is heavy. It will crush him."

Suddenly an idea popped into Jordan's head.

"And do it fast," the fortune-teller added. "You don't have much time."

The man grinned. "Now, your twenty dollars is up."

"I gave you forty dollars."

"Then your forty dollars is up. Good luck, Mr. Stone."

The fortune-teller escorted Jordan to the door and gently closed it behind him with a smile.

Jordan knew his next stop. It was so obvious, he reproached himself for not thinking of it before.

Wally left the fingerprint card on the kitchen table as a personal reminder that Jordan Stone had reneged on a promise one more time. Jordan, Jordan. It would have been so easy had the hands been Jordan's. Then Wally could have at least considered releasing Timmy unharmed. What was wrong with Jordan anyway? Did he think he was smarter than Wally? Was he trying to humiliate him? If Jordan didn't value his son's life, then why should Wally? Perhaps Jordan was far more spineless than Wally had imagined. What a disappointment. What fun would it be to celebrate a victory over such a weak opponent?

Wally picked up the fingerprint card and compared it again to the print he had taken hastily in the airport bathroom. Even the untrained eye could tell that the print of who-knows-whose index finger didn't match Jordan's print. The moment he had inked the finger Wally knew, but he gave Jordan the benefit of the doubt. He returned to the van in the airport parking lot where he studied both prints side by side. Not even close. Wally had thought about going home and doing Timmy right there and then. But he calmed down. He wasn't going to allow Jordan and the Bureau to fluster him. Not now.

Wally drummed his fingers on the kitchen table and gazed out on the rows of corn. And another thing. How foolish those FBI nerds were to assume they were going to capture him. Who did they think they were dealing with here anyway, some drug runner or slobbering child pornographer? No wonder the federal government was in such a bad state. Bureaucrats, all of them.

For these reasons, Wally thought it tremendously ironic, not to mention divinely auspicious, that a little boy of Timmy's age should be found murdered near Jordan's house. Wally felt blessed again by the perfect timing of the event. God was with him.

Wally flicked on the evening news. It was Wade Deply reporting a story titled "Jordan's Close Call."

"The father of true crime stares true crime in the face." How poetic, Wade.

Wally found particularly gratifying the clip of Jordan walking back from the body. His pale face, blank expression, Wally was sure that as Jordan walked to the car, reporters firing questions at him, he was wishing more than ever he had cut off his hands. Wally chuckled over the coverage, so immediate, thorough, just like the news' promos always promised. Thank God for the media.

Still, Wally found himself in a quandary. He couldn't simply demand another drop-off, that would be absurd, self-abusive. Trick me once and you're a fool, trick me twice and I'm a fool. Plus how could he ever replicate a moment as consummate as Prince Andrew's arrival had been. He could kill Timmy, but that would put an end to the lesson, dreary as it was getting, and would be so uncreative. Wally fancied himself a classier operator than that. Still it might be the only option left, considering the circumstances.

Wally heard the boy knock on his bedroom door. Ever since Timmy's escape attempt, Wally had opened the door but once, to deliver the last box of Twinkies, a six-pack of Yoo-Hoos, and a roll of toilet paper.

Wally was angry at the boy for attempting to flee. Just like his father, Timmy had looked for the easy way out, had failed to uphold his promise. Hadn't Wally made a deal with Timmy that no harm would come to him if Timmy didn't try anything foolish? Well the deal was off, little boy.

The smell of urine wafted under the doorjamb as Wally turned his attention to the room. The potty must be overflowing by now, but the boy deserved it. He deserved a lot worse, but being a thoughtful man, Wally refrained from meting out due punishment this time.

"What is it?"

"I want to go home."

"Okay, you can." Wally smiled.

"Really?" Timmy's eyes lit up.

"Only kidding." Wally chuckled. "No, your father doesn't want you back. Neither does your mother."

Timmy burst into tears.

"Oh, come now. Don't be prissy. Can I help it if your father is a coward? Of course, you can't pick your parents. I couldn't pick mine and my children didn't pick me, though they wish they could have picked someone else at times, I'm sure."

"Will I ever go home?"

"Perhaps not, how should I know? It's up to your father, and he doesn't seem to care."

Timmy couldn't keep his lip from quivering.

"I miss my cat," Timmy blurted out. He didn't know why he said it, but he did miss his cat.

"Your cat, huh?" Wally said. "You'd like your cat here?

"Yes."

"What's your cat's name?"

"Capote."

"Where does Capote sleep?"

"In Sarah's room. She's my sister."

"I know who Sarah is, silly. Is she pretty?"

"Yes."

Suddenly Timmy got a bad feeling, like he was telling too much.

"Capote. What an appropriate name. It would be nice to have a cat around here, liven up the place a little bit. I'll see what I can do, okay? In the meantime, let's empty your potty, it must be full by now."

Wally made the boy carry the potty to the toilet and flush the contents down.

"Now get down and scrub the floor. I can't stand the smell."

Timmy did what he was told. Wally stood over him then marched Timmy back to his room.

"Now go to bed or something."

Wally pulled the door shut and clasped the lock tight. He looked at the wall clock, not realizing how late it had become. He rushed to turn on the television. It was nearly time for his newest favorite show, *Crime Current* with Wanda Gentry, the seductive anchor in love with him.

EIGHTEEN

Behind the scenes, every television show like *Crime Current* operates alike. Low-level producers spend too many hours in cramped cubicles enticing reluctant guests to appear with promises of justice, fame, revenge, and, if all else fails, money. The anchor owns the hallowed set with its rarefied air, miles of thick cable creeping along the floor, and the heavy cameras wheeled on trolleys like portable cannons. The director sits high above the set in the control booth pressing buttons and switches. Don't mind the wizard behind the glass curtain. Editors fry in cramped editing bunkers that reek of body odor and hum with the electricity of editing decks and rubber rollers working overtime in an eternal effort to splice drama out of tidbits of tedium.

It was in an editing suite that Jordan found Wanda at ten minutes to seven in the evening, huddling over an editor, reviewing tape for an upcoming show. As if she sensed a story behind her, Wanda turned to find Jordan waiting at the door, a miffed assistant at his rear.

"I asked him to wait in the lobby, but he wouldn't," said the assistant. "Should I call security?"

"No, that won't be necessary. Thank you," said

Wanda with a smile. She looked Jordan up and down. "I knew you'd come."

"I want to go on," said Jordan.

"How delightful, we'll take you onto the set and shoot a one-on-one for tomorrow night's show. We can postpone a segment, or two—if you have something interesting to say."

"I want to go on tonight, live. And I do have something to say."

Wanda let out a spontaneous chuckle. "It's been a long time since you've surprised me like that Jordan. I'm glad to see you still have it in you."

"I'm serious."

"I would love to shoot you tonight, but you know that's impossible. Our affiliates already have tonight's feed. We go on in the East in nine minutes. This isn't the *Ed Sullivan Show.*"

"Then good-bye," Jordan said, turning to leave.

"No, wait," Wanda ran after him. "Let me think."

Wanda's eyes darted back and forth searching for a quick solution.

"I don't know if we can do it, but if we do, you'll have to promise me it's an exclusive."

"I can't promise you anything. And I want no cutaways, no voice-overs, no seven-second delays, or whatever you call them."

"Jordan, come on," Wanda pleaded. "We need at least the seven-second—that's FCC regulation."

"Sorry."

Wanda bit her lip. "I could get into big trouble over this."

"Take your chances."

"You've got to let me ask you some questions."

"Two."

"Ten."

"Three."

"Eight."

"Good-bye."

"Okay, three," said Wanda. "This is exciting."

Wanda punched two digits on the phone pad and cupped the receiver to her lips.

"Mort, alert the affils, we may have to go live."

She looked up at Jordan to make sure her good fortune wasn't skipping out the door. "I *do* have a good explanation, Mort. I have Jordan Stone sitting right in front of me, so close I can smell him."

She dialed two more digits. "Who do we have in makeup? Good, don't let her go. We're on our way." She hung up. "Let's go, Jordy. Your wish is my command."

Wanda led Jordan down a series of corridors to the makeup room adjacent to the set.

"Gloria, do Jordan first. He may cry, so nothing drippy. I'll start on myself."

Gloria examined Jordan's face for weak spots, shadows, blemishes. Jordan glanced in the mirror and saw all the imperfections.

"You should have shaved. You look like Nixon," Gloria said.

Wanda pulled a tube of red lipstick out and applied it carefully. "So, what is it that you want to announce to the world tonight?"

"You'll have to wait to find out."

"Does anybody know? Does Allie know?"

"Nobody knows."

"You're getting me hot."

Jordan felt the thump of his heart as the moments ticked away. He hated the shallow eye of the cameras, hated the forceful heat of the high-powered lights, hated the blank stares of the camera operators, directors, and assistants as they gathered around to catch "the show," like horny old men at a peep booth. He hated the thought of millions of viewers encroaching on his personal life, his personal tragedy. But most of all,

Jordan hated the demand to perform. Because with every demand came the fear of failure.

"Four minutes." An assistant stuck his head in.

Beads of sweat gathered on Jordan's forehead. They felt heavy and unstable, as if with one shake a stream of water would drown his eyes. His hands were moist and his mouth parched. He noticed his hands trembling. He tried to calm them but he couldn't. Breathe deep, he told himself.

Jordan glanced at Wanda dabbing cream on the crow's-feet around her eyes. She moved so assuredly. He wondered if she ever had had a vulnerable moment in her life. But then he remembered her past, or the tidbits she had shared with him, and he realized she had had many vulnerable moments. The set, the show, the performance, all were Wanda's ways of fighting back, of staying in control, of never experiencing vulnerability again.

"Three minutes."

Gloria ran a comb through Jordan's hair. "Have you ever heard of the Men's Club for Hair?"

Jordan wondered what had attracted him to Wanda all these years. It wasn't love, certainly. Perhaps lust at the beginning, but not for the last few years. Intimacy certainly had nothing to do with it. His encounters with Wanda were at times as antiseptic as a visit to the dentist's office. So what was it? Why had Jordan jeopardized his marriage all these years to sleep with her? All he could think of was how similar he and Wanda were. Sure, she liked the limelight and he didn't, but that wasn't the attribute that defined them both. It was their need to control, their fear of winding up on the short end of the stick. As he watched Wanda gracefully pull a brush through her red hair, Jordan came to the sobering conclusion that he was in essence fucking himself when he fucked Wanda. Their love was mutual masturbation, the ultimate act of control.

Mort popped his head in.

"We got sixty-two out of our sixty-nine affiliates with us," said the executive producer. He looked as frantic as Jordan felt. "This better be good, Wanda. Damn good. What do we got?"

Wanda reached in a drawer, pulled out a pack of smokes and lit a cigarette. She blew a smoke ring and paused to admire it, all the more so, it seemed, because of its transitory nature.

"We're simply having a conversation with Jordan Stone."

"Very nice, shall I fix you some tea?" Mort said derisively. "What's he going to *do,* for God's sake?"

Mort spoke as if Jordan were an animal act whose mysterious billing had gone too far.

Wanda inhaled deeply, drawing in strength. "We'll see."

Mort was not amused in the least. "What about camera angles, breakaways? I've got Pete piecing together a backgrounder. You've got to give me a clue as how to take this thing."

"No," shouted Wanda. "Not one inch of tape. This is me and Jordan."

"You're giving me shit to work with."

"You won't be disappointed." Wanda smiled.

Mort vanished, replaced quickly by another assistant. "Two minutes, show time."

"Shall we?" said Wanda. Jordan followed her along the short walk to the set, where he was blinded by a bombardment of the heavy lights. An assistant stuck a monitor in his ear and pinned a lapel mike on his chest, feeding the wire through his shirt.

"You want the last-minute instructions?" Wanda didn't wait for a reply. "Talk to me, not the camera. Pull your jacket down occasionally, and wipe your forehead when the camera is on me. Don't speak loudly, and don't tap your fingers on the desk, the mike is very sensitive."

"We got ten seconds."

"And don't lie or get angry," added Wanda. "It never works and it doesn't look good."

"Six, five, four."

Wanda leaned over to Stone. "Don't worry, I'll use kid gloves on you."

"Three, two, one."

Jordan heard the theme music roll and watched in the monitor as the flying title announced the show. Wanda's manner didn't change one bit when the on-air sign flashed on.

"Five days ago, seven-year-old Timmy Stone was abducted from the front yard of his home in Rocky Cliff, Long Island. Timmy, of course, is the son of renowned author and the king of true crime, Jordan Stone. To lose a child is a parent's worst nightmare. And for five days the country has witnessed the Stone family's horror and grief as they desperately search to get him back. The kidnapping has baffled the FBI and has transfixed a nation on the most infamous kidnapping case since Patty Hearst. I'm Wanda Gentry coming to you live in this *Crime Current* exclusive. Ten minutes ago Jordan Stone walked into our studios and asked to go live on national television. He is here with me now. Thank you for coming, Mr. Stone."

"Thank you."

"Mr. Stone. Before you address the nation. Tell us, how is the investigation going?"

"We have some leads of course, the Bureau is working night and day, but that's not why I've come here."

"And how is the family doing? I know that Timmy has a brother and sister."

"Well as you can imagine this is a very stressful situation. I think the country has already seen how stress can affect siblings. But we are hanging in there. Doing the best we can as a family. We *will* survive."

"And Mrs. Stone, how is she doing?"

"Mrs. Stone is fine, thank you."

Wanda paused, changed tone.

"Forgive me for asking, but there have been reports and allegations, Jordan, that somehow you were involved in the kidnapping. That it is all some sort of pretense to increase sagging book sales."

"That is absolutely and categorically false. And you know that, Wanda."

Jordan realized immediately his personal attack was a slip. He had intimated a closer than professional relationship with Wanda and challenged her integrity.

"If you'd like, we can find the audio tape of the unnamed FBI source who gave us that information."

"That won't be necessary."

"And isn't it true that you were arrested years ago for disorderly conduct?"

"During a First Amendment rally, and I was never convicted."

"But you were guilty of destroying government property, were you not?"

"That's open to interpretation."

"Isn't it also true that you plagiarized while at your old job at *Newsday?*".

"What does this have to do with Timmy?"

"It has everything to do with your credibility."

"My credibility isn't at issue here."

"It is the issue for the FBI, and apparently for whoever took Timmy."

"How can you say that?"

"Why else would someone take Timmy? We already know it's a vengeance kidnapping."

"Maybe because I told the truth. Have you ever thought of that?" Jordan felt a bead of sweat break free and run down his temple.

"Tell us the truth now, Mr. Stone. Have you always told the truth in your books?"

"I've never falsified or maliciously slandered anyone."

"That's not the question."

"I've had to dramatize, of course, take some liberties, but that's the nature of the beast. Everybody does it. You do it."

"Obviously, Mr. Stone, not as well as you."

Wanda turned to face the camera and gathered blank paper in front of her for effect. "We'll be back in a moment."

The on-air light flashed off, and the set exploded with movement. Jordan remembered the sweat on his brow and wiped it clean. The cloth came back moist and colored with foundation cream.

"Why are you doing this to me, Wanda?"

"It's my job."

"To trash people on air?"

"Do you want to guess our ratings tomorrow? They'll be through the roof. I bet we'll pick up a 40 share by the end of the show."

"You don't care a thing about me."

"What gave you the impression I did?"

An assistant whisked by. "In thirty."

"Have you got your little speech prepared?" Wanda asked.

"I do."

"Then don't say I never did you a favor."

"You're wicked."

"Last time you said that you were fucking my brains out. At least you thought you were."

"In ten!" shouted the assistant.

"Better wipe the sweat, honey pie."

Jordan dabbed his forehead. He felt woozy, unsure, but he thought of Timmy. He was doing this for Timmy.

"Four, three, two, one."

"We're back with Jordan Stone, author and father. Mr. Stone, I believe you have something you want to say to America here on *Crime Current.*"

"I do."

Jordan took a deep breath.

"I know there are millions watching out there, but I'm talking to only one person now. Whoever has my son. First, please don't harm him. Whatever you do, please don't hurt Timmy. He has done nothing wrong, he deserves no punishment. He has already suffered enough. Please, for the sake of all children, do not harm him."

Jordan felt emboldened now, oblivious to Wanda, to the camera, to his fear. His only thought was of Timmy. This is why he came. For Timmy.

"I know you've been very clear with your demands. And I know I have not been forthcoming. But that is only because I took the advice of the FBI. I can assure you, with God as my witness, that won't happen again. The Bureau is out of it. Do you hear me? The police are out of it. Everyone is out of it. Everyone but you and me. I promise. Contact me. Send me a sign. Talk to me. Whatever you say. Whatever you want. I'll do it. I'll give it to you. You have my word. Just tell me what it is you want."

Jordan sensed a commotion on the set.

Wanda pressed her fingers against her ear monitor to better hear instructions coming in. She appeared flustered, surprised. Jordan glanced to the left of the set and saw Mort in a furious argument with Dick Slater, the network's VP.

Jordan stopped talking and Wanda missed a beat. One second, two, three seconds of dead silence passed. What was going on? This was not like Wanda.

"We have a caller," said Wanda. "Please stand by."

Wanda brightened her eyes and shrugged her shoulder to suggest to Jordan that this was not her idea, this was not planned.

Jordan glanced over to the side. Slater had vanished from the set as quickly as he came. Jordan saw Mort give Wanda a nod. Wanda touched her earpiece, an indication to Jordan that he should listen closely. Something important was happening.

"Okay, we have him on the phone." Wanda's eyes brightened. "I believe we have . . . Timmy Stone on the line."

Jordan froze.

"Daddy? Hi, daddy. Is that you?"

God almighty. It was Timmy.

"Timmy! Where are you?"

"I don't know. I don't know where I am."

The voice was muffled as if Timmy was speaking through a cloth. But it was Timmy for sure, Jordan had no doubt about it. It was Timmy, and he was on the phone.

The cameras crept closer.

"Timmy, thank God," said Jordan. "Timmy, are you all right?"

"I miss you. I miss Mommy."

"We miss you so much, too. We love you so much."

"Daddy?"

"Yes, Timmy?"

"Would you please come and get me?"

"I want nothing more."

"I want to come home."

"I'm trying so hard, Timmy."

"And Daddy?"

"Yes, Timmy."

"I'm scared."

"I know Timmy. So am I."

"Daddy?"

"Yes, Timmy?"

"Would you do what the man says?"

"Yes, Timmy, anything. I'll do anything to get you back."

"Promise?"

"Yes, Timmy."

"And Daddy?"

"Yes, Timmy?"

"I love you."

"I love you, too," Jordan gulped.

"Is the man there now? Can I talk to him?"

"I don't know."

Jordan heard a muffle, a conversation he couldn't understand.

"Daddy?"

"Yes, Timmy?"

"I have to go now."

"No, Timmy."

"I love you, Daddy."

"Don't go, Timmy!"

"I love you very much."

"I love you, too, Timmy."

"Don't forget to get me, okay?"

"I won't forget, Timmy. Don't go, Timmy. Please, I beg of you. I beg of him."

"I miss you, Daddy."

"I miss you, too, Timmy."

"Good-bye."

"No! Timmy. Timmy?"

But Jordan's plea was of no use.

"Speak to me! Timmy!!!"

The line fell dead and Timmy's voice was replaced by a dial tone and then nothing at all.

A tear traced down Jordan's face. But Jordan did not wipe it away. Instead he looked directly into the camera.

"Whoever you are, you win. You win. Just give me Timmy back. You win."

Jordan covered his face with his hands. He no longer

noticed Wanda, the lights, the staff gawking at him like a freak. He cared nothing of the millions of people sitting in front of their TV dinners, in bars, prisons, and hospitals watching him cry. He didn't notice the studio cameras zooming in again on his pain or the long, conspicuous silence, intended to drive home the emotion of the moment. Jordan didn't notice any of these things, only the sweet voice of his child lingering like a lullaby in his ear.

Wanda captured a breath then spoke softly. "This *Crime Current* exclusive will return after these messages."

The house lights went up, and Gloria came over to refresh Jordan's face. But Jordan stood abruptly, unclipped his microphone, and walked from the stage.

"Don't go," said Wanda. "We're not done."

"Oh, yes we are."

Mort jumped on the set. "Jordan, my man. Let's think this through. Maybe he'll call back. America has a right to know how you feel, what you're thinking."

"Get out of my way or I'll kill you."

"Let him go," said Wanda. "He's spent."

Mort stepped aside, and he and Wanda watched Jordan depart.

"What a show," said Wanda.

"Unfucking real."

"I bet we'll hit a fifty share," Wanda said.

"The phone lines are flooded. Koppel's begging for tape. We'll lead every newscast in the nation. This is unfucking real. The jackpot, baby."

"How did you know it was Timmy?" asked Wanda.

"What do you mean?"

"It could have been a prank kid or something."

"Funny you should ask. I don't know. The kid just sounded real. Gut feeling, I guess. We were lucky."

"Lucky? Scoop of the year," said Wanda with a high-five.

"Wait a minute. There was one thing odd about the call," Mort said quizzically.

"What's that?"

"I just remembered. It came in on your private line."

PART III

NINETEEN

The breeze at dusk soothed Jordan as he left the studio. With rush hour over, the city felt less clamorous, and the sky's pink hue made the sharp angles of the narrow buildings soft and forgiving. Jordan walked by a few subway stations to work off the numbness. When he finally did catch a downtown train, Jordan noticed many of the riders gawking at him, the impression of tonight's television entertainment, those who had watched it, fresh in their minds.

Jordan felt like telling everyone to leave him alone, gape at somebody else, read your *National Enquirer.*

As Jordan returned the gaze of the subway riders, he fully expected to see the eyes of condemnation from the riders, but instead Jordan detected something strange in their faces, something Jordan had never experienced before. Sympathy.

The train lurched to a stop. The faces followed Jordan as he rose to depart. Jordan could hear their necks creaking as the spectators tracked his path. The riders, the strange and normal, the wealthy and impoverished, all reached out silently, sadly with their gazes. What a strange, peculiar sensation, sympathy. How oddly comforting.

"We're with you, Mr. Stone," said a lady with a wink and a smile.

"Thanks," said Jordan.

Suddenly the passengers erupted in applause and many stood and cheered. Jordan was stunned and nearly missed his stop. He stepped out of the car, the doors nipping at his heels. As the train gained speed, Jordan stood motionless watching the impromptu audience ramble down the track, their applause drowned out by the chatter of the steel wheels echoing loudly in the narrow tunnel below the craziest of all cities. Jordan hurried to the parking garage, his car, and across the bridge home.

It was dark when he arrived. The media circus had grown exponentially since before the show. Where once there were four microwave trucks now there were ten. Mrs. O'Keefe across the street had apparently negotiated with the media en masse, since a new scaffold had been set up on her lawn at the point closest to Jordan's home. Reporters in their baseball caps lounging on lawn chairs sprung to attention when Jordan's black Porsche veered around the sharp curve for the final lap. Jordan slowed considerably, fearful of hitting one or more of the throng of cameramen and reporters pressed against his car, angling for a shot, pleading for a statement. No sympathy in these faces. Uniformed police officers cleared a path and Jordan pulled into the driveway.

As Jordan stepped from his car, the barrage of questions reverberated so calamitously that Jordan didn't see the front door of the house burst open and Allie run toward him. The embrace was carried live across the world.

"I love you, Jordan."

"I have something to tell you," Jordan whispered.

"About Timmy?"

"Let's go inside."

The soundmen strained to aim their long-distance mikes at the conversation, but the Stones spoke in whispers too soft for them to hear. Allie closed the blinds and shut the porch light. It did nothing to stop the television reporters from skirmishing as they battled to use the house as a backdrop for their latest dispatches.

Inside Agent Waters waited, fuming, his thick neck ready to burst from his starched collar as he paced the floor. His frustration stemmed not only from Jordan's gamble, but because the investigation was no better for it. Their immediate inquiries to the studio had yielded little, only a tape of Timmy's conversation. Waters' men were unable to trace the call. They were this close to the kidnapper with nothing to show.

"I should have you locked up," said Waters.

"You had your chance. Now I want my son back," Jordan said.

"And what do you think you can do that we can't?"

"Give him what he wants," Jordan said.

"You promised to keep out of it."

"And you promised to get Timmy back."

"Be careful, Stone. You have a short leash."

Jordan didn't care to respond. He and Allie walked up the stairs to the bedroom, hands clasped.

Agent Russo watched the couple vanish up the stairs. He moved closer to Waters and whispered. "Why don't you just lock him up?"

Waters nodded no. "I need him. That man's going to lead me to my kidnapper."

Upstairs, Allie put her arms around Jordan's neck and kissed him.

"I don't know what's going to happen, and I don't even know if I agree with what you did tonight, but I want you to know how proud I am of you. You did a very brave thing."

"Anything for Timmy."

"I love you, Jordan, very much."

Jordan could wait no longer. His heart pounded with the truth ready to burst.

"I have something to tell you," he said.

He sat down on the edge of the bed and fiddled with the ring his father had given him long ago.

"What is it?" asked Allie.

"I haven't been truthful with you, and I need to come clean."

"What?"

"It's about Wanda. And me. I lied."

"What are you saying, Jordan?"

"We were seeing each other again, sexually. The last time was the day of Timmy's birthday party."

It was out, ugly as a monster. Allie withdrew her arms and stepped back.

"How many times?" she asked.

"Many. Dozens, I don't know. It didn't mean a thing. I know that's a cliché but it's true. It only served to make me feel dirty and guilty, that's all."

"That's all?" Allie said.

"I'm sorry."

Allie bit her lip.

"How can you do this to me? How can you do it to me now?"

Jordan had no answer. "I know this is all wrong, the timing is all wrong, but I can't hide things anymore, Allie. Not from the people I love. And I love you."

Only Allie's anger suppressed her tears. She paced the room and returned to face Jordan.

"Tell me what I should do now," she said bitterly. "Because I don't know. Do I kick you out? Tell you to leave? Do I tell Sarah and Cal that their father has been fucking that woman on television, you know, the one who says all those nasty things about our family? Do I hold a press conference? Get a lawyer? Or do you expect me to take you in my arms and say, oh baby, you've been through so much, come here and let's forget about it all. Tell me what to do Jordan, because I don't have a clue."

Allie sat on the edge of the bed and fought back the tears.

"I wish I could help. All I can say is I'm sorry, so truly sorry."

"Oh, Jordan. You couldn't be sorrier than I. Now get out."

"Please, I—"

"Get out!"

Jordan retreated to his office above the garage. The late television news passed without his watching. Jordan stared at the ceiling wondering about so many things, about Allie and Wanda, and how he got into this whole mess. But he wondered most how the kidnapper would respond to his plea. For the first time since Timmy's abduction Jordan felt a glimmer of hope, that the worst was behind him, that somehow he would recover Timmy and all would be well. Whatever it took, Jordan was willing.

Through the window, Jordan heard ten thousand cicadas sing a serenade in the fragrant night air. The sound was deafening, fading in and out of consciousness like a mantra. Jordan fell asleep with the images of the train load of passengers applauding him as he stood motionless on the platform and of Allie's wounded expression after his untimely confession.

Allie didn't know where to go at first, what to do. She found herself wandering the house until she found herself in the kitchen fixing a cup of tea. Deleese swung open the door and smiled.

Allie tried to smile, but her pain was obvious.

"Don't give up hope," said Deleese softly.

"Hope?" Allie said sarcastically. "Sometimes life takes so many unexpected turns."

Allie poured him a cup of tea and they gathered at the kitchen table.

"May I ask you a question?" said Allie. "I know you haven't been married, but I'm sure that sometime in your life someone must have violated a trust with you, unequivocally. Has that ever happened?"

Deleese nodded yes.

"What did you do?" Allie continued. "I mean, how do you start to love, or trust, or care for that person again?"

"When I was a child. My mother drank. And she brought men home often, in the middle of the night, dr-drunk and rowdy. One year, I was seven, one of the men decided to stay. But he didn't like me very much. And he told my mother to get rid of me."

"What happened?"

"She put me on a train the next day. I lived at my aunt's house in Lincoln until I left high school. She was good, my aunt, but there's no getting over the pain when your mother sends you away."

"Is that when you got your—"

"Stutter? Yes it is."

"Did you see her again, your mother, I mean?"

"When I was twenty-two. She was dying of emphysema. She could hardly breathe. She was hooked up to a tank all day. I quit college to take care of her. She died eighteen months later."

"Why did you do it?"

"Why? Because she needed me."

"But you didn't owe her anything. She betrayed you."

"She still was my mother, and nothing in the world could change that. Nothing."

Allie finished her tea and looked into Deleese's true blue eyes, so sad, so kind, without a trace of bitterness.

"You're a better person than I," she said.

He smiled. "We'll let the Lord be the judge of that."

Deleese looked at his cup. It was empty. "I better go home. Get some sleep. I got the morning shift."

"Good night, Mr. Deleese. And thank you."

"For what?"

"Just thank you."

Allie returned to her bedroom and fell asleep thinking about Deleese, his words, and why she could never be as forgiving as he. Never in a million years.

Outside the reporters and cameramen shut off lights, powered down generators, bolted shut trucks, and went home, leaving a skeleton crew behind bivouacked for the night. The rhythm of the story had been set days ago. There would be no more news tonight. Not from Sand Castle Drive.

Only one agent was left to man the house, aided by a pair of uniformed officers posted out front by the driveway.

At 3 A.M., against his better judgment, the agent inside indulged an overwhelming urge to rest. He laid his heavy head on the couch pillow in the den. He didn't want to fall asleep, and as he felt himself dozing off, he promised it would be for just a few minutes.

No one was stationed out back. There was no reason since all vehicular access was from the front. All the action happened out front. Perhaps that's why no one, not the media, not the police, not the sleeping agent, nor any of the Stones, heard the soft slapping of oars on the inlet behind the house.

No one heard Wally tie up the small row boat or throw out the foam bumpers to keep the boat quiet as the waters gently lapped at its sides. No one saw him scurry up the path to the rear of the house, or heard the tapping and clicking as he finessed the porch door open. The alarm wasn't on, why should it be with agents and cops on duty. No one caught Wally sneaking through the darkened kitchen, past the snoring agent, up the stairs to the second floor. No one heard the creak of the knob as he slowly opened the door to the master bedroom. Allie slept soundly as Wally set down an envelope on Jordan's dresser and retraced his steps.

He tiptoed into the hallway and pushed open Sarah's door slowly. No one noticed Capote sit up at the advance of a visitor, or his purr as he accepted the gentle strokes of the stranger. No eye caught the glint of the hypodermic syringe as Wally uncorked it and tapped the air from it before squeezing the needle into Capote's neck. Sarah didn't stir as Capote let out a little moan before falling into a stupor. Sarah didn't hear the compact surgical saw sing as Wally slipped it from its sheath.

The Stones slept, the media's million eyes looked elsewhere, the agent downstairs dreamed of the chase, the uniform cops out front listened to the radio. No one heard the crunch of soft bone as Wally sliced off Capote's front paws, and arranged them carefully on Sarah's vanity. The blood dripping on the soft carpet hardly made a sound. Wally cradled Capote in his arms, then slipped him into a canvas bag. He retraced his steps and snuck out the back door as silently as he had entered.

No one witnessed the moon cast its rays on the tiny fishing boat as Wally pulled back the bumpers and unhitched the rope. No one heard the reprise of oars dipping rhythmically in the black waters of the Sound as Wally returned to the landing a half mile away where his car awaited him. No one certainly, save for Wally, heard Timmy's lament the following morning when he awoke to his cat curled up at his bedside, as pawless as he was dead. No one.

Allie made it to Sarah's room first, followed quickly by Jordan, who heard the shrieks all the way in his office. They imagined another of Sarah's nightmares. But Allie saw the tiny blood drops dotting the carpet, and Jordan noticed the grotesque arrangement on the vanity. And they knew.

It took a moment for Sarah's hysteria to subside. Then it started all again. There was no room for comfort. Deleese, back for the morning shift, ran up the stairs and instantly caught sight of the abominable shrine. He wanted desperately to cover up the paws, to remove them from Sarah's sight, but he feared that evidence would be destroyed in the process. Instead he instructed Allie to take Sarah out of the room, leading mother and daughter around the drops of blood on the carpet to the door.

It was a half an hour before Jordan returned to his room and noticed the strange envelope on the dresser, addressed in hand to Jordan Stone in curiously small and awkward print. His tongue grew thick with adrenaline when he realized the handwriting was Timmy's.

"Deleese!" he shouted. Jordan instantly regretted his reaction.

"What is it?" asked Deleese, rushing to the room.

Jordan hid the envelope behind his back. "Nothing, I'm sorry. Just thanks for being here, before, with Sarah."

"You're welcome," said Deleese, puzzled by Jordan's uncharacteristic response.

When he was certain Deleese was busy again with the latest crime scene, Jordan tore open the envelope, carefully at first for fear of disturbing any fingerprints, but then with abandon after realizing the kidnapper would never be so foolish as to leave prints, if indeed this missive was from the kidnapper.

Jordan's question was answered immediately. The first item to emerge from the envelope was a swatch of cloth from Timmy's tye-dyed T-shirt, the handmade one he wore the day of the kidnapping.

Jordan smelled the cloth. It was Timmy's. He cursed the kidnapper for bringing Timmy so close again.

A note came out next. It was computer-generated, the same fuzzy dot-matrix typeface as used on the label of the original ransom demand.

The page was folded in four equal squares, and Jordan unfolded it hastily. The paper contained only one line of text, not even a complete sentence. It read: "Local Library *Orthopedic Amputation and Prosthetic Management of the Hand.*"

Jordan folded the instructions and the envelope and slipped them deep into his pocket. When he returned to Sarah's room, Bureau technicians worked meticulously, attempting to coax fingerprints and shoe prints from unforgiving surfaces. But it was no use, and Jordan saw the frustration plainly on Waters' face as he directed the campaign.

"We followed the blood path to the inlet outback. He came by boat. We're on foot looking for leads," Waters said.

"There aren't many places to launch a boat around here. Just Robert's Landing and Harrows Point," Jordan said.

"Unless he trespassed on a private boat dock."

"You think it's him?" Jordan asked innocuously.

"We don't have proof yet, but I can't believe anyone else would care to pull a stunt like this. Then again, this case. . . ."

"Meanwhile," Waters continued. "Not one word to the press. This, we're going to keep to ourselves, understood?"

For once Jordan was in complete agreement with Waters.

"If it is him, it doesn't bode well," said a female voice.

Jordan turned to see Agent Fortunato, the psycholinguist. She attempted a smile but her concern prevented one from emerging.

"Small animals are one step away from small children. He's escalating. That's not good."

Jordan appreciated the honesty, all the more reason to clutch tightly the letter stashed in his pocket. It was his work order for the deed he so desperately wanted to commit.

"Are you okay, Jordan?" asked Fortunato.

"Yes, why?"

"You look lost, preoccupied."

"No, I'm just thinking what all this means. Last night, the show, this. My mind hasn't processed it yet."

"You're not up to something, are you?" Waters inquired.

"Me?"

"Yes, you."

"Why would you think that?"

At her desk overlooking the East River, Wanda Gentry made a list of everyone who knew her private telephone number. The list wasn't very long. Her bosses, coworkers, attorney, and agent knew it, but they were under strict instructions not to pass it along. A few paramours possessed it, and occasionally she gave it to show guests, though usually just very prominent ones.

And then it dawned on her. She had given out the number twice in the past few days, both to guests on the slam–Jordan Stone show. She hurriedly pulled up her files, then jumped on the phone and dialed Mort's extension.

"Mort, you've got to come in here. This will blow you away."

Mort's jaw slackened when Wanda told him the news. "Let's not rush to conclusions. Maybe there's another explanation."

"Like what?"

"Like the kidnapper got your number from an associate or something," said Mort.

"I can hear the conversation with my agent now. 'Hello, Mr. Peele, I'm Timmy's kidnapper, would you happen to have Wanda Gentry's private number.' "

"Very funny. How about Jordan? Did he have the number?"

"Yes," said Wanda. "What are you saying? That Jordan gave the number to the kidnapper?"

"Not at all."

"Then what?"

"What if that wasn't Timmy on the line last night. We have no confirmation it was really him, only Jordan's reaction. Maybe the call was some sort of charade or ruse orchestrated by Jordan or the FBI."

"For what possible reason?" asked Wanda.

"To anger the real kidnapper, lure him out."

"Impossible. I know Jordan, and I'll tell you one thing. He wasn't faking it last night. He couldn't pull off a performance that good in a million years."

"Then what's your theory?"

"We had the kidnapper on the show the other night. I only gave out my private number to two people. The first was Bill Kincaid, the prison lover of John Tibett from Jordan's book *The Tended Garden*. The second guest was Arthur Hedlund. You remember, the father of Josh, one of the three boys convicted of killing a teen-aged girl in *Slaughter Alley*. Both came on the show, both have axes to grind with Stone, and both had my telephone number."

Mort leaned back to muse the possibilities.

"How do we proceed?" Mort asked.

"We call them both back and try to set up follow-up interviews. We'll do some background checking in the meantime. We'll see what happens. Take it one step at a time."

"We've got to tell the FBI, don't you think?" asked Mort.

"No. Not yet. This is only a hunch, after all. Let me follow it up, please."

"I don't know."

"I'll deliver you ratings so high, you can personally pull the plug on the competition."

"Wanda, if you're right, you know what this means, don't you?"

"You bet. The ultimate exclusive."

Agent Bales, as obvious as ever in his brown Chrysler, was back on duty as designated tail for Jordan Stone. Rather than attempt to lose him, Jordan meandered through the streets of Rocky Cliff checking his rearview mirror to ensure Bales could maintain surveillance; after all, Jordan was merely taking a trip to the library.

The small town's local library was housed in an historic Victorian on the banks of a picturesque duck pond. Jordan knew William Martin, the librarian, well. In his quest to celebrate local authors, of which there were many in the upscale village, Martin had convinced Jordan to give a number of free talks to book club members.

"Jordan, what are you doing here?" said Martin.

"I need to see a book. It's called *Orthopedic Amputation and Prosthetic Management of the Hand.*"

"Never heard of it."

"It's a medical text."

"Obviously. But we don't carry technical books of any kind."

"Well, where would it be if you did carry such a book?"

Martin picked up a copy of *Books in Print*, and suggested a call number. "Need help?"

"Yes. I need you not to say a word to anyone about this."

"I understand."

Jordan noticed Agent Bales enter the library and

scout for Jordan. Jordan gave him a wide smile as he
sauntered to the row Martin had suggested. No book.

He scoured the adjoining shelves moving well into
other subjects with no luck. He was ready to leave when
he noticed the oversized books on the top shelf. There,
squeezed in between two consumer medical guides, was
the heavy tome.

Jordan opened the book and a cassette tape spilled
out, turning heads as it toppled to the floor. Jordan
picked it up and slipped it into his jacket pocket, hoping Bales hadn't noticed. He flipped through the pages
filled with concise illustrations and medical terminology
Jordan couldn't begin to understand.

The book had no call number attached to its spine,
nor stamps indicating it belonged to the Rocky Cliff
Library. For the sake of Agent Bales, Jordan quietly
asked Martin to go through the motions of checking
out the book.

"Anything else?" asked Martin.

"That will do it."

When Jordan returned to his car he slipped the tape
into his cassette player and drove the winding back
roads of the pastoral North Shore. The tape was cued
up and Jordan's hair bristled when he heard the altered
voice of the man he hated more than anyone on earth.

*Jordan, considering your pitiful performance last night,
I'm extending you one more chance to accommodate my
wishes. You were rather touching, I must say.*

*Here is what I need you to do. Go to the corner of Glen
Cove Road and Old Northern Boulevard. There's a phone
booth on the southwest corner near the gas station. You'll
find a paging device on top of the phone booth.*

*Now, do you think you can follow these directions, nit-
wit? Find someone to take the Montauk train tomorrow.
They can take the 12:06 P.M. train in Rocky Cliff and
change at Mineola. That's P.M., as in post-mortem. Give
them your hands, well packaged, and the beeper. When*

the pager beeps, have them throw the package from the moving train. Follow these instruction and maybe, maybe you'll see Timmy again. Fail to follow these instructions and you will most certainly see Timmy again, in approximately the same condition as that poor little rat of yours, Capote.

I'm counting on your word that the Bureau won't be involved. If I find one indication to the contrary, all bets are off. This is your last chance, Mr. King of True Crime. Last chance.

Jordan glanced at his watch. It was a 10:12 in the morning. He had a little less than twenty-four hours to slice off his hands, package them, and find an accomplice to take the Montauk train.

Good-bye hands.

He rewound the tape and played it again, making certain he had the instructions clear. Jordan checked his rearview mirror. Agent Bales followed dutifully. Jordan would have to lose him now. He speeded up, taking turns with a degree of abandon he hadn't attempted since his teenage years. At first Bales dropped behind, but despite his disadvantage, he quickly caught up.

Jordan's mind raced with possibilities, challenges, not the least of which was devising a way of cutting off his hands, a challenge that had bewildered him so far. But the end was hours away and Jordan rejoiced in being one step ahead of Waters and the Bureau.

At least Jordan thought he was one step ahead.

But at the Stones' home, at the de facto headquarters around the dining room table, Agents Waters and Deleese listened intently to Radio Channel 3. It was receiving a signal from the hidden transmitter taped on the underside of the dashboard in Jordan Stone's car.

Even as Jordan listened to the kidnapper's message for the first time, the Bureau tape machines recorded the kidnapper's instructions, and Agent Fortunato jotted notes concerning the state of mind of Mr. X. The radio transmission was muffled by the sound of the Porsche's engine whirring away, but the words were clear enough, and even before Jordan heard the last of the message, Waters barked out his first order.

"Get me that beeper before Jordan gets his hands on it. I want it, and I want it now."

TWENTY

"Bales," Waters shouted into the radio as if the current crisis was all the agent's fault.

Waters' voice thundered throughout the first floor of the Stones' home, and the agents floating around the dining room table recoiled at the intensity of his command.

"You stick to him but good," Waters continued. "And I mean but good. We need time. The longer you're tailing him, the longer he'll have to steer clear of the intersection."

Waters thanked the Lord he had listened to Deleese and planted a global positioning device in Jordan's car as well. Even if Bales were to lose Jordan's trail, Waters could track him on the screen of Deleese's laptop. The agents were still frozen in their tracks when Waters hung up.

"What are you looking at?" he said. They quickly returned to their stations.

Bales floored the accelerator. The engine responded with a cacophony of clanks and knocks as the Chrysler's big engine churned out more horsepower than the suspension could ever hope to manage. At times Bales lost sight of Jordan, but then Bales caught a flash of the black demon slipping around the next corner.

About four miles from the intersection, the inevitable happened. Bales veered around a corner onto a straightaway. He saw majestic maples forming a canopy as far as the eye could see. But not a sign of the elusive Porsche.

"He's gone," Bales called in.

"Shit," Waters replied as he slammed down the phone. "Where are the beeper boys?"

At the same moment, and several miles closer to civilization, Russo and Lewis slammed their car to a stop on the curb in front of an electronics store. Russo flashed his badge as the two men stormed inside.

"We need a mobile messaging unit and we need it now."

"What kind?" The kid behind the counter was intrigued by the two men in a state of panic.

"That one," said Russo pointing to the first pager he saw below the glass counter.

"What kind of service plan would you like?"

"We don't want it activated."

Russo yanked the pager from the counter and left the store. Lewis flipped his card on the counter. "Call this number to get paid."

The clerk looked at the card and smiled.
"Stone case, eh?" he said.

The agents didn't answer but the clerk knew from their expressions it was true, and he would have a story to tell forevermore.

The lunchtime traffic crawled along the main thoroughfare en route to the intersection. Russo weaved his way in vain, until he pulled out his mobile cherry top and suctioned it atop the car. Still, traffic only reluctantly gave way.

Deleese kept his eyes peeled on the computer screen. Its blinking cursor indicating the ever-changing location of Jordan Stone as he zipped along the back roads.

Lewis picked up the radio handset. "We are one traffic light away. Where's Jordan?" he asked.

"He's at Four Rivers Road, two miles away from Highway 25," said Deleese. "You have a three-minute lead."

Russo pulled in the flashing light, not wanting to alarm Jordan if they happened to find each other in adjacent lanes.

Russo pumped the gas and horned his way through the traffic.

"There it is," said Lewis pointing to the booth, which, much to the dismay of the agents, was occupied. The car squealed to a halt inches from the glass booth and the agents jumped out.

"Move it, ma'am," said Lewis. He pulled the receiver from the caller's hand, hung up the phone, and escorted her away from the booth. Russo, meanwhile, vaulted on the hood of his car and swapped beepers—his deactivated model for the kidnapper's. As fast as they had pulled in, the agents jumped in their car and vanished from the scene, leaving the caller mystified.

The woman had just started redialing when Jordan downshifted and drew his car to a halt on the very spot the agents had occupied moments earlier. She watched in puzzlement as Jordan climbed aboard his car and felt around the grimy roof of the booth for the beeper.

He leaped down, fired up his car and veered away, a smile on his lips and the beeper in his lap. The wrong one.

It was midafternoon, and Wally was half awake, half asleep. He had grown tired, weary of the entire affair, depressed like before. He thought about killing the boy after receiving Jordan's hands tomorrow. Jordan deserved it. All the trouble he had put Wally through, risking his cover again, this time at the Rocky Cliff Library, not to mention Jordan's impudent attitude during the course of events, last night's *Crime Current* show notwithstanding. And Timmy was nothing special either. Then he remembered his commitment to society and the lesson he had been chosen to teach, he and Jordan Stone.

The ring of the phone startled Wally back into consciousness. He waited for the fifth ring.

"Hello," Wally answered as demurely as possible. "Ah, Ms. Gentry, what a pleasant surprise."

Wally perked up. He had forgotten about the lovely Wanda, the only bright spot in this tedious affair. Obviously she hadn't forgotten about him. "What can I do for you?" asked Wally.

"As you can imagine, we're still very interested in your story. I found your performance so . . . thought provoking the other night. You're so articulate that I was able to convince my producer to do a follow up report—just on you. An exclusive. What do you think?"

Wally loved the idea. A segment alone with Wanda Gentry, touching toes under the table, gazing into her big blues.

"Sounds great. When should I come in?"

"Well," Wanda took a deep breath. "We were thinking how nice it would be to do a show from your place. It would add warmth to the piece. Don't you think?"

That changed everything. "I see. I'm afraid that won't be possible. You see, I'm in the middle of remodeling. Plus, I'm sure you wouldn't want to drive all the way out here."

"You're in Manhattan, aren't you?"

Wally had forgotten about call-forwarding. Wanda had dialed locally, the 212 area code. She had no idea where he really was. He could meet her at the apartment, of course.

"All right. When?"

"How about tonight?"

"Tonight, that's kind of soon."

"Please," Wanda pouted. "For me?"

"Well, I am kind of busy tomorrow. So tonight would be the best opportunity."

"Great."

Wally gave Wanda his city address. "Seven o'clock, then?"

"How about eight," he said. "If I'm a little late, just wait."

"Oh, we will."

"And Wanda?"

"Yes?"

"I'm doing this for you."

"He's losing it."

Agent Fortunato shook her head despairingly. She had spent the last hour analyzing the content and speech pattern of the kidnapper's message to Jordan.

"He's flippant, irrational. He's free-associating and rambling. His articulation is marked by pronounced rises and falls in pitch. He's even nasty. This is a dramatic departure from his first tape during which he exhibited astounding discipline and irreproachable manners. I would say he's entering a period of disassociation. If I may sum up my report in very nonclinical terms, this guy is falling off his rocker."

Waters listened carefully. Fortunato's assessment matched his. It didn't take a Masters' degree to figure this one out.

"And Timmy?" he asked.

Agent Fortunato shook her head again.

"How much time?" asked Waters.

"I don't know. I don't believe the boy was dead at the time of the taping. But hours have past since then. It's entirely possible he has been killed. If not, we're on borrowed time."

The news was as dreary from the criminalists who analyzed the beeper. Their preliminary examination of the device yielded few clues. Tracking the pager's telephone number was impossible; the serial numbers had been sheared off. And, not surprisingly, there was not a single trace of fingerprints, just the residual latex dust consistent with rubber gloves, the same as found on other materials touched by the cunning kidnapper.

"Looks like we're stumped again," said Waters. He leaned back in the chair and gazed through the one-way window onto the reporters and cameramen. Some were throwing around a football.

"Well? Do we let Stone go through with it?" asked Russo.

It was the question on everyone's minds but no one's lips. Waters turned to analyze the kidnapper's pager, which occupied a place of honor in the center of the dining room table. He hoped to uncover with his naked eyes what the criminalists were unable to detect with their delicate instruments.

"It's a problem," Water's said. "A public relations problem. What if Jordan gives up his hands and the kidnapper doesn't deliver? We'll look like fools for letting Stone do it. We'll never live it down."

"If we don't let Stone do it, the kidnapper will kill Timmy. We can be certain of that," argued Russo.

"I just can't take the risk. I want Timmy back as much as anyone, but I'm not going to put the reputation of this force in jeopardy for what I perceive to be a slim chance to begin with."

"It's the only chance we have," said Russo.

"We still have twenty hours. Lots can happen. We have a drop-off, a pickup, there are still plenty of opportunities for the kidnapper to make a mistake. Meanwhile, I want agents on duty throughout the night protecting this house and digging up whatever crumbs we have left. No one goes home. I'm going to get this guy even if I have to cut off my own hands to do it."

* * *

Jordan approached his home with his sunglasses down and not a shade of mercy as he cut through the sea of reporters. He marched straight to his office above the garage and closed the blinds tightly. A little-used rear door in the office connected to a staircase that led to the garage downstairs. Jordan freed the lock and walked down the creaky stairs. One side of the musty garage was reserved for Jordan's car. The second side was a clutter of boxes, toys, tools, and assorted junk accumulated over the years. Jordan pushed away cartons filled with old books, Barbie dolls, and clothing for two-year-olds, until he reached a low shelf where he kept the tools he had taken from his father's home when he left years ago. Among the dusty hand tools, there was but one electric tool, a table-top scroll saw, designed for craft enthusiasts.

Jordan's father had purchased it after awakening from a alcohol-induced stupor one morning and announcing to the family he was ready at last to work with his hands. The commitment lasted about as long as the hangover.

The arm of the saw was long and the saw blade thin, but Jordan remembered the blade working just fine during that miraculous moment when his father fed a piece of plywood through it to make a hotplate shaped like a teapot. That was the last Jordan's father had ever used the tool and it sat idle in his garage and in Jordan's garage ever since.

Jordan yanked the cord free from a crush of heavy boxes. He examined the relic as if it were a long-lost archeological find. Then he picked it up carefully and maneuvered through the debris back up the stairs to his office. Once he sponged away the dust accumulated over thirty years, the saw shined brightly in its original paint. Its hundred tiny upturned teeth sparkled like diamonds in the fluorescent light. Jordan placed the unit firmly on a filing cabinet and plugged in the thick cord.

He flipped the red switch and the saw came alive with a grunt and a whirl. The blade jittered up and down until it gained speed and became a blur of vibrating metal.

Jordan selected a paperback book, one of his own, from the shelf and carefully fed it through the blade. The saw ripped through the book without a tug. The baby sang. Jordan examined his handiwork, then flicked the switch off and listened as the saw descended in pitch until it cycled slowly to a stop.

The medical text, gratis of the kidnapper, was of little use to Jordan except for the section on emergency aftercare of accidental amputation. Jordan learned how to apply a tourniquet and relieve the effects of shock. Loss of blood was the big problem.

Jordan prepared tourniquets with bed sheets from the office's pull-out sofa. An emergency medical box kept on hand provided the antiseptics that would be required. There would be no anesthesia.

Only when fully prepared did Jordan drape the instruments with a blanket and call on the intercom to the house for Allie.

Wanda bussed up her gear and headed to her first appointment. The apartment was upscale, West Side, doorman. She checked her watch, five minutes before the hour. Wanda hadn't wanted to spook her guests with a crowd of faces, so she traveled with only Phil, her trusted cameraman. Even before she knocked, the door was opened by Bill Kincaid.

"Come on in," Kincaid said with a smile.

The apartment was light, clean, and impeccably decorated. Kincaid seemed overly eager to supply his guests with drinks, and while away in the kitchen, Wanda spied a coffee-table book hastily covered by *National Geographic*. She flipped through the pages of men dressed in S&M garb, engaging in mock, almost comic, scenes of bondage and domination. Kincaid returned with ice teas for all.

"I felt like a nitwit when you called." He smiled. "I was half asleep. I'm glad the time worked out for you."

Wanda studied Kincaid hard. He was a bundle of paradoxes. His arms were as thick as a longshoreman's but his disposition was sweeter than an old aunt. He had thick Mediterranean lips and a strong Roman nose but his skin color was delicate Irish, almost white. He was as large as lumberjack but soft like a cherub.

After the warm up chitchat, Wanda got started.

"Why don't you tell us again why you have a personal grudge against Jordan Stone."

Kincaid again attested to his lover's innocence, maintaining that it was really the freed Greek who killed John Tibett's wife. And Jordan's efforts to free the Greek were motivated solely to create a sensation around an otherwise mediocre story saturated by the time Jordan's book hit the stand.

As he spoke, Wanda responded with concern, interest, and sincerity. Boring shit, all of it, but she wanted him to loosen up, feel that she was an ally. Then she got to the heart of the matter.

"And what about Timmy?" she asked.

Dead silence.

"What about him?"

"How is this affecting him?"

"I feel sorry for the boy I guess. Doesn't everyone?"

Wanda employed the oldest technique in the how-to interview book. She remained silent, forcing Kincaid to continue talking to relieve the embarrassing silence.

"How should I feel? This entire episode is Jordan Stone's doing. He did it to himself, in effect. Sure, the boy is a pawn. I feel for him as much as you do, I'm sure."

"If you had the power to release him, would you?"

"Of course, but the power's not in my hands. It's in Jordan's."

"Why do say that?"

"The demand is clear, isn't it? Why doesn't Jordan simply give up his hands?"

"Would you?"

"Would I what?"

"Cut off your hands in exchange for your son?"

"Absolutely."

"And would you release the boy if Stone complies?"

"Yes, I would," said Kincaid. "But then again, we're speaking hypothetically."

Allie cringed at the sound of Jordan's voice spilling from the intercom. After his confession, she had spent most of her time in the den conferring with the agents, speaking occasionally with friends, and writing in her journal, a practice she had long abandoned but now felt compelled to resume to sort out her emotions. Allie's anger toward Jordan had given way to numbness and then to a feeling so alien to Allie it took her awhile to identify it. It was not one of the emotions she had anticipated: bitterness, consternation, or sadness. Rather it was the peculiar sensation of resignation, both hollow and heavy at the same time.

Allie's mind played with the many ways she could announce to Jordan that he must move out. She formulated her responses to his likely pleas of unity for the sake of the family. She practiced silently not feeling guilty when the children would undoubtedly complain about being abandoned. She readied herself for the ridicule she would take in the press for the divorce, predicted with such accuracy by television psychologists. Her mind raced with contacts she could call to start the process of finding a job after all these years. She regretted not stashing away some money of her own. The faces of a few old boyfriends rushed through her thoughts and she wondered, if only for a moment, what they were doing now.

One thing was certain, she wanted nothing to do with Jordan outside of Timmy's rescue. And she knew Jordan well enough to know he would not call her now unless it concerned this subject only. She didn't answer the intercom query. Instead she walked to his office, silently promising herself not to succumb to any stray feelings of regret that would surely stab her heart.

Allie rapped on the door as if she were a visitor. She felt cold and strange, and battled an overwhelming urge to leave.

"Come in."

"This better be good," she said.

Allie averted Jordan's eyes.

"I have something for you," Jordan said. He pulled the tye-dye swatch from his desk's top drawer. Allie's jaw dropped.

"Jesus, that's from Timmy's shirt," Allie exclaimed. She rubbed the cloth against her cheek and drew in its scent. It smelled so good. "Where did you get this?"

"Listen."

Jordan punched the tape recorder and the kidnapper's warped message began to play. A jumble of fear, anger, and hatred streamed through Allie's body. Everything centered now on Timmy.

"What are we going to do?" she asked.

"We have no choice. We'll do exactly what he says."

"You can't be serious."

"He's not fooling this time, Allie."

"Has Waters heard this tape?"

"He has no idea." Jordan told her about finding the pager on top of the phone booth as promised.

"We must give it to Waters," Allie said.

"We can't, don't you see? Didn't you hear what he said? He said no police. None. Waters can't know. We have to do this alone, together. I need your help."

"You need my help." The irony was not lost on Allie.

Allie walked to the window, squeezed a finger between the blinds and panned the scene outside. A pair of cameramen squirted each other with water bottles to relieve the heat. Her mind swelled with so many emotions. Revulsion for the kidnapper, anger toward Jordan, desire for Timmy, and a sinking feeling of helplessness reserved for herself.

"I want Timmy back so bad," Allie confided in Jordan. She hated him even more for putting her in this position, for being the only one she could talk to at a time when she never wanted to talk to him again. Allie straightened her spine and banished her emotions.

"It will be over soon, I promise."

"It seems so wrong," she said.

"What?"

"Everything."

"It's our only choice. Don't you want Timmy back?"

Allie pictured Timmy, as she had so many times these past few days, waiting patiently for her and Jordan.

"If we did it. And I'm not saying we will. But if we did, how?"

Jordan took two steps backward and uncovered the equipment he had prepared.

"Oh, Jordan. You can't be serious. This is barbaric." Allie averted her eyes, repelled by the sight of the contraption with its ungainly arm and surgical blade.

"Do we have another choice?"

"How about Emerson or a doctor?"

"I've tried. No one will do it. Plus we can't take the risk of being discovered by the FBI or the press. We have to do it here."

"Absolutely not. We have to tell Waters."

"You heard the kidnapper. We have to keep Waters out of this if we want to get Timmy back."

"Jordan, this is nuts. You could go into shock, bleed to death."

"I've got it all figured out. The kids can spend the night at Emerson and Judy's. We'll call an ambulance even before it's done. You'll have to help with the second hand, of course, but I'll show you how to apply the tourniquets. We'll throttle the blood loss in no time. Then you'll be out the door with my hands. I've timed it. We're talking two minutes."

"Do you hear yourself?"

"Loud and clear," said Jordan.

"And do you realize what you're asking me to do?"

"Just imagine having Timmy back. Hugging him and kissing him. Knowing he is safe in your arms. Just imagine."

Allie had imagined it, a million times. She kissed the cloth of many colors and felt its softness again.

"And what about the kidnapper?" she asked.

"He'd go free."

"So he can come after us again, terrorize us?"

"I want it that way. I've given him my word. Look, this is not about the kidnapper, it's not about my hands. It's about our son. If we get Timmy back, who cares about the kidnapper."

"And you're willing to part with your hands?"

"Absolutely."

"*If,* and I say *if,* I say yes, when would we do it?"

"Tomorrow morning, right before eleven. That would give you enough time to elude police and take the train."

"And you?"

"I'll be at the hospital, stabilized, long before you hear the train whistle."

"We have until tomorrow morning, right? Let me think about it."

"Do you want your family back?"

"You know I do."

"Then think about it." Jordan pointed to the band saw. "But believe me, *this* is our only salvation."

Wanda's next meeting was just two blocks away. Arthur Hedlund possessed a coolness that bordered on clammy, a characteristic of many doctors she had known. He held the door tightly as he invited Wanda and Phil in, then he looked behind her for others.

"That's it?" he said.

"I thought we'd keep it personal."

"I see." He smiled.

Hedlund's apartment was the opposite of Kincaid's. It was dark, filled with laboriously ornate antiques of mahogany, and thick carpets that hadn't been shaken out in years. The art was cheap impressionist reproductions made to look respectable with gilded gold frames. The windows were shuttered and the walls looked like they hadn't seen light in centuries. Wanda's allergies kicked in immediately, and she pulled a handkerchief from her purse.

"It was my mother's place," Hedlund explained. When she died five years ago, I didn't have the heart to sell or redecorate."

"Then you don't live here?" asked Wanda.

"I do. It's just that between work and play, I don't get to spend much time here."

Wanda took the measure of the man. Slightly bald, he looked remarkably fit for someone in his mid-fifties, well-groomed, bright blue eyes, everything about him was right, except for his breath. When he spoke he emitted a sour stench of rotting teeth or decaying flesh. It was putrid and loathsome and Wanda did all she could not to appear physically repelled.

After setting up the lights and arranging chairs, Wanda used the same tactic she had with Kincaid, and asked Dr. Hedlund to recount the events leading to his son's suicide.

"He killed himself the night after the TV movie based on his story aired."

"You're kidding?" asked Wanda. "Why didn't you say that the other night, during the show?"

"I didn't want to—I don't know, it slipped my mind, I guess. The whole thing is so upsetting."

"I guess Timmy must be upset these days, don't you think?"

"I know he's scared."

"How do you know?"

"Wouldn't every little child be scared, I mean to be cooped up in a room out in the middle of nowhere. What a tragic irony, don't you think?"

"If you had it in your power to release him. Would you?"

"I don't know."

"You wouldn't harm a child, would you?"

Hedlund smiled. "I'm sure the Stones' are hoping he doesn't end up like their little cat, Capote."

"Capote?" asked Wanda, puzzled.

"You know the Stones' cat that got his paws torn off this morning."

"I didn't hear anything about that," said Wanda. She turned to Phil. "Did you?"

Phil nodded no.

"Well, I'm sure it was on one of the news stations," said Hedlund. "I've been watching all day."

Wanda had been monitoring reports all day too, nothing had come up about the cat, certainly that would be headline news.

She smiled. "I must of missed it."

"You must have," said Wally with a nervous smile.

TWENTY-ONE

Allie helped Cal and Sarah pack overnight bags, making sure each had enough clothing for three nights. Due to last night's incident she didn't need to dig deep for an explanation. Nor did the children object to staying at Emerson and Judy's.

Jordan waited until Allie had cleared out before he came in to say his good-byes. He entered Sarah's room first. She was sitting bravely, Jordan thought, at her vanity, brushing her hair. Sarah had placed a photo of Capote on the very spot where his paws were found earlier in the day.

"I'm never going to move that picture," she said.

Jordan put his hands on Sarah's shoulders and rubbed gently. This was the last time he would have the opportunity to touch her this way and he savored every moment. Jordan was sure Sarah felt the trembling in his fingers, he only hoped she felt the love as well.

"What's going to happen to us? To Timmy?" she asked.

"We'll get Timmy back."

"Oh, Daddy, I'm so scared." Sarah turned and buried her head in her father's chest. Jordan ran his fingers through her soft hair, feeling the silkiness for the last time.

"We'll make it through. I promise. This will all be over soon," Jordan said.

"God, I hope so."

"Sarah, I want to say I'm sorry."

"For what?"

"For everything. For this happening to our family, for bringing fear into your life, for Capote, for all the times I've yelled at you, or not trusted you, or didn't give you the time you've deserved."

"I think it's me who owes you an apology, for the other night with Jimmy. I feel so selfish," Sarah said.

"That's ancient history. Look, we're all having trouble dealing with this. I guess there's no manual on how to deal with the kidnapping of someone you love."

"I didn't do anything with Jimmy, I mean . . . you know." Sarah blushed.

"I love you, Sarah. And I trust you."

"I love you too, Daddy."

Jordan took a deep breath before entering Cal's room. Cal was stationed at the Nintendo at his desk, firing volleys at grotesquely large bad guys. A baseball game was playing on the radio, the Dodgers were beating the Mets 2-to-1.

"Can I come in?"

"I guess," said Cal.

"Cal, I know these past few days have been difficult for you. For what it's worth, I just want to say I'm sorry. I've acted foolishly. I've made demands on you no son should have to endure."

Cal kept firing.

"But there's one mistake I won't make," Jordan continued. "I won't let you go. Not without a fight. I'm asking you, man-to-man, please, forgive me."

Cal loosened his grip on the joystick.

"I have something to give you," said Jordan. He wore a gold ring fitted with a black onyx stone. He twisted it off his right ring finger and buried it deep into Cal's palm.

"You're my oldest son," said Jordan. "I want you to have it. Wear it proudly if you choose. And if you don't, I understand."

A Met hit a home run and the sound of cheers filled the room. Cal race to his father's arms, a tear tripping down his cheek. When Cal realized he was too old to be hugging his father he backed off. Jordan extended his hand.

"Friends?" said Jordan.

Cal smiled. "Friends."

Jordan shook long and hard, but then he couldn't bare the regret or withhold his love any longer and he kissed his son on the lips. "I love you, Cal."

The car horn beeped.

"Let's go," Jordan said.

Jordan wrapped one arm around the boy and the other around Sarah as she emerged from her room. At the front door, he caressed Cal's pimply face one last time and brushed the hair out of Sarah's eyes. He tried to smile. He never realized how much he would miss his hands until now.

Jordan prayed he would see Timmy again, but whatever the outcome, the kidnapper would not succeed in breaking Jordan's family apart. Jordan knew now where his strength lay.

"I love you, kids."

Emerson and Judy tried to put on a happy face as they entered the house. Jordan had always discounted Emerson due to his persistent honesty bordering on the extreme. Now Jordan envied him more than he could ever know.

"Let's go, guys. The car is running," said Emerson, extending his hand to carry Sarah's overstuffed overnight bag.

"They really need to get away from all this," said Allie. She hugged her children good-bye.

"Now, you're sure you have everything you need?" They nodded yes.

"We're so happy they're coming. Hey kids, what do you say we go to the video store?" Judy said, trying to pump some life into the room. "Your choice. R-rated if you want."

Cal and Sarah attempted a smile. Jordan gave each of them one last bear hug. Then Jordan pulled Emerson over to the side.

"You know that book idea you had, the one about medical ethics?"

"Oh, that. Just a fantasy of mine. It will never happen," said Emerson.

"I hope it does. I really do. I'll talk to my agent, get some ideas. I'd like to help you."

"You mean it?"

"Yeah, I do."

"That would be nice. Thanks," said Emerson.

"It's my pleasure."

"Okay, let's go gang or we'll never get out of here," said Judy.

"I'll walk them to the car," said Allie.

Jordan stood at the threshold waving good-bye. The last wave.

Allie waited in the driveway as the car backed out. " 'Bye kids. Have a good time. We'll call as soon as we hear anything."

The few reporters hanging around didn't know what to make of Allie. It was the first time they had seen her in days. She didn't care what they thought as she stood in the driveway enjoying the sweet evening air. Then the breeze from the Sound sent her walking back to the house.

She couldn't see the faces of the agents behind the one-way glass or the dining-room curtains, but she could hear their muffled voices speak in serious tones. She crept to the house and pressed her ear against the window. Now she could hear remarkably well.

"It's one hundred miles between here and M-Montauk," she heard Deleese say. "The kidnapper could activate the beeper anywhere along the way. There are miles of f-farms and dirt roads out there. We can't cover it all."

Waters' distinct baritone voice was easy to identify. "But he'll want the package right away. He'll be waiting at or near the pickup spot. He's not taking chances. I know it."

"So how do we do it then?" an unidentified voice asked.

"We start with a package that is virtually impossible to open, so he can't pull the same stunt as last time. Then we chuck it from the train when he signals."

"But the train will be moving, how can we pursue him?"

"A second train," Waters continued. "We follow the noon train by one minute with a second train carrying a SWAT team. He'll have a one-minute lead, but he'll waste most of it trying to open the box. He'll be frustrated and preoccupied by the time the second trains pulls to a stop. We'll ramp down officers on foot and on motorcycles. We'll put another team in cars. They'll ride the highway. It parallels the tracks for most of the way. And we'll have a helicopter trailing. We'll get him from all sides, surprise the hell out of him. Thank God we got that beeper before Jordan."

"And what about Jordan? What if he tries something himself?" asked Deleese.

"First move he makes, we lock him up. Any objections?"

Silence, then Waters added, "Okay, let's get working on the logistics."

Allie drifted away. She could hardly believe what she

was hearing. Jordan had told her that Waters had no idea. But they knew everything. At first it alarmed Allie terribly, but then she felt greatly relieved. Now the weight of telling or not telling Waters about Jordan's plan was off her shoulders. And perhaps it was better that the Bureau did know. They were professionals, they knew what they were doing. They had promised to get Timmy back. Deleese had promised.

Allie slipped into the house. Jordan was watching the news from the edge of the couch in the den. He looked tired and beaten and Allie felt a wave of sympathy wash over her.

"Not one station has picked up on Capote," said Jordan.

Allie's first reaction was to tell Jordan that his plan was in jeopardy, that the Bureau knew all about the beeper, the train, and the drop-off. But then she remembered that she had until tomorrow morning to think about it, and as long as Jordan thought the plan was set, he wouldn't do anything foolish. Better wait until the morning to tell him. Then he would have no choice but to let the Bureau takeover. It would be too late, then.

"What is it?" Jordan asked. "You look pale."

"Nothing," she said. "You won't do anything until tomorrow, right?"

"Right."

"Good night, then."

As soon as Wanda returned to her car, she ordered Phil to pull around and stake out Hedlund's apartment. The story about the cat could be an outright lie, a misconception, or even a fantasy on his part, Wanda thought. But Hedlund had let slip on one other count, which Wanda hadn't picked up until she listened to the tape recording of the interview in the car. Wanda rewound her tape and listened again.

"I guess Timmy must be going a little crazy these days, don't you think?" Wanda had asked.

"I know he's scared." Hedlund replied.

"How do you know?"

"Wouldn't every little child be, I mean to be cooped up in a room out in the middle of nowhere."

How could Hedlund know that Timmy was in the middle of nowhere. Perhaps he was in the city, in an apartment.

Even if there was a logical explanation for Hedlund's telling remark, there were other white lies. He had said on the phone earlier that his apartment was under renovation. It hadn't been touched in years. And he said he lived there, but Wanda had seen no signs of occupancy whatsoever.

Most importantly, Wanda's sixth sense told her that he was the kidnapper. It wasn't his blunders, his mannerisms, or his breath. No, it was something intangible, a malevolent quality that transcended description.

Wanda got on the cell phone to check if any media outlet had reported an incident with the Stone's cat. No one had. But a call to a source at the Nassau County Police Department paid off. The source would not divulge any details, but did confirm that Hedlund had the story right.

"Hey, look!" Phil said. "It's him."

Hedlund strolled out the front door of the apartment and turned left, an overnight bag in his hand.

"Follow him," Wanda ordered. Phil fired up the car and stayed as far back as possible, pretending to hunt for a parking spot. They crept along behind Hedlund, but apparently he felt a presence lurking and he speeded up and turned quickly down a one-way street. Phil zipped around three corners, ignoring traffic lights along the way. But when they turned onto the one-way street, Hedlund was nowhere in sight. There was, however, an open parking space, a rarity that suggested a very recent departure.

A homeless man was crouched near his bundle of possessions on the sidewalk nearby.

"Can you tell me what type of vehicle was parked here?" inquired Wanda.

"You mean the one that just left?"

"Yes, that one."

"What's it worth to you?"

"Twenty bucks."

"Then I can tell you."

The man approached Wanda for the money. She deliberately dropped the bill out the window rather than hand it to him for fear of touching the filthy wretch. The note fluttered to the ground into a puddle of wash water. The man stooped to pick it up, fully aware of the intent of Wanda's action.

"Well, what did you see?" Wanda asked impatiently.

"I didn't see nothing," said the man. He slipped the bill in his pocket and returned to the kingdom of his belongings.

"Not a thing at all."

"Street people," Wanda complained in a whisper.

"We should call the FBI," suggested Phil.

"No. We still only have a hunch. Plus, I have a plan. Take me home."

Phil crossed town and dropped Wanda at her house. She plopped her keys on the table and flicked off her pumps. Two messages awaited her, both from Mort pleading for her to call. But Wanda didn't return the calls because she knew Mort, Slater, and everyone at the network would prohibit her from doing what she planned the following morning.

She turned the ringer off, took a hot shower, and set her clock for 5:45 A.M. Then she turned in for a sound night's sleep.

* * *

Wally drove the Parkway through Nassau and into Suffolk County. He felt queasy about the interview tonight, that slipup with Capote. Had he gone too far? Had his vanity brought him too close to danger? He got home feeling sick and lonely and wanting company, but there was no one around him but Timmy.

Wally unbolted the door to Timmy's room, letting free the stench of feces and urine. The boy slept soundly on the bed. Wally held his nose and emptied the potty in the toilet then sprayed the room with air freshener. The Twinkies were gone and a fly buzzed around the top of the half-empty Yoo-Hoo bottle. Wally stood over the boy and watched his rhythmic breathing.

Wally pulled up a chair and sat by him. His boy was little once. Joshua. Sometimes Josh's mother called him Joshy, but Josh hated the nickname and his friends teased him tremendously until the seventh grade. Joshua liked to be called just that, Joshua. He loved the bible story of Joshua and the blaring trumpets when his mother sat him on her lap by the fireplace.

Wally remembered the words to this day. "And the Lord said to Joshua, march around the city, all the men of war going around the city at once. And it came to pass the people shouted and the trumpets were blown and the wall fell down flat. Then they utterly destroyed all that was in the city, both men and women, young and old, oxen, sheep, and asses, with the edge of the sword."

Too bad Joshua had possessed that bad seed. Wally had no choice but to crush it. So much was wrong with the boy. When he was a baby he cried too much, demanded attention, wanted to sleep with his parents until he was four. Squabbled with playmates. Wet his pants too many times. Got scared over nothing. Wally tried to help with a consistent dose of stern discipline, but to little effect. Even those hours Josh had been

banished to the closet to reflect on his wrongdoing did
him no good. He only grew worse. In fifth and sixth
grades Josh fought frequently with neighborhood boys.
And lost. Though Wally never caught him, he suspected
Josh of stealing money from his wallet. Wally detested
the belt more than Joshua could have known, but spare
the rod and spoil the child. That's what his father had
taught him.

The boy had no smarts, that was the problem. He did
miserably in school, a truant, and a derelict. He tried,
yes, but he never applied himself fully, always flitting
away, no power of concentration whatsoever. In high
school, Josh experimented with drugs, Wally was sure.
He found a pack of cigarettes on the boy in the ninth
grade and Wally had little choice but to whip him good.
And the hooligans he hung out with. Petty thieves and
sniveling drug addicts all of them. No wonder he fell in
with that murderous bunch, though he was never man
enough to admit his errors.

When Josh was arrested, his mother fell apart. Wally
didn't tell his wife how secretly pleased he was that
their son had been arrested. Put some fear into the boy.
Joshua's mother actually believed Josh's sorry excuses.
He said he did not participate in the rape and murder.
He said he had tried to stop the offense. But Wally
knew better. His son didn't have the courage to speak
up to anyone, let alone the bullies he counted as his
friends. Joshua always feared bullies so much, the
spineless wimp.

During the divorce, Josh's mother attempted to lay
much of the blame for Josh's troubles on Wally. She
said his stern ways and denial of genuine love and affection had damaged the boy. Nonsense. The boy was a
bad seed from the start. If blame was to be had, it
rested with her. She caused the boy to be a sissy with
her soft, sentimental ways. If anything, Wally's discipline had delayed the boy's descent into delinquency.

There was no explaining to her that Joshua deserved the fear of jail, the uncertainty of a trial.

True, Wally had never expected it to end as it did. He planned on stepping in at the last moment and paying an attorney to plea-bargain the sentence. Wally figured five years would do Josh good. But the trial never came. Josh killed himself first, strung himself up from his jail cell and choked to death. The coward. They say Josh was raped in prison, and that his shame led him to suicide. That's what they said, but Wally knew better. The death came the night after the movie of the week based on Stone's book.

It was Stone's fault. Stone and his putrid filth.

And so Wally had no choice but to devise a plan to revenge the death of his son. How dare Stone intrude on the intimacy of Wally and his family. How dare Stone profit from Wally's pain. Wally's suffering was his and his alone and he had given permission to nobody to share it with the world. Stone had to suffer. There was no choice.

The original idea came after Josh was buried. Revenge was all Wally had in mind. But as the days passed, revenge gave way to a larger, nobler cause, ridding society of vermin like Stone. As the plan unfolded, it gave Wally untold pleasure. He took delight in the planning of each step. Then everything fell into place: Prince Andrew's trip, the media stumbling onto the case, Wanda Gentry and her kind invitation, the ease with which Wally was able to invade Jordan's house and leave the latest message. The plan was blessed by God, no doubt because it was just and fair.

Wally gazed down on Timmy. The boy stirred slightly. He smiled until his drowsiness lifted and he realized under whose shadow he lay.

"I had a son once, a lot like you," said Wally. "Not a bad boy, I guess. He had his moments."

"What happened to him?"

"Your father killed him."

"My father didn't kill anyone."

"Don't you talk back, boy. Your father didn't kill him outright, not with his hands, but with his words. Your father is an evil man. He needs to accept guilt for his sins."

"My father is a good man."

"I said don't you talk back." Wally lifted his hand to strike the boy but stopped himself in midair.

"You're lucky, young man. I have a greater calling than to inflict deserved punishment on you. Very lucky."

Any sympathy Wally had harbored for the boy vanished. No, to do away with him properly and humanely was the only solution still. His original vision had been correct.

Wally picked up the Yoo-Hoo bottle and Twinkie wrappers and left Timmy to his own devices. No use opening another bottle for the boy. He wouldn't be alive this time tomorrow.

Jordan sequestered himself in the office. He thumbed through his personal files, pulling out folders that contained his will, life insurance policies, investment portfolios, royalty sources, and important phone numbers.

Then he sat down to pen a letter to Timmy, just in case, God forbid, Jordan didn't make it through the day.

Dear Timmy,

I want you to know that my first choice was to live for you, to see you grow into a fine a young man, which I'm sure you will do. As your life takes you to unexpected lands and as you stumble upon surprising revelations about yourself, remember always that I loved you, that I tried my hardest to get you back, that you, Cal, Sarah, and Mommy were my life.

Here are the things I remember most about you. Your sense of wonderment and joy. Your concern for all living beings. Your gift of perception. And, above all, your gentle spirit.

Don't take revenge or remain bitter about what has happened. Be kind to others. Pursue happiness and your dreams, whatever they are. Stand tall and be proud of yourself, and for God's sake don't blame yourself for what has happened to me. I blame myself for what you had to endure.

Take care of your brother and sister. And always remember that I love you, Timmy. My father never said that. At least I never heard it. So I will tell you again and again now, so that if the Devil should take away your memory, the last shred of remembrance to go will be that of your father's love. As you grow into manhood, you will better understand the meaning of these words.

Now I put myself in the hands of God. Forgive me, Timmy, and in the days to come, remember your father who loved you so much, who still thanks God for the privilege of having you, the precious moments spent with you, and the opportunity to sacrifice myself so that you may live.

I love you. And God bless you.

Love, Daddy.

Jordan sealed the letter in an envelope and covered it with a towel, so that it would not get stained tomorrow by stray blood spatters spit from the saw.

When Jordan returned to the house he found Allie asleep, dreaming fitfully. He tried to close his eyes knowing he would need his strength for tomorrow. But his anxiousness kept him awake. The clock read well past four before he was able to shut his eyes.

At 6:07 A.M. the telephone awakened him abruptly. He fumbled for the receiver and forced his mind awake.

"Hello?" he answered in a groggy morning whisper. The voice on the line was alarmingly familiar.

"Jordan. It's Wanda. We need to talk."

TWENTY-TWO

The morning broke hot, as if the sun had returned prematurely from its journey to the far side of earth. The dew had evaporated from the grass and the squint was back in the eyes of the vigilant press outside. Allie stirred awake and Jordan sat up in bed, wiping the sleep from his eyes.

"We need to talk," Wanda repeated on the telephone.

"About what?" Jordan returned to consciousness.

"I can't tell you on the phone. I'm sure the FBI is listening."

"What is it, Wanda? I don't have time for this."

Jordan glanced over and saw Allie's eyes open at the sound of Wanda's name.

"I have some information. It's worth your while, believe me. But you'll have to meet me someplace. Alone."

Wanda was many things, but a spoiler she was not.

"Where?" he asked.

"At the first place we made love. Do you remember?"

Jordan thought back. It was the Breakers Motel in Hempstead, a seedy little place not far from the *Newsday* offices.

"Yes, I remember."

"Meet me there as soon as you can. I'll be in Room 16."

"Don't mess with me, Wanda."

"You won't regret it. I promise."

Jordan hung up the phone and turned to face Allie. Not anger as much as amazement filled her eyes.

"You're not going to go, are you?" Allie asked.

"She says has some information."

"After all she's done to us?"

"This isn't about us, it's about Timmy. She says she knows something and I believe her."

"What about your plan?"

Jordan checked the clock. "We have time."

He jumped from the bed and pulled on some trowsers.

"Jordan, wait, I have something to tell you, too."

Allie didn't want to, but there was no delaying it anymore. If Jordan left without knowing, how could she prevent him from cutting off his hands somewhere else, on the run. She had no choice. Once again, Wanda had changed everything.

"What?" asked Jordan.

"They know. Waters knows about the beeper, about the train, about everything."

Jordan stopped dead in his tracks. "What are you talking about?"

"I heard them talking last night. They have the kidnapper's beeper. Yours is a decoy."

"Allie, are you sure?"

"I'm positive."

"How did they find out?"

"I don't know. But they know. I'm sure of that."

"Tell me what they said. Tell me everything."

Allie recounted the plans she had overheard, the second train, the SWAT team, motorcycles, helicopter, the indestructible box.

"Why didn't you tell me?"

"Why? Because I want my son back, that's why. And I'm not sure you're the one who can do it.".

"You were stalling me."

"Should I still have faith in you? Is that what you're asking?"

Jordan ran down the stairs tucking his shirt in. He anticipated resistance upon passing Waters, but instead Waters simply followed Jordan out of the house as he left.

Jordan fumbled for his keys and jumped into his car. He turned the key.

The car was stone dead.

A police officer smiled as he held up the Porsche's battery cable.

Jordan stepped out. "What the hell is going on?"

"You didn't think they were going to let you leave, did you?" asked the officer.

Jordan heard footsteps behind him. He turned and saw Waters fast approaching, a set of handcuffs dangling from his grip.

"Now Jordan, you have to understand," said Waters as he lunged for Jordan. The weight of his large frame slowed him down. Still he caught a piece of Jordan's pant leg and wrestled him to the ground. But in his haste to slap on the cuffs, Waters released his grip a moment too soon and Jordan kicked Waters in his gut and wiggled away.

Now the uniformed officer blitzed Jordan like a linebacker. Jordan faked left then juked right and the officer went sailing by, tackling air.

Deleese watched from the window, but by the time he dashed outside to help, it was too late. Jordan ran around to the back of the house and to the maze of paths that tunneled through the thorny brush and cattails of the wetlands. Deleese knew them well, having searched them for evidence of Timmy, but Jordan knew them better.

A media van driver stepped out of his van to stretch. It was his good fortune to wake up just as the altercation began, and he sent up a holler through the ranks. Within moments the media whipped itself into a frenzy, and sleepy-eyed cameramen, reporters, drivers, and others commandeered vehicles of all descriptions for the chase. The buzz began to circulate on the AM dial even as Jordan vanished around the house and down the path. The media vehicles vigilantly patrolled Sand Castle Drive, passing each other time and again as they circled like sharks smelling chum.

Jordan bypassed the path that led to the Silversteins' house next door. Instead he slipped down a little-used trail that veered inland onto drier footing. But his muddy footprints betrayed his turn and Deleese, accompanied by a posse of officers, followed closely behind.

Jordan gasped for breath as he reached the road several hundred yards from his house. A van with station call letters plastered on its side squealed to a halt. Jordan had forgotten about the media.

"There he is!"

A cameraman spilled out of the van and aimed his camera at Jordan.

"Jordan, over here," the female reporter called.

Jordan darted across the road and into the woods not stopping to reply, but the cameraman was delighted nonetheless to have captured a few seconds of Jordan on the run. The reporter wore high heels and was in no shape to give chase. The cameraman, weighted with a Portapak, tried a few steps but was no match for Jordan's fleetness.

Deleese and his troops emerged from the path moments later and the reporter directed them up the hill, proud to be of service. Bureau reinforcements came by way of sedan, and the fresh legs darted into the woods.

Jordan didn't know these paths as well as those around his house. But he caught a second wind, made a few calculated guesses and found himself just where he wanted to be, on Woodbury Road just over the ridge. Jordan hugged the manicured hedges of the posh homes, wary of every vehicle that drove by. The early-morning commuters shared the road with the media and police responding to the call. Jordan dove under a mulberry bush upon hearing a helicopter thunder overhead.

When traffic cleared, Jordan jogged a few houses down and dashed across the pavement. Then he walked up to the front door of a ranch home and buzzed the doorbell.

"Jordan, what the heck are you doing here?"

Arnie Sinkowitz, Jordan's *Newsday* friend, nearly spilled his coffee at the sight of his neighbor at his front door.

"You said to give you a ring if I ever needed help. Well, I need it now."

"What's going on?"

"I can't say. But, please, trust me."

"What do you need?"

"Your car."

"Are you a fugitive? I have to know that."

"I haven't broken any laws."

Arnie studied Jordan, almost wheezing now. "All right, let me get the keys."

"Can I step in for a moment?"

"Sure, of course. Would you like a cup of coffee?"

"I'd love one."

Jordan closed the door behind him just as a patrol car cruised by. As Jordan waited in the foyer, Arnie's children dragged themselves down the stairs. Lydia was the youngest, and Shoshonna was in Timmy's class. Jordan hadn't seen them in months. How they had grown.

Arnie returned. "Anything else?"

"A pair of sunglasses."

"In the glove box. Are you sure I should be doing this?"

"No."

"Then I won't ask what this is all about."

"Thanks."

"Good luck."

Jordan waited until the coast was clear then made a dash for the car. The Honda had tinted windows, that was good. Jordan fished for the sunglasses and pulled down the visor. As he drove through Rocky Cliff he passed three media vehicles, six patrol cars, and two unmarked sedans weighted down with agents. With coffee in hand he looked like another weary commuter bracing himself for the long haul ahead. In minutes he was headed south toward the L.I.E. and the motel. Only then did he take a moment to let out a sigh, take a chug of coffee, and wake up to face the day.

From a block away, Jordan saw the tired neon sign for the motel. Wanda didn't own a car, so Jordan didn't know what to look for. He parked around the corner just in case. The digital auto clock read 7:23.

Jordan peeked inside the motel office. Not a soul in sight. The motel rates, measured in hours, were posted plainly above the registration desk protected by a thick plate of glass.

Room 16 was on the bottom floor, one of a handful of squalid rooms behind a stucco wall of peeling aqua paint. An air-conditioning unit protruded from the front of the room. Years of dripping had left an orange splotch on the concrete walkway below. The unit was on full blast, a sure sign Wanda was in. This better be good.

Jordan knocked lightly.

"It's open."

Wanda sat on the edge of the bed, dressed to the nines, smoking a cigarette and flicking the ashes in an ashtray beside her. The room reeked of smoke and perfume.

"What took you so long?" she asked.

"What do you want?"

"Don't be so brusque, Jordan. Tell me, how are you doing?"

"I don't have time for chatter."

"Then I'll get to the point," said Wanda, tapping her cigarette. "I know who the kidnapper is."

"Don't think you can fool me."

"I do know. I can prove it." Wanda took a drag of her smoke.

"Prove it, then."

"Capote, your cat. His paws were chopped off yesterday."

"How did you know that?"

"The kidnapper told me. No one knows it outside of the police."

"So maybe one of your inside sources told you. You've got plenty of them, I'm sure."

"I confirmed it with a source, but that's not how I found out. I wouldn't lie, Jordan. You know that. I wouldn't be here if I wasn't sure myself. I care about Timmy. I really do."

Jordan sat himself down on the far side of the bed and pondered the possibilities.

"Who is it then? And why are you telling me, why not the FBI?"

"Because the FBI doesn't have anything I want."

"Tell me who it is, goddamn it."

"Not so fast. You don't think I'd offer it up for free."

"You're making a deal?"

"You get what you want. I get what I want. What's so wrong with that?" Wanda smiled.

"Prostitutes make the same argument."

"I can walk out of here, Jordan, no skin off of my back."

Jordan paced the floor. He filled a plastic cup with water and quenched his thirst.

"What do you want?" he asked.

Wanda put down her cigarette and walked the few paces to her briefcase resting against the dresser.

She pulled out a sheath of paper and chucked it on the bed.

"What's this?" Jordan asked.

"It's a contract. For the life rights to your story. It covers books, movies—theatrical and television—news magazines, news programming, everything, exclusively and in perpetuity. Sign it and I'll tell you who the kidnapper is."

During the past week, each stunt pulled by Wanda had blindsided Jordan. With hindsight he realized that she had always remained in character. He was foolish to be surprised now.

"You are the scum of the earth," he said.

"Just doing my job."

"And if I strangled you right here, I'd be doing mine."

"Don't be so melodramatic, Jordan. It's only the rights to your story. Just think, you can have your son back. I'm sure by now you've given more than one maudlin speech on how you would gladly trade anything for Timmy. Well, here's your opportunity."

Jordan picked up the contract and scanned the pages. The terms were merciless.

"You know that if I sign, it will be under duress and it won't hold up in a court of law."

"I'll take your word that you won't contest it. Obviously your moral character is far greater than mine. Plus, somehow I can't envision the manly Jordan Stone standing up in a court of law complaining that he was coerced by a little old lady like me."

"And if he's not the kidnapper?" Jordan asked.

"Then the contract is null and void. That's in there, page twelve, you can check."

Jordan did check, and she was right.

"I don't see that you have any option here," said Wanda.

"How do I know you won't tell the FBI?" asked Jordan.

"You have my word. I've arranged to work away from the office today, remain elusive."

"You promise?"

"Promise," said Wanda.

Jordan felt the pressure of the seconds ticking away.

"I'll agree, with one addition," said Jordan.

"And what's that?"

"You never reveal the identity of the kidnapper to anyone. Even after it's over."

"Certainly people will find out."

"Not from me, not from you."

"But, Jordan, that's half the story."

"I'll walk. You know I will. I have to have that."

"Why?"

"That's my business."

"Okay, deal," said Wanda.

"Write it in the contract. Add it now."

Wanda drew a pen from her purse and penned the addition, adding her initials to the margin.

"See how accommodating I can be?"

Then she twirled the pen in her fingers and handed it to Jordan.

"Wanda, you will live to regret this."

"The sequel, eh?" she said with a smile.

With a flourish Jordan etched his name on the dotted line and dated it.

"Now, you tell me, and you tell me everything."

"It's Arthur Hedlund. Dr. Arthur Hedlund. I visited him last night at an apartment in the city, but he doesn't live there. No one does. We checked it. Here's the address. But Timmy's not there, I'm sure of that. We tried to track him down, but no luck. He mentioned that Timmy was being held out in the middle of nowhere. He told me about Capote and the paws. The slip showed on his face like egg. I have it on tape. He's weird, Jordan. It's him. I'm certain of it."

"What else do you know about him?"

"Here's his phone number, but the calls have been forwarded to an undisclosed location, we checked it. And here are tapes of our interview last night."

Wanda handed him an audio and video tape.

"See how much I care about you? Anyway, listen closely, you'll see what I mean. It's him."

"What else?"

"That's it, honestly."

"Now I never want to see you again," Jordan said, turning to leave.

"Wait, Jordan."

Wanda took out her checkbook, tore off a check and handed it to Jordan.

"What's this?" he asked.

"It's a check for one dollar. Consideration for your signature. It's necessary to make the contract legal. Take it, please."

Jordan snatched the check from her hand. He tore it up in little pieces and scattered it over the motel parking lot as he ran to his car.

Alone now, Wanda picked up the contract and admired Jordan's signature. Then she kissed the contract and returned it into her briefcase.

In the car, Jordan slipped the cassette into the tape player and listened. Wanda had been right about Hedlund's demeanor. He sounded guilty as hell. But it was something else that convinced Jordan that Wanda was correct.

He rewound the tape and listened.

Wouldn't every little child be scared, I mean, to be cooped up in a room out in the middle of nowhere. What a tragic irony, don't you think?

It was that term "tragic irony." Jordan had heard it before recently. He racked his brain, and then it dawned on him.

"No tricks, and this tragic irony will end. I will allow no second chances." That's what the kidnapper had said in his original ransom message. He had allowed a second chance, but a tragic irony it remained, and the peculiar phrase turned twice, convinced Jordan that Hedlund indeed was the man.

Now came the hard part, finding him before the 12:06 train blew its whistle. Four hours to go.

The confusion around her induced Allie to seek the serenity of the back porch. During these past days, the few assumptions Allie had held had crumbled like castles of sand. She hesitated to hope for anything at all, fearful her desire would be dashed by yet another unexpected turn. With the deadline four hours away and her husband out chasing a lead that could be as spurious as its source, how would it all end? Allie didn't dare to guess.

She was deep in thought when she felt Deleese tap her on her shoulder. Suddenly she was awakened to the sounds coming from inside the house: the agents calling around furiously gathering information about Wanda, attempting to track Jordan, arguing with network executives, fielding press calls, and Waters enduring dress-downs from the hierarchy above him—from the supplicant tone of Waters' voice—way above him.

"Sorry to interrupt," he said.

"Please," said Allie with a wave of her hand.

Deleese's presence had always grounded Allie, and it succeeded in doing so again now.

"We need your help, Allie."

"My help?"

"I'm afraid so."

Allie didn't wait for the invitation. She took a deep breath and began her confession.

"Jordan knows everything. He knows about your plans to drop the box from the train, the SWAT team, everything."

Deleese was rattled by the news. "How? How did he f-find out?"

"It was me. I told him. I overheard you preparing last night in the dining room. I had to tell him. He has an electric saw in his office. He was planning to slice off his hands this morning and he wanted me to help. I couldn't let him do it."

"Why didn't you tell us earlier?"

"I don't know. I promised him. I don't know, I just needed time to think about everything."

"I understand. Tell me, what did Jordan say to you when he left this morning?"

"Just that Wanda had some information and he believed her."

"Where was he going, did he say?"

"No."

Deleese seemed hesitant to speak, as if what he was about to say was distasteful. "What do you know about Wanda and Jordan?"

"What do you mean?"

"About the k-kind of relationship they had."

"If you're asking me if they slept together, the answer is yes. But what does that have to do with anything?"

"I'm just protecting you."

"From what?" asked Allie, truly puzzled.

"Listen."

Deleese flipped on the recording of Wanda and Jordan's phone conversation earlier. Allie shuddered at the sound of Wanda's voice.

I have some information, Wanda had told Jordan. *It's worth your while, believe me. But you'll have to meet me someplace. Alone.*

Where, Jordan responded.

At the first place we made love. Do you remember? said Wanda.

Deleese switched off the machine. "I'm sorry. It's just—"

"Don't be sorry, I would look inside the gates of hell to get my boy back."

"Do you know where, by chance, that place may be?"

Allie remembered back to the moment she first discovered the affair between Wanda and Jordan. It happened all by chance. She was in Hempstead, for a podiatrist appointment for Sarah's pigeon toes. Sarah was young then, two, maybe three, and the impediment was easily remedied. But that day, coming back from the doctor's, Allie got lost and ended up in an uncomfortable part of town. As she searched for a gas station to ask directions, she past a rundown motel and spotted Jordan's car. He was driving a Chevy at the time, undistinguished except for a bumper sticker not fully scraped off. It read "The First Amendment. Your right to think."

Jordan at a motel in the middle of the day? Allie was sure he would have an explanation and since she passed the *Newsday* offices on her way home, she decided to stop. Allie and Wanda had been on their way to becoming casual friends by then. They had been introduced at a noisy office party, then Wanda came to the house one Sunday. They even had lunched together a few times, always with a promise of seeing each other again. That day, with Sarah on her lap, Allie waited at Jordan's desk, which abutted Wanda's, a coincidence Jordan had neglected to reveal. The two lovers walked in. Wanda's expression was clueless, but Jordan had guilt written all over his face like newsprint.

Later that evening Jordan tried to deny everything. But Allie was no fool, and Jordan eventually confessed that he and Wanda had had sex a few times, always at the motel during the day. Allie intuitively felt that it had been more than a few times, but there was little use in arguing numbers. The damage had been done.

Remember that motel? Allie even remembered the cheap blue paint peeling from the exterior. Nor would she ever forget the name of that place, apropos as it was.

"The Breakers," she told Deleese. "It's down the island, in Hempstead."

"Thank you."

"Just bring me back my son alive."

TWENTY-THREE

Jordan hadn't been gone but two minutes when Wanda heard a knock on the motel door. She glanced around for car keys, thinking Jordan must have forgotten his, why else would he return?

When she opened the door, she didn't find an absent-minded Jordan as expected, rather she cast her eyes upon a thick cluster of grim-faced FBI agents, commanded by the intimidating Waters, seething with anger. Waters skipped the usual introductions and led with an open hand that extended around Wanda's throat and thrust her backward until she was pressed against the rear wall of the motel room gasping for breath.

"Now, you listen and you listen good," said Waters. Spittle flew from his mouth.

"You tell me everything that you know, and everything that you told Stone or I will put you away for as long as the law allows."

"Get your hands off of me." Wanda coughed out the words.

Waters loosened his grip. "Now talk."

"Don't you ever touch me again like that, ever."

As the agents groped through the room, looking for anything of interest, Wanda dusted herself off, and with palms facing outward she reclaimed enough personal space for her to breath. Then she deliberately spent more than a few seconds tapping out a cigarette and lighting it up. Time and space were hers again.

"Now, perhaps we can start over, politely," she said.

"I'll give the orders around here."

"You don't scare me, Agent Waters. I'm surprised, frankly, to find you are still on this case, considering the rumors I've been hearing."

"Save the antics for someone else. Let me put it to you plainly. You tell us everything you know or we will slap an injunction on your program that will last until menopause."

"How dramatic. Did you rehearse that little speech coming over here? Good job. Unfortunately, I have nothing to say. I have a constitutional right to protect my sources."

"And I have a constitutional right to throw you in jail."

"Tit for tat. We can play all day, if you'd like," said Wanda with a puff. She sat on the bed and crossed her legs.

"Ms. Gentry," Deleese said, stepping in between his boss and Wanda. His voice was soft, almost reverential. He looked at the floor as he spoke.

"I don't know how much you know about the kidnapper. But he is a very sick man, mentally. We have good reason to believe he is preparing to kill Timmy at this moment. I respect your right to protect your sources, but we have a little boy out there who is in danger of losing his l-life. We have a far better chance of finding and stopping the kidnapper than Jordan could ever have. Please, for the sake of the boy, tell us what you know."

Wanda dragged hard on her cigarette.

"Well, it's nice to see someone knows how to communicate around here," said Wanda.

"Please, help us," Deleese implored.

"All right. But I'll want favors in return."

"No favors," retorted Waters.

"Well, we'll talk later about that," said Wanda. "Anyway, I could be wrong, of course, but I think I know who the kidnapper is."

"Who?" Waters demanded.

"His name is Kincaid. Bill Kincaid."

Wanda proceeded to tell the agents all she knew about Kincaid, including the tidbit about the B&D book on his coffee table.

"But don't take my word for it," she added. "I would hate to be the source of erroneous information."

Jordan tried to think of all the methods of finding people he had used before he was spoiled by the luxuries of a computer and a deadline measured in months not hours. He pulled into a 7-Eleven store and checked the phone book. No residential listing for the Hedlunds, but he did find a professional listing not far away for Dr. Arthur Hedlund, orthopedist. He jumped in his car and burned up no more than twelve minutes getting there.

The office was crowded with the elderly and mothers with their children. Everyone instantly recognized Jordan as he strolled up to the reception desk, and the cacophony gave way to a rare silence.

"I'm looking for Dr. Hedlund. Dr. Arthur Hedlund."

"I'm sorry but he hasn't had a practice here in over a year," said the receptionist.

"I realize that, but do you know where he has gone? Where I might find him?"

"Wait here one moment," she said.

Jordan turned to the stares of the patients in the waiting room, some holding copies of *Time* and *Newsweek* with his grim photo on the cover. Young children stared at him as if he were Big Bird. A young doctor appeared with a stethoscope dangling around his neck and a lapel pin of a smiling face.

"Dr. Hedlund left our offices abruptly. We've been attempting to locate him, too. We have some papers we'd like to serve him with. But no luck, I'm afraid."

"When did he leave?"

"Last year, right after the death of his son."

As he drove through town, Jordan tried to conjure up the faint recollections he had of Arthur Hedlund. There wasn't much. Jordan had done precious little research while writing *Slaughter Alley,* extracting most of the story from court transcripts. He had attempted to contact Hedlund but with no luck, though Jordan had to admit his attempts had been half-hearted at best.

As it were, all he could rely on was Wanda's audio tape, the faint recollection Jordan had of Hedlund's performance on Wanda's show, and the taped ransom messages from Hedlund, if, indeed, he was the kidnapper. The man seemed so ordinary in every way, his looks, persona, even his voice was monotonous and dull, as if—and the thought sent a lump to Jordan's throat—as if he were a robot, void of emotion, understanding, or empathy.

Jordan stopped at a phone booth to pull a risky stunt. He dialed his novel-writing friend, Fred Griff, at the detective division of the Nassau County Police Department.

"Fred," said Jordan. "This is your mentor."

"Jo-," said Griff. But he stopped short, realizing the ramifications of uttering Jordan's name on a phone line that was perpetually tapped.

"What the hell are you doing calling here?"

"Help me, please. Arthur Hedlund. H-E-D-L-U-N-D," Jordan said. "Please give me what you got on him. I'll call back in five minutes."

Jordan hung up before Griff could reject his plea, then drove across town just in case the cops were perceptive enough to recognize the voice and trace the call back.

Jordan looked at his clock, 9:37. Not much time. How would he cut off his hands now? How would he deliver them? Perhaps he should return to the house, tell Waters everything, and let the Bureau handle it. But then he remembered his promise to the kidnapper not to involve police.

Jordan plunked in a quarter and redialed Griff's number. The detective answered before the first ring finished.

"It's me," said Jordan.

"Nothing, and the records were recently checked by the FBI, too."

"How recently?"

"Last couple of days."

"What do you mean nothing?"

"The guy just vanished. The mortgage holder is looking for him, his partners are looking for him, credit card companies up the ass are looking for him. He dusted his tracks pretty good."

"Fred, thanks."

Jordan ached with panic. Then suddenly it dawned on him, the oldest trick in the newspaper business. He fed a quarter into the phone and called *Newsday*.

"Accounts receivable," said the voice in a pleasant tone.

"Who's this?" Jordan asked.

"Terri."

"Oh, hi Terri. This is Arnie Sinkowitz up in Editorial. I'm doing a story and I'm looking for someone's number, but for the life of me, I can't find it. I'm sure they subscribe. Could you check it out for me?"

"Sure, Mr. Sinkowitz."

"Great. It's Hedlund. Arthur Hedlund." Jordan gave the spelling.

Jordan dripped in sweat as he heard Terri clicking

the keys on her computer. He peeked around the convenience store. No one had yet recognized him.

"I'm sorry, Mr. Sinkowitz. No Hedlund."

"Should I try another spelling?"

"No, that won't be—yes, please."

Terri tapped away gingerly.

"Ah, here it is, Arthur Hedland, he spells it L-A-N-D. You want it?"

"Yes."

Jordan hastily jotted down the address, but to what avail, he thought. Arthur Hedland with an *a* could very well be a different person altogether, someone as far removed from the kidnapping as Terri on the other end of the line. What were the chances that the spelling discrepancy was a simple data entry error, or even a deliberate slip by Hedlund designed to keep creditors at bay. Not good.

"Hey look, while I've got you on the line, do you have his address, too? Just in case," asked Jordan.

"Sure, it's 18746 Route 43, Sag Harbor, New York."

"Sag Harbor? That's out in Suffolk County, isn't it?" asked Jordan.

"Way out, almost to Montauk."

Bingo.

"Thanks, Terri."

"Hope I've helped."

"You have."

Jordan thought about calling the number just to see who would answer, but he decided against it. His calling card certainly was being tracked for usage, and he would have to go inside the convenience store for change to make the toll call. And why alarm Hedlund. With the mention of Montauk, Jordan was willing to take the calculated risk that it was, indeed, Hedlund. *"Out in the middle of nowhere,"* the kidnapper had told Wanda. Sag Harbor certainly fit the bill.

There was time yet to make the delivery as promised.

* * *

Wanda was pleased with her performance with the FBI, and was dying to call Mort and give him the news now that her scheme was a fait accompli. But she hesitated to call from the motel room for fear the Bureau may have tapped the line. Instead, she waited for the cab to take her to the train station, where she chose a pay phone on the platform and dialed in.

"You won't believe what as just happened, Mort." In a whisper Wanda told her boss briefly about the interviews last night with Kincaid and Hedlund.

"We had the kidnapper on the show, Mort! Hedlund. It's Hedlund. That tape is worth millions."

She proudly talked about her deal with Jordan, how she fooled the FBI and left Jordan to his own devices, a much better story in the end.

The train rumbled into the station.

"Gotta go," she said.

Still smiling, she picked up her briefcase and boarded the train to Penn Station.

Wanda couldn't know it, but Waters and Deleese heard the train chug away. They listened to the transmission coming from the hidden microphone Deleese had planted in Wanda's briefcase while Waters held her neck up against the wall. Nothing like a little diversion to plant a microphone.

"I told you she was lying," said Waters. "Kill the stakeout on Kincaid. It's all systems go on Arthur Hedlund. And get a Bureau attorney to start filing charges against that woman. I want her hanged."

Arthur Hedlund gazed out upon the rows of orderly corn crackling under the late-morning heat. Hedlund couldn't remember a hotter summer.

He unlocked the door to Timmy's room and saw the boy prostrate on the bed, suffering the early effects of dehydration. The heat seeped through the walls like a liquid. What the hell, Hedlund thought, and he brought the boy two Yoo-Hoos. Timmy drank lustily and the chocolate drink ran down his cheeks onto his pajamas.

"You see," said Hedlund, "I'm not so bad after all."

"Thank you," said Timmy.

"Now listen, young man. I'm going to be leaving soon for a few hours. I want you to remain calm and relaxed. It's a hot one. When I return, you'll be able to shake your father's hand."

"Really?" Timmy's eyes brightened.

"Really." Hedlund chuckled. "So nothing foolish, okay?"

"Okay."

"I don't have time to buy more Twinkies, so you'll have to wait."

"I'm very hungry."

"I said wait," Hedlund said angrily. "You're so petulant. Every time I try to be nice to you, my God, you snap back. You're just like my son. You're all the same."

Hedlund closed the door and double-checked the lock. Everything had to be perfect now. No room for mistakes, no place for uncertainty. He picked up a ratty Long Island train schedule and calculated again just when he expected the train to cross Waring Road, a desolate dirt lane that bisected a pumpkin patch and was as far from civilization as one could get in these parts. His cellular phone had been in the recharging cradle all night ready to call the beeper number, and his .38 was cleaned and loaded. He stashed the handgun behind his back and patted it affectionately.

He checked his watch, it was coming on noon. Jordan's hands would be boarding the train in minutes. Another hour-and-a-half and Hedlund would be in possession of Stone's hands. The thought of actually holding them now excited Hedlund to no end. He longed to actually touch the decaying members, to pos-

sess Jordan's power once and for all. It would have to
be for only a moment, for surely the Bureau would
conceal within them a positioning device.

He brought along all the tools necessary to check the
fingerprints on the spot, just like last time. Only this
time he also packed his battery-operated surgical saw.
He figured the FBI would pack the hands tightly this
time, so he couldn't rip and run, so to speak. No matter
how well-packed the hands, the saw would rip through
the packaging, and with the train moving at sixty miles
per hour, it would be virtually impossible for the Bureau to predict the moment of release. They could follow with a helicopter, but Hedlund had a plan for that,
too. He would park the van some two miles away and
hide underneath a culvert with a moped, just large
enough to get him cruising at 40 miles per hour and
small enough to cross the thin and weak bridges he had
constructed over the irrigation ditches along the route
back to his vehicle. Should the agents come out with
motorcycles, the weight of their heavy machines would
crush the wood planks and send the men tumbling to
the sloppy mud below. The end game was near and
Hedlund thrilled at the thought of winning.

As he went over his plans one last time, he thought
about turning on the television for the noon news but
decided against it, preferring instead to watch the sun
climb to its zenith. The news would be a distraction at
this moment when reverence and prayer were required.
And he did just that.

He bent on one knee, pressed his hands together and
silently thanked God Almighty for choosing him as his
agent of truth in a world so dearly in need of justice.

As he flew east on the Southern State Parkway, Jordan
flipped on the radio and listened to the shock jocks run
with the story.

"Jordan Stone, where are you?" the jock yodeled to the tune of Car 54.

"If you're out there, Jordan, tell us what it's like to drive with stumps. Hope you're on a straightaway, old buddy. Sudden turns could be disastrous. And while you're at it, wave at the good people of the state of New York, let them see those bandages, will you? Let's have some fun here. And let's go to the phones. Mildred in Babylon."

"I think you're disgusting," said Mildred in Babylon. "This is a tragedy and you're making it a joke. You—"

Click.

"Ah, shut up, Mildred. Go ask your old man to take his hands out of his pants and put them on you for the first time in twenty years. Next call, Monty in Bay Ridge."

"Why don't Stone trust the FBI? Why is he on the run? I'll tell you. They're all a bunch of friggin' liberals now. They can't shoot straight."

"Monty, let me ask you something. Is everybody in Bay Ridge named Monty? Oh, excuse me, there are a few Tonys out there, too. My apologies. But does everyone share your low I.Q.? You're a dumb ass, Monty. You hear me? A dumb ass. Go drink a Bud and stick your wong in that hole in your mattress because your wife is out screwing your boss. You're an idiot. Can you spell that, Monty? E-D-E-I-T, Monty. Go practice."

"Now, Stumpy, listen to me. Get on that cell phone and call us, will you? Use your nose to press zero if you can't punch those numbers. I'll tell you what. Let's have some fun here. I'll give $1,000 cash to anyone who spots Jordan Stone on the road, confirmed, and two tickets to my New Year's Eve ball. Go get him, New York."

Jordan pulled down the visor and tightened the fit on his sunglasses. Jordan was sure the couple in the next car was gawking at him, but he didn't dare turn to acknowledge their stares. Instead, he slowed down and let them move forward. When they finally exited ahead, Jordan speeded up and changed lanes.

"Jordan, is that you on the Southern State Parkway moving east?" said the jock.

"Phil and Joanne Angelides of Patchogue thought they saw you driving a late-model Honda Accord, silver in color. Jordy, we got you."

Shit. Jordan saw a sign for the Sagtikos State Parkway North and he veered off quickly. He would hook up again with the L.I.E., but the detour would lose him fifteen minutes. He had no choice now. He slumped down in his seat and turned up the radio.

"Come out, come out where ever you are," howled the jock. "Jordan, we love you. We'll give you an escort, O.J. style. We *want* you to find what you're looking for. We're on *your* side."

In the distance Jordan saw a police helicopter thundering south toward the Southern State Parkway. Jordan eased down to the speed limit and the helicopter cruised by without a pause.

When he noticed the gas gauge on one-eighth of a tank, Jordan turned the air conditioner on low. He estimated he had sixty miles to travel still, and no way could he afford to stop at a gas station.

He picked up speed and turned east on the expressway, traveling through Ronkonkoma, Holtsville, and Medford. Then he took a secondary road south, where he saw his first sign for Sag Harbor, 20 miles away. He checked the gas gauge. It had fallen below empty and strayed perilously into the red zone. The highway ended at Shinnecock Hills, and Jordan had no choice but to travel a two-lane road through a series of languid intersections, only a few of which were punctuated with stop lights. Finally, he reached the small village of Sag Harbor.

Jordan checked his watch, 12:02. Now the problem

was finding Route 43. He pulled over at an intersection on the near edge of town. On one corner gleamed a newly sprouted Shell station with a dozen pumps. Across the way, stood an old-fashioned filling station manned by a lone teenager drinking an RC Cola as he leaned back on a lawn chair. The kid was preoccupied with swatting away buzzing flies and reshaping his baseball cap. Jordan pulled into the pump and stuck his neck out slightly.

"Route 43, do you know where it is?"

"About a mile down, turn right. Hey, ain't you Jordan Stone? Shit, I could win $1,000 bucks."

The teenager ran inside and jumped on the pay phone. Jordan followed him inside and wrapped his fingers tightly around the boy's neck.

"You listen to me, kid. If I find out you made any call to anyone, I'll come back here and shove my stumpy hand up your ass so far you'll burp blood. Do you understand me?"

The kid gulped for air and nodded yes.

"Good. Now, I want you to go out there and pump my car with gas, full service. Got me?"

The kid gulped again and Jordan let him down. He filled the Honda and returned inside dutifully. Jordan kicked him in the balls for good measure, then dashed to his car and sped away.

The AM station was fading now, but Jordan heard the caller through the breakup.

"Scott in Sag Harbor, you're on the line."

"He just kicked me in the balls and made me fill his tank."

"Whoa, slow down there, Sonny. What are you talking about?"

"Jordan Stone. He said he'd shove his stump up my rear end if I told anyone he was here. Honest."

"Scotty, fess up. You got your friends with you. You're drinking beer. You're all bored out of your simple minds. You're looking to pull a prank. So you call us. Well, beam yourself up to the *Starship Enterprise,* Scotty, because I'm wise to your crap. The FBI just issued a statement on the wire. It said they've caught Jordan Stone and he's in their custody, or care, or whatever they call it."

"I'm not lying," said Scotty. "I want my thousand bucks."

"Hey, Scotty, dork brain, do me a favor would you? Piss on someone else but not on me, okay?"

Click.

Scotty pulled his boom box outside, and as he filled tanks and wiped windshields, he tried to figure out exactly what was going on.

His preoccupation prevented him from noticing the brown sedan roll through the intersection carrying four men in suits. His balls hurt too much for him to notice anything at all.

Jordan slowed to a crawl as he took a right onto Route 43, a narrow two-lane with a phantom yellow line that only occasionally marked the center of the pavement. The road undulated gently as it passed through fields of leaning corn stalks, broken and angular. He passed occasional farmhouses, relics of a bygone era save for the giant television satellite dishes installed near each house. Jordan followed the addresses on the mailboxes, some painted black-and-white like Holstein cows, others decorated by crafty welders, and others unadorned altogether, except for the fading street numbers painted in the simplest of type styles.

There was no mailbox in front of house that rightly should have been 18746. Jordan traveled to 18752 then turned and drove the quarter mile back.

The house was little more than a cabin with a tar roof. So much green paint had peeled off the clapboard siding that the shack was more gray than green. The screen door had a hole the width of a raccoon, and the windows were shuttered tight. A tan van was parked out front, and the morning's *Newsday* lay folded on the crumbling asphalt driveway.

Jordan rolled past the house and parked his car behind a small crest shaded by an elm tree. Then he walked to the front door, blood red in color, and knocked politely.

TWENTY-FOUR

After his moment of prayer, Hedlund indulged his lesser urges and zapped on the television news. If he had to endure the tedium of the wait, he might as well do so accompanied by the unending spew of tales of corruption, sex, and murder, which ran together like an intravenous feeding of some second-rate narcotic. His wristwatch told him it was 12:23, another hour before the train would speed by. He had prepared too early, foresaw all the possibilities, and now he was left with time on his hands, that was the problem.

Hedlund perked up when he saw Stone's photo flash on the television screen, followed by a bumpy video segment of Stone running across a road near his home and up a footpath with FBI agents in hot pursuit. Now here was worthy programming.

The tape shrank to a small square on the upper right-hand corner of the screen as a somber-faced anchor picked up the narration.

"The FBI is reporting that Jordan Stone is back in custody this afternoon after fleeing from his home early this morning following an altercation with Bureau agents. Unconfirmed sightings from motorists had spotted Stone as far away as New Jersey, the eastern edge of Long Island, and southern Vermont.

"It's not known what caused this morning's altercation or how or where Stone was apprehended, but sources close to the Bureau have hinted that Stone indeed had attempted to cut off his hands this morning to comply with the ransom request of the kidnapper. The sources would neither confirm nor deny reports that Stone was successful. We'll break into programming as updates warrant. Be sure to catch a complete recap of the day's events in the kidnapping of Tiny Tim with your *Live at Five* news team tonight.

Hedlund chuckled. There it was, his answer. The hands of Stone were on the train and soon would be his. *Triumphant Lord, I am your servant.*

With the bounce back in his step, Hedlund tidied up a little and even ventured to whistle a tune. He flipped around the stations for more news of Stone, but found only soap operas and talk shows, two even more feeble narcotics, thought Hedlund.

Then came the knock on the door.

Hedlund lowered the volume on the television. Had he heard correctly? A knock on the door? No, it must be a mistake. He remained still, hoping to banish the gremlin cruel enough to play such a trick.

He waited in anticipation and heard nothing, and with each silent second grew more confident that the knock was merely a figment of his imagination, a subconscious fear manifesting itself in this disturbing manner. No one would knock on this door. No one ever had.

Knock, knock, knock.

God, no. The reverberations coursed through his nerves.

No way. Not now.

Hedlund remained still for what seemed like minutes. He hoped, prayed the visitor would lose faith and leave. *Make them go away,* he implored silently to the

God that had benevolently blessed his mission until this moment.

Another soft but insistent rap on the door sent a dull dose of dread through Hedlund's body. He crept to the window and stretched his neck to cop a peek outside, but the view was obstructed by the shutters he had fastened so well over the front windows.

Goddamn it. Please, no.

Another knock. Who could be so insistent, so rude as to knock a third time? An intrepid salesman? An evangelist? A lost motorist? Please go away, Hedlund pleaded. Go away.

But again the gentle rapping of a hand.

There was no choice now. Hedlund had to answer. All else would provoke suspicion when none was justified. He collected his thoughts, rehearsed his alibi. He was alone, enjoying the solitude of a cabin that belonged to his dead ex-wife's family. Nothing more. A friendly smile and a knowing nod were all that were necessary to send the visitor away satisfied. Hedlund emboldened himself and wiped the sweat from his hands.

And then he remembered Timmy. What if the boy shouted, cried. The boy could ruin everything. Hedlund crept to Timmy's room and pressed his ear against the bolted door to listen for sounds of life. Nothing.

"You stay quiet, boy, or else. Do you understand?"

Timmy offered no response and Hedlund could not take the time to drive home his threat.

Again the rapping on the door. Hedlund approached. The floorboards creaked. He cracked his lip practicing a smile. He breathed deeply and toweled off the sweat from his forehead with his sleeve. His hands felt clammy and he decided not to shake hands no matter who he came upon. Make it easy, make it fast, make no mistakes.

He unfastened the chain. At first he thought to peek

the length of the chain. But no, he had nothing to be afraid of. He could not show fear.

With a gulp, he opened the door wide. The white light of the midday sun blinded him. He squinted to adjust. At first he saw nothing more than the murky outline of a human being. But as his eyes grew accustomed to the glare, the outline surrendered to detail.

Hedlund reeled back on his heels. His hand instinctively reached for the .38 nestled in the small of his back.

"Freeze!" Hedlund shouted, his fingers trembling on the trigger. "Freeze, or I'll shoot."

Jordan Stone obliged.

His eyes, too, were adjusting, to the shadows inside. And when the darkness and light merged, Jordan took his first look at the abductor. His eyes were filled with fear, apprehension, loneliness, not the monster Jordan had imagined.

With a quick glance Jordan surveyed the lay of the living room: the overstuffed chair, the television, the kitchen beyond. He instantly recognized the telltale wallpaper pattern, which he had memorized from hours of staring at the photo of his imprisoned son. And he saw a publicity photo of Wanda Gentry pinned to the wall above the TV. Jordan redirected his stare at Hedlund, locking on the eyes full of fright.

"Here," Jordan said gently. "I've come to give you these."

Jordan extended his hands, both of them, palms upward.

"Turn around." Hedlund yelled. "Hands up. Against the wall!"

Jordan moved slowly inside, a willing captive. He spread his feet and pressed his palms against the flower designs of the wallpaper, one hand per flower. He felt the odious breath of Hedlund as he patted Jordan down, first his arms, then legs, crotch, and abdomen.

From the corner of his eye Jordan spotted the thick padlock on the bedroom door.

"I have no weapons," Jordan said.

"Turn around." The voice trembled.

Jordan turned slowly and again he extended his hands.

"Here. You asked for my hands. I give them willingly. Use what you will. Cut them off. Just give me back my son."

Hedlund gawked at Jordan's hands as if they were alien matter. How could it be possible that Jordan Stone stood before him with his hands attached and not a trace of trepidation in his voice? How, at this hour so close to triumph? Hedlund had never prepared himself for such an improbability.

Suddenly it dawned on Hedlund that Jordan must not be alone. This was a setup, a snare. He peered out the door, searching up and down the road for cars, action, any sign of conspiracy.

"What about the police?"

"They don't know. They're still looking for me."

"On the news . . ."

"It's a lie. They want everyone out of the way. They have your beeper. They intercepted your message. They're out to get you. But they don't know who you are or where you live. Only I do. I've come alone. To meet your demands. You have my word."

Hedlund studied the man he had spent so much time plotting against. He was a man, a tired, grizzled man in need of a shave and a nap.

"Why should I trust you?" Hedlund said.

"Do you think the FBI would let me come here unarmed if I was with them?"

"What do you want?"

The answer was simple. "I want my son," said Jordan, eyeing the padlocked door.

"You want your son," Hedlund said. "You think you can come in here and walk out with him."

"Take my hands." Jordan extended them again, baring his wrists ready for the slashing.

"Take them. That's what you asked for. I'm ready to give them. That was the deal. Wasn't it? My hands for my son."

"I could kill you, that would be easier."

"You're not a killer. You're a giver of life, a doctor. A good doctor, I understand."

"Don't patronize me," said Hedlund.

"And I'm sorry about your son. I truly am."

"No, you're not," Hedlund snapped back. "You didn't even know my son, yet you wrote about him like he was scum. You killed him, Stone. You."

"You're right," Jordan said.

Hedlund tightened his grip and grinded his teeth.

"Don't patronize me, I said. You make me sick. You'll say anything, do anything to get what you want. You're just like them. All of them. You didn't know my son. He didn't even do it."

"Tell me what happened, then."

"Tell you? Okay, I'll tell you. He was there when the girl was raped and murdered. But he didn't do it. He tried to stop them. Him, Josh, my little coward. He tried to stop the killing but he couldn't, he didn't have the power. You should see how he cried afterward. You didn't know my boy."

"I was wrong, hasty. I admit it. I'll accept blame willingly for my part in his death."

"What good is your apology to me now?" said Hedlund.

"Only you can answer that. But I want my son back, and I'm willing to pay the price you set."

"You must be crazy, Stone."

"You would do anything to get your son back. To have a second chance. So would I."

"I don't have that luxury anymore. You have a son still. Do you want to hear a story? I guess you don't have much of a choice, do you? The last time I saw Josh, we got into a fight, and I kicked him out into the snow. The following morning on my way to work, I saw him asleep at a bus stop. I don't even know which one. Huddled and cold, like a tramp. He killed himself soon after—shamed by your book and that filthy movie they made of it. Where is Josh's name? Where is it? It exists in your words, on your pages. It was his good name and you painted it black. That's what is left of him, Jordan Stone, your dirty words. Sometimes I feel like—"

Hedlund lifted the gun. He squeezed the trigger ever so slightly, lifting the hammer from its rest.

"Then you know the pain of losing a son. I lost my son, too, once. I looked out the window and he was gone," said Jordan.

But Hedlund wasn't listening, his regrets held center stage.

"You think you know loss? You don't know loss," Hedlund continued. "Even Timmy isn't lost. Not yet. Loss is when there is no hope left. When there is nothing but pain."

"I can't bring Josh back. All I can do is give you what you've asked for. Here. You win. You made your point, to me and the whole world. I was wrong. I apologize. I can't do more. Take them. My hands. They're yours."

"Mine," Hedlund mimicked.

Hedlund remembered the portable surgical saw waiting on the kitchen table. He walked backward into the kitchen, taking his eye off Jordan for one brief second. Jordan saw the opportunity to run, jump, fight. But he chose not to resist.

"Put your hands on the table, palms up."

Jordan moved slowly over to the dark wood table near the door. He kneeled before it. He laid down his left hand and then his right. The veins in his wrist pulsed with tension. His fingers trembled.

"You deserve this, Stone. You had it coming. You owe the world this sacrifice and you're lucky I've asked for nothing more."

Hedlund hit the trigger of the saw, and it cut through the air with a whine. His finger pressed firmly against the trigger. He lowered the saw slowly, inching closer to Jordan's wrists.

"Wait. Please, tell me, before you cut. How is Timmy? Please tell me that much?"

Hedlund shot a glance at the padlocked door. "Timmy? Timmy is alive."

"May I see him? May I hug him once before I lose my hands, maybe my life."

"You're out of your mind, Stone."

"Please, let me see him, just to see that he is all right. Let me hug my son one last time. Only you have the power to grant me a last wish."

"Forget it."

"I'm giving up my hands. Show me that you're fulfilling your end of the bargain. Show me that he isn't harmed."

"You think I'm lying?" Hedlund asked angrily.

"Prove that you're a man of honor."

Hedlund wavered. "I don't lie."

"Good. One look is all I ask," said Jordan.

"That's it. One look."

"Okay."

Hedlund laid down the saw. He dug in his pocket for the key to Timmy's room and unfastened the padlock.

"Any wrong moves and I'll kill you both."

Jordan nodded in agreement. His hands tingled, crystals of sweat sparkled in his upturned palms.

Hedlund kicked open the door. The doorway was empty, a frame without a picture. Then, like an apparition, Timmy moved into view. Calm, gentle, and more beautiful than Jordan had ever remembered him.

"Daddy!"

Timmy reached out. His face awakened with joy. Jordan rushed to him. Hedlund be damned.

"Oh, Daddy I'm so glad you're here."

Jordan wrapped his arms around his son, reveling in Timmy's scent. His breath. His tiny body quivering like a bird.

"Thank God."

Jordan pressed Timmy against his chest. He kissed his face and neck. It felt so good to have his son back, like coming home.

Timmy wrapped his hands around his father's neck and vowed never to unwrap them again. Then he began to cry.

Jordan pulled back and studied Timmy for signs of abuse. He was emaciated, pale, tired. His right foot was wrapped with blood-stained bandages. Jordan wiped the tear from Timmy's cheek and kissed him once more.

"Don't worry, everything will be okay," Jordan whispered. He tried to smile.

"I just want to go home. Please take me home."

"I will."

Jordan stood and faced Hedlund.

"I gave you my word. You can have my hands."

Jordan waited obediently, ready for the cut. "Go ahead, cut them off."

Hedlund placed one hand upon the saw.

"But before you begin, think about this," said Jordan.

"Don't try to stop me, Stone."

"I won't, but think about the consequences of your action. Surely, I will die here today. And you will have to kill Timmy. And then they will have all the time in the world to find you. And they will. And they'll arrest you, and put you away for the rest of your life."

"What are you saying, Stone?"

Jordan pulled Timmy closer.

"There is another choice," said Jordan softly.

"And what is that?"

Jordan lowered his voice as if someone was listening in on this secret.

"Let us go. Let us walk out the door, and I promise no one will ever find out who you are. You will go free, Doctor, free instead of chained."

Hedlund's grip on the revolver did not waver.

"Do you know how many nights I've laid awake thinking about you, what I've wanted to do to you. This is bigger than even me, Mr. Stone."

"Yes, you're a big man. But you'll be small in prison. Why spend the rest of your life confined to a cell, at the mercy of inmates? You're a man of nobility. You deserve better."

"What a web you spin, Stone, with your silver tongue. You're a deceiver by birth. It's in your blood."

"What I'm saying is true."

"And how do you know they would catch me?"

"Sooner or later they will. You know that. I know it. Let us go. Save yourself."

Hedlund felt so unsure. Jordan was never supposed to be here. He was never supposed to find out. Everything had changed in the last few minutes. Everything had happened so fast. Hedlund's head swelled.

"Save yourself, Dr. Hedlund."

"I don't know. I can't think. Give me a minute."

Jordan saw the waver, however slight.

"I'm leaving now. And I'm taking Timmy," Jordan said.

He clutched his son tightly and took one step toward the door.

"Hold it right there!" ordered Hedlund. "I give the

orders around here. I'm in charge. Timmy, come here.
Come here now."

Timmy looked up at his father for guidance. Jordan's
tightened grip told Timmy to stay put.

"Timmy, you come here or I'll shoot your father."
Hedlund raised his gun. "You wouldn't want that,
would you? I'll shoot, I swear."

Timmy slipped from his father's grasp and ran to
Hedlund's side.

Hedlund stroked the boy's head. "See how quickly
the tide turns, Stone." Hedlund smiled.

"Go ahead then, shoot," Jordan said. He took a deliberate step toward the two.

"Get back!"

Jordan moved closer. "I'm not leaving here without
my son."

"Get back or I'll shoot. I will. I swear I will."

"Shoot, then." Jordan's gaze grew stronger.

"I'm warning you, Stone." Hedlund stepped back
and clasped the boy tighter.

"Shoot, I dare you."

"Don't do it Stone, you'll be sorry." Hedlund smoth-
ered Timmy's face in his thigh.

"You won't shoot me," said Jordan firmly.

Hedlund back pedaled until he reached the wall with
Wanda's photo tacked to it. He wanted to shoot. He
tried to pull the trigger. He tried so hard.

"I'm taking Timmy now," Jordan whispered.

"No you don't."

Jordan clasped Timmy's hand and gently pulled him
away from Hedlund.

"You'll be sorry," said Hedlund.

Hedlund's hand trembled under the weight of the
heavy revolver.

"Live, Doctor."

"I'm warning you, Stone." He wanted to shoot. Why
couldn't he shoot?

Jordan maneuvered himself between Timmy and Hedlund.

"Don't walk out on me, Stone."

"I will never let anyone know who you are. That is my promise."

Hedlund trembled with uncertainty.

"Wait. Stop. How do I know it's not a trap?"

"You have my word. That's all I can give."

Jordan moved methodically, inching closer to the bright path of light streaming in.

"Don't do it," Hedlund pleaded.

Jordan and Timmy stepped into the brilliant light. Timmy shielded his eyes from a sun he hadn't seen for days. Jordan slipped his son's hand in his.

"Don't go."

Hedlund tried once more to pull the trigger. His head felt light, his gut churned with regret. He felt everything come tumbling down, his grand plans to teach Stone a lesson, his scheme to enlighten the world. What had gone wrong? How had he failed? Why had his God turned on him so fiercely?

"Please, wait."

He aimed the gun once more, but it was useless.

"No clues, Stone, do you hear? No one finds out."

"No clues."

"I'll come after you if they find out. I'll kill your wife, and your babies, and you Stone. One word, Stone, and I'll kill you, I swear."

Jordan reached the driveway. "Stay calm," he whispered to Timmy. "Do exactly as I say. If anything happens to me, you run. Do you hear me? You run and don't stop."

"You're a lucky man to be walking away with your son, Mr. Stone. A very lucky man."

Jordan reached the road, Timmy limping beside him. Jordan slipped his hand into his pocket and searched for the key.

"I'm not so lucky, Stone."

Five paces to go. Five paces separated Jordan and Timmy from the shelter of the waiting car. Jordan pushed Timmy in front of him.

Four paces. Jordan strained to hear any final revocation from Hedlund.

Three paces. He gently nudged Timmy ahead.

Two paces. He quickened his step.

One.

"Get down!"

The voice rang out like a cannon shot.

Jordan pushed Timmy to the hot asphalt and spread over him for protection. Jordan searched for the source of the command. It came from behind him, down the road.

It was Waters.

"Get down!" he repeated, sidearm drawn.

Waters barked another order, but Jordan couldn't hear. The words were squelched by the rumble of the helicopter overhead. It appeared from nowhere. Streams of armed men spilled from the corn fields across the road. The glint of gun metal stung Jordan's eyes. An endless line of police cars, their lights flashing, sped closer from both directions. The air filled suddenly with the crackle of walkie-talkies, the grunts of troopers, and the trample of jackboots crushing dried cornstalks.

"No," Jordan whispered. A squad of men rushed toward Jordan and Timmy.

"No," he repeated.

A SWAT team flowed from the back of the house and converged around Hedlund. A second team shattered windows and poured into Hedlund's house from all sides. Hedlund stood helplessly surrounded, desperately aiming at everyone and aiming at no one instead.

"Drop the gun!" a voice ordered. Hedlund stumbled.

"Drop it!"

It wasn't supposed to happen like this, dear God. You said it wouldn't.

"Drop it or we'll shoot!"

Hedlund let the revolver slip from his fingers. It hit the hard earth with a thud.

Slowly Hedlund raised his hands.

The SWAT team swallowed him up, forcing him to the dusty soil and cuffing his hands behind his back.

"No," Jordan said. His pace quickened.

"Let him go. I gave him my word. You don't understand."

The helicopter swung down, whipping up a hot, deafening wind. Cars squealed to a halt on the barren lawn, unleashing torrents of dust.

"I promised," Jordan implored all of them. "Go away, get out of here."

But Jordan's words fell like flies in heat. Hedlund lifted his cheek and stared at Jordan.

"I didn't know. I swear I didn't know," Jordan mouthed the words, shaking his head.

Jordan couldn't hear Hedlund's response above the din, but he could see the pain of betrayal in the man's eyes. Jordan beseeched understanding with his hands. But to no avail. The deed was done.

The agents whisked Hedlund away to a dark sedan at the far end of the yard, forcing him into the backseat. Four agents stationed themselves at each corner of the car. The sentry had begun.

Jordan wanted to banish the agents from the site, to turn time back two minutes and drive away with Timmy, leaving Hedlund to his own devices, fulfilling the promise he swore to keep. But Jordan knew it had to end this way, the final plot twist.

A tap on his shoulder snapped Jordan back to reality.

"It's over," said Waters.

"I made a promise," said Jordan, kicking the dust. But he knew he couldn't blame Waters.

"Just doing our job."

"How did you find out?" Jordan asked.

"Can't reveal my sources," said Waters with a smile. "Anyway, it's a long story. And you have a visitor."

Allie jumped from Deleese's car before it rolled to a stop. She rushed to Timmy and clutched him to her breast, anointing him with her kisses. Jordan waited a moment, then he went to them.

Allie averted her eyes, afraid to look at her husband for fear of breaking down, giving in. She nodded her head and kissed Timmy some more.

Jordan turned to leave. Then Allie spoke.

"Thank you, Jordan. Thank you for bringing my son back home alive."

The car carrying Hedlund rolled off the lawn, spitting gravel as it began its long journey back. As Jordan watched the departure, he saw a convoy of microwave dishes bobbing in the air.

Jordan tugged at Allie's sleeve and nodded toward the approaching assault. She rose. They faced each other and for an instant their eyes met. Jordan took a chance and embraced his wife. She didn't resist. He felt a flicker of affection in her touch, not more. It was enough for now.

"Let's go," he said, placing one arm around Timmy and the other around Allie. "Let's go home."

EPILOGUE

August's tyranny was overthrown by the gentle breezes of September. The winter that followed was among the mildest in memory and spring came early. In May, amidst predictions of the hottest summer ever, Jordan Stone took the opportunity afforded by an unseasonably warm afternoon to sit in an outdoor café in Rocky Cliff. And as he had all winter and spring, he reflected upon the events of August past.

Minutes after the rescue, following a preliminary examination by a doctor on the scene, Timmy was granted his only request, to drive home with his parents. The ride back was the most exhausting and satisfying moment Jordan had ever known. The three remained nearly silent in the back of a Bureau sedan. Jordan and Allie took turns caressing Timmy's cheek and cuddling him. Timmy smiled and acknowledged the reassurance. During the ride through the cornfields and back into the thicket of suburbs, Jordan dozed in and out of consciousness, awakened occasionally with a start by the burning desire to rescue Timmy, only to find him safe in his arms. Allie asked Timmy a few questions but knew instinctively now was not a time for words.

During the evening, Timmy was questioned briefly by

Waters and Deleese. Then a therapist was asked to determine first if Timmy had suffered any sexual or physical abuse and, second, any emotional abuse or torture.
The answer to the first question came back negative.
The answer to the second question was far more difficult to determine. The events as Timmy recounted
them certainly led the therapist to conclude that emotional abuse bordering on torture had indeed occurred
in the form of solitary confinement, false hopes about a
rescue, nutritional deficiency, and the devastating incident with Capote.

Oddly, Timmy displayed little anger or resentment
over the abduction. After subsequent sessions, the therapist was convinced that Timmy had yet to deal with
the trauma, and thought that its inevitable effects
would emerge later, perhaps in months or years, as a
neurosis or phobia, as was often the case with trauma
victims.

Jordan disagreed, believing Timmy's gentle character
helped him transcend the ordeal. Whenever Jordan
needed a model of true grace, he looked no further
than his youngest son.

One of the most emotional moments of the first day
occurred when Timmy was reunified with Sarah and
Cal. Before the kidnapping, the relationship between
the three children had been based on the obvious: common parents, a few similar interests, and a shared
household. But after the kidnapping, from the moment
they embraced, their relationship underwent a subtle
but dramatic change. Now they were a unit of three,
not separated from their parents, but separate from
their parents. They had forged a partnership as mature
as one held by brothers and sisters in maturity, who had
seen the cruelties of the world and realized that siblings
were the greatest gift of God.

The media maintained, even intensified, its vigil the
week following the kidnapping. The clamor for reaction

from the family grew to a fevered pitch. But to no avail. Through the Bureau, Jordan and Allie issued a statement of appreciation for all those who helped in solving the case and thanks to the nation for its prayers. All media requests for anything were denied. The parents even rejected personal pleas from the anchors of the national network news programs for interviews.

Like nature, the media abhor a vacuum and the rumors began to fly. One such tale held that Jordan had indeed cut of his hands and doctors had been furtively shuttled into the house to fit prosthetics. Another rumor posited that Hedlund had subjected Timmy to terrible and perverse sexual torture. And yet another went so far as to suggest that Jordan had negotiated to get Timmy back and was well on his way home before the FBI even arrived at Hedlund's house.

The day after Timmy's rescue, one television station was lucky enough to get a brief shot of the family as they huddled in the backyard to bury Capote, a ritual that perplexed the media to no end as news of Capote's death still had not circulated. The consensus had it that the family was burying Jordan's hands, though no one had an explanation as to why it appeared Jordan's hands were intact during the ceremony.

As the days passed, the media grew tired waiting for a press conference or statement from any of the Stones. Attrition dwindled their numbers until only a few reporters remained, largely from outlets with budgets large enough to afford a presence without a guaranteed payoff. Finally the last crews packed up and left to cover a gruesome sex slave murder near Buffalo, a development that also served to bump Timmy's kidnapping from the tabloid front pages and the opening minutes of every newscast for the first time in weeks.

Jordan's only contact with the outside world was a call to Goodwill Industries, which dispatched a truck to pick up the Stone's generous donation of the wide-

screen television. During a family meeting everyone
voted to get rid of the television, everyone except
Timmy. But the majority ruled, and no one paid mind
when the burly men hauled it away.

September came and the kids returned to school, ce-
lebrities at first, but then just struggling students after
the burden of classes began. Their routines were interrupted occasionally by reporters looking for a follow-up
story during unusually slow news days.

In the weeks and months following the rescue, over
seventy producers from as far away as Tokyo and Ri-
yadh called the Stones' house seeking the rights to the
story. Jordan forwarded all calls to Wanda, per their
agreement. The contract never stipulated, however,
that Jordan was required to divulge any information to
Wanda, just that he couldn't divulge the information
to anyone else. Accordingly, Jordan never spoke to
Wanda again, despite protestations from her attorney
and a lawsuit claiming breech of contract.

Despite Jordan's reticence, Wanda parlayed the contract into three television movies, two feature development deals, four paperbacks, and seven "exclusive"
tabloid interviews, not to mention a month's worth of
Crime Current opening segments that propelled the
show to number one status in its time slot, a crown it
had yet to relinquish. Jordan read in a business section
of the *Times* that Wanda was planning on leaving the
show soon to create her own production company
based on the clout and profits derived from the case.

The first television movie aired just nineteen days
after Timmy's recovery, a record. Hedlund was portrayed as a pathological liar and brute, and Jordan as
the defender of truth, justice, and the American way.
The second television movie, three weeks later, re-
versed the order. Hedlund was a misunderstood victim,
and Stone a devilish incarnation of the media.

Based on a request from the FBI, the Department of

Justice opened an investigation into Wanda's conduct during the days preceding Hedlund's capture.

"What did she know and when did she know it?" the media demanded to know, while the investigators deposed Wanda and others at the network. For the better part of the week, Wanda became the whipping girl for the media's guilt over its coverage in the case.

By week's end, the investigators released their findings. They found that "while Wanda Gentry was in possession of circumstantial evidence as to the identity of the alleged kidnapper several hours before his apprehension, the nature of the evidence, in and of itself, was not substantial enough to prompt an indictment under federal statutes concerning the withholding of evidence. While this board in no way condones the actions of Ms. Gentry, we cannot find her culpable of any punishable crime."

Privately the investigators labeled Gentry's action "reprehensible" and "unconscionable," quotes that were picked up and seconded by many of the same media outlets that were secretly negotiating with Wanda for her coveted rights.

Wanda's legendary status as "Queen of Prime-Time Crime" was sealed when she wrangled the only interview granted by Arthur Hedlund. Hedlund insisted on the time for the live interview, which just so happened to precede the President's State of the Union address. The President's advisors protested publicly but were secretly pleased that the President would be preceded by the most heavily watched lead-in in the history of the State of the Union.

The interview turned out to be somewhat of a disappointment. His trial still a month away, Hedlund had been advised by his attorneys not to talk about the kidnapping or his relationship with Jordan Stone and his family. Hedlund did speak at length, eloquently if not convincingly, about his ideas about the deterioration of values and the banality of the media. His reflections prompted offers from publishers looking to cash in on the popularity of celebrity musings in book form.

Jordan, meanwhile, quietly negotiated with his publishers to cease publication of all his books. The publishing houses dashed off new runs before negotiations could be completed. The agreement cost Jordan every penny of royalties due him and then some. Once news of the agreement hit the streets, copies of his books, particularly *Slaughter Alley,* flew off bookstore shelves, and collectors offered up to ten times the cover price for any copy, thirty times the cover price for first-print copies, and a hundred times the price for signed copies. Libraries across the nation reported an epidemic of "lost or stolen" Stone books.

Just as coverage began to die down, Hedlund's trial began. After weeks of posturing, pretrial hearings, and jury selection, the trial finally began under the full scrutiny of the media, impatient to learn the juicy details of the kidnapping that Stone had sealed inside him.

The prosecutor laid down a seamless case. He didn't hit a snag until Jordan Stone took the witness stand, the first time Jordan had seen Hedlund since the kidnapping. Jordan testified truthfully but far more tersely than the prosecutor had anticipated. So much so that the prosecutor asked the judge to stipulate Jordan as a hostile witness, so that he could use leading questions to coax the events of that afternoon from the reluctant witness. At the end of his testimony, Jordan pleaded for leniency. Hedlund's action was reprehensible, Jordan said, but he argued that he shouldered a portion of the blame for Josh's death. When the judge finally got Jordan to shut up, he instructed the jurors to disregard everything Jordan said. Apparently they did, because they brought back guilty charges on all thirteen counts, including felony kidnapping in the first, second-degree child endangerment, and cruelty to animals. When the judge handed down the life sentence, Hedlund cried.

Allie didn't share Jordan's sentiment and was pleased with the verdict. She was more than ready to rebuild her life. After the kidnapping, Allie had asked Jordan to move into his office, the pain of his affair, now common knowledge, still sharp. After a few weeks, however, she asked Jordan to return, for the sake of the children, she said. In truth, she saw the changes in Jordan and realized what had happened with Wanda could never happen again, that Jordan was a changed man, and she a changed woman, and their ordeal would only serve to bond them. As they made love for the first time in months she confessed that she wanted to try one more time. Jordan said one more time was all he needed.

Following the trial, Jordan vowed not to remain a hermit. He circulated in Rocky Cliff and Manhattan regularly, at first causing quite a stir, then as the months passed he was a familiar oddity in his frequent haunts and a ghost of TV past in those places he visited occasionally.

He hadn't sat at his computer or penned a line, outside a letter here or there, since the kidnapping. He spent his days reading the classics and the list of books he vowed to read someday but never had. Now with winter and the trial over, Jordan decided it was time to pick up a pen again and hear what his inner voices had to say.

As he drank coffee on the patio of the Rocky Cliff Café, Jordan felt good about the future, though he had no idea what it held. He knew he had write. It was after all his vocation and his love.

It was by coincidence that Arnie Sinkowitz walked by the café and saw Jordan Stone jotting notes at the small table up front.

"Well, if it's not the illustrious Mr. Stone."

"Sink, what a nice surprise. What's up?"

"I'm off the crime beat."

"Fantastic," said Jordan with a high-five. "What's the new assignment?"

"Features, 'in-depth looks at significant issues,' as the boss puts it. Fewer stories, lots of inches."

"Congratulations."

"Thanks."

"And what are you doing, writing another book?" Arnie motioned to the notebook on the table.

"Yes, I think I will."

"Another best-seller?"

Jordan chuckled. "I don't think so."

"Don't keep me in suspense. What's it about?"

"You know, I don't even know yet."

Arnie understood. "How's Timmy and the family?"

"He's great. Really great. We all are. Though we're selling the house," said Jordan.

"Selling, why? It's a gorgeous place."

"The bend in the road. I never want to live by one again."

The Dollmaker was a serial killer who stalked Los Angeles and left a grisly calling card on the faces of his female victims. With a single faultless shot, Detective Harry Bosch thought he had ended the city's nightmare.

Now, the dead man's widow is suing Harry and the LAPD for killing the wrong man—an accusation that rings terrifyingly true when a new victim is discovered with the Dollmaker's macabre signature.

Now, for the second time, Harry must hunt down a death-dealer who is very much alive, before he strikes again. It's a blood-tracked quest that will take Harry from the hard edges of the L.A. night to the last place he ever wanted to go—the darkness of his own heart.

THE
CONCRETE
BLONDE

"Exceptional...A stylish blend of grit and elegance."
—Nelson DeMille

THE CONCRETE BLONDE
Michael Connelly
_____ 95500-6 $5.99 U.S./$6.99 Can.

Head coach Vance White's brutal regimen encourages a viciousness on the field that shocks even the most hardened NFL veterans. But when the mysterious ingredient fueling the Ruffians' aggressive fury leads to tragedy on his own team, tackle Clay Blackwell rebels. Now, trapped between his conscience and his desire to join his teammates on their steamroller ride to the top, Clay faces the most agonizing choice of his life.

RUFFIANS

TIM GREEN

"Like *NORTH DALLAS FORTY* crossed with *THE FIRM*."
—USA Today

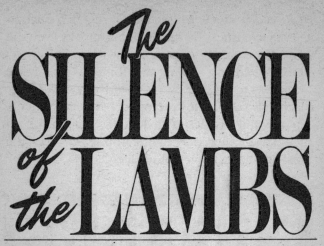

The SILENCE of the LAMBS

THE ELECTRIFYING BESTSELLER BY

THOMAS HARRIS

"THRILLERS DON'T COME ANY BETTER THAN THIS."
—CLIVE BARKER

"HARRIS IS QUITE SIMPLY THE BEST SUSPENSE NOVELIST
WORKING TODAY." *— The Washington Post*